"*Jane Lark has an incre...*
from the first page ...
Cosmochicklitan Book Revi..."

"*Any description that I give you would not only spoil the story but could not give this book a tenth of the justice that it deserves. Wonderful!*"
Candy Coated Book Blog

"*This book held me captive after the first 2 pages. If I could crawl inside and live in there with the characters I would.*"
A Reading Nurse Blogspot

"*The book swings from truly swoon-worthy, tense and heart wrenching, highly erotic and everything else in between.*"
BestChickLit.com

"*I love Ms. Lark's style—beautifully descriptive, emotional and can I say, just plain delicious reading? This is the kind of mixer upper I've been looking for in romance lately.*"
Devastating Reads BlogSpot

JANE LARK

I love writing authentic, passionate and emotional love stories. I began my first novel, a historical, when I was sixteen, but life derailed me a bit when I started suffering with Ankylosing Spondylitis, so I didn't complete a novel until after I was thirty when I put it on my to do before I'm forty list. Now I love getting caught up in the lives and traumas of my characters, and I'm so thrilled to be giving my characters life in others' imaginations, especially when readers tell me they've read the characters just as I've tried to portray them.

http://www.janelark.co.uk/

@JaneLark

The Dangerous Love
of a Rogue

JANE LARK

Harper*Impulse* an imprint of
HarperCollins*Publishers* Ltd
1 London Bridge Street
London SE1 9GF

www.harpercollins.co.uk

A Paperback Original 2015

First published in Great Britain in ebook format by Harper*Impulse* 2015

A catalogue record for this book is
available from the British Library

ISBN: 9780008125271

Automatically produced by Atomik ePublisher from Easypress

Prologue

It was a renowned truth, that any world-worn rogue, without a feather to fly with, must be on the hunt for a wife, or rather her dowry. As the parody of Miss Austen's verse, from her charming little novel about country life, ran through Drew's head, a sound of mocking humour rumbled through his chest and he leaned a shoulder against the false pillar in the Earl of Derwent's ballroom watching town life.

The pillar was wooden, painted to look like marble. Like everyone in this damned room, it was a farce. A shallow image. A performance… Nothing here was what it seemed. Society lived a damned lie and he had lived it for a lifetime.

He was a bastard, sold by his mother to her husband as worth the risk of giving her naturally born son his family's name to keep up the façade and to save the reputation of the Framlington title.

Damn the title… Damn the bloody name… Drew had no interest in either.

He was bored of this. Bored of pretence. Bored of the games these people and he played. Bored of the face he displayed to the world and bored of the man who suffered all this behind a closed door.

He wished to escape it. He had a plan. Of course plans required money. But his plan covered that. He was seeking a well-dowered young woman to take as his wife, and therefore earn himself an instant fortune. A fortune which he would use to pack up his bags and retire to a quiet life, away from town, away from this… Perhaps he would experience life then just as Miss Austen wrote it. Or was 'Country Life' an equal façade? Never mind wherever he went, he would not live behind a façade. He'd had his fill of charades.

"Have you seen Marlow's daughter?" Mark leaned to Drew's ear. "She would be a prize."

Drew looked at his friend and lifted his shoulder away from the pillar, straightening up. "I have."

"She looks remarkable."

"She does indeed." He'd been watching her. She was on his list of potential wives.

"Are you intending to try her?"

"I would be a fool if I did not. Look at her…" Yet the she in question, Miss Mary Marlow, was as far above his reach as the sun. The step-sister of a duke – with a bastard… It was not a match that would be desired by the sweet young miss's mama and papa.

Yet Miss Marlow was the most appealing to the eye and Drew had been awaiting his moment to explore his opportunity with her. The time had come. He'd not been standing here for his pleasure. He'd been standing here waiting for Miss Marlow to complete her dance.

"Then what are you waiting on." Mark laughed, spotting the same opportunity.

Not a thing. Drew glanced over his shoulder and gave his friend a wicked smile before turning to walk about the edge of the room.

Miss Marlow was in a set close to him and the dance was drawing to its conclusion. Drew positioned himself so that when it ended her back was turned him. She stood three feet away; he could feel her exuberance even though he could not see her face or her smile. Yet he knew she was smiling, she'd smiled throughout every dance tonight.

Mary Marlow was in her first season, newly launched upon the marriage market, and he was here to trade. But what his friends did not know was that as much as he desired her money, he desired innocence. His heart and mind were jaded and bitter. He longed for the refreshing invigoration of innocence. God knew, he'd never been given the blessing of innocence in his life; he'd been born into the world of sin. Born of sin and raised in sin.

Miss Marlow's partner lifted her hand to his lips and bowed.

Drew stepped forward. "Miss Marlow." He said her name as though they'd been introduced and he had a right to use it, speaking before the man had chance to offer to lead her back to her mother.

She looked at him, her expression confused, but then she smiled, and it was as though the sun rose in the room which was already illuminated by several hundred candles in the chandeliers.

Her smile said, "I am not sure I know you, sir." Yet a young woman like her would never be rude enough to ask.

When her companion let her go, Drew captured her hand, as if he had a right to that too. He felt as though he did. She had become his favourite choice as a bride the minute she'd smiled at him and not turned away. "May I have the next dance?"

He did not push things too far, he did not kiss her hand, yet he let his gloved fingers slide up her wrist a little to touch her skin, as if the gesture was accidental. She lowered into a sweet perfectly correct curtsy and looked up an instant before she rose.

Beautiful.

Her eyes were an unusual blue, an extremely pale rim of colour surrounding the dark pupils that looked at him in question. *"Who are you? Do I actually know you, sir?"* Too polite to ask those questions she simply continued to pretend they had been introduced. They had not.

If he could have picked a tune it would have been the waltz, but the first waltz was not until later and he had no wish to lose the chance of the distance from her family. They were at the far end of the ballroom, in their usual pack. The Pembrokes. Although Pembroke was not the name the family went by as a whole, the old Duke had had four girls, and they'd all married exceptionally well, apart from Mary's mother, who had at first married a soldier, who'd died, and then settled on the second son of an earl. But the son from her first marriage had inherited the title and given Miss Marlow a very attractive dowry, and so Mary was simply a Miss and yet a powerful match as a duke's sister, and innocent.

"I believe you should stand here, and I there…" Drew said to her look of confusion.

There was another quick smile, which was far more fleeting than the first. She was perhaps realising she had made an error. He smiled to ease her concern. "I shall admit we have not been introduced. You must forgive me for taking the liberty of breaking the rules, Miss Marlow." The music commenced.

He stepped forward and took her hand in the format of the dance, then completed a shoulder to shoulder turn.

"I should walk away immediately."

"Indeed you should. But is it such a sin for a man to find you so utterly beautiful he cannot wait even another moment, or at worse another dance, to find some party who might introduce him?"

"That is the course of a gentleman."

"It is indeed." He leaned to her. "There you have me; perhaps I am not a gentleman…" He said it in a voice to tease her, the voice he knew earned him a little more money from the women who asked for his favour. Her head turned instantly, but then her gaze dropped to the lopsided rogue's smile he threw at her and she laughed.

"You are a gentleman. You would not be here if you were not."

So innocent… so blind. Such a novelty.

What he would give for that blindness.

"So are you enjoying your season, Miss Marlow?"

Her answering smile was softened then. "Yes. I have had to wait patiently, because we've been in mourning for my grandsire, but I cannot tell you how wonderful it is to finally be out. My cousins, who are older, have been full of stories and made me long for this. Now finally I have my moment."

Yes, she did. "Tell me how it compares to the things you must have dreamed…" As they talked their steps followed the intricate country dance, but the blessing of it was, he had by chance chosen a country dance that did not separate them.

"It does not compare, I could not have imagined this…"

"You lie, surely you knew you would be in a room full of young men making fools of themselves for young women, and old men being bores, and young women who giggle at the slightest word." *and older women…* like his mother… he did not even wish to think of them.

"So you think I giggle like an idiot." There was a little annoyance in her voice.

As they made another turn he took the opportunity to press his palm against her side, below her breasts. Her body slid across his fingers as she followed the pattern of the dance. He only touched her for an instant, as if it was to stop her stumbling, yet her whole body jolted.

"Forgive me. I thought you'd missed a step."

"You thought—"

"No I did not." He leaned to her ear as he stepped forward. Her hair brushed his cheek. "I simply wish this were a waltz and I had the opportunity to hold you."

He stepped back. There was a sparkle in her dark pupils, and he saw her heartbeat flickering beneath her skin at the base of her neck.

The woman was charming.

"Yet it is not a waltz, and so you should refrain…"

Finally he was challenged, her pause awaited his name. It had taken her long enough. "Lord Framlington."

As they walked around the back of the couple beside them she looked as though she searched her memory for his name, yet when they came into the middle of a ring of six there was no light of recognition in her eyes. The Duke of Pembroke had not mentioned his name to her then.

"I like you, Miss Marlow. You are pretty and sensible," he said, as they came back together – *and innocent and wealthy*.

"I cannot say I like you in return, I do not know you."

He smiled at her little jab. "Know you or not, I like and admire you." It was true, the girl was claiming his entire interest the more the dance progressed. She was perfect.

"Indeed." She laughed, a light, jolly sound, not a forced jubilant creation developed to draw attention.

The girl was doing something to his soul, he felt as though he was bathing in her innocence, baptised in it, his sins washed away. "It is no jest, and no falsity, you are charming. A man would be a fool if he did not see it."

"So you are telling me you are no fool."

"I have never been a fool, Miss Marlow." Another step forward brought them together. "I am interested in you." He whispered it into her ear.

Her head pulled back. "Interested…"

He let his lips tilt into a smile. "Yes. Very. Immensely. As I said I like you."

"My Lord, you may speak as though you know me, but you do not."

"Such a sensible head, you only interest me more…"

Damn it, there was probably only a dozen steps left and beyond those dancing Drew saw her father in a discussion with her brother, Pembroke. The Duke must have recently arrived. They both glanced across the room.

Drew looked at Miss Marlow, his time with the beauty was at an end. "I am the son of a Marquis…" In theory, and yet if he was to sell himself he must sell his best side. "You may hear bad things of me, but disregard them. Judge me by the man you see. Admittedly I am not like the young men I see you dancing with—"

6

"You have been watching me."

"Did I not already say that I admire you? Why would I not watch you to learn more about you and be sure what I think is true?"

"What do you think?"

"That I shall be a very lucky" *and wealthy*, "man, if I were to win you... You are a beauty." He would guess if she looked about this room she would only see the light, the flowers, the beautiful dresses and people's smiles. Like looking at that damned wooden pillar, unless you touched it, or tapped it, unless you knew, you would not know the lie beneath the paint.

Damn it, if he chose to marry her he would lock her up to protect her innocence.

The music ceased; her fingers were in his as the dance was completed. She would have pulled them free but he refused to let go.

She lowered in a curtsy.

Half the room would be laughing behind their smiles as they watched his game play, thinking the poor woman the fool he'd just told her he never was. He did not wish her thought a fool either, though.

As she rose, she smiled.

Her eyes said she liked him, even if she had not said it with her lips.

She'd taken him at his word, and she was judging him by what she saw, not by the history that had woven around him like a web for years... Rogue... Rake... Bastard... Unwanted son... Unwanted entirely...

"My father," she breathed as her hand slipped from his. He felt the loss like something had been taken from him.

"Remember me as I am."

She gave him another tentative smile and then her fingers gripped her dress to lift it away from her feet and she turned towards her father.

Drew watched her cross the floor then join her family. Her

7

father leant to her ear and spoke hurriedly. She glanced back. Drew smiled. She smiled in return but it quivered with uncertainty. She knew now. Her father had just told her.

Do not dance with that rogue…

Damn the man, and damn these people. Drew turned away, to return to his friends, to return to his life, but he had ambitions, and now his ambitions leaned heavily towards Miss Mary Marlow, though winning the girl would be a challenge, there was no denying that.

"Drew, come to my room tonight…" for God's sake, he had just bathed in innocence and now he was dirty again. He'd lied when he'd said he was unwanted entirely, one element of society welcomed him willingly. Women of his mother's ilk.

Her removed Lady Worton's hand from the front of his trousers, pressing his thumb into her palm so she would yield her grip on his crotch. "I am afraid I am not inclined, Bets. Find another toy tonight."

He did not wait to hear the woman's reply. He was so damned bored of his life. He'd fallen into it, never chosen it. Been damned well born into, like a whore into a brothel, and for years he'd enjoyed the sex, and the money and gifts the women gave him, but there had come a point he wished to be able to do as he chose – be free to live as he chose – and the only way to achieve it was to marry money.

"Drew!" Another of his friends, Peter, lifted a hand. Drew did have some people he appreciated.

"Peter. You are late. Where have you been?"

"I have been…" As Drew listened to his friend, he turned to face the room.

Miss Marlow was not dancing the next, she stood with her father receiving a scalding by all appearances, while her brother was with a woman in a knot of the family who crowded around them.

Drew looked at Peter. "Who is that with Pembroke?" The Pembroke women, including Miss Marlow, were all dark haired, it was one of the strongest characteristics of their beauty; jet black hair and pale skin and then pale blue eyes about onyx pupils, but this woman was blonde.

"Pembroke's bride. I came in just before them. He's taken a wife."

Good Lord. That was a lark. No one would have expected the man to marry for years. He was not like his sister, his heart was made from stone, and he was no more innocent than Drew. They had travelled in the same circles on the grand tour. Pembroke had been one of the women's toys too. But he'd walked away from it years ago. Yet he'd been tarnished by it even then.

"Why?" Peter gripped Drew's shoulder.

"Oh for no reason, I simply wondered."

"I thought you were interested in the sister, you will hardly have a chance there if you pitch for the man's wife."

Drew laughed and looked back over, Mary's father had ceased talking to her but now her mother was speaking to her. Miss Marlow glanced across the room, her eyes seeking Drew out.

An odd sensation leapt in his chest. He would have said it was his heart, but like Pembroke, he did not really have one. That had been kicked far too many times in his life. Her mother said something else and Miss Marlow looked away.

Drew looked at Pembroke again. Drew liked Miss Marlow. She fulfilled all that he was seeking. Yet Pembroke would never let Drew near his little sister. That thought was a punch in the gut. Another rejection, and a rejection from a man who could have no moral standing over Drew.

It was bloody tempting to pitch for Pembroke's wife, solely to kick the man back.

If Pembroke had earned himself a wife and a second chance, than why could he not offer Drew the same?

"Stop drooling over the fair Miss Marlow, come and play cards."

"I ought not, I ought to dance with every woman with a dowry if I am to find one fool enough to take me."

"There is no hurry for you to choose a woman. If you need

funds I'll pay. Come and play. I am need of your company; Mark and Harry are already playing so I need another man I trust for my pair."

"Very well."

Drew played a few hands of cards at the tables with his friends for an hour; they did not normally attend such affairs, but Derwent's wife was in Drew's mother's set, and so any young man with ill-morals had been encouraged to attend. It would end in an orgy later, but by then he and his friends would be gone. He had never been into those sorts of games.

"I am out." He'd played for long enough.

If he wished to escape his current life, he must return to the task of looking for a new one.

"Then you must settle what you owe."

Fortune had played against him. Drew looked at Peter who nodded as a hand moved to his pocket. Drew rose. "Good evening, gentleman." he said to the others about the table, but then he shared a look with Peter that said I shall see you in a while. His friend smiled.

It was all well and good to have a generous wealthy friend, but how could a man respect himself when he lived off his friend like a leach, or from services rendered to the older women of society. They saw society's untitled sons as a pack of male whores. The devil take this life. He no longer wished for it.

Of course there were lucky untitled sons, those who had fathers who paid for a commission in the army, or the clergy. Framlington would never have deemed to give Drew that. He had given Drew nothing bar his name, his food, and limited clothing, from Drew's birth until his fifteenth birthday. Then Drew had learned a way to earn freedom from his false father's house. Only to tie himself up in a new hell.

He should have saved the money the women gave him and paid for his commission into the army, but he'd been young, and greedy, and he'd celebrated his new wealth playing hard at the tables and buying whatever he wished. Of course then the debt had begun, and the debt had sucked him deeper into the power of his mother's set of friends; though friends was an ambiguous word. Yet they had paid his duns for years, but never enough to fully clear his debt.

He returned to the ballroom to look for his prize – a young woman with a dowry of reasonable size, one that would clear his debt fully, and finally, and enable him to set up his life as he wished.

His eyes were immediately drawn to Miss Marlow's dark curls, which bounced against her shoulders as she skipped through the steps of another country dance. He truly liked the girl. She'd become his preference tonight.

But he should not put all his eggs in one basket, as people said. He looked across the room at another debutante, a lady with auburn hair whom he'd danced with thrice. She was not as pleasing on the eye as Miss Marlow and yet her dowry was equally substantial.

As he passed a set, a woman was spun out of the last turn of a dance breathing hard. Her gaze met his.

Pembroke's newly acquired wife.

She had blue eyes, but they were not as pale a blue as her sister-in-law's.

Damn it, but he was tempted to play a game. He knew if he settled on Miss Marlow, then Pembroke would fight him all the way. Pembroke had turned his back on the life Drew led, and now treated all those who'd no choice but to live it, as if they were scum. Drew could teach Pembroke a lesson with this.

As Pembroke's wife's partner bowed over her hand elegantly Drew saw Pembroke speaking with Lady Elizabeth Ponsonby, Drew's sister. She was older than Drew, older than Pembroke, and of Framlington's blood, and she'd adopted and thoroughly enjoyed their mother's way of life.

She was the one who had pulled Pembroke into their set on the grand tour. Pembroke had been as innocent and stupid as his little sister then. Like a baby, newly born, presented to the women in a linen cloth. Here is another young male for you to mislead.

Drew never spoke to Elizabeth. They did not acknowledge their connection.

Yet on this occasion Drew was grateful to her.

Pembroke would be occupied for a while; if Elizabeth was interested in him again she would not let him escape easily.

"Your Grace." Drew grasped the fingers of the Duke of Pembroke's hapless young bride as soon as her former companion walked away. The woman looked a little lost… a lost sheep… "Would you dance with me?"

She had large blue eyes, which looked her confusion.

"Oh, of course…" Just like her sister-in-law she was too polite, too innocent and naïve, to deny him.

Of all the dances, it was a waltz.

Perfect.

He took her hand and brought her close, so her breasts pressed to his chest. She stepped back.

This was going to be amusing at least, and perhaps if she was so newly innocent, if she could be persuaded, sharing a bed with her might actually be enjoyable.

He span her several times, gripping her firmly as her hold was so light it felt as though she tried not to touch him at all. "So where did you meet Pembroke?"

"I… Near Pembroke Place, Lord Framlington."

She did know who he was then.

"Is your marriage as blissful as you hoped…" he was being sarcastic.

Her mouth opened, but she did not answer, as though she didn't know what to say. Well there it was then. Another cold loveless society marriage that would end in shame, and sin. He did not wish it for himself. He wished for more in the marriage he sought, underneath all else, he sought loyalty too. He may have cuckolded dozens, but he did not wish for that from his wife.

12

Drew saw Pembroke over her shoulder, whispering with Elizabeth, already perhaps agreeing to play his poor wife false. Drew had an urge to play the same game, why should Pembroke have what Drew wished for and then treat it ill.

Besides Drew had been brought up to be wicked. He leaned to the Duchess's ear speaking as he spun her again, toning his voice to the pitch of seduction. "Pembroke is dull. Perhaps when you tire of him you might think of me. I would be willing to warm your bed if it is cold."

The woman snapped her head back, as though he'd slapped her, and the look on her face implied horror. "I will never tire of my husband, my Lord…"

Her rejection was an insult, another kick. He wished to be good enough for a woman like this. "But there is much to be said for variety, my dear, and your husband knows it, look, see, he's speaking with my sister, an old flame he probably wishes to rekindle."

She looked as he turned her, her head turning as he turned, so she could keep looking at Pembroke. When she looked back at Drew pain shone in her eyes, pain and something else… She cared for Pembroke. Truly cared. Her eyes were shimmering with tears, and she had bitten her lip to stop them falling. Her fingers clawed on his shoulder and gripped his hand a little harder as though she was saving herself from falling as much as trying to prevent her tears.

His hand, which had been seductively spread across her back to feel the movement of her body beneath her gown, now slid a little downwards, to hold her up if needs be, as they took the last few turns.

He did not know what to say.

When he looked beyond her, unable to look at her eyes filled with sparkling tears, he saw Pembroke coming. The man had disposed of Elizabeth and was crossing the room with a look of thunderclouds in his eyes, walking through the dancers for God sake.

Pembroke did not in general show his emotion. Drew had truly believed him no more movable than stone. He had thought this woman had been selected to be a future Duchess and was on the verge of a life of hell. But the look in Pembroke's eyes, the anger, implied the man felt as much for his wife as his wife clearly felt for him. Drew had made an error in this.

Fortunately before Pembroke collided with a couple the dance came to its natural end, and when he reached them, as the last notes played, he gripped his wife's arm, with a force that said, she is mine and no one else will touch her. Then he hissed at Drew. "I'd already made a note this evening to warn you off – I do not want you dancing with my sister – and now I see I must also warn you off my wife. Just so that you know, Framlington, hunting my sister is pointless, I would not agree the match and never pay you her dowry, and if you touch my wife again, I'll kill you."

Drew smiled as he stepped away from the Duchess. He wished to laugh. Well who would have known that Pembroke had a heart? And who would have known that Pembroke could make a woman fall for him so deeply.

As Drew walked away he saw Miss Marlow, Pembroke's sister, being returned to her parents, by her latest partner. Her gaze turned to Drew, as it had earlier. He smiled and nodded slightly in recognition.

She had not heeded her brother's and her father's warnings.

He returned to the fake marble pillar and watched Miss Marlow. She spoke with her family as her dance partner walked away.

Several of the men in the Pembroke group had hands resting at their wives' waists, and the couples stood close, barely inches between them. Some of them had been married for years…

The Earl of Barrington turned and said something to his wife, then kissed her lips. Barrington was Mary's uncle on her father's side, and Drew had heard he'd been a rake, as wicked as they came, until he'd married. Now he was never in town unless he was with his wife.

Wiltshire, another Duke, The Duke or Arundel, who was as hard-nosed as Pembroke, laughed about something, then mid-conversation he turned and looked at his wife, lifted her fingers to his lips and kissed them, then merely turned and continued the conversation.

Drew saw Marlow lean and say something in his wife's ear and she looked up at him and smiled then shook her head laughing, her answer from him was a kiss on the cheek and another whisper as he gripped her fingers and then kept a hold of her hand.

They were all affectionate. Every pair. Mothers with their husbands, and the elder daughters with theirs. He was looking at a utopia. Of course it could be as false as the damned pillar he leaned against. But if it were true…

If it were true then there was no doubt about his choice. If Miss Marlow was as capable of constancy as the other woman in her family, why would he choose another?

Yet it would not be easy to win her. They would wrap her up and keep her away from him now. But he wished to be sure of this. He wanted to be confident in the fidelity of his wife, and he now wished for something new, after tonight… How could he expect a loyal wife if he did not ask the same of himself? He wished to know that he could be faithful to the wife he chose too. He knew exactly what he wanted now. He wanted what the Pembrokes had. Commitment… Exclusivity… Constancy… Even affection… perhaps…

He had made his choice, for a wife. He wished for Miss Marlow, but he would wait and not rush – to be certain. He had a little more credit he could call on, his need for her dowry was not desperate.

"Are you ready to retire?" Peter's hand settled on Drew's shoulder.

Drew also had a friend with generous pockets.

"Aye." Drew straightened, looking back at his friends, Peter, Harry and Mark, his brothers… His family. "Did you fair better than I?"

"Richest of us did." Mark quipped. "The man who does not need it."

"I won back your losses and more." Peter clarified. "So I say that earns us a drink and a pretty bird of paradise each."

"I'll take the drink, but I shall pass on the whore…"

Spending the money he'd earned from the women he now hated, on younger, prettier women of his choice, had been the way he'd balanced his soul for years, a little silent kick in the teeth of his mother's friends. But now he was done with women until he took a wife. The thought of sleeping with a woman other than the one he'd chosen for marriage was now abhorrent.

"Then I shall have yours as well as mine." Harry laughed.

Drew smiled at his friends, but as they walked from the ball, he glanced at Peter. The only one of them who usually attended these sorts of events with Drew. "What do you know of the Pembrokes? The sisters, and their daughters…"

* * *

Mary was sitting on her bed, with her knees bent up and gripped in her arms. Her bare toes peeped from beneath her nightgown. She watched her mother put her garments away; she'd dismissed the maid.

"Mama, why did you favour, Papa?"

She was placing Mary's earbobs into their box. She hesitated and did not speak for a moment as though the question shocked her. Perhaps she'd guessed why Mary asked. Mary had asked because one particular gentleman's light brown eyes had hovered in her mind all evening, along with the particular lilt of his smile.

"There you have me. Perhaps I am not a gentleman…"

No. So her brother John had told her father, and her father had told her. "Framlington is a fortune hunter. A rake. A man to avoid…"

16

"Remember me as I am…"

"When I met your father…" her mother sat on the bed, "our eyes met across a table and I just knew he was right for me." She was blushing a little.

"Do you think I will know?"

"I hope you will. I hope you find a man who shall sweep you off your feet and love you with all his soul."

"That is what I hope for too." Lord Framlington's eyes, his face, returned to her mind. There had been something fascinating about him. He was different to any other man who'd spoken to her.

"Did you truly enjoy the evening? You have been quiet tonight." Mary smiled. "I did."

"Come along then, let me tuck you in—"

"I am too old to be tucked into bed, Mama."

"You will never be too old. Come along." Her mother rose.

Mary slipped off the bed, then lifted the sheet and slid beneath it. She plumped the pillow with a thump before she lay down her head.

Her mother leaned down and kissed her cheek, then tucked the sheet in beneath the mattress so the sheet was tight about Mary. "Sleep well…"

"Would you give Papa a kiss from me?"

Her mother smiled. "I love you, Mary." She bent and pressed another kiss on Mary's cheek, then her cold fingertips touched Mary's cheek too.

"I love you too, Mama."

Mary's mother walked across the room and extinguished the candles in the candelabrum before turning to collect a single candlestick. Then she walked to the door. "Goodnight."

"Goodnight."

Her mother turned once more as she opened it. "Sleep well."

Mary smiled, and then her mother left and closed the door. The light disappeared with her.

Mary saw Lord Framlington in the darkness, as he stood against a marble pillar, watching her across the room. She ought to feel nothing for him. She ought to never think of him again. He had been courting her dowry, nothing more.

Yet there had been something about him.

I like and admire you, Miss Marlow... She had felt the same. There had been something calling her towards him.

She'd looked for him thrice after they'd danced, on one occasion he'd not been in the room but the other times, he'd looked at her too, and smiled.

But John was adamant he was unsuitable and if Lord Framlington were seeking her dowry he would smile.

Then why did she feel pulled towards him? Her thoughts drifted into dreams. Dreams that included Lord Framlington.

Chapter 1

The following year…

Miss Mary Rose Marlow's whole body jolted with surprise, "Oh!" and she nearly fell down the short flight of garden steps she'd just climbed. A masculine chest faced her.

Lord Framlington caught hold of her elbow, saving her, only to pull her towards the chest which had caused her exclamation.

He'd appeared from behind the hedge to block her path.

Her fingers pressed against the solid muscle beneath his day coat. Unladylike longings besieged her. She had never forgotten him.

Irked by the desire she should not feel, Mary pushed him away, anger flaring and overriding the unwanted attraction that constantly pulled at her, urging her to look for him, to listen for his voice.

She looked up and met his gaze, ire burning a flame she hoped he saw in her eyes.

If he did, the deep, dark amber brown of his absorbed it with cool, quelling disengagement.

Her stomach wobbled like aspic with an unwilling hunger for the reprobate.

"Miss Marlow." He let go of her arm, then raised his hat a little.

Mary stepped back, careful to avoid the shallow steps.

"It is my good fortune to collide with you."

Bobbing a hardly recognisable curtsy Mary's gaze reached beyond him seeking a way past. But the garden path, lined by tall yew hedges, was barely wide enough for one. She could not pass him without further contact unless he moved aside.

"Lord Framlington." Her voice rang sharp with irritation. "If you will excuse me, I really ought to be getting back." She moved to sweep past, but he blocked her with his broad chest.

"No haste, Miss Marlow, the party was still in full swing when I left, no one will notice our absence, they are busy playing Lady Jersey's outdoor games. Have you tried the archery butts? You could aim an arrow at my heart if you wish, I would not complain, and perhaps you might snare me if it came from Cupid's bow."

Her gaze lifted to his. "Do not be absurd?" The snapping words leapt from her mouth. His comment was far too close to her secret wish. "You know my brother advises against you."

"The Duke of Pembroke?" Condescension sharpened his words, while a roguish smile played with his lips. Oh she remembered that smile, it had hovered in her dreams for a year… "What do I care for his opinion, and what do you care. I have often thought the man did me a favour, warning you off. You have been enamoured ever since."

"I have not." Mary's hands balled to fists. The man was infuriating. Why on earth did she find him so interesting? Because on one evening, nearly a year ago, he had danced with her, and talked and flirted, and smiled and laughed as no other man had.

He grinned. "Careful, or I shall think you protest too much. Besides I know because I have seen you watching me. Whenever I turn, there is Miss Mary Marlow staring across the room."

He leant forward, his face inches from hers. "Your looks call to me, Mary. You whisper to me, come, come, Framlington, closer." His husky pitch made her skin tingle with awareness and possibilities course through her blood.

He straightened, his gloved fingers gently bracing her chin. "Well here I am, Mary. Come to you. What will you do with me?"

Run away.

She backed away a step, lifting her chin from his grip. "Nothing." She forced the denial from her lips, when internally she longed to know how his kiss would feel. "Let me pass. I should not be speaking with you."

"But you are." He stepped forward.

When she'd danced with him last season his glittering light brown eyes had melted her bones. He'd held her gently, while making her laugh, like he was a jester, and as they'd parted he'd asked her to remember him.

She'd fallen in love during that dance. Irrevocably in love. She had not forgotten.

But afterward her eldest brother, John, the Duke of Pembroke, had advised that Lord Framlington – her beauty – was a beast. A fortune hunter, chasing dowries.

Worse, he was a rake, a philanderer, a seducer, not to be trusted in the least.

It is folly talking to him.

"Then let me rectify that." She tried to pass him. But he caught her upper arm, stopping her and turning with her. She stood facing him in the narrow gap between the tall yew hedges.

"Stop running and stop pretending you do not like me. I am not blind. Besides, run, and my predatory instincts say, chase." On the last word he leaned forward, pulling her closer and then his lips pressed down on hers and his other hand came to her nape urging her to stay, to allow, to give, as his lips brushed across hers.

Mary's instinct screamed, run. But his lips urged so beautifully her body cried, take, longing to devour, to the point that she was no longer sure who was the predator, him or her. This was her first kiss.

Gripping his shoulders, she clung to him, opening her mouth at his urging, and when his tongue invaded her lips a rush of desire slid through her stomach reaching to the central point of femininity between her legs.

This was what she'd imagined and longed for – this enchantment and desire.

He moved her back a step, against the yew hedge, as his kiss increased in intensity, the movement of his lips and the caress of his tongue growing in determination, intriguing and intoxicating.

His grip left her arm and closed over her breast, squeezing it through the thin muslin of her gown.

A sharp, sweet pain travelled from her nipple, catching her breath. It was delicious, but still it was pain and it was enough to rip her focus from his kiss to rational thought.

What am I doing? What am I letting him do?

Breaking the kiss suddenly, she caught him off guard and it gave her the chance to escape.

Slipping from his grip, she fled, not daring to look back for fear he'd follow.

"Miss Marlow!" he called after her, a note of humour in his voice. "I know you feel the same for me as I feel for you! Stop running and come back to me!"

She did not even look back.

"Well then, if not now, whenever you wish, simply give me a sign and I shall find a way we can meet! Or look for my signal!"

Her fingers gripped her dress, holding it from the ground, as she ran along the path, her breathing heavy and her lips burning, while her breast ached from the pressure of his hand.

When she reached the end of the path, she slowed to a walk letting her dress fall and stepped out on to the open lawn where a crowd of elite society had gathered for the garden party.

Her fingers pressed against her breastbone.

"Mary, there you are." She turned as her brother's voice cut the air. "We were coming to find you. Katherine was concerned."

Mary looked to the lady who held her brother's arm. Her sister-in-law was kindness incarnate, but Kate was Mary's chaperone today. A blush burned beneath Mary's skin. She had let him kiss her. A man her father and brother had explicitly warned against.

"I walked down to the Jerseys' grotto. I wished to see it and I did not like to bother you, you were talking."

John's and Kate's eyebrows rose. They did not need to say, *Mary you should not have gone alone*, she knew it was an error now.

But his kiss had been beautiful. She had not known that a combination of lips and tongues could cause her body to ache... and ache in unspeakable places.

Lord Framlington appeared from behind the hedge. Mary looked back, the heat in her skin increasing.

The rogue smiled at her, then walked on across the lawn, implying, without a word, that something had happened between them. Heat swept over her.

"What were you doing?" John whispered, in a harsh condemning tone. Mary met his pale blue gaze; it was chilling, like ice.

What indeed? "I did not plan it," she whispered back, tipping up her chin to stand against her domineering brother. "I bumped into him." Literally. "I did not intend to."

One of John's eyebrows quirked. "Well I assure you, he did. Do not to speak to him, Mary, and certainly, never in private. If you are compromised, you will be tied to him. That is what he wishes. If you do not want to be forced into marriage with a grasping rake, then have more care; no wandering pathways alone. You're lucky he did not ravish you and wait on someone to happen along and see the two of you together. His situation is even more desperate than last year. The man cannot curb his spending, his debt is spiralling. There is not a prudent bone in his body. He's fortune-hunting, hard."

Mary's gaze fell to John's diamond cravat pin. She did not argue. Lord Framlington had proved John right – and her wrong. Very wrong.

Every word John spoke was true, she knew that, but something within her burned for Lord Framlington. He'd lit a flame in her a year ago, and it refused to be snuffed and if her heart had longed for Lord Framlington for a year, now it screamed… He had kissed her and fulfilled every expectation fostered in her dreams.

She shut her eyes to escape a giddy sensation. Simply thinking about his kiss caused her to ache for him.

She opened her eyes, denying her inner clamour. "I know, John, it was a mistake. I will not do it again."

"Do not fret, Mary, no one saw." Kate linked her arm with Mary's. "Did Lord Framlington do or say something to frighten you? Has he upset you?"

"No." Mary looked at Kate. There was no need for her family to know he'd kissed her. She did not wish John, her father, or her uncles, calling Lord Framlington out. It was only a kiss after all, no harm, not really. Except, if she'd stayed, she did not think it would have ended there. John was right: Lord Framlington was trouble. He had intended ravishment.

Why did her silly heart have to make her stomach flutter at the thought?

"He did not touch you?" John's fingers rested on her shoulder, his voice filled with concern, but there was an edge of anger to.

Her eyes turned to his. "No." Guilt thrust its knife into her breast. "Honestly, John, Lord Framlington merely frightened me. I know I made a mistake."

Lord Framlington had made her lie.

John's fingers fell away from her shoulder. "Well, if he's scared you, you will hopefully never make such an error again."

"Yes." She would not, she had learned her lesson. This could have ended with awful consequences. She felt torn in two, he heart pulled one way, towards danger, while her head and her family pulled another. She must listen to her head and heed common-sense.

If I'd been seen with him?

The blood drained from Mary's head. "May we go home?"

"If you wish." John looked at her, his gaze deep with concern, as though he only half believed her assurance. "I'll send for the carriage." He turned away.

"We shall say our goodbyes, John." Kate drew Mary closer and began walking across the lawn to where Lady Jersey stood among a knot of friends.

"He did disturb you," Kate whispered, "and I'm sure it was over more than nothing. You do not have to tell me, but just mind what John says and do not allow yourself to be drawn in by Lord Framlington's charm."

Mary looked at the woman she thought of as a full sister. "It was nothing, really, just nonsense." She was lucky, her family may caution, but they would always support her. Mary smiled. Kate smiled too, but her eyebrows lifted again.

"Nonsense to a woman, Mary, is manoeuvring to a man. Beware, males are predatory and determined when they choose to be, and Lord Framlington is of that ilk. Avoid him."

"I was… I am… I just… I never thought he would follow."

"Well, doing the things we never expect, is what they do," Kate advised conspiratorially. "But I will convince John not to tell your father and mother of this. No need for you to listen to this lecture twice."

Mary's smile lifted a little. "Thank you."

"Now let us get our goodbyes over with, and then, shall we stop at Gunter's for an ice; the day is so hot, I am positively melting." With that Kate flicked open her fan and began to waft the warm early summer air over them both, looking towards Lady Jersey.

Mary's gaze spun away scanning the lawn full of people for a gentleman with dark brown hair, a head above the rest. She spotted him in seconds she was so used to searching him out.

Lord Framlington stood among a group of men, laughing.

His head turned and his gaze reached across the open space finding her. He knew she'd been watching. He smiled, a self-indulgent smile and nodded before looking away.

Her heart raced, against her better judgement, her imagination whirling with images she should not see.

Chapter 2

"The game is on with Pembroke's little sister. I have settled on her. She is my choice." Lord Andrew Framlington, fourth son of the Marquis of Framlington, in name only, leaned back in his spindle chair, self-confidence flooding him. He hooked one arm across the chair's back and raised an ankle to settle on the opposite knee, modelling the pose of a dissipated rake. That was what he had been for most of his life.

"Marlow's ice maiden? Are you serious, Drew? The girl who freezes out all of dubious character? She has not allowed you near her since last year." His friend, Harry Webster's speech slurred a little.

"The same," Drew's gaze passed around his small group of loyal friends.

Harry sat forward in his chair. "Have you spoken to her?"

"Yes, and as you know I have been improving my character." He smiled at Harry. They knew he had kept himself away from whores for nearly a year – the kind to be paid. Yet he'd also kept away from the kind who paid. His friends did not know the latter fact. "You'll see. She'll be mine in a month, three at the most. She's taken my bait, a kiss, and I shall charm her into submission. She will be begging me to wed her at the end."

"She'll be yours within a week, knowing how women fall for

27

you." Mark Harper commented, his concentration still on their game of cards. He tossed a four of spades onto the table.

Drew looked at his hand of cards. No spades. He would trump them all with a heart.

"But didn't Pembroke warn his little sister off you?" Harry persisted.

"He has warned her off every man with a speck of dust in his closet. A man must have a spotless reputation to be considered." Peter Brooke, Drew's closest friend smiled.

"As if Pembroke can judge," Harry pressed. "That man is no saint, he is not spotless himself."

"But reformed," Drew answered. He un-looped his arm from the chair, leaned forward and set his card on the table, then looked at his friends, a wry smile twisting his lips. "Maybe the woman has a little contrary in her soul, though. Ever since he warned her off she's been watching me. Or perhaps she just has a taste for risk or badness hidden beneath her cold denials, or likes being naughty – any of which appeal, they are all to my advantage."

The group laughed.

Peter leaned forward to lay his card. "Well, I would not cross Pembroke or any of her family for that matter, they are far too influential. She calls a quarter of the House of Lords Uncle, even if her father is only a second son."

Drew did not need reminding.

Yet he intended winning her. He had waited a year, given her, and himself, the time to be sure. He was sure. She had come back to town this season and her eyes had still searched for him across the ballrooms, and the first time he'd seen her again he'd felt slain. The girl was beautiful, rich, innocent and his best hope of constancy – and ever since the night he had danced with her, he'd felt pulled into choosing her. It was a physical feeling, not simply a mental choice.

She had lived with him for a year, in his dreams, both in the day and at night.

Yet as certain as he was of his choice he was equally certain her family would not allow it. They would say no if he asked for her.

His contrary streak itched. He did not like being told no. No, was temptation. Like the girl running, it only made him want to chase. But he did not think she would run, not now – unless it was towards him. He smiled at his silent humour.

"You are going to wed her then?" Mark clarified.

"I've no choice. The duns are on my tail. I need to marry money. She's interested, available, and she has it. Plus she is remarkably kind to the eye."

"Kind to the eye." A sarcastic smile twisted Harry's lips. "That is lacklustre. The girl's the darling of society. They all fawn over her. She's stunning. I would have a go at her if I thought I stood a chance, but she'll not look twice at me. You however…"

"You have the looks and the knack, Drew," Peter expounded, "while we are all left to petty jealousy."

Drew laughed. "I have not won her yet, and you are just as capable."

"No. But we all know you will win her. I would not even waste a wager on it," Mark enthused.

"The question is, what will you do with her when you have her?" Harry laughed. "Now that is what I would like to see, however, after that, what on earth will you do with a wife?"

Drew looked past his friends at his small living quarters.

His rooms in the Albany were a decent enough bachelor's residence, but he would need something more once he'd wed. He longed for a property of his own. Somewhere outside of London and he would need space to lose a woman in. He did not wish to be crowded. In the last year, when he'd thought of marrying Miss Marlow, he had never considered the detail beyond the wedding night and receiving the cheque.

Still once he'd wed, he'd have her dowry and he could buy a bigger property, perhaps something with land, to make a profit from. She would understand that life and fill her time without his assistance.

His hands itched to be out of town and free of his reliance on Peter. His debts had swelled in the last year, barely anyone allowed him credit now and so more and more he'd become reliant on Peter's kindness. It unmanned him, but he refused to return to earning his living through sex.

But how the hell would he fit in a life with a wife... He had not one daisy petal of an idea how to manage land, let alone how to manage with a wife.

All the wives he knew spent their time cuckolding their inattentive husbands.

But that was why he'd settled on Mary, chosen Mary – he thought her different to those women. He'd watched her family for a year. They were all in what society deemed love matches.

Love – that word was false, in his experience. A non-entity. People did not love. They used the word to wound and hurt.

His mother declared she loved the Marquis, but cuckolded him constantly. While on the occasions the Marquis came to town he spent his hours with chorus girls. His mother's favoured companions were the sons of society and she was regularly in town.

Their behaviour was typical; he knew that because his mother's friends had begun his initiation into their world of fornication when he'd been fifteen. Ten years on and society had not changed.

But he had changed.

"Drew, I'm sure you're thinking of what the woman will be like in your bed, but you will not be saying goodbye to her come morning. I said, what will you do with her once you're wed?"

He had no idea. *What the hell will I do with a wife?*

Lock her away somewhere so she will not lay with other men. Or could he truly trust her.

She was not like them. Miss Marlow was his best hope of fidelity and yet she would not be in love with him... and he would not be in love with her. Theirs would not be a love match... He did not know how to love, he did not even really believe in it.

30

Perhaps if all failed he would follow his false-father's path and leave her to get on with it, find a country sanctuary for himself and rooms in town for her.

But quiet words whispered in his head, she would not be false. Deep down, he hoped so hard.

That desire was another secret he was keeping from his friends. They thought him a pleasure loving rogue. He was still, in a way, but…

God, how they'd laugh if they knew a man with his reputation hated the women he was meant to seduce. He could not stand female promiscuity anymore. Not since he'd discovered a group of women who abhorred such things.

The Pembroke women had become like idols to him.

He met Harry's gaze, his friend waited on his answer with an inquisitive grin, as the others carried on playing cards.

A self-deprecating smile twisted Drew's lips. "The devil knows."

"Pass her on to me!" Mark laughed. I'll entertain her when you're bored.

Drew's jaw stiffened, his hand itching to form a fist.

He threw down another heart, the knave, and claimed the trick.

Then he forced his shoulders to relax and leant forward, to pull all the cards towards him. But while he did so, he shook his head. It was an adamant, no.

"Why not share, you're hardly the monogamous type." Harry laughed.

Drew tidied the cards into a pile at his elbow. Then looked at Harry, and Mark. "Perhaps not. However, I require that quality in a wife. She shall be monogamous, and if any of you touch her…" His gaze passed to Peter too, "I shall call you out."

They all laughed.

Drew did not. It was not a jest.

"My God, Drew, have you fallen for her?" Peter charged. He knew Drew too well. They'd known each other since they were six.

Drew made a face at Peter, calling him ridiculous. "No, why

31

would I? That is hardly my style. I just do not fancy being done to—"

"As you have done to others… Chickens coming home to roost, Fram?" Harry threw Drew a broad smile.

"Exactly, I'll not be made a fool of." He'd willingly admit that much.

Let them know he would insist on a faithful wife, he just did not wish them to know how important it was, or that he planned to be faithful to. They would think him a fool.

* * *

A week had passed since the Jerseys' garden party, a week to contemplate her foolishness. Yet no matter how stupid Mary knew it was she had not ceased looking for Lord Framlington at every event. Her traitorous body refused to heed the frequent warnings of her conscience and her common-sense.

She had not seen him, but tonight, as she walked into the crush of another ballroom, on her father's arm, her eyes immediately identified her heart's quarry.

He stood in the far corner, with his elbow on a marble bust, leaning forward and speaking with a woman, the Marquis of Kilbride's wife. A beautiful blonde woman. Mary's heart sank and she looked away before Lord Framlington felt her observation as he always did.

John is right. She'd told herself so a thousand times in the last few days, and yet even as she said it her mischievous mind recalled the press of his lips and the feel of his hand cradling her breast.

Heat rose across her skin and awareness leaked into her senses, prickling along her nerves.

Why am I so attracted to him? This emotion never clawed at her when she looked at other men, and she had danced with dozens. It was just Lord Framlington her heart and body craved.

Ninny! her common-sense screamed. But her senses still

whispered Lord Framlington's nearness.

He walked past, barely feet away as if he knew his proximity made her senses sing.

Yet he did not look at her.

Mary gripped her father's arm more firmly. *I will overcome this attraction.*

There must be some man she could feel as much for. A man who did not have a wicked reputation. Who she could trust not to treat her ill.

"Miss Marlow, I would be extremely honoured if you will allow me this dance."

Mary turned and faced Mr Gerard Heathcote, one of her staunch admirers. He bowed deeply. He was a wealthy merchant's son who'd courted her last season. Her family liked him. He was charming, in a genteel way.

He'd made her an offer last season. She'd refused, saying it was too soon to settle on a husband. But that had been kindness. He was good natured, blonde-haired and blue-eyed. But her heart craved dark brown locks and laughing brown eyes with a wicked glint.

However Gerard was a good dancer and he'd become a friend, as were many of her beaux. But none of them were anything more. She felt nothing beyond like.

Mary swallowed back her growing impatience, letting go of her father's arm. She offered her hand and Gerard drew her away. Usually she enjoyed dancing, but tonight it was one endless boring whirl.

Since when did I become so jaded?

Since the rogue kissed me.

From this moment on, unless Lord Framlington repeated his kiss, her life would be dull.

* * *

Arms folded across his chest, with one hand loose, the stem of his wine glass dangling between his fingers, Drew watched the dance floor.

She was dancing again. Her hand held that of the young heir to the Earl of Warminster as she skipped along an avenue made by their set. It was a boisterous country dance. The boy was smiling as was Miss Marlow, brightly, giving her beau all her attention, and Drew had none of it.

He was beginning to wonder if instead of increasing her interest he'd jumped his fences with that kiss and made his horse bolt. He'd not once caught her looking at him tonight. She was instead doing everything she could to avoid looking at him.

She'd spent the entire night amidst a gaggle of youths – a mix of her female friends and their beaux.

The child she danced with laughed at every word she said. Drew suspected the boy would laugh no matter what she said, and undoubtedly Miss Marlow was bored. But even so her eyes focused intently on her idiotic companion while her female friends fluttered their fans, along with their eyelashes and cast their gazes about the room seeking to hook some unsuspecting male.

Irritation burned in Drew's veins.

He'd expected Miss Marlow to at least come closer. He'd even given her a clue earlier, by walking past her, suggesting a silent game they could play, passing close without touching, in secret acknowledgement. She had not picked up his gauntlet. She'd left it where it lay, kiss and all, and instead blatantly ignored him.

He leaned his shoulder against the wall silently seething. He'd thought this the victory leg but despite her youth and innocence Miss Mary Marlow was not going to be easily caught.

A challenge. He sighed, suddenly, letting the tension in his muscles ease with his outward breath. A challenge was like a chase, it whispered to his male instincts. He liked to be challenged. What fun would there be in life, if everything came easily?

Raising his glass of wine to his lips he watched her let go of young Warminster's hand.

Then she turned to take her place in the line of the set. Her eyes lifted, and her gaze reached across the room. It was literally a glance, only an instant, but in that instant their gazes collided. She had looked for him. She had known he was watching her all along and exactly where he stood.

A smile curved his lips as she looked away and began to clap, watching another couple skip along the middle.

You will be my wife, Mary Marlow. You will. And you will beg me to offer for you, when I do.

He was going to change his tactics, though, perhaps she needed a little less subtlety and a little more urging.

* * *

Lord Framlington's gaze made Mary's skin prickle on the back of her neck as she looked along the line of dancers. He'd stared at her for an hour. What he expected her to do she did not know. Perhaps he thought she would seek an assignation with him. She could even hear his words in her head, "Come and meet me, Mary, outside where it's cooler, where it's quiet".

It was nonsense of course, she was not psychic. It was her urge. Yet he'd applaud her weak conscience if he heard it and say, "Listen to it, do what you want to do, not what you should". It was his voice she heard.

"I know you feel the same for me as I feel for you! Stop running and come back to me!" he'd called when she'd run away from him, along the pathway.

How could he know, and how had Lord Framlington managed to invade her thoughts so utterly after one kiss? But it had not just been since his kiss, ever since she'd danced with him she'd heard his voice and seen him in daydreams, and when she slept.

His gaze left her, like a physical touch slipping away.

Mary looked to see him set his half empty glass on the tray of a passing footman before he strolled away, leaving the ballroom, and she presumed the ball.

A sense of desertion tugged somewhere in her stomach and an odd ache settled like a cloak about her heart.

Was that it then? Was it over? Had she spurned him successfully? That had been her intention, to cut him dead and she'd succeeded until that final moment when she'd dropped her guard and glanced his way.

Perhaps he'd taken the hint regardless and tired of playing with her. There were a dozen other heiresses on the market, she was not his only choice.

But you are his choice. Her traitorous, wicked heart thought it a compliment that a man of Framlington's looks and reputation wanted her as his wife.

"Idiot," Mary said aloud, to her heart. Unfortunately as the dance drew to a close, Derek heard it too when he took her arm to walk her to her parents.

"What have I done to deserve that charge? Did I step on your toes?"

Patting his arm she shook her head, forming the false smile she'd relied on tonight. "I was speaking to myself, sorry. I agreed to dance with two partners for the supper set, I will have to apologise to someone."

He accepted the excuse, without hesitation. Why would he not? Mary had not been in the habit of lying, until the day of the Jerseys' garden party. Now she had lied twice.

When she reached her parents Lord Derek gave her knuckles a chaste kiss and bowed. The kiss did nothing to her innards. Unlike the kiss on her lips that had twisted in her stomach like someone hurriedly coiling embroidery threads.

Physical memories clawing at her soul, the room spun and Mary longed for home. The burden of pretence was too tiring.

"Mary, is something wrong?" Her gaze lifted to meet her father's.

"I have the headache." If sulking made her pathetic she did not care. "May we go home?"

"Already, we have not even eaten supper?"

"I know, Papa, but my head hurts." Her fingers pressed to her temple. It throbbed with the pain of bottled up tears. She wished to cry over her insanity.

His brow furrowed and his fingers stroked her upper arm gently. "We will get you home."

"I must use the retiring room first though, Papa."

"Very well, you go up. I shall have the carriage called for, and tell your mother. We shall await you in the hall."

Mary turned away, her head pounding. She felt a little sick as she climbed the stairs. The retiring room was quiet. Her mother's maid was not there; she must have already been told they were leaving.

As Mary left the room, her fingers shook and she walked along the silent hall, with her thoughts screaming.

"Miss Marlow." Her arm was gripped, firmly and she was pulled aside, into an alcove, and then pressed back against the wall as Lord Framlington's mouth came down on hers.

She lifted her arms about his neck instinctively kissing him back with a longing that raged through her and took away the pain in her head, but then common-sense prevailed and she let him go, gripped his shoulders and pushed him away, whispering. "What do you think you are doing?"

"You have been playing a good game of ignoring me, but we both know you cannot. As I cannot ignore you." His breath brushed over her lips his voice low and quiet. She would have turned and walked away but he gripped her wrist and held her still.

"Miss Marlow. Mary. Darling. Do not deny this. I know what you feel, because I feel it too."

"I feel nothing."

"And that is why you kissed me a moment ago, and at that garden party. You feel. You want. But I cannot come to you in a place like this, so if you want what I can give you, you will have to come to me..."

"What you give—"

37

"Kisses, darling. Happiness. A life filled with moments like this. You know I am looking for a wife, I know your brother has told you—"

"Most men do not look for a wife in the shadows of a hallway, or a narrow garden path—"

"I am not seeking any wife, I am seeking you, and if you wish to explore that, you will have to come to me, Mary."

"No." She pulled her wrist free, and turned away, her heart pounding as she began to run.

She heard his deep voice echo down the hall. "You may run but I know you do not wish to… You will come back when you have had chance to reflect and understand what you will miss… I will give you time, Mary, and then we'll see."

* * *

Drew watched her hurry away. She was scared but interested despite her better judgement. She had kissed him back. Her denial was pretence. He'd felt her attraction in her body, her breasts had pressed to his chest, as her slender arms had clung about his neck.

He sighed.

The power of emotion in him had caught him off-guard. At the garden party she had answered his kiss hesitantly, but tonight, it was as if she had longed to kiss him again. In the first instant when the shock had silenced her fears, she had thrust herself at him, and thrown herself into the kiss.

He smiled.

She had kissed him with innocence on both occasions.

His hand gripped the back of his neck for a moment, then fell. What if he had been the first man to kiss her? God that thought pierced through his chest, like a spear surging through him.

The first to press his tongue into her mouth.

Lord. The idea floored him with a sudden punch. But then he smiled, as the novelty of it bloomed, uncurling in him like a shoot from a seed, it rose up. Hope.

He walked along the hall; she had already reached the stairs and disappeared.

She was becoming more and more essential to his future. No other woman would do. She was his choice, and he was not going to be deterred.

She simply needed time.

Hell she had kissed him back with hunger tonight, albeit a little clumsily, but who cared. Who cared when he had been the first man to claim her lips – like a pioneer, and he intended to claim much more.

There was only one way he knew how to woo women, and that was with his body, he could teach the woman things she could never have imagined.

Innocent. He could not even remember how that had felt. But he knew how to make her feel good. He would give her the gift of sensual discovery and then she would never be able to refuse him. He would have her then.

But if she was running from kisses, she was not ready for that yet.

He needed another approach for the present and he had one; if the girl wanted to play hard to get, let her. If she wished to fain disinterest, then so could he.

He laughed.

He would give his little fish more line. Let her have some time to contemplate her choices. He doubted any of her young beaux made her heart race, or her bones melt. He doubted she had thrown her arms about their necks, and he had a very strong feeling she had never kissed any of them.

He would reel her in in a week or two when she'd had chance to realize his kisses were better than a hundred dances with the children she had danced with here.

What he had said to her was true, he felt the same... He knew she desired him, as much as he desired her.

Mary sat in her family's coach bowling towards her brother's town mansion.

The coach swayed on the uneven cobble. Its motion made Mary feel sick.

"It is unlike you to suffer with headaches, Mary, is something wrong?" her mother whispered.

Mary shook her head, then stopped as pain hammered in her skull.

"You look pale," her father stated. "Has something happened?"

"I just need to sleep," she whispered. She'd done very little of that in recent nights, and she feared she would not sleep tonight. The strength of Lord Framlington's kiss still trembled through her nerves. "I will be well tomorrow."

Leaning forward her mother pressed Mary's knee. "We will be home soon. Would you like me to sit with you a while when you retire?"

"No, thank you, Mama." Their kindness was cloying when Mary knew she was living a lie. She was not who they thought she was, she was not good, she was bad, or rather, she wanted to be bad. Everything Lord Framlington had said was true, she wanted to meet him, and kiss him again. He tempted her.

Now she felt as though he had poured himself into her blood, her body throbbed from the memory of their sudden encounter in the dark, and she could still feel his gentle grip on her wrist.

When they reached home, Mr Finch, her brother's butler, opened the door. John and Kate were at a private dinner. Her younger brothers and sisters were all in bed. Her mother came upstairs with Mary, helped her undress and then tucked her in to bed, even though Mary had not wished her to.

"May I fetch you anything? Something for the headache?"

"No, Mama, thank you, I just need to sleep."

Her mother smothered the candle then pressed a kiss to Mary's forehead.

"I am not a child, Mama," Mary whispered into the dark, although she longed to be held and for the turmoil inside her to ease.

Her mother sighed. "I know you are now nineteen. But you are still my daughter and you always will be, no matter your age."

Her mother's fingers touched Mary's hair. "Goodnight, sweetheart."

Mary rolled to her other side, feeling guiltier than ever, and wept.

She'd done nothing wrong, not really, not yet, it had only been kisses that she had allowed, but she had a dreadful feeling she would. She could not quell this longing for a man she should not want.

* * *

For the third night after she had kissed Lord Framlington for a second time, Mary looked for him with no success. Her heart ached. She longed to see him. She missed the rogue, with his little knowing nods in her direction, and his charming smiles.

He had asked her to meet him but then disappeared and made that an impossibility. While his kisses continued haunting her…

She wished for wickedness. She wished for kisses and embraces.

"Miss Marlow. Damn it, you stood on my foot." Mr Makepeace was a wealthy landowner, but he was double her age and as dull as working on embroidery. He was boring, and he was rude. She may have missed a step, because she had been daydreaming, about Lord Framlington, but it was ungentlemanly to curse at her for it.

"Forgive me." The heat of a blush touched her cheeks as people along the line of dancers looked over at them. Oh, she longed for a dance she had shared with a man a year ago, she had barely heard the notes of it; her thoughts had been too absorbed by the colour of his eyes.

They were hazel; a light shade of cluttered brown, but when the

41

light caught his eyes it turned the colour to honey, a soft amber or gold. It had literally gilded his eyes.

The men she danced with were young and weak in nature, and silly compared to him, or too old for her, like Mr Makepeace, and dull, or in between but so busy seeking to portray a fashionable ennui that they had no personality at all.

The dance came to its conclusion, thank the Lord.

Breathing hard Mr Makepeace walked her back to her parents. She smiled at her mother. Then turned to Mr Makepeace. "Thank you." He nodded in return then walked away.

Good riddance…

She looked about the room for Lord Framlington, he still was not here. She was becoming angry with him now. Why? Where was he?

She huffed out an unladylike breath. "Mama, I wish to go to the retiring room."

"I will come with you."

"That is not necessary, the hall is busy; I will not be alone."

"Very well."

Mary turned away and then pressed a path through the crush of people out into the hall and then across to the withdrawing room. She had foolishly hoped to discover Lord Framlington hiding somewhere. He had not been hiding anywhere.

The rogue had known how she would feel, how she felt… *You feel. You want, but you know I cannot come to you in a place like this, so if you want what I can give you, you will have to come to me…* But how could she come to him if he was nowhere to be found!

She hated him.

He was playing with her.

She loved him too, though. No one she spoke to or danced with compared to him, they were all a mile beneath him.

He was beautiful, witty, charming… and poor… A fortune-hunter, and a rake.

Her heart thumped as she hurried back to the ballroom still

looking for him. He was not there. She did not return to her mother, she sought her friends. Someone to talk to. Though she had not spoken to them of Lord Framlington, they would think her mad. Everyone would think her mad. She could not even explain to herself why she liked him so much. But she did.

Her heart pounded harder even at the thought of him.

"Mary!"

"Emily," Miss Smithfield was one of Mary's more recent, less confident, friends. She had looked lost one evening, sitting out a dance against the wall, and so Mary had befriended her.

"Mary. You poor soul, I saw you had to dance with Mr Makepeace." Lady Bethany Pope kissed the air beside Mary's cheek.

Mary made a face. Bethany and Emily laughed.

"Hasn't he asked you to dance every night this week?"

"Good heavens, yes, but hopefully never again, I stood on his foot."

"Deliberately…"

"Perhaps." They all laughed but Mary heard the hollowness in hers. Her life no longer interested her. She was bored. She missed the sense of danger hovering across the ballroom when Lord Framlington watched her. He made her feel different from everyone else, special. Every other man she danced with, danced with a dozen other women, she was no exception to any of them, and yet she had never seen Lord Framlington dance with anyone since he'd danced with her. Nor did he stare at anyone but her…

Although he had talked to that blonde woman the other day…

She sighed.

Had she lost him, by not conceding? Had he given up on her?

"Miss Marlow." Mr Gerard Heathcote bowed before her. "May I have the honour of this dance?"

She wished to scream. No! She had danced with him ten dozen times, he was nice, polite… Boring.

Oh, her father had never spanked her, but he would wish he had done if he knew how wrong-headed she had become.

She dropped a shallow curtsy and then gave Gerard her hand. "Of course." In reality she wished to run from the ballroom and out into the dark garden. It was raining outside, she quite fancied a thorough soaking. Perhaps it would bring her to her senses.

On the twelfth night after her second kiss with Lord Framlington, when she returned home with her parents, she stopped at her bedchamber door, and refused to let her mother in. "Please, Mama, I can retire alone. You cannot treat me as a child forever."

"Yet—"

"I know it is only out of love, but I wish to retire alone, Mama."

As soon as she shut the door, the tears came. They had been hovering all night as she had looked for Lord Framlington almost constantly. When she'd waltzed her gaze had spun about the room searching every corner. Her dance partners must have thought her mad.

But she had come to the conclusion that it was over. He'd given up on her, and so she ought to listen to common-sense if the man was so fickle.

But her bitterness was washed away by tears. The maid in her room unbuttoned the back of Mary's bodice, and then unlaced her stays. Mary looked at her, the stains of silent tears still damp pathways whispering their presence on her cheeks. "Pray tell no one that I have been upset. You may retire."

"Are you certain, Ma'am."

"Yes absolutely certain."

When the maid left, Mary did not even bother to strip off her clothes or blow out the candles, but tumbled on to the bed and cried. Not only because she had not seen him, and may not see him ever again… but because she was a complete ninny for wanting to see him.

"Fool." she breathed into the sheets.

Chapter 3

Pride in his self-discipline burned in Drew's chest as he strolled into the Wiltshires' ballroom. He'd avoided Miss Mary Marlow for two weeks and now the moment to return was ripe.

Lord Wiltshire, The Duke of Arundel was her uncle. The girl would be feeling relaxed among her family and find it harder to be false and he hoped easier to establish a moment to escape as she'd done at the Jerseys'.

Looking down from the top of the entrance stairs, at the end of the Wiltshires' ornate ballroom, he briefly scanned the crowd of heaving humanity, the *ton, England's elite,* in all their shining glory.

If her uncle knew Drew's intent he would never have received an invitation, but he 'd kept away from Miss Marlow in public since last year and so, to her family, he was simply another name on a list to fill the room and enable every society hostess's wish for a crush.

He saw Miss Marlow; she was not far from the foot of the stairs and when his name was called she looked up. He rarely entered a room without drawing the attention of women, he ignored the others and smiled at her, holding her gaze.

She had been looking for him, for two weeks, and she had missed him, he could see it in her eyes; they were sparkling bright with relief.

He smiled at her, and for the first time in nearly a year she gave him a little self-conscious, confused smile back.

Her eyes asked him questions as she kept looking. "Where have you been? Should I seek you out and ask?"

Yes, you should, Mary.

He let her gaze go and smiled at the room in general to avoid her family noticing the exchange. If they whisked her away to the country to avoid him, his game would be off entirely for this year.

Drew wasted his first hour in the card room. This early in the evening she would be too much in demand to risk slipping away.

The supper bell rang and the music died, then guests surged into the room set aside for refreshments. Drew sauntered in a little late, at the rear; a gentleman acquaintance with whom he'd been playing cards at his side, a friend he'd picked out for the sole purpose of gaining entry into Miss Marlow's family group.

If he was going to tempt her he needed to throw her at least a little more bait. His companion was an old mutual friend of Drew's and Pembroke's, from their days in Paris, during their dissipated grand tour. Days the Duke of Pembroke preferred to forget. Like Pembroke, Roger Harris had turned prude, and therefore Harris was the perfect camouflage, he would be welcome even if Drew was not.

On cue Roger called, "Pembroke!"

The family group were sittting about several tables. Drew ought to be daunted, but daunted was not within him, what he felt was a swell of anticipation, exhilaration. This was a bold move. He was walking a line, willing Miss Marlow to notice him while he wished her relatives to spot nothing out of the ordinary.

His quarry sat amidst her uncles and aunts on her brother's table.

"Roger! I did not know you were in town." Pembroke rose and strode the few steps towards them. "Is your wife with you?"

With Pembroke's attention focused on their mutual friend, Drew let his gaze deliberately meet Miss Marlow's. He caught it just for an instant, a moment in which his heart forgot to beat as her pale blue gaze struck his – summer skies and azure Italian seas. She was still deliberating. "Should I seek you out?"

Yes!

Her beauty literally kicked him at times. He forgot to breathe.

"No, I'm afraid Miriam is in her last month and not fairing too well…" Harris babbled on about his family.

Drew nodded marginally to Miss Marlow. A blush stained her pale skin red. Drew let a hint of a smile form at one corner of his lips then looked away, nodded to Harris, lifted his hand in parting and walked on. He wanted her to watch him; it was his signal.

Satisfied the bait had been set. Drew helped himself to items from the buffet, but did not bother with a plate, he did not wish to spend the supper hour eating. He stopped to acknowledge a few acquaintances, and then extricated himself from several ex-lovers, before turning to walk from the room.

He glanced at Miss Marlow as he passed.

She was watching. Would she follow?

He gave her an encouraging echo of a smile.

"Should I?" The thought shone in her eyes.

His absence had done its job, all her pretence had gone.

Striding on across the empty dance floor he looked back. Her gaze followed him still. He smiled again and nodded. *This is your chance, Mary, darling…*

Deliberately picking his path to keep within her view he walked to a set of open French doors and stepped into the tepid night air, looking back one last time, throwing her a calling card.

He was too far away now to be sure she still watched, but something in the turn of her head told him she did.

Come on little beauty, follow.

Outside he walked to the end of the Wiltshires' stone terrace, he could not go too far, she would not find him.

The terrace, like the ballroom, was deserted.

He leant his buttocks against the stone rim of the balustrade.

The dark house walls framed the empty ballroom and the view into the dining room, like a picture, with huge chandeliers illuminating the scene within.

It made the terrace darker.

He withdraw a slim cigar and a match from the pocket of his evening coat, lifted the cigar to his lips and struck the match on the stone beside his hip, then held the flame to the tip of the cigar and sucked until it caught.

At least he had an excuse to be out here if he smoked.

Taking the cigar from his lips he let the smoke slid out of his mouth.

Miss Marlow smiled at her sister-in-law, the Duchess of Pembroke, nodding at something the other woman said. Then her face turned to someone else across the table, a gentleman, one of her uncles, and she laughed. Pembroke spoke to her. Drew could see the Duke smiling at her, at something she must have said, before he laughed with her too.

Her father approached behind her, stopped and pressed a hand on Miss Marlow's shoulder. He leaned and kissed her temple.

Drew took another long draw on the cigar he held between his fingers.

It was as unreal as watching a play at the theatre. Drew did not understand a family like that. They moved in a pack, a pride, like lions, closing to defend and protect one another whenever the need arose, all the men prowling about their lionesses.

I really ought to be daunted. He was not, very little dented either his ennui or his ego.

But Miss Marlow dented his ennui.

That was good. He hardly wished for a wife who'd bore him.

He sucked on the cigar again, relishing the flavour of tobacco in his mouth. He knew how to enjoy things. He'd learned to make the most of every little gift life gave him when he was young. He would enjoy making Miss Marlow his.

Rising, smiling at her brother and her father, and then passing the sunshine of her beauty about the others at her table, Miss Marlow then bobbed a slight curtsy.

Drew smiled, sensations dancing a bloody jig in his chest; his little fish had taken the bait.

Strolling away from the table she weaved a path through the other guests, stopping occasionally.

Drew's heart beat a steady elated rhythm. He felt as though he'd been dealt the most superb hand of cards, but there was still a risk that if he laid them wrong he'd waste their benefit. There was still a requirement for skill and caution. He had to be careful now.

When she reached the ballroom instead of turning towards the open French doors, though, she disappeared through a door at the side of the room near the entrance stairs.

Shutting his eyes Drew urged her with all the will power he had, to… *Come to me!*

But damn it, if she did not, he was not giving up; he would simply have to find a new tack.

Drew opened his eyes lifted the cigar back to his lips and sucked in the smoke, then looking up to the stars he blew out a circle.

The night was clear, a blanket of very dark blue with thousands of sparkling pin pricks of light. He loved night, like he loved storms. His soul had always turned to the dark and wild.

As a lad he'd lain outside for hours, looking up at the endless pitch black and he'd loved swimming in the dark, clothed only in moonlight. That had always been his purest escape. It had been a whole other world.

A small dark shadow flew like a dart in the air over his head. Bats. He smiled, watching them swoop and turn. Now he'd spotted one, he saw more, they were after the moths which had been drawn to the light spilling from the windows.

"What are you doing? Where have you been?"

His own little moth came to the flame. Her wings would be burned. But, God, he could not believe how much his heart thumped, and exhilaration coursed through his blood.

49

Her voice had come from the foot of the steps which descended from the terrace to his right.

Lifting his weight from the balustrade, his eyes searched her out in the darkness.

He caught the movement of her pale lemon dress about two feet away from the bottom step.

"I am waiting for you," Drew answered her first question as he descended the steps, feeling the tug of her presence pull at him.

She was young, six years his junior, but he'd never seen her behave as a girl. She did not fluster or giggle. No, Mary Marlow had a serene womanly grace, she was kind, sensible, confident and extremely beautiful.

His eyes adjusted to the darkness.

"Tell me where you have been. I have not seen you for days."

A few teasing curls of her ebony hair had fallen to lick her jaw and throat where he'd like to place his lips; and her eyes sparkled diamond bright as they caught a shaft of moonlight and challenged him.

His game of patience had been a brilliant hand.

"I have been giving you time to make your choice. Does this mean you have made it?"

"This…"

He'd confused her. Hell he was confused himself.

The movement of her fingers clasping together before her waist pulled his gaze lower.

She was anxious. She should be. But he was too. The emotions inside him were eclectic. Hope. Desire. Need. Desperation. But there was respect and pride too… When had he ever felt respect for a woman? Never before.

"You being here – is this your answer? If it is you took your time." He stepped from the bottom step to stand in front of her, aware of the hardness in his voice and a stiffness in his body, but both were due to the bewildering mix of emotions causing turmoil inside him. He did not know this ground; did not know how to speak with a young innocent woman.

"I could hardly get up the minute you walked out. I do not even know why I am here."

Ah damn it, he needed to forget his anxiety, forget his own fears. He did know how to woo women. She was a woman.

"Because you want to be here." He moved closer. "With me." He dropped his cigar on the dew damp grass.

"Do I? I barely know. All I know is that I missed you watching me."

When he lifted a hand, she stepped back.

He smiled, his fingertips brushing her cheek. "You want more kisses, Mary. You can hardly have them if you do not let me near." Damn it, he needed to persuade her to stay and not run again, to persuade her to be his wife – and the only way he knew how to do that was through sex. He needed her to let him close.

* * *

Is that why I am here, to let him kiss me again? She had not been able to define the pull which led her here.

She had seen him enter earlier, and her heart had leapt at the sight of his splendid figure as he stood at the top of the stairs. But she'd wanted to know where he'd been. Why he'd stopped following her?

To give her choice…

But choice had left her with a desperate, quivery feeling inside. Choice, separation from him, had been painful – and yes, she longed to be kissed.

He had a magnetic quality. When he'd walked out his gaze had called follow, and an invisible thread had pulled her here.

Lord Framlington pulled that invisible thread again and it drew her nearer still.

His fingers trailed across her jaw, then his thumb brushed over her lips.

She met his gaze, though she could barely see him in the darkness beyond a silhouette. The smell of tobacco carried on his breath.

This is madness. Why did I come to him? Why am I doing this?

"Not here," she breathed as his lips neared hers. "Anyone may see us."

She could not see his lips curve and yet she sensed they did. His fingers opened, spreading to cradle the line of her jaw while his other hand gripped her waist. He pressed her backward.

In a trance she let him back her into the darkness, into the corner where the wall of the house turned at the side of the steps, and met the high yew hedge bordering the garden beyond the terrace.

They were deep in the shadows, she could not see him at all, but she could feel his tall frame against her and his strong hand half holding, half caressing at her waist, while the hand cradling her jaw slid to her nape and pulled her mouth to his.

Oh heavens.

His lips were firm then soft against hers, coaxing her to kiss him back.

A sensual ache spiralled through her stomach, sliding down between her legs. Her arms lifted and her fingers settled on his broad shoulders as she leaned into him, clung to him, and gave herself up to kissing him back.

It was delicious and wicked, and utterly stupid. But she didn't care, she didn't want to think, she just wanted to feel. Her body fitted to his perfectly, her back curving, her hip bone pressing to his, her breasts crushed against his chest.

A groan rumbled deep in his chest. She felt it in her mouth and her breasts.

His tongue slid between her parted lips, tentatively at first, then deep, then tentative again, tempting her, encouraging her to seek more.

She wanted more with a bone-deep longing; his kiss dissolved her senses.

Her fingers clasped his hair as he pressed her further back, the wall grazing one shoulder while the sharp clipped bows of the yew hedge pierced her other.

The sound of the orchestra spun into the night air. The supper hour was over.

He did not stop, his tongue danced about hers as his fingers cupped her bottom and pulled her hips more snugly to his.

A ridge of hard flesh in his trousers pressed against her abdomen, it ought to have scared her. It did not.

His grip stayed tender and gentle while the play of his tongue enchanted.

"God, Mary, you're beautiful," he whispered into her mouth. "Better than I imagined."

His fingers slid up over her hips and her waist, then settled at her ribs and his thumbs brushed the first curve of her bosom.

"Mary," he said her name again with a dizzying awe. Then he kissed her jaw and her neck, while his palms settled over her breasts, kneading her flesh through her gown.

Voices spilled from the open French doors onto the terrace. People would be dancing again soon, crowding into the ballroom and walking out on to the terrace. Her heart pounded hard, fear, excitement and bewilderment mingling.

He didn't stop, his teeth nipped her neck while one hand left her breast and slid downwards.

Oh.

He touched between her legs, stroking inward over the material of her gown pressing it to the warm wet flesh at the juncture of her thighs.

She knew men and women joined there. That was where she craved him.

His strokes were tender, careful, like his teeth and lips on her skin, and the grasp of his hand on her breast.

Anticipation and desire climbed, as if her body sought a peek.

Her breath quickened and a sob broke from her lips as delicious sensations wove a spell in her blood.

The hum of conversation seeped from the ballroom along with a melody the orchestra played.

She should tell him to stop, but wrapped in the darkness, hidden from view, the danger had become exhilarating.

His hand clutched her breast harder and his thumb swept back and forth across her hardened nipple, while his fingers stroked forward and back in the cleft between her legs caressing her aching flesh.

Her hands clawed on his shoulder and his neck, clinging, as a whimpering sound left her lips.

He silenced her with a kiss.

She could not kiss him back, she could not think as whatever peak she raced towards approached as if she flew on a firecracker. *Goodness. Oh heavens.*

She exploded, and fell from the sky, then the sensation inside her was carried on a flood of water swirling beneath her skin, reaching out to her toes and fingertips as she gripped hard at his neck and shoulder, afraid she would truly fall.

A sound of amusement, half laugh, came from his lungs, slipping into her mouth as he drew away.

He looked down at her, but she could not see his face, or his eyes. His fingers touched her face and his thumb ran back and forth across her cheekbone.

"I could make a sound and have someone find us like this." he whispered.

"Is that what you want?" His thumb touched her lips as she breathed heavily, still a little disorientated. He was breathing heavily too and through her grip on the back of his neck, even through his neckcloth, she could feel his heart racing hard.

She was not afraid, nothing about him spoke of danger, *but I do not know him at all.*

"I want you," he answered, in a hushed voice. "I want you as my wife."

"You want my dowry."

"I want you, and your dowry. I know your brother hates the idea of a man in need of a fortune, but he has one. It's hardly a crime to need to marry wealth, just circumstance. But any of three dozen heiresses could bring me money. I want you, Mary."

She smiled, knowing the darkness hid it. "You could choose a military career and work for your living."

His thumb swept across her cheek. "I have not even enough to buy a commission. Besides would you wish to follow the drum?"

"The clergy then…"

"Me, a vicar? Are you mad? That would never work." A scoffing rumble of amusement growled in his throat.

"I must be, I am here with you."

His thumb and forefinger gripped her chin, then tilted it up. "Do I have your interest?"

"To be your wife?" Mary fought a desire to kiss the lips lingering over hers. "I barely know you. All I know is you are a rogue."

This time his amusement erupted as a proper laugh which someone might hear. "Guilty as charged, I'll not deny it, but now I'm looking for more than amusement. I did not do this with you for that. I wish to marry you. I am trying to persuade you."

"For money…."

He shook his head. "Money, yes. I need it. I'll not lie to you. But I want you, too, not only your fortune." His lips brushed hers, weaving enchantment, fogging her mind.

She forced herself to cling to common-sense. "And if I had no fortune…"

He did not answer. He'd said he would not lie.

He would not choose her if she was penniless. But that was the way of life. There were three dozen men in her uncle's ballroom without expectation of inheritance, or the desire to be shot at on a battlefield, or the inclination to preach… All of those men were in need of a fortune.

She pushed him away.

As he moved back, his hands slipped to her waist.

"I have to go. I will be missed."

"When can I meet you again? Where? Do you ride in the morning, in Hyde Park? What if I were there at nine, would you come?"

Male voices drifted on the night air, rising in volume, they came from the terrace.

"I don't know. I have to go." She slipped from his hold, both physically and mentally, and hurried back across the grass to the courtyard entrance she'd come from, then returned to the ballroom via the servants' entrance.

He was not in there. He'd gone.

Mary found her father, who commented on the length of time the maid had taken to fix her hair. It was only teasing.

She'd lied to him, deceived him and disobeyed. She had never done any of those things until the Jerseys' garden party.

Insanity had claimed her.

What had she done?

Her heart raced, her blood running thick with the memory of their intimate caress.

"Miss Marlow, will you dance?"

She turned to face Lloyd Montague, another of her usual set.

She liked him, she liked them all, but they did not intrigue or enchant her. The only man who did that liked to make her dance with danger.

She accepted Lloyd's arm and let him lead her into a waltz. But she longed to be outside with Lord Framlington again.

Would she go tomorrow? She could, if she took a groom.

But would it be wise?

Of course it would not. It would be anything but wise. But she wanted to go.

Where would this lead if she went? Not to marriage. Her family would never permit it. It could only lead to disgrace.

She would not.

Chapter 4

Drew sat astride his horse, waiting by the gates of Hyde Park. Miss Marlow was thirty minutes late. She was making a fool of him.

Impatience bit hard. His hands on the pommel of his saddle he shifted his weight, and as he did so, he thought of her in his hands last night. Something gripped within his stomach, something which was not lust. She had melted him. Entirely. He had been ice and now he was water… She flowed in his veins, he'd never had an encounter with a woman which was so… beautiful… so real

God his heart had thundered as hard as hers at the end, and he'd wanted to yell out with jubilation. She would have thought him insane, and of course, it would have meant they may have been caught.

His friends would think him insane too if they knew how he felt.

He'd smiled for the rest of the night, like a damned green youth who'd just discovered the sport, and he'd still been smiling this morning.

She had been all that he'd hoped of in an innocent woman.

He, Drew Framlington, had been the first to show the beautiful Miss Marlow what true pleasure could be!

Yet she had not come this morning. He was not smiling anymore.

Damn it. Waiting on a woman was not Drew's forte. He'd rather walk away than wait. But he craved her now, he could never choose another woman now. Not after her beautiful response last night… and he needed to marry someone, he needed a bloody fortune too. He refused to go back to his former life and give pleasure to his mother's friends for money, yet if he did not come into money soon the dun's would have him in jail.

Devil take it, she'd shattered in his arms last night…

He'd not thought she would allow him so near so soon, but she'd been willing him on, kissing him back with an un-virginal fire.

He wished this courtship over and Miss Marlow in his bed, just as much as he wished for her damned money.

But it seemed he'd lost his touch.

After the climax he'd given her last night, and it had undoubtedly been her first, she had been shocked by it, he would have thought she'd be here begging him to marry her.

He lifted his watch from the pocket of his morning coat. Five minutes more had passed.

She'd stood him up.

Bloody hell. He would never live it down after he'd bragged to his friends that they could begin their celebrations.

Women, damn them, they were all fickle.

He saw her.

Lord. Something bit into his chest. Relief. Desperation. Then came the flood of hope on a wave of a storm of sensations even deeper than he'd experienced before.

She rode along the street outside the park, a peacock feather bouncing above her head, to match her vivid blue habit. The colour a sharp contrast to her pale skin. She sat the horse extremely well, her spine rigid and her grip on the reins firm. She looked magnificent riding the glossy jet black stallion.

A groom rode beside her, keeping guard over the Marlows' precious package.

Drew smiled and tugged on his reins, turning his mare away from the gate and setting it to walk across the lawn.

58

He could not let their meeting appear planned. It must look accidental. His heart raced as though he was galloping, not walking the horse.

A clear blue sky stretched from one horizon to the other.

Drew kicked his heals and stirred his horse into a canter, giving her time to enter the park and his heartbeat a chance to recover from the sight of her.

It was not busy but there were others about.

Once he'd ridden a few hundred yards he swung back, turning on to the outer path. She was a couple of hundred yards into the park, rising and falling in a trot.

She'd seen him, he could tell. She was not looking his direction, but he somehow knew from her stance.

Riding nearer he slowed from a canter to a trot and lifted his hand as though he'd just noticed her. "Miss Marlow! Well met!"

With his raised hand he lifted his hat and bowed his head in greeting, ignoring the groom who gave him a hard glare.

"Lord Framlington!" Her voice rang with a bright false pitch as she turned her horse towards him.

She was worried. A surge of something he was not used to feeling for anyone other than his younger sister, Caro, surged through his blood – a need to reassure and protect her

He slowed to a walk as she did, then stopped, his horse facing hers.

"You are out riding early, Miss Marlow?"

"I thought to come out while it's cooler."

"May I ride a little way beside you?"

"If you must."

Drew smiled, as she turned her horse. He turned his, walking the animal close beside hers.

She looked over her shoulder and signalled for the groom to stay back.

The man's glare bored into Drew's back.

"You are late."

"Well, that is a woman's right."

"Is it?" He glanced sideward.

Her habit hugged the curve beneath her breasts, the arch of her lower back and her slender delicate arms. He was falling into the enchantment of her innocence, fast and hard. His hunger was intense. He no longer even cared that she'd kept him waiting. She had an aura which pulled him close, winding around him like a charm. She gave him life, he felt different in her company.

It was probably just her beauty affecting him... All men must be dazzled by her. She was exceptional.

"Let us race?" she said, flicking her whip and setting her animal off, not waiting for agreement.

He kicked his heels, following her into a gallop as her horse tossed divots of grass at him.

The sharp rhythm of horse's hooves pounded on the earth, and her laughter played on the air between them.

He gained ground and pulled ahead. She did not concede but tore on towards the lake, laughing still.

When they neared the lake, he pulled up, a full half leg in front. She stopped too and her horse turned a full circle.

"What was that?" he called to her.

"Fun!" she breathed, laughter dancing in her pale eyes as he rode closer. "I was not going to come you know."

Her groom had been left a quarter mile back, but he could see them.

"So that was why you were late then, a change of heart?"

"Not exactly. I always behave. I always do as I should. Perhaps I just wished to kick up my heels."

"Then this is not to be taken as any indication you agree to my offer."

"Definitely not." She shook her head. "If my family knew I was here with you, they would—"

"Slaughter me. I know."

"Then, you cannot, for one moment, imagine they would agree

to a match. They would think I had run mad."

"You would be mad not to." He held her light blue gaze. "I gave you a glimpse last night of how good it could be."

She smiled, her eyes catching the sunshine. "In your bed you mean. That says nothing of how we would get along. Marriage is more than that, my Lord. Much more. And my family would never agree. They neither like nor trust you."

"No… Then why did you come?" Drew did not intend to seek consent. He knew he would never be approved, the only one he sought to convince was her.

She stopped her horse from prancing and her gaze locked with his.

Those eyes. Who was seducing who?

His gaze fell to her lips.

"I have no idea. I think I am insane." Her words kicked him firmly in the chest, and a soft ache hovered in his middle, as his gaze lifted back to her eyes.

The girl was a breath of fresh air, a light summer breeze. Sunshine.

"Could you not sleep, Miss Marlow, for thinking of me?" He laughed, feeling hope swelling inside him.

She blushed slightly. She had spent the night awake then. He hoped he'd hovered in her dreams as she had in his.

"So where do we go from here?" He encouraged her to take another step towards commitment.

"Where…?" A frown marred her beautiful brow. She had genuinely not thought about his offer then, merely their embrace.

"What next?" Drew clarified.

She shrugged, a dainty little gesture on her slim shoulders. "It should be nothing."

"But it will not be nothing, because you want more, don't you?" She needed more persuasion. Drew leaned forward and gripped her hand as it held her reins, holding both her and the animal steady. "Where will you be tonight?"

Her gaze clung to his. Maybe her common-sense told her there should be nothing more but other parts of her, that he had sway over, bid her answer. "I am attending Lady Frobisher's musical evening."

Musical evenings were a rogue's curse, he could do nothing untoward when seated in a row of chairs. The game was off then, for tonight.

Nor could he meet her again in the park, once could be deemed accidental, but twice would draw attention. Without doubt the groom would mention this encounter to someone in the house.

"Miss Marlow!" A timely call came from their rear.

Drew glanced back. Her groom had come to retrieve his damsel from the beast.

Drew let her hand go and straightened. "Tomorrow then, where?"

"I shall be at the Phillips' supper party." Her gaze passed over Drew's shoulder to the groom.

"There then. They have a large glass house in the grounds, to the right of the house. I'll meet you there at midnight." Drew's eldest brother had been at school with the Phillips' son, he could obtain an invitation.

Mary nodded. She had begun an intrigue. She had definitely become foolish.

"I shall look forward to it, immensely. Until tomorrow then, Miss Marlow." His fingers reached for hers. Instinctively she released the reins, letting him take her hand. He lifted it to his lips, turned her hand, his thumb pressing into her palm, and kissed her wrist, above her glove.

Her heart skittered, its rhythm racing violently.

When he let go a smile lifted his lips and glinted in his eyes but the gleam turned wicked as his gaze shifted to her groom before he turned his horse and rode away.

Mary ached for him. She'd wanted this for a year… to give in to longing. But she should not have agreed to an assignation; it could mean nothing more than kisses.

"Forgive me, Miss," Evans spoke when he drew near, "you should not speak with gentlemen."

"I shall speak with whom I wish, Evans." She sounded like John, and she was not normally harsh with servants.

"Miss Marlow." The man lifted his fingers to his cap and tipped it forward, "Forgive me, but it is my duty to inform your father."

"That I met a casual acquaintance in the park by chance and spoke with him? There is hardly anything to tell, Evans." She ought to feel guilty. She did not, not yet, perhaps later.

It was as though she no longer knew herself.

She had lied to her family, and a friend, and now she was widening the net of deceits to the servants. It would trap her in the end if she was not careful.

She turned her stallion in the direction of the park gates. *I cannot continue this.* Tomorrow must be the last time she spoke with him and allowed his kisses. Unless she chose ruin.

Her heartbeat flickered and her stomach somersaulted. Was she fool enough to do that?

But John had increased her dowry as a gift to broaden her choice of husbands. Why did it matter if she chose a man who needed it?

Because John thought him heartless.

She rode out of the park gates beside Evans. Lord Framlington seemed sincere. He had not hidden his need for her fortune, just said he'd chosen her over other wealthy women.

Mary knew he'd chosen her, he'd chosen her a year ago; she had not needed to hear him say it, because her heart had chosen him too, and since then they'd watched each other through the crowds.

Whether she believed him or not, though, it did not matter. John did not like him and therefore nor did her father, and therefore Lord Framlington could never be hers.

You are a fool Mary. End it tomorrow. It can go no further.

When she drew her horse up before her brother's front door,

Evans swung down from his saddle and offered his hand.

She took it, lifting her knee from the pommel of her side saddle. Then he made a step with his hands so she could descend.

Before leaving him, she said, "You need not trouble yourself to tell tales, Evans, I shall inform my father."

Bowing he tilted his cap again. "Miss Marlow."

Lifting the hem of her riding habit from the ground, Mary ran up the steps to the front door which a footman held open.

Her family would be in the breakfast room. She headed there, stripping off her hat and gloves and passing them to a footman on the way.

Her youngest brothers and sisters ate in the nursery, but those who could sit sensibly shared the adults table and so the breakfast room was full and noisy. She smiled at her father and mother when she entered, and then at John and Kate.

Mary loved her family. She'd never lacked a thing. She'd always felt secure. So why did the danger Lord Framlington dangled draw her away?

"Mr Finch said you were riding, Mary," her mother said with a gentle smile, "that is unusual for you." It was a subtle question.

"I slept poorly and the morning was so sunny I could not resist." Mary bent and kissed her mother's cheek, then moved to take a seat among her younger brothers and sisters.

"Had you asked I would have ridden with you," her father stated.

"It was a momentary decision, Papa." Her eyes focused on the spout of the coffee pot, as a footman filled her cup, a blush warming her cheeks.

"Was Hyde Park busy?" John asked from the head of the table.

Her gaze lifted and met his.

John was older than her by a decade. He behaved more like a second father than a brother. Looking away she helped herself to bread from a plate a footman held. "Not very, I saw Lord Framlington, though. He stopped and spoke." She let the words fall as though the incident meant nothing.

"Then you must not go again without a chaperon."

"John," Kate spoke from the other end of the table. "Mary took a groom and I'm sure she is able to cope with Lord Framlington. She was in the open, and she is sensible."

Mary smiled at her sister-in-law.

The footman dished up some scrambled eggs and smoked fish.

"I have no concern over Mary's behaviour," John answered. "It is his I worry over."

Mary looked back at John. "Why do you dislike him?"

The question made her father look at her too. "He's a fortune hunter."

John's eyebrows lifted. "And a man of his ilk, is not for you."

"His ilk?" Mary could not help pressing. She wanted to understand. She wanted to convince her heart it was wrong.

"This is why, she needs a chaperon." John looked at Kate. "He speaks to her, and now she is asking foolish questions." He looked back at Mary. "What did he say to you?"

Heat burned under her skin. "Nothing beyond courtesy."

"So he put on the charm. Do not believe any of it. It is feigned."

Mary set down her knife and fork. "I cannot see—"

"Mary!" Her gaze passed to her father. "This is an inappropriate conversation." He glanced at her younger sisters. "I trust you to be sensible. But I agree with your brother, no more unaccompanied rides."

She held her father's gaze for a moment, before looking back at John.

He nodded.

What had Lord Framlington done to be deemed such a villain? Many men needed to marry for money, Lord Framlington was right, that in itself was not a crime. He was a rogue too, but many men were that also, they lived recklessly then grew up – as John had done.

But surely if he intended marrying her his rakishness did not matter, he was not planning to seduce and desert her. Her father's and brother's arguments were groundless.

Mary focused on her breakfast. Perhaps John had some vendetta against Lord Framlington; he had not spoken against any other man so adamantly.

Perhaps she would ask Lord Framlington why her brother disliked him tomorrow.

The thought of meeting him made her appetite slip away and a dozen butterflies take flight in her stomach.

Chapter 5

Drew strolled into White's, his gentleman's club, seeking masculine company, a game of cards and conversation.

He found his friends in their usual place. Harry Webster, Mark Harper and Peter Brooke sat in the first salon.

"Fram!" Harry called. "I thought you were hunting Miss Marlow..."

Drew smiled. "She is attending a musical soiree, a place where it is impossible to pursue the chase."

His friends laughed. Drew signalled to a footman to bring him a glass of brandy.

"How goes the seduction?" Mark asked when Drew sat beside him.

"If it were simply seduction it would be done, but as I am seeking a wife the game is more complex. Despite allowing me certain favours, Miss Marlow has given not a single indication she will agree to become my wife."

"Favours?" Peter laughed.

"Tell," Harry added.

Leaning back into the winged leather chair and letting his hands fall onto the arms Drew grinned at them all. "I am hardly likely to share. If all goes according to plan she will be my wife."

"I cannot see why that prevents you," Harry pressed, his gaze darting across the room then back. "Your brother never keeps his triumphs in the dark."

Drew looked over his shoulder, sure enough his eldest brother sat a distance behind him, accompanied by their brother-in-law, Lord Ponsonby. Ponsonby had married Drew's eldest sister. Neither man was an example Drew wished to emulate. A sneer touched his lips. Drew's sister, Ponsonby's wife, was no better.

The only member of his family who had not broken their marriage vows was his younger sister, Caro, Lady Kilbride. However, her husband, the Earl, had. That man had a violent nature too which poor Caro constantly lived in fear of.

Caro was the only member of his family Drew felt close to.

Drew looked back at Harry, glowering.

"I take it you will not then," Peter quipped.

Drew's gaze spun to his best friend. "Definitely not!"

The others laughed.

A footman appeared with a tray bearing Drew's brandy. Drew took his drink, then looked over his shoulder at his eldest brother, who was now looking at Drew.

Drew lifted his glass, in mock salute, then turned back to his friends.

* * *

Raising the dress of her ivory satin gown, Mary hurried along the garden path.

She'd left at the commencement of a set, hoping her family would not notice her absence. They were all busy dancing or talking.

There were no lanterns to light the way, deterring couples from strolling into the garden but the night sky was clear and moonlight shone through the leaves of shrubs in places so she could see the route.

Etched in the moonlight Lord Framlington's figure formed a

vivid silhouette in the darkness when she reached the glass house.

"Miss Marlow," he called, stepping forward when she drew near.

Her heart skipped and her stomach spun like a top. She'd barely been able to eat since she'd last seen him, and she'd not slept last night; as her thoughts danced a reel.

She had to end this. It was beyond foolish.

But she wanted to be alone with him one last time.

He looked dangerous in the darkness, she ought to be afraid of him. She only knew him by reputation and that was bad. Yet she'd never been so pulled towards anyone – surely her heart could not be wrong?

His lips lifted in a half smile when she reached him and his fingers touched her face. He'd removed his gloves. "I was not sure you'd come. You've barely given me a glance this evening."

Her fingers captured his and drew them away from her face, as she smiled too. "I did not wish to make my family suspicious. I'm already in the mire for speaking to you in the park."

His other hand lifted suddenly, then gripped her nape and pulled her mouth to his.

He kissed her long and hard while he braced her nape with one hand and his fingers also weaved between hers and twisted her arm behind her back.

When he released her she was short of breath and her heart thumped.

But he was short of breath too.

His dark eyes held her gaze for a moment. "We should go inside in case someone walks this way."

She'd forgotten the risk. "Yes." They should not be kissing on the garden path where anyone might find them. But then she should not be alone with him.

Her hand clasped in his, he pulled her into the conservatory and closed the door.

Orange, lemon, olive and fig trees, in terracotta pots, lined the pathways in the huge glasshouse and the scent of warm earth merged with the floral aroma of the delicate flowers dangling from vines above them.

The grip on her hand claimed her. It said he treasured her. She was not anyone to him.

She felt special.

Was it an illusion? If she believed John, Lord Framlington thought nothing of her; he only cared for money.

He turned to face her, illuminated by moonlight through the glass above them, his starkly handsome face painted silver. He smiled, a smile that shone in his eyes too. He stepped backward one pace, then another, pulling her with him, leading her deeper into the glasshouse. "The exemplarily Miss Marlow has fallen from her pedestal." His tone teased.

"Or perhaps a certain Lord has pulled her from it."

His smile lifted again, this time it had a wicked lilt. "I accept the charge. I am sure it was deadly dull upon it anyway."

Yes, yes it was, and lonely at times.

Perhaps that was why he tempted her. She should not feel lonely in such a large loving family but she had no space to be an individual. She wished to be loved singularly, to be the most special person to someone, to him. Like her father was to her mother, and her mother to her father.

She looked beyond him, closing her lips on her disloyal thoughts.

A small wrought iron table stood on a paved area among the plants, with a few chairs gathered about it. Beyond it she saw the river Thames through the glass. She'd forgotten the garden bordered it.

Ripples ran with the current of the river, shimmering in the moonlight. While dots of light sparkled from windows and lanterns on the far bank. It was a scene from fairytales.

Lord Framlington lifted their joined hands, pulling her awareness back to him as he brought her fingers to his lips, then kissed them. His dark eyes gleamed staring at her glove, then he freed the button at her wrist, and then began to pull each fingertip free.

Once the glove was loose he stripped it off and tossed it on the table where his gloves laid. Then he removed the other too.

She should not allow him to touch her skin, but beautiful sensations skipped up her arm as his lips pressed on her bare knuckles.

Was everything which felt good wicked?

"What are you thinking?" He pressed a kiss on each of her fingertips.

Her heartbeat stuttered, she could not find words to reply while his breath warmed her skin.

Pain circled low in her stomach.

His gaze lifted to hers, "What, Mary?" then lowered. He slipped the tip of her little finger into his mouth and sucked it gently.

She pulled her hand from his grip, a blush burning. "I should not allow you to do this."

"You should not be here, come to that." His voice was deep and low.

"No…"

"But you are." His hands braced her waist.

The danger she faced reared. They were a long way from the house. No one would hear her cry out if he forced himself on her.

Her heart raced harder as her fingers gripped the muscle of his arms through his evening coat and her breath caught in her lungs as she looked up at him.

"You do not trust me." It was a statement, not a question.

She did not. How could she? "I barely know you…"

"Apart from your brother's tales."

His face had moved into shadow. What had seemed an enchanted place, suddenly felt like a gothic novel.

"I'll not hurt you," he whispered. "Don't heed him, I am no monster, Mary, darling. I do not wish you harm. I want you to be my wife, why would I hurt you?"

"I… I…" She struggled to find words as his gaze dropped to her lips.

She turned her head, so he would not kiss her. He merely kissed her cheek instead.

A tremor raked her muscles as his lips touched her earlobe too, then her neck.

Her fingers clasped his arm. "Why does John dislike you so much?"

His head lifted, moonlight catching as a glimmer in his eyes, which were dark here. "Pembroke sees himself in me. He was not always a saint. He had an affair with my eldest sister."

"With your sister…"

He smiled. "I suppose he did not mention it. Yes, he cuckolded my brother-in-law, Lord Ponsonby, not that I think Ponsonby cared. It was when we were in Paris."

"You were in Paris with him…" His palms felt heavy on her waist.

"Yes." The deep masculine burr tingled over her skin.

John had spent seven years abroad. She'd written to him, but he'd rarely replied and she'd been too young to hear much of how he'd lived. He'd married Kate soon after his return.

"If you do not believe me, ask him. I doubt he'd lie. A young man's recklessness is part of life – a part your brother now claims to be above. But he has no cause to judge me ill beyond my lack of wealth."

"But you have a reputation."

"Yes. Ignore it, it is irrelevant to us; your brother had a reputation. Now he has a wife. This is about the two of us, no one else. You and I shall be all that counts."

Her heart ached. But her common-sense whispered. "Only because you need my money."

"What I need right now, Mary, darling, is not your money. I need you."

A muddle of turbulent emotion writhed inside her but longing overrode them all, as his lips pressed down on hers.

She forgot doubt and responded as his tongue slipped past her parted lips. Her fingers gripped his shoulders and when she slid her tongue into his mouth, he caught it lightly in his teeth, for an instant, before sucking it deeper.

It was so intimate.

Her fingers slid up into his soft, thick hair.

I love you, the words whispered through her thoughts unbidden. She did, she loved him, no matter what John said, no matter the risk. She loved him.

His hands held her, resting against her back.

She remembered everything he'd done the other night. His lips left hers and began travelling a path of kisses along her jaw then down her neck.

"You're beautiful," he said, against her skin.

She shivered. "And rich," she whispered to the air above her, forcing her mind to return to reality.

His head lifted and a soft laugh left his lips as his finger tapped beneath her chin. "Yes you are rich but there is far more to you than money."

His fingers fell to either shoulder and slipped beneath the short sleeves of her gown then slid them down. They hung loose on her arms and her bodice sagged

His gaze dropped to her breasts, and his heated palms cupped them.

Mary's mouth dried and she looked up at the glass roof above. It reflected her image, against the jet black wash of night.

She saw his dark hair against her pale skin as his lips touched the hollow at the base of her neck where her pulse flickered.

When his fingers slid into the fabric and gripped her breasts, she shivered again.

Oh dear Lord. A sweeping sensation plunged down to the place between her legs. She ached for him there.

He eased one breast free, then his lips brushed her nipple before covering it and then sucking it; cradling her nipple on his tongue.

Her bones dissolved and her fingers clasped in his hair, as she watched the mirror image above them.

This was wicked, but delicious; the sensations intoxicating.

Her breath came in pants. He made her body ignite.

Still sucking her breast, his hands slid to her hips, and began lifting her dress.

Cold realisation drenched her, he was not going to stop. He did not simply expect kisses. "No."

Her fingers, slid from his hair, gripped his shoulders and pushed him away. "No." She had not completely lost all sanity.

His gaze cut through the darkness, meeting hers, his heavy breaths echoing against the glass. "Mary." His fingers unclenched, letting her dress fall.

But when she would have stepped back his hands slipped to cup her buttocks, and pulled her closer still.

A column within his trousers pressed against her stomach through their layers of clothing. "See what you do to me."

Her grip on his shoulders urged him away. "Let me go."

"You have no need to be afraid of me." His hands slid back to her waist then fell as he stepped back.

Her fingers shaking, Mary righted her bodice and lifted her short sleeves, unable to look at him.

"I would not hurt you." His voice hit a hard tone.

Fear and wariness slashing at her foolish soul she met his gaze. What if her instinct had been wrong? She had good cause not to trust him. It was not only John who thought ill of him, he was an outcast, ignored by most.

"For God sake, Mary." His pitch lifted to anger.

Her chin titled defiantly. She had to stop this before it became too late to turn back. "I will not meet you again."

"I did not hurt you." Irritation brimmed in his voice.

"I know you did not." She stepped back – away. This was the end. "I did not say you did, but I cannot… I will not meet you again. I won't hurt my family. I cannot keep betraying their trust."

"Then what are you doing here?"

"I came to tell you… I would not—"

"You took your time saying no. If that was your intent. You came to be made love to…" he growled.

Mary held up a hand, to ward him off. "Love is not involved in this. I may be innocent, but I am no fool either, Lord Framlington. You may convince me you are attracted to me but you will not persuade me this has anything to do with love." *At least not on your part.*

That was her downfall. She'd let him take liberties because she did love him.

* * *

Silver moonlight caught in Mary's eyes.

Pain shone there.

He'd said he would not hurt her, but he had. That cut at him. He thought of Caro… and himself as a child… The only time when perhaps he could compare his feelings to understand Mary's. He never wished to hurt Mary.

Damn, he was unused to women with a heart – a woman who knew love. A woman who'd been surrounded by it her entire life.

His error glared him in the face. He should not have wooed her with passion. It was not her body he had to persuade – it was her heart. She wanted to be loved. Of course she did.

"Andrew," he stated bluntly.

Why had he given her his full name?

Her chin tilted higher, reminding him of her brother's stubborn countenance.

How the hell do I make her love me?

"What?" Her tone rang sharp and challenging.

She did not even know his name. He'd wooed her physically and not even let her in so far as to tell her his name.

His voice dipped to a calmer conciliatory pitch. "My name is Andrew, although most people call me Drew."

"Oh." She looked confused. Perhaps she also realised how many favours she'd allowed him without even knowing his name.

"Say it." His voice held the undercurrent of the desperation humming in his blood. He could not let her walk away. Everything hung on him winning her. The idea had fermented in his head for so long, he could not choose to change his path, not now. He could not bear to be with anyone but her.

She took a breath. "Andrew."

A fist gripped hard and firm in his gut.

"Or Drew… That suits you more, it is more dangerous."

"You deem me dangerous… I'm not the devil, Mary, just a man. A man looking for a wife, you, and once we are wed, every morning when you wake, you will say my name; and when we retire, I'll make love to you, slowly and thoroughly so you know it is not a marriage solely for money."

Uncertainty flickered in her eyes. But he knew he could not progress. He needed to regroup, and think of a new strategy. To make her love him?

Damn. He knew nothing about love.

But an odd sensation seared in his chest.

If she came to love him, he'd rejoice. It was what he wanted – a faithful, committed wife. He had no idea how Mary would fare once they were wed, but surely if she loved him it could not go awry. "I want you, Mary. If you need to be loved, I will love you, I swear it. I'm half in love with you already." It was surely true, the emotions inside him were a turmoil of desperation, need and hope.

Her eyes turned cold. "Or half in love with my dowry…"

Her stubborn insistence that he desired her money made him angry. "You were right earlier, you don't know me. Money is not all to me." He picked up her gloves and thrust them at her.

She took them, then turned.

But he caught her elbow before she could leave

"I have to go. I am promised for the next dance."

"Next time—"

"There will be no next time!" Her elbow slipped from his grip, and then she was gone, her ivory clad figure disappearing into darkness.

Bloody hell, he'd lost more ground than he'd gained tonight. If she would no longer come to him then how the hell was he to progress? He could not approach her, that would make her family suspicious. They would remove her from town.

Striding from the garden he didn't bother heading back to the ball, instead he headed to his club. He needed to drink, and think.

Chapter 6

After breaking her fast, Mary retired to the drawing room with her mother, her sister-in-law Kate and her sisters, while the boys were at lessons upstairs. She chose to sit on a sofa in the sunshine, beside her younger sisters, Helen and Jennifer, who were busy working on embroidery samplers. Mary guided them.

"Excuse me, Your Grace."

Mary looked up. Mr Finch stood just inside the door, a small silver tray balanced on his fingers.

Kate held her son on her lap, and had been amusing him with a wooden rattle while Mary's mother sat on the same sofa, with Mary's youngest sister, Jemima. They'd been studying a picture book.

They all looked up.

"What is it Finch?" Kate asked.

"A letter for Miss Marlow," Mr Finch intoned.

"Mary?" Her mother looked in Mary's direction, a question bright in her eyes. Who?

Mary stood, heat flaring in her cheeks. She received letters regularly from a variety of friends, and her cousins, but they came with her father's and John's post.

She took the letter from the tray, her skin glowing.

Mr Finch turned to leave.

The writing was unfamiliar. But… Surely not…. It was large, bold strokes. She broke the blank seal and looked at the bottom of the page.

D. F.

Drew Framlington.

Her heart pounded against her ribs.

Her family had noticed her absence last night. She'd told them she had gone to the retiring room. Even so her father had admonished her for not telling her mother. They had warned her of rousing unnecessary gossip.

Kate had interjected then, saying she'd experienced such things and would not wish them on Mary.

By the time they'd come home, Mary had been thoroughly chastened, and been made to feel painfully guilty. She'd cried herself to sleep, then woken barely an hour later, thinking of the things she'd let him do, and what he'd said.

Holding the letter she crossed to the window.

"Who is it from?" her mother asked.

Mary glanced back. "Lord Farquhar." *Daniel*, one of her friends, she'd known him since her come out, her mother knew him too.

Her mother smiled with a fond look, before turning her attention back to Jemima and the picture book.

Mary longed to take the letter up to her room but that would look odd. Instead she sought seclusion on the window seat, slipping her feet from her shoes and then lifting them on to the cushion before her.

My dear Miss Marlow,

Has any man told you what a treasure you truly are?

The rogue, he actually referred to her fortune in a pun. She smiled, more amused than angry.

What I would give to make you mine, you cannot imagine. I am yours, a hundred times over. I adore you. Your ebony hair and your alabaster skin. Your eyes, as blue as a summer sky, or an azure sea, so pale they are like ice. They make me shiver when you turn your gaze upon me, turn it my way often and forever, Mary dear. Make me yours, make me love you. If love is what you want, bring me to your heel. I will come. I will beg for you if that is what you wish, only never turn your smile away from me, that is what I live for, to see your perfect smile.

And your lips, I have not yet spoken of those…

It was nonsense of course, all nonsense, and it went on and on, profoundly expressing her beauty and his adoration, while not once claiming to love, but pleading for her to give him the opportunity to fall in love. It begged her to tame him. It asked her to show him how. Then he finished it all with a silly poem.

When she folded it and lifted her gaze, a smile curved her lips.

He'd not been deterred by her dismissal yesterday. That gave him credit. He was more serious about choosing her than she'd thought. He could have simply transferred his attention to another wealthy woman.

"What did he say, Mary?" her mother asked.

Mary looked across the room. "He is gushing, Mama." It was becoming far too easy to lie. She rose from the window seat, and slipped her shoes back on.

Her mother smiled. Her sister-in-law Kate looked up and smiled too.

"Are you interested in Lord Farquhar?" her mother asked, with a curious look.

Mary laughed. "Heavens no, but it is flattering."

"Let me see!" "Let me read it!" Her sisters cried.

"No!" Mary clutched the letter to her breast as they rose and rushed over.

"It's personal," her mother admonished. "Helen, Jenny, sit back down and leave your sister alone."

Fortunately her parents were not in the habit of reading her post. They trusted her.

A sharp pain cut deep into Mary's chest.

She did not deserve their trust anymore.

She'd been beyond foolish last night. She would have lost her family's respect forever if she'd been caught with Lord Framlington. She would have been utterly ruined. She would have had to marry him.

But, then, surely, his discretion was another point in his favour. Even his letter did not contain anything which would force her hand.

Last night he could have had what he wished, her hand in marriage, her money, if he'd arranged for someone to discover them.

Surely that he had not arranged it – that he would not act without her consent – meant he was honourable despite his reputation. Then he must also – to some degree – care for her.

"May I take this letter up to my room, Mama, so I can put it in my travelling desk?"

"Of course, sweetheart." Her mother gave her another fond look.

Mary fled the room with sinful, wrong notions, spinning in her head. If only she knew his address she might write back.

No! No! I have finished with this foolishness.

* * *

Fate played an odd game on Mary at the Fosters' ball; as Mary stood talking with Miss Emily Smithfield, Lord Farquhar asked Mary to dance the first set.

She accepted with a shallow curtsy, smiling at him, then glanced back to give Emily, who invariably ended up the wallflower once more, an apologetic smile. Emily was the shy type, too quiet, but as she had only come out this season, she was still finding her place in society.

Mary looked back to see if Emily had found another companion to speak with, and caught her mother watching. The look in her eyes resembled the one in the drawing room that morning. Her father's eyes glistened in the candlelight when she looked at him.

They thought she carried a torch for Lord Farquhar and he for her.

Mary turned away.

Lord Farquhar carried his torch for her good friend Lady Bethany Pope.

Oh heavens, lying never brought any good. It was always found out. The only time she'd lied in her childhood was when she'd accidently broken her mother's perfume bottle. She'd hidden the broken bottle and claimed no knowledge of it. They'd known because she was the only one who smelt of the perfume.

She'd been in more trouble for lying than for breaking the bottle.

She'd never lied again – until the day of the Jerseys' garden party.

Lord Farquhar's eyes twinkled with good humour as he led her on to the floor. She liked her friends. She'd formed a good set last season. She glanced back at poor Emily. She was sure Emily would become settled, her friends were loyal, happy people, and generous in nature, all of them – yet none of her male friends carried an air of mystery, as Lord Framlington did. She selfishly wished for a life that was more exciting than this.

Her heart ached with a bitter sweet sadness. Lord Framlington made her long to unravel all the things he kept hidden. He was exciting...

Yet she had not even known his given name until she'd been about to leave him in the glasshouse.

The image of his eyes as he'd asked her to say his name aloud caught in her memory.

He was... vital... consuming heat... danger – and mystery. All other men were bland compared to him. How could she carry a torch for a bland man when there was Lord Framlington to compare to?

She would probably never marry, and then if she never married her whole life would be dull.

"You do not look quite the thing this evening, Mary. You look distracted. Is anything wrong?"

Lord Farquhar's fingers gripped hers as they passed each other in the format of the country dance.

She had not even spoken to him since they'd walked on to the floor. "Nothing is wrong. But thank you for asking. I am merely tired, I have attended too many entertainments..."

"You can never attend too many... Are your shoes pinching? You may have too much dancing if your shoes are pinching..."

Mary laughed at his attempt to cheer her but stupidly it sent her tumbling into the doldrums.

If she never spoke to Lord Framlington again she would have to endure an entire life of dullness?

"I should be honest. It was not I who noticed. Bethany did. She sent me to cheer you up."

"Ah." Mary glanced at Bethany, who now stood beside Emily, then she looked back and smiled at Lord Farquhar.

She must cease longing for Lord Framlington. This was enough to make her happy. It had to be, and happiness was enough. Even if inside she spent her life screaming for excitement.

When the dance drew to an end Lord Framlington entered the ballroom, as her group swapped partners then formed the next set.

He walked with a group of men. They stopped and looked about the ballroom.

One gentleman's gaze passed over her, then jolted back, stopping on her for a moment before he turned to the man next to him, his lips tilting in a smirk. Then they all looked at her.

She turned away.

Lord Framlington had spoken of her to his friends, then. What had he said? She hoped he'd not told them anything.

"Mary?" Philip Smyth took her hand and pulled her into motion as the music began. She was one step behind everyone, her heart racing as nausea tumbled in her stomach and light-headedness made her feel as if she might collapse.

But she did not give in to her weakness for the dark-haired, vibrant brown-eyed Lord Framlington, she lifted up her chin, caught up the step and continued, focusing on Philip and smiling as hard as she could.

When the music drew to its crescendo and ended in a brisk flurry, relief and a desire to reach the safety of her mother swamped Mary. But before she had chance to ask Philip to take her back, a shadow fell over her. She turned. John's cousin, from John's father's side, stood beside her, Lord Oliver Harding, with another man.

"Miss Marlow."

She had met Lord Harding at several events but he'd never paid her any particular attention. He was older than John and not interested in John's young half-siblings.

Mary curtsied. "Lord Harding."

He smiled, bowing only slightly then he turned to the gentleman beside him.

Heat burned beneath Mary's skin. He was one of the men who'd entered with Drew.

"May I introduce Mr Harper to you Miss Marlow, he begged an introduction. Mr Harper, Miss Marlow, is my cousin's sister."

Mary searched for a memory of the man's name but could recall nothing. She'd never seen nor heard of him before.

He gripped her hand, then kissed the back of her glove. Goosebumps ran up her arm, like a cold breeze had swept in to the room.

Bowing her head, to avoid his gaze, she curtsied a little.

When she rose and looked at him, she met piercing, assessing, blue eyes.

His blonde hair gave him a look of innocence, but his eyes denied it entirely. He was a rogue, of the worst sort, the sort who did not even bother to court wealth. That was why she'd not seen him before, because he was not the type of man to attend sedate functions. Even the card room here, she was sure, would not play deep enough.

He was a man who danced only with sin – and Lord Framlington's chosen companion…

"May I have this dance, Miss Marlow?" If she refused it would be obvious to everyone around them as the sets had already formed and she would have to leave the floor alone. Philip had turned away.

Her mouth was too dry to answer. She nodded, anxiety spinning in her gut. Why would he single her out? What had Lord Framlington said?

"You're very beautiful, Miss Marlow. More so than I'd thought, I admit. Now I can see why he is so smitten."

"He?" Her cheeks heated with a deeper blush as they took the first steps of the dance moving forward then back. Then they turned to make a ring of four with the couple to their left.

Mary faced Lord Framlington.

Ah. So this was the game?

They completed a full circle, hands joined as a four and then she turned, looking at Lord Framlington and walking towards him as the dance required.

"Miss Marlow," he acknowledged her with perfect formality.

Her fixed smile faded.

The next move was a closer turn, shoulder to shoulder, he pressed close. Heat scorched down her arm, and burned inside her, her heart thumping hard. She opened her mouth to breath, but there was no air.

"Mary," he leant a little to whisper to her ear. "Did you receive my letter?"

"Yes."

"Will you write to me?"

There was no time to answer. They were parted by the figures of the dance.

She faced his friend again, her heart pounding as she sought to watch Drew through the corner of her eye. There were no other moments to speak with him, and the rest of the dance seemed endless as the complicated patterns moved Drew further and further away.

* * *

During supper, Drew stood apart from everyone, hands in pockets, as he watched those eating. Miss Marlow was in the bosom of her family, again, surrounded, laughing and happy. Happy? Now there was a word, a word like, *love*. Had he ever known what it was to be happy? How the hell did he know who was happy?

He'd laughed last night, though, laughed and got very drunk. He'd called at White's after he'd left her, searching for his friends.

They'd not been at White's, but he'd tracked them down in a gambling den not far from St James.

He'd dragged them all from their game, and Peter and Harry from the whores draped about them, and taken them back to his bachelor residence for a more intimate night of masculine companionship.

On the way there he'd explained his plight.

How was he to convince the girl to love him? How did a man use romance and not sex to woo a girl?

Harry, particularly, had laughed heartily.

Drew could see the humour in the situation, the renowned seducer smote by a lack of love.

What the hell did he know of love?

His friends had spent the next three hours in drunken hilarity, advising him on the subtleties of love, and its difference from desire.

The letter had been Peter's idea.

He'd leaned back in his chair, lifting his glass of brandy and grinning. "What you need my friend, is a bloody good poet. Prose is your key. All women fall for it. They like to be told their eyes are like this, their lips like that, they love to have their beauty praised."

Between them then, through much laughter, they'd constructed the basics of the letter. The prose, had in fact, been mostly Peter's. This morning Drew had re-written it with a sober hand and sent if off.

Yet, having played a part in the game of catching Mary Marlow, his friends had declared their interest in attending the next ball. They were eager to see the outcome of this new, more tactical, game. They'd considered it brilliant luck that Mark knew the Harding twins, Pembroke's cousins, and then another plot had begun to spin, one to gain Drew access to Mary at the ball.

The Hardings were not as high in the instep as the Pembrokes. Lord Oliver had not even lifted an eyebrow at Mark's request.

The plan was, once Mark had the introduction he would introduce the others and then they'd all dance with her, and if Drew merely passed her during moving sets, her family would not suspect any particular intent.

But the reality proved frustrating. He could only speak to her for an instant here and there.

He'd asked if she had the letter, if she'd write, if she'd missed him, she'd had no chance to answer anything to any real degree. Then he'd resorted to brushing her shoulder with his fingertips once.

It was hardly enough to win him a wife. He was not going to be able to convince her to take him like this.

Turning on his heel he walked from the supper room, he needed to think, he needed to settle his mind. He'd go for a smoke. Then he realised, suddenly, in a blinding thought, he'd asked her to write, but she didn't know his address. He could hardly put it in a letter, her parents might see it.

Changing direction then, he searched out a footman in the hall, and asked for a quill, ink and paper to be brought to the gentlemen's smoking room.

He let her dance with her friends, for the first and second dances after supper, but then he asked Peter to lead her out.

The dance was a pattern of four. Drew picked a quiet little wall-flower of a woman to partner him.

Two movements into the dance he and Peter swapped partners. It was not a requirement of the dance. He'd agreed the move with Peter to gain longer access to Mary.

Of course Mary realised instantly what they'd done and her jaw dropped on the verge of exclamation, but he caught her fingers in his as part of a turn and squeezed them hard. It effectively silenced her. The little wall-flower seemed to think they'd made a mistake. She was smiling at Peter as though she thought him foolish, but then knowing Peter, he was probably charming the girl and making her think he was the one who'd planned the swap.

"Lord Framlington," Mary whispered in a harsh tone. "Why are you playing this game?"

He bent his head and although he felt like being harsh in return because she had returned to distancing him with the use of his surname, he softened his voice to honey. Some elements of seductive skills could still apply when making a girl fall in love… by convincing her you suffered the same condition… "My dear, it is no game. I told you, I want you for my wife. I am not backing down. Steadfastness is surely an element of love."

Lord Framlington bore arrogance tonight. He obviously did not like losing. She had enough brothers and male relations to know how stubborn they could be.

"It is no statement of love to want to win at any cost." She did not like being used like a puppet.

"You are on your guard, Mary, darling. I told you, I will not hurt you."

"Anything between us will hurt me, when it will hurt my family…"

"But what if it hurts you and I more to be held apart. Does my steadfastness not express my heart's devotion?"

"You are determined, Lord Framlington, I give you that. But devoted, I question, I do not think you devoted to anything beyond my dowry."

"Call me, Drew—"

"Lord Framlington."

His eyes shone with condescending humour. "Must I be set back so far?"

"You have not been set back at all. There is simply no going forward. Is there? Our—"

"Affair…" He leaned forward and whispered the word. It vibrated through her nerves.

She took a breath. "Hardly that, but whatever it is; it is over – and was always folly. I cannot hurt my family."

"Folly," he whispered. "I have heard it said, Miss Marlow, that each of us has a soul mate, and if I am yours, if we are each-others, would you throw that away because your family did not like the man of your heart, and hurt that man, who ought to be higher in your heart – your future husband. Families rear us; then they are meant to become second in our lives."

His words struck her like a slap – *and if I am yours, if we are each-others, would you throw that away because your family did not like the man of your heart, and hurt that man…*

That was bloody prophetic. Where the hell had it come from? Drew would be spouting this drivel as second nature soon. But he would do anything to win her, including prattling, idiotic, poetic words.

The dance separated them for several movements. But his gaze clung to her face.

She was intoxicatingly beautiful. Whenever he looked at her a jolt sparked in his chest as well as his groin. His thoughts were forever transfixed by the woman while he was in her close proximity and even when he was not.

He had to win her.

He did not want to choose another woman. He'd chosen her

last season, nearly a whole year had already passed, he would not wait another year and he'd no intention of letting her slip through his fingers.

He refused to accept no from her.

He needed her and not simply for her money.

Did she not understand that?

Aware his gaze had hardened to glaring, he whispered, harshly, "Am I not good enough for you? Did you not like my verse?"

Her lips parted slightly. They drew his gaze. If they'd been alone, he would have kissed her, drawn her into his arms and never let her go. She was his. She just didn't know it yet, but he knew it. His eyes lifted to hers again. "You are meant for me. Why can you not see it?" Forget the drivel about souls and fate and love, this much was true. He was certain that she was the only woman he would be happy with. Lord, without her, he would never even be able to claim the word, happy!

Her lips pursed.

"I tried to tell you in that letter, what I think, how I feel—"

Her fingertip grazed his lips, to silence him, as she passed him in a turn.

Good God! Did she not know he would give anything to have her?

"I read your letter, I know what it said."

Drew's heart missed a beat. The look in her eyes spoke of sympathy.

Did it mean he had hope?

"Write to me," he urged. "I'll speak to you when I can, but in the meantime write." The notes of the dance drew to a close.

"I do not have your address, I—"

He captured her fingers, lifting her hand to kiss it, and as he did so, he slid the small folded piece of paper he'd written his address on into the wrist of her glove.

"You do." He met her gaze over her bent knuckles as he gripped her fingers. Then he let her hand fall and bowed briefly before turning away.

* * *

Mary watched him return to his friends, her heart racing.

"Miss Marlow." The man who had led her into the dance, Lord Brooke, was at her side offering his arm.

She lay numb fingers on it.

They'd orchestrated the whole night, he and his friends.

"There are a dozen other heiresses he could court..." she said.

"But none as beautiful."

"So that is what draws him, wealth and beauty?"

They walked across the floor, towards her parents, slowly, as people formed sets for the next dance.

Lord Brooke leaned closer. "Is it not his looks which draw your eyes to him?" It was not a whisper, his deep baritone made her skin prickle, and the note of condescension stirred anger inside her.

"Miss Marlow." He straightened, lifting her fingers from his arm, as her parents came into view. "It has been a pleasure." He bowed.

Then like Drew he walked away.

"Who were you with?" her mother asked, coming forward.

Mary, glanced across the room. Lord Brooke, Lord Framlington, Mr Harper and Mr Webster were leaving the ball.

Mary faced her mother. "Lord Brooke, Mama. Oliver introduced his friend to me and his friend introduced Lord Brooke."

"And his friend was?"

"Mr Harper." The slip of paper tucked within Mary's glove itched. Had the whole endeavour been to slip her his address?

"Mr Harper? I think his father's money came from sugar plantations." Her father had moved beside her.

She shrugged. "I have no idea, Papa. We danced, we did not share life histories."

He smiled. "No, I suppose not, but if it was that Mr Harper, avoid him, he has an appalling reputation, and Lord Brooke too.

Avoid them both in the future."

"Yes, Papa."

She had been right; Lord Framlington consorted with men whose reputations matched his. His had been earned then, surely.

Her breath slipped out through her lips – and, he'd left his address within her glove. She would be the worst fool to communicate with him.

Her father's fingers, tapped her beneath the chin. "Cheer up, sweetheart, there are plenty of decent men about, and here is one. I believe Lord Farquhar wishes a second dance."

Mary turned. Daniel was approaching with a broad smile.

Why could not cupid aim steady arrows at her heart, ones which led to trustworthy men, rather than dangerous predatory rogues?

Chapter 7

Drew crawled into bed, three sheets to the wind. They'd retired to his bachelor apartments for a second evening, and it was now almost five of the clock. The first light of dawn crept about his curtains.

His friends had spent half the night commending him on his choice. The second half they'd spent constructing more verse, only this time Peter had said it should praise Mary's nature, not her eyes. Apparently Mary did not take kindly to being complimented on her looks. She wished to be appreciated for more than her appearance. It was another credit to be notched in her favour.

A considerable amount of laughter had followed, and an inevitable quantity of wine.

When he woke he was hot and sweaty, his body thrumming with need for Mary Marlow – in his dreams she had not said no the other night.

He looked at his watch on the side. It was only mid-day but there was no way he would be able to sleep again.

He threw the covers aside and got up, then washed and shaved, planning to ride in the park and vent his frustration. Rewriting the latest letter would have to wait until he'd dealt with his painful surge of desire.

He could seek a willing woman to assuage it, but if he wanted constancy with Miss Marlow the idea seemed traitorous; he had abstained for a year, he would not break that now.

He was not interested in other women anyway. Not any more. Mary consumed him, mentally and physically. It was Mary he needed, no-one else.

His mouth dried, filling with a bitter taste, and it was not from last night's excess of drink, it was from fear he'd fail and lose her.

On his ride he stretched out his mare, hurtling across the open meadow of Green Park, leaning low, hugging his body to the horse, pushing his bodyweight into his heels, and keeping balance with his shins, and his thighs, riding like a mad man.

He felt close to insanity – desperate.

Still, if she was easily caught he'd be bored of her in weeks. No, her determination to withstand him only bore out his belief that she was the woman for him.

She had strength of character, and that was to be admired.

Returning home he rewrote the letter his friends had constructed in their cups last night, and as he reached its end found his own words flowing from the quill, a diatribe falling from his mind onto the paper as the words had last night when they'd danced. He blotted the words briskly then folded the paper before he lost the courage to include his own words and sealed it with wax.

He found a young lad he trusted in the street and sent the boy off to deliver it.

* * *

"Miss Marlow."

Mary sat alone in the family drawing room. She looked up at the butler who carried a silver tray.

"A letter."

When the butler bowed to offer it, Mary saw Drew's handwriting and her wicked heart flooded with joy.

Her mother and father, with John and Kate, had taken all the children on an outing to the park. Mary had declined accompanying them and bidden Mr Finch to say no one was at home if anyone called. She was not in a mood to entertain, or be social.

Images and memories of Lord Framlington kept spinning in her head.

Her heartbeat thumped when she took the letter.

She had a foolish heart.

When Finch had left she opened it, slipping her feet from her shoes and curling her legs sideways on the sofa.

It began with another poem, commending the extreme good nature of her soul, and then enthusing on her charm, her eloquence.

She smiled.

Lord Brooke had been telling tales.

The following paragraphs spoke of commitment, of life long happiness. They were only words. They meant little in reality.

But the last paragraph… The strokes of Drew's writing seemed somehow sharper, and the words on the page lifted out with feeling.

My Mary, you are you know, mine. You always will be, accept me or not. You and I are meant to be one, half to become whole. Put us together Mary, darling, make us one, a single being. I want you. I cannot say I love you, not yet, I do not even know what on earth love is, but I do know that I cannot sleep for thinking of you, or avoid dreaming of you. I think of you and I lose my breath, I see you and my heart begins to pound, I hear you and my spirit wants to sing. I am yours, Mary. Be mine. I cannot simply walk away. I will not.

Think of the possibilities. If this is love? If this is our only chance? If we are meant to be, would you throw that away? Throw me away?

Do not! Let us be.

   Yours truly,

   D

The words were spoken as though he stood with her and read them.

She barely knew him and yet she felt as if she'd known him all her life. She had not been drawn to any other man – perhaps it was true, he was meant for her.

A sigh slipped past her lips. If she let him go he'd marry someone else. He needed an heiress. He could not wait forever.

Her gaze drifted to the window. Birdsong permeated the glass. She would not marry unless someone else made her heart race as he did. If no one ever did, she would definitely never marry. She sighed again. She had thought that last night, and yet she had not thought about what he would do… She may never marry but she'd be forced to watch him with his wife.

Oh, why did her heart have to fall for someone forbidden?

He was mystery. Challenge. There was so much to learn about him.

Her heart was caught up with him and she did not know how to break free. *I don't want to be free. I want to be his wife* – to understand the complexity in his eyes.

She didn't see a bad man in his eyes.

Was that a dreadful admission?

John would be furious if she chose Drew. Her father and mother would be disappointed. But they would not disown her. They'd forgive her, because they loved her.

She folded the letter and took it to her room. There, she searched out the paper on which he'd written his address. Then she sat at her writing desk.

Her quill hovered over the paper. She could not make promises yet. She was afraid to do what her heart wished and say yes.

Could she have her family and Lord Framlington?

Could she trust him to look after her and love her?

How could she bear to hurt her family?

Yet how could she bear it if Drew turned to someone else?

Make me believe, if you wish. she began to write. *You make us be. Prove that I may trust your words. Prove that you will love me and not hurt me.*

She wrote no more. She could not think of anything else to say. His ego was too big to offer him compliments. He'd only bask in them.

Folding the letter she reached for wax, and melted a little to seal it. She smiled when she rose from the desk.

Was she really doing this?

It appeared so.

Her feet carried her downstairs, the letter fluttering in her fingers to dry the wax.

When Mary reached the hall, avoiding Finch, and any unwanted questions, she carried on into the servants' stairwell, heading for the stables.

There she found one of the boys who fed the horses and cleaned the stalls, gave him a half-penny and sent him to deliver the letter.

Less than an hour later, the boy burst into her private sitting room with a broad grin, waving a reply in his grubby hand. "The gent sent this back, Miss. I brought it up meself 'cause he said it was a secret between you and me. I've snuck through the house. No one saw me, Miss."

Fortunately.

Mary rose and took it. Then found out another half-penny for the boy.

Drew had probably given him one too – the price of deceit.

"Wait here a moment."

Breaking the seal, she turned and walked into her bedchamber then sat on the edge of her bed.

How may I prove it to you? Tell me, and I will do it. Anything. I will climb the highest mountain for you, swim a lake or run across a continent. Only tell me and I shall prove it, Mary, darling.

Are you alone? How long for? Look from the window.

Oh heavens! He's outside!

She went to the window.

Carriages passed in the square below and people walked the pavements. She saw him. He stood against the central railing of the square on the far side of the street from John's house, looking up and smoking a cigar, in a nonchalant, blasé, pose, the rim of his hat tipped forward shadowing his eyes.

She returned to the sitting room where the stable lad waited. "Let the gentleman in, Tom, please. Take him to the summerhouse and tell him to wait there. But remember this is a secret. I will reward you for your silence later. No one must see him, you understand?"

"Yes, Miss." The lad gave an awkward bow, tugging his forelock, and then he raced out of the room.

Mary hurried back into her bedchamber, checked her hair in the mirror on her dressing table, tucked a loose strand into the comb holding up her hair, then raced downstairs, gripping her blue muslin day-dress to lift her hem from the ground.

A dozen butterflies took flight in her stomach when she saw Finch in the hall. She slowed immediately, half-way down the stairs.

He looked up and bowed, as did the footman he spoke with.

Mary stepped from the bottom stair. "I'm taking a book out to read in the summerhouse, Mr Finch. I may sleep, please don't let anyone disturb me."

"Of course, Miss Marlow," the old bulldog answered. He was her family's guardian, and now she was deceiving him too. Her parents would send her home to the country if they knew.

She went to the library and picked up a book from a side table, without even looking at its title, then let herself out through the French door into the sunshine.

Heat touched her face as she crossed the lawn. She had not put on her bonnet. But she didn't hurry in case Finch watched from the house.

The Summerhouse was at the end of the garden, tucked away amongst tall shrubs. No-one could see it from the house and no-one could see anyone approaching it from the stables.

A beautiful Wisteria archway covered the path Drew must have walked through.

When she reached the summerhouse, he stood at the far end of the narrow wooden veranda, with his back to her. He'd removed his hat and he'd ruffled his hair.

"This is very bad of you," she stated as she climbed the steps of the veranda. Then she leaned back against the post at the opposite end to where he stood, the book she carried tucked behind her.

He turned with a broad smile on his lips. The same smile danced in his eyes. "But exhilarating. What if we are caught? Think of the repercussions!" He was teasing. She saw laughter in his eyes. She had not seen him in daylight since the morning they had ridden together. She had forgotten how sunlight gilded his eyes, and made the hazel shine like gold.

"I would rather not," she answered, watching him and smiling.

"But you feel the exhilaration. Otherwise you would not have ordered the lad to let me in." He walked towards her pulling off his gloves. "How long do we have?"

"An hour, perhaps more."

"A whole hour to ourselves..."

He threw his gloves aside. They landed beside his hat on a low table.

When she looked up, he stood a foot away.

"So tell me..." His fingers touched beneath her chin. "...how may I prove that we are meant for one another?"

She could not find any air in her lungs to answer as she looked into his eyes. But then it didn't matter; his lips pressed to hers. It was unlike any other kiss they'd shared – it was not urgent or hurried, or persuasive. It was just a kiss, a touching of lips.

A sigh escaped his mouth when he pulled away as if he'd been longing to kiss her.

Mary leaned around him to put the book down beside his hat and gloves.

He caught hold of her hand when she straightened, and gently pinned her back against the post. "I've thought about you all night…" His words caressed her ear sending tremors down her spine, then his lips touched her earlobe and the sensitive skin behind her ear.

Her head tipped back, and she said to the air above them, "So we are back to this."

His head lifted as he laughed and his hand let hers go. But then both his hands braced her waist gently and he shook her a little. "God, I love you, you have convinced me of it. You're the only woman who can say no to me. I adore you more because you fight me. But you are tempted none the less. You just do not trust me enough…"

"Enough to do what?" She held his gaze, fighting the urge to believe him. His hands made her feel safe not in danger, but the words I love you were easily said and they'd been spoken with a pitch of frustration and laughter not from any depth of feeling, they did not sound as though they had come from his heart – and he had said in his letter he did not even know what love was…

"To become my wife. I was not talking of physical intimacy, sweetheart. I am speaking of marriage."

"What would it be like to be your wife?" She had never looked into his eyes in the daylight this close, the hazel had now turned to the depth of light shining through amber. She looked beyond the colour trying to see into his soul.

He looked back at her with as many questions as she wished to ask. But she could not see any artifice.

Did he feel for her?

Put us together Mary, darling, make us one, a single being. I want you. I cannot say I love you, not yet, I do not even know what on earth love is, but I do know that I cannot sleep for thinking of you, or avoid dreaming of you.

Were the words true?

"I hope we would be happy. I want to make you happy. We will buy our own estate and make it a home. It needn't be large. It will take time to become profitable, but I will make it so."

I think of you and I lose my breath, I see you and my heart begins to pound, I hear you and my spirit wants to sing. I am yours, Mary. Be mine.

"And children?" She longed for her own life and her own family.

His smile dropped, and his gaze turned inward, no longer looking at her but lost in thought.

Didn't that prove his earlier words true though, if he could not hide when he needed to stop and think to answer?

She touched his cheek. For the first time believing she saw something real in him, a hidden reality. This was not the Lord Framlington of dangerous rakehell fame. This was Drew, the man who had written those impassioned words.

His gaze came back to her. "I have never thought of children." He spoke in a solemn voice, as if the thought shocked him.

She pressed her palm to his shaven cheek. He was a man, human, as vulnerable as any other, no matter his reputation.

"But I would like them, with you…" His tone said, only, with you.

Mary lifted to her toes and kissed him, touching her lips to his – as he'd kissed her.

His grip at her waist firmed. "We will have a dozen children." A broad smile parted his lips and his eyes shone with a new light. "You must teach me how to be a father, as you'll need to teach me how to love you. I am no good at this."

He was good. He just didn't know it. But she could teach him.

"Are you tempted?"

"To marry you?"

He shook his head the smile playing on his lips. "Stop doubting me. I am not speaking of a physical relationship. Of course to become my wife."

"Yes." The word slipped out before she had chance to consider it. Her heart said it. It was the truth, but she defined it. "I am tempted."

His lips pressed to hers in a strong kiss.

When he broke it, he whispered to her mouth, his nose rubbing hers, "I love you. I really think I do."

And I love you. She did not say it. She did not dare. Her head did not trust him enough. Not yet. But her heart…

He picked her up. She grasped his shoulders as he swung her into his arms, one about her shoulders and another beneath her knees.

"You are perfect for me, Mary."

She laughed unable to prevent the sound, as he smiled broadly.

His eyes gleamed gold and then shone amber, changing in the changing light, as he carried her into the summerhouse, and then dropped her on the soft cushions of a sofa.

Smiling like a fool she sat up and spun around.

She did love him, she adored him, but her head was still too afraid to let him join her upon the sofa.

His smile tilted, but undaunted he dropped to one knee. "Mary…" He took her hands from her lap, gripping them gently. "Marry me."

Her stomach performed a somersault.

She took one hand from his, and pressed a palm to his cheek.

His eyes were so earnest, she believed him. He wanted her, not just for money. He bore affection for her, whether it was love or not, he cared for her.

But her family? "I cannot answer yet. I'm sorry. I need to think."

His eyes turned darker. "But there is hope. I have hope you will say, yes?"

"You have hope." Mary bit her lip, afraid of what she'd said, of what she wanted to say. She loved him – her body pulled her towards him.

His fingers lifted and gripped her nape, then they urged her mouth to his, as he remained on one knee, a supplicant before her.

This time his kiss seared her, like a fire, as his mouth opened and caressed hers with hunger and thirst. The same hunger and thirst ran in her blood.

When he drew away, his eyes looked into hers. "Let me touch you. Let me love you. I will not take your virginity I swear that I will leave you choice, but let me show you how it can be between us. You are right marriage is more than a physical thing, but this is what I know, let me give you this and show you..."

She could not answer with words, her head wished to refuse – yet her heart... Agreement spiralled in her stomach, coiling to the point he'd touched between her legs that first night, and her fingers slid into his hair, pulling his lips back to hers.

This kiss was hard and ruthless, pressing against her mouth, as he rose from the floor, leaning her backward.

His warm hand gripped beneath her knee, lifting, encouraging her to move her legs on to the sofa so she lay down. Then the weight of his knee dipped the cushion beside her, a moment before his other knee settled on her dress between her thighs. She was trapped beneath his masculinity, smothered.

She didn't care. His weight on top of her was beautiful – dangerous and arousing. His tongue came into her mouth, invading and caressing, and the heat of his palm slid upward from her waist.

What if my parents return?

He stole the thought away as his palm covered and caressed her breast.

Her nipple hardened and a sharp pain ran from it into her breast.

The thrill of that night beside the terrace, in the darkness, with people talking nearby span through her memory. There was no darkness to hide them now, everything shone clear and visible.

He broke the kiss and knelt up. She sucked in a breath as he took off his morning coat and threw it on to a chair across the room. Then he moved his legs either side of hers, and began sliding up her dress watching her face as if he feared she might stop him.

Her heartbeat thundered. She should stop him – but she wanted to know…

She pressed her heels into the cushion so the material could slide up easily, her gaze clinging to his as if he was a cliff and she might fall.

When her hem slipped over knees he stopped, and the air trembled in her lungs as he came back down on top of her.

Just the weight and feel of his hard muscular body was a caress, it made the place between her legs throb with moisture.

One of his hands pressed on the cushion holding some of his weight, the other settled over her breast.

Her fingers shook as she swept back the hair from his brow, looking into his brown eyes, there were so many different shades within them.

People were not all one shade, one thing; they were a myriad of elements. He could not only be bad, there was good too. She longed to unravel the good in him and prove to her parents it was there.

A firm column within his trousers pressed against her hip.

Need coiled through her abdomen again.

Like this, she could imagine how it would be to lie with a man, with him. Her mother had told her very little, but Mary knew what happened. He mother had said not to listen to anything she might overhear implying it was unpleasant; it was not unpleasant if you loved the man you married.

She loved Drew, and it did not feel at all unpleasant to be beneath him, letting him touch her.

He kissed her again, urging her to reciprocate as his tongue pressed through her lips.

She did, her fingers clasping in his hair as their tongues played a breathless weaving and dancing game, and her hips pressed upward against his.

His fingers undid the couple of buttons securing her bodice free, then his hand was within, beneath her chemise clasping the flesh of her breast.

She wanted to feel him.

Her fingers left his hair reaching between them running over his waistcoat, searching for buttons, she found them and fought to free them.

A sound rumbled in the back of his throat, and his hand gripped her breast more firmly, but his body lifted a little to let her slip his buttons loose.

When his waistcoat opened her fingers slid beneath, brushing over his cotton shirt and the architecture of his muscle beneath it.

She arched against him as her hands moved to his back beneath his waistcoat, she wanted the release he'd let her experience in the dark.

His kiss left her lips. She shut her eyes, shut out embarrassment, as his lips touched her chin then travelled down her neck, nipping and biting gently.

"You're beautiful, Mary, within and without. I do love you."

I love you too.

Her fingers slid down his back and pulled his shirt from his trousers, as his lips touched her breast.

A summer breeze swept in through the open doors, caressing the naked skin he'd revealed.

He said nothing as she pulled his shirt loose and touched his silky skin, and the firm muscle beneath it. With her eyes closed she hid in the darkness as they'd done in the garden.

He sucked her nipple with a sharp tug, and the pain of desire struck like a dagger between her legs. She wanted him there. To know how it felt.

Another moan left her lips as instinctively she arched again, pressing her breast towards his mouth.

Then the warmth of his mouth was gone.

She opened her eyes, sensing him looking at her. The brown amber had become dark, his onyx pupils wide. "Let me touch you fully." His voice flowed over gravel.

She didn't understand at first, but then his hand slid from her breast to her dress clutching the fabric.

"Will you allow it?" he breathed.

Her eyes held his gaze.

"Yes," again the word fell from her lips without thought. But it was what she wanted, desperately wanted.

He held her gaze, and drew her dress higher, his fingers brushing the smooth inner surface of her knee.

A shiver raked her body.

A smile lifted his closed lips, but he did not look away.

She wished to hide behind closed eyelids but she could not while he watched, it seemed cowardly. His fingers slipped beneath the hem of her drawers, playing across her inner thigh.

Her lips fell open. She wanted to weep, whimper and cry out with pleasure all at once.

Then with a single movement his fingers swept up and touched her there, between her legs, pressing against her flesh for a moment.

She bit her lip holding onto his gaze, imprisoned by it, as her fingers gripped the skin at his sides above his hips.

"You're wet for me, darling." His fingers slid forwards and back, as they had in the dark over her dress only now he touched her flesh, slipping through the slit in her drawers.

She could not breathe; a part of her could not believe she was letting this happen, another part wished for so much more. She wanted him to stop and she wanted him to continue.

If my parents find us like this?

Again the thought was swept away as his fingers slipped into her, only slightly, but…

She died, closing her eyes, the world crashing in on her, as her fingernails cut into his flesh, gripping him hard. She cried out. His lips covered hers, brushing them again and again, taking the sound.

"Good, God, you are perfect. I cannot believe how well we are matched."

His fingers worked a charm within her, withdrawing a little and pressing back, gently stroking and provoking. Sensory delight danced through her nerves. The day was so hot; she wanted to be rid of all her clothes, of all of his and lie naked with him.

The column of his arousal pushed against her hip as he worked. She wanted to touch him, but embarrassment held her back, and yet… And yet… She could not hold herself back… She pressed her hips into his hand searching for a deeper invasion, but he would not give it. Desperation pulling at her nerves, her fingers hunted for the buttons on his waistband then she fought to free them as a soft laugh left his throat.

His lips touched her breast then sucked as the buttons came loose.

She bit her lip, afraid to open her eyes, afraid of his judgement, hiding in the darkness, and not wanting to face what they did because then she would have to admit she was committing a sin. If she did not face it. It did not feel sinful.

Her fingers dipped within his trousers to touch the hard column of his flesh.

The skin felt like velvet.

She clutched it, holding firm, not knowing what else to do.

"I'll show you." His voice brushed her cheek, answering her unspoken thought. Then his hand covered hers; his fingers damp with her essence. "Like this."

She opened her eyes and met his gaze, as he drew her hand down and then up.

His eyes were pools of emotion, sunlight shining through honey.

I love you.

She should feel embarrassed by this intimacy. She did not.

After a moment he let her hand go, and then his fingers were back between her legs, and they touched each other, watching each other. He had a hand about her heart too, and a fist in her stomach, the emotion caught so tight within her.

His head bowed and his hair brushed her skin as his lips touched her breast again.

Drew.

He sucked her nipple, his fingers working their charm between her legs.

Drew.

Her fingers clasped tighter about him.

Drew.

The hunger and thirst inside her surged on a high tide, rising in a pool in the place between her legs, impatient for more. She wanted his weight, his strength, his pressure there.

Her thoughts lost in the turmoil swirling through her senses, Mary's thumb brushed the tip of his erection.

A shiver racked his body.

How heady, to know she could move him as he moved her.

His suck pulled hard on her breast, then he released it and his head came up, a rogue's smile twisting his lips. "Mary, darling, I'm trying to be good."

"And if I do not want you to be good." The breathless words tumbled from her dry mouth.

His eyes lost their rakish glint. "Sweetheart, you do. I made you a promise. You can trust me. I shan't break it." The caress between her legs grew more intense as he spoke, utterly entrancing her body.

His head bent and his lips brushed her temple, then his kiss touched the skin beside her eye. Her eyelids lowered.

He kissed her cheek, her nose, her chin.

Her fingers gripped his erection, just holding now, with one hand, while her other clutched his shoulder as her breathing quickened and her heartbeat raced.

"Let go, sweetheart, trust me," he whispered to her ear in a husky voice.

A tide rose within her, like it had done in the dark. He knew… He knew how he moved her.

His fingers stroked, pushing inside her a little before withdrawing while his thumb played over a sensitive spot and the sensations flowed like ripples through her body, reaching even to her fingers and toes.

"Please, I want you." Her fingers clasped more tightly about him.

"You'd regret it, darling. You would. Just let go." His voice urged as it had done in the dark. "Come into my hand."

Thoughts and feelings shattered, splintering into a thousand pieces that were swept away on a surging, rolling wave. It washed through her blood like a boar tide, ripping through her veins, stronger than she'd felt in the darkness.

"That's it, sweetheart... Just... That's it..."

Then his fingers were gone from inside her, and she felt him touch the tip of his erection, spreading her moisture there, before his hand closed over hers.

She opened her eyes, her vision focusing on his face, then his eyes. He was looking at her. She held his gaze. "I'm sorry, darling. I'm sorry, but I need this."

His hand covered hers, moving her fingers.

His gaze clung to hers, fixed and hard.

His hips moved, pressing into their joined grip and then withdrawing.

The pattern aroused her as his deep brown amber eyes shone, his gaze sharpening with a dark intent, their onyx centres dilating.

She understood the heat in his eyes, she could see the sensation he'd taught her echoed there.

His movements quickened, and his fingers gripped more tightly over hers, it became a painful embrace. Then he stopped, suddenly, as though every muscle in his body locked, a cry of revelation broke his lips, rasping from his throat and his gaze was lost then. She saw ecstasy there for an instant before his eyelids fell, then he pulsed in her hand and wet heat spilled from his tip.

The intimacy and vulnerability of it gripped at her soul. It spoke of his humanity. He was not a monster, just a man. A man she loved, and a man who'd said he thought he loved her. A man who did care for her. A man who'd just been isolated and labelled *bad* by society. They were wrong.

When he opened his eyes, they shone with gratitude. "You are divine, Mary, thank you." His forehead rested on hers for a moment before he rose up, lifting off her, though his gaze still held hers. "When you're certain, my darling, when you say, yes, then we'll join, but not before. You can trust me."

Her heartbeat had slowed. She felt cold, despite the hot day.

"Here…" He'd reached to his coat and withdrawn a handkerchief, to wipe her hand clean, then he wiped himself.

Her fingers lifted to brush back his brown hair as she sat up. She felt uncertain now, and her touch was tentative.

Had they really just done what they'd done? Had she really begged him for more?

He looked as if he feared she'd bolt.

She would not. She'd made her choice. But she was embarrassed and self-conscious.

He slid the soiled handkerchief back into his pocket, then rose to secure the buttons at his flap and tuck his shirt into his trousers.

He looked down and smiled. "You look gorgeous. Do you want to tempt me back?"

Heat absorbing her skin, Mary pushed her dress down, then swung her legs from the sofa, to sit upright before pulling up the neck of her chemise and securing the buttons of her bodice with shaking fingers.

He bent, and his fingers wrapped about her nape, tilting her face up so he could press a hard kiss to her lips – a thank you kiss.

Her heart fluttered and her stomach flipped.

When he straightened, letting her go, she stood up too, awkwardness besetting her, uncertain what to say or do.

He smiled as he buttoned up his waistcoat.

He was a stranger to her in so many ways and yet her soul knew him… It had been waiting to find him. She trusted him, regardless of what her father and John said. Had he not just proven himself? He could have taken everything from her. He'd not. He'd left her the choice.

She'd made it.

Lifting up on to her toes, and wrapping her arms about his

neck, she kissed his cheek before saying to his ear, "I will, yes."

He pulled away sharply, his eyes full of questions as his hands braced her elbows. "Yes?"

She smiled. "Yes. I will marry you."

His brow furrowed, as though he did not believe her.

If she had needed more proof he was not the rogue he seemed, here it was. His surprise and doubt only showed he was not as self-confident as he appeared. He needed her as no other suitor had. He needed her to help him show people he was not what they thought.

"You're sure?" he whispered. "I feel as though I have done nothing to prove myself."

"I am sure," she answered, holding his gaze and stepping from the cliff she had clung to earlier – faith her bridge. "I think I can trust you."

His eyes softened, the rich, deep, honey brown glowing behind dark lashes. "You think you can trust me, and I think I love you. Is it a good enough foundation?"

Her hand cupped his cheek. "Do you wish to dissuade me now? You are only proving yourself worthy of my…"

His lips tilted to his roguish half smile, when she stopped. "Of your what?"

She shook her head, losing courage.

"Of your love? Do you think you love me too…" His voice rang with surprise and hope.

"I would not have done what we did, if I did not?" Vulnerability trembled through her nerves. She lifted her chin in defiance of it.

His fingers brushed her skin as his gaze bored deep into hers, looking for something. "Let us be in love then. Let this be a love match." His voice rolled through gravel. Then he pressed a hard brief kiss on her lips, before catching hold of her hands. "I'll make arrangements."

She nodded.

"You know we must elope, your family would never agree to a

match while your brother is so against me."

"I know." The weight of her decision settled heavily on her shoulders. This would be hard, she would break their hearts. But surely they would come to see the good in Drew.

His fingers tenderly brushed a lock of hair from her brow.

The muscle within her core clenched, aching at the memory of his more intimate touch.

"I'll write to you. Send the boy to me in three days and I'll send word."

She nodded.

His lips brushed hers, another brief touch, then he breathed across her mouth. "Sweetheart, I cannot believe you said yes."

She could not believe it either.

Her fingers clasped in his hair as she kissed him. She did not want him to go.

He broke it. "You will have me hard for you again but I must go."

She nodded. Her parents would be home soon.

He gripped her hand and squeezed it for an instant before letting go and turning to pick up his coat.

"I'll walk you to the gate," she said as he put it on.

He threw her a smile across his shoulder, then picked up his hat and put it on, before picking up his gloves too.

Her heart thundered.

He held out his hand. She took it. It held hers firmly, the leather of his glove now a barrier between them.

She pulled gently, leading him from the summerhouse into the cover of the trees and then beneath the arches draped with sweet scented flowering wisteria.

When they reached the gate which opened onto the alley leading to the mews, she stopped and looked up at him.

His gaze held hers, then he bent, bestowing a brief hard kiss on her lips. When he broke it, his eyes shone. "I'll write. I'll tell you where and when."

Nodding, she caught her lower lip between her teeth as tears clouded her vision.

He smiled, and his gloved fingers brushed her cheek. "We will be together soon."

She nodded again, unable to speak for fear she'd cry. He turned and slid the bolt loose, opened the gate and threw one last roguish smile across his shoulder, then he left.

It was still clear and bright, but without him the sun had gone. "Mary!"

Her heart raced as she turned back to the garden.

"Mary! Mary!" Several voices lifted on the air shouting her name, her brothers and sisters.

Her parents were home and her siblings had tales to tell about everything she'd missed.

She longed to tell her own news. *I am engaged.*

A smile suddenly parted her lips. *I am engaged, I am going to marry him.*

Her brothers and sisters came into view, charging towards her at a run, all shouting at once.

* * *

As Drew jogged up the steps of White's, he grinned from ear to ear. When he walked into the room where his friends were ensconced a few moments later his grin had dropped to a smile but joy was lodged somewhere deep in his chest and exuberance hovered. He had said the words I love you. God knew if they had been true; he did not, no one had ever taught him what love was. But his feelings for Mary had been so much more than physical.

She had been without guile, without powder or paint, without artifice, beautiful, honest, and her soul had been naked for him. She had let him touch her. But more than that, she had given him her complete trust… and hope… and love… She had inferred that she loved him too.

His feelings had been more than lust, it was not just a physical

113

desire he felt for her, and so the word love had come to his lips, the word he'd never thought he'd say… Even if it was not true, it did not matter. He cared for her. He knew that.

He cared a great deal.

He saw his friends.

Strange new feelings still whizzed about through the nerves in his chest, like fireworks exploding. Pride. Happiness. Hope. Excitement. His life had become something to look forward to, he saw a horizon in the distance, and Mary there.

"Success." He stated the single word as he joined their group and dropped into one of the leather armchairs about a low table. Their eyes turned to him in question. "You may congratulate me gentlemen, I am engaged to the fair Miss Marlow."

"No!"

"You dark dog!"

"Bloody hell, old boy!"

All three exclamations broke at once, his friends rising to their feet, then they slapped his shoulder and shook his hand.

"The prose did its job then," Peter intoned.

"It was more than the prose, my friend. It appears I've not lost my charm after all."

Peter laughed. "You did not? It's the middle of the day. How the hell did you get within ten feet of the girl?"

Drew smiled. *That is for me to know…*

Peter laughed again, shaking his head before sitting back down.

The others sat too, but as they did, Drew caught sight of Pembroke across the room. Mary's half-brother sat among his influential uncles, looking Drew's way.

Drew sent him a twisted smile. Let the bugger squirm, he would find out the cause of their exuberance soon enough.

But Drew needed to be wary, he could not let her family find out. They would stop this instantly if they knew, and he'd have her father, her brother and her uncles baying for his blood. But they would be anyway when the truth was out.

Looking away Drew leaned forward to pour himself coffee. He was in for a fight, but it was a fight worth having. He would need a day alone with her. It would be best to leave in daylight then they could travel more easily and cover more miles to find somewhere they could be private for a night. There, he would fix their fate, so when they were found, there would be no going back.

Chapter 8

When Mary saw Lord Framlington enter the ballroom with his friends two nights later she could recount how many hours and minutes had passed since he'd left her at the garden gate. Their secret had been bursting to break from her lips ever since. She wished to scream it aloud, to grip her friends' arms and whisper in their ears, to take her mother and father aside and say, *I am engaged.*

Her fears had slipped away and instead her heart brimmed with a tentative joy.

Her family would be disappointed, and angry, but she would make them understand.

Last night she'd claimed a headache and kept to her room rather than eat dinner amongst them; not wishing to face the guilt but to hold on to happiness. She had not slept, or eaten since then, she was not tired or hungry. Her body hummed with energy, waiting impatiently for the moment they would elope, jubilant yet terrified the lies she'd told would start to unravel.

Her mother had come to her room to talk this morning, sat on Mary's bed and taken her hand, then asked, "What is wrong?"

Mary had denied anything was. But then her mother had said she'd heard Lord Farquhar had announced his engagement to Bethany last evening. She'd thought Mary upset because of it.

She had kissed Mary's cheek and promised she and Mary's father would always be there.

Mary hoped they would forgive her.

She hoped to elope with Drew soon, before any more of her lies came to light. But oh, she wished they could be like Bethany and Daniel as they were now, surrounded by her friends all congratulating them. Mary longed to open her mouth and say, I am engaged too, but she was unsure how her friends would receive the news. They only knew Drew by reputation. They would probably call her mad.

Her gaze left her friends and looked for him as love coursed through her blood. He stood among his friends, and it was as if they stood either side of a battle field, the chasm between their lives too wide. But she would cross it.

He probably could not see her as she stood among her friends.

A confident smile hung on Drew's lips then he said something to his friends and the group broke into laughter.

Something tight gripped in her stomach.

Lord Brooke and Mr Harper looked over their shoulders, then Drew's gaze lifted and searched the room. She guessed they were looking for her.

What had he said to them? Why had they laughed?

A woman approached the group.

Mary recognised her, Lady Kilbride, the Marquis of Kilbride's wife, she had seen Drew speaking with her once before. The woman laid a hand on Drew's forearm. He bent towards her, letting her whisper in his ear. His friends turned away, talking amongst themselves. Then Drew turned.

Mary's heartbeat stuttered.

Lady Kilbride held Drew's arm, her fingers gripping it as he escorted her outside through the open French door, disappearing into the darkness.

Mary's stomach froze.

She'd heard rumours of Lady Kilbride, of her unfaithfulness.

Was Drew one of her consorts?

Nausea ate at Mary's empty stomach.

Were her parents, and John, right?

She did not dance the next set, claiming her slippers rubbed. Daniel stood out with her while Bethany danced and shy Emily sat with them, as she was playing wallflower again.

Utterly numb, Mary fought to make conversation.

Drew returned with Lady Kilbride twenty minutes after he'd left, and Lady Kilbride clutched his handkerchief in her fingers.

Mary had been talking but the words slipped from her mind as tears filled her eyes. She wiped them away quickly, the void of pain inside her filling with anger.

"Mary, what is it?" Daniel looked over his shoulder, following her gaze.

But Drew was already hidden by the dancers.

Would he do that? Would he make love to her yesterday afternoon and this woman now?

I was warned.

Daniel looked back to her.

"Mary, what is it?" Emily queried her silence.

"Nothing is wrong, sorry I lost my thread."

The set ended, *thank God*, and their friends returned before either Daniel or Emily could pursue their questions.

Mary turned away, speaking to someone else as she looked for Drew again.

He'd returned to his friends and stood with Lord Brooke. Lady Kilbride had walked away.

As Lord Brooke spoke Drew's gaze caught hers, reaching across the room, hard and fixed. A bitter smile twisted his lips.

He knew she'd seen him, Lord Brooke must have seen her watching.

I will not be his puppet.

"Emily." Mary turned back to her friend.

Emily was uncertain of her place in society and she hated

to offend, she made a good confident. Mary caught her elbow and whispered. "There is someone I wish to talk to, a group of gentlemen I met the other night. Mama will skin me alive if she thought I was being so forward, but you will keep me company won't you? There is safety in numbers after all. There will be no harm in me speaking to them if you come with me. I'm sure your Papa will thank me for introducing you to Lord Framlington and Lord Brooke."

Emily's naivety and newness to their group meant she would not know Drew and Lord Brooke were to be avoided.

Emily nodded, conceding rather than actively agreeing.

Mary added another sin and another lie to her list, threaded her arm through Emily's and drew her across the room.

Lord Brooke noticed Mary approaching before she reached them and turned to Drew.

"You had better look sharp. You are about to become the victim of your fiancée's wrath. The lady bears daggers in her eyes." Peter smiled, then laughed.

Drew's friends had joined him tonight not at his asking but of their choosing, insisting he should be given the opportunity to converse with his future wife.

Really they'd come to watch Drew demean himself before her and act the lover. To laugh at him.

Of course he had not told them, his affection, to whatever degree, was genuine. That was for Mary to know and no one else. He would not make himself vulnerable and declare his affections to the damned world.

But his friends' presence was welcome, especially as Peter had been able to warn Drew that Mary had seen him leave with Caro. Mary had clearly misunderstood.

Drew turned as she approached. The pale blue satin she wore enhanced her eyes and made her hair and eyelashes look even darker, while the skin above her neckline and the pearls about her neck, made his fingers itch to touch her.

His gaze met hers.

Peter was right, a thunderstorm raged in her eyes. She probably didn't even know Caro was his sister, only a few people knew of their relationship. His family never acknowledged either of them in public.

Kilbride had been up to his vicious games again and Caro had needed a shoulder to weep on. The poor girl had been desperate.

Ever since childhood they'd turned to each other and neither of them spoke to any other members of their family.

He'd promised to intervene in her marriage a dozen times but she was too afraid of Kilbride. But soon he would have the money to both get her away from Kilbride and hide her, and then he intended to be very insistent.

Drew held Mary's gaze as she walked the final steps, laughter tight in his throat. He smiled.

Her family be damned. The girl had courage, to come across the room and tackle him.

He liked it.

But the poor little mouse of a woman on her arm…

"Lord Framlington." Mary dropped a shallow insulting curtsy, her friend lowered much further. Then Mary turned to Peter and dropped deeper too, saying. "Lord Brooke."

Bless the girl, she was mocking him before his friends. The little firebrand.

His future wife had a spirit beyond his hopes.

She acknowledged Mark and Harry too, then introduced the mouse she'd used as her cover. "May I introduce Miss Emily Smithfield."

It was like tossing a lamb into a dog pit. The poor child curtsied again. She was no match to Mary's magnificent beauty, but she was pretty, with brown hair and brown eyes. She would be of interest to his non-fussy friends.

"Lord Framlington." Mary ruthlessly dragged his attention back to her.

His smile broadened as he contemplated fighting over who wore the trousers in his wedded bliss.

"Miss Marlow." He bowed as insultingly as she'd curtsied to him.

She opened her mouth to speak—

"Before you begin, Lady Kilbride is my younger sister." He kept his pitch cold, for the benefit of his friends' ears.

The storm in her eyes blew out instantly.

He laughed.

"Your sister?"

"Yes, my dear, my sister. You may wish to rescue your friend. It is rather rash of you to throw her to the wolves, Mary."

She glanced at Miss Smithfield, then back to him. Then she stuttered. "Forgive me, I'm sorry, I…"

His smile lifted. "I am not sorry. Your jealously heartens me. It bodes well for our future, darling – that you care so much." A rakish pitch rang in his voice, but he cursed internally when he saw her eyes cloud with uncertainty – yet his friends were in earshot.

She blushed and his fingers itched to stroke a curl back from her brow to reassure her – but he could not touch her here.

The first notes of a waltz began. Peter asked Miss Smithfield to the floor. The poor girl didn't stand a chance.

Drew looked at Mary, longing to ask, he thrived on risk but he'd be a fool to take such a step now. His gaze lifted to catch her father's glare; it stretched across the room.

Exactly why he should not take the risk. Her father had seen them.

Drew looked back at her and said quietly to avoid Mark and Harry hearing. "Your father is watching, you had better go, but tell me one thing first. Are your family busy any days in the next week or so?"

Her eyebrows lifted. "Not that I know."

Drew caught Harry glancing at him, but continued. "I think it best if we leave after breakfast so we can travel during the day.

Contact me when you know your absence will go unnoticed from morning until at least the dinner hour?"

She bit her lip and nodded, her gaze searching his expression, looking for proof of his loyalty.

A part of her still urged her to be cautious then.

His fingers lifted and touched the bare skin above her long evening gloves, his action hidden by her body so her father could not see.

She shivered.

"You may trust me. I love you." He was desperate for her to believe him, even though he did not believe himself… *Who knows what love is. But if I do not have you as my wife now, I would rather not live…*

She nodded. "I'm sorry, I mis—"

"It does not matter." The whole world misjudged him. "Things will be good between us. I promise…" It would be true.

Mark moved closer. Drew threw a look at him to say stay away.

"I will organise something," she answered.

Drew nodded. "When you have a date, I'll send you the arrangements. But let's not wait too long, sweetheart… I want to be with you." The last he said in a hoarse whisper.

A shallow smile touched her lips. "Yes."

The look in her eyes said she would kiss him if she could.

Glancing past her shoulder Drew saw her father striding towards them. "Your Papa is coming, darling."

She did not look back nor turn away, as if she was reluctant to leave him.

Something clenched hard in his chest. "Go, sweetheart; write soon and set a date; then no one can separate us."

"Goodbye, I love you." she whispered as she gripped her dress. Then as the words struck his gut like a punch, she span away sharply as if she'd been insulted and had just given him a scalding.

The words sank into his soul and pride bloomed – good God, someone loved him. Someone who understood those words to their full depth. Lord, he adored her strength and resourcefulness.

He smiled, his gaze following her movement, then he met her father's glare.

The man could fume all he wished, he'd lost, wherever they hid Mary now Drew could reach her.

Her father turned to follow Mary back; to guard her and his wife.

The man could hardly judge. Marlow was a second son who'd married money. He'd taken the daughter of a duke.

Drew laughed.

Mary's mother was no better, she'd eloped, but not with Marlow, with Pembroke's father, Captain Harding. Harding had been another lower son. The old Duke had cut her off then. How she'd come back into her wealth after her first husband's death, and married Marlow no one knew. But neither of them had a right to judge him and he would take the greatest pleasure in giving her family's arrogance a hard kick.

"I am wondering who has seduced who." Harry leaned to Drew. "Are you smitten?"

Drew turned. "I have to look smitten; the girl wants a love match. Was that not the whole point of our letter writing? I need to convince her I am affected or she will not have me." Harry's needling cut. What Drew felt, or did not feel, was his own business, he did not like people knowing who he was beneath the rogue's façade. Beneath the rogue's façade was the boy who'd only known rejection as a child, and had become a toy and a thing to be hated.

Mark grinned. "Well, I was convinced."

"Think what you will."

Laughing, Mark and Harry walked off, probably to find somewhere to play cards, or a woman to torment.

Marlow's judgement irked more than Drew cared to admit. Pembroke had cause to be against him, but her parents had none. Marlow's views were based on hearsay; he ought to wait until he knew Drew to make a judgement. It was another seed thrown to grow in the bitterness that was a tangled forest inside him. He hated being rejected by people who thought themselves better than him. Marlow was not even trying to look for good. He'd judged Drew on ill-founded gossip.

Drew glimpsed his elder sister Lady Elizabeth Ponsonby across the room.

His reputation had been sealed before his birth. His damned name had dictated it – his family. Their reputation had preceded him and become his. He'd never had a choice. Failure and wickedness were expected of him.

While Mary's family tended towards happy-ever-after his family raced towards hellfire and Elizabeth was one of the worst.

She sat on a sofa, set in an alcove, with her latest adoring youth beside her. She collected young men like other women collected hats. The poor child leaned over the arm of the sofa handing her a drink. While the tip of her fan slid up and down his crotch. Drew's elder sister was crass, but no doubt the boy thought himself in love as Pembroke had once.

It was no wonder Pembroke judged Drew ill when he'd been entrapped by Elizabeth's games in France. But Drew was not like Pembroke, Pembroke had arrived in Europe sheltered and blind – Drew had known from birth that promiscuity was not about love.

Nor was he like Elizabeth. He never spoke to her but he was tarred with her brush and his mother's, and scarred by his father and brothers and ruined by his mother's friends.

Faithlessness, uncaring, arrogance and self-gratification, were all expected of him and he had lived up to every expectation until he'd met Mary and been rejected by Pembroke's duchess.

He wanted to be different now; he just did not know how to be different.

Looking at Marlow again Drew saw Mary being subjected to an interrogation. She shook her head again and again, clearly denying everything.

A vicious anger, which had plagued Drew since childhood, sliced into his gut.

He liked her lying through her teeth on his behalf and fighting with her father – standing up for *him*. A satisfying surge of pride gripped in his chest. He was important to her, he had become most important. It was a sense of domination. Control. He would ram Marlow's ill opinion down his throat.

Mary would be Drew's to protect and care for. Her family could go to hell if they did not accept him. Mary had accepted him, and if Marlow wished to throw stones then, he would be throwing them at Mary too. That would teach the man to judge – when it was his daughter he judged. Maybe then Marlow would open his bloody eyes and look for the truth.

Peter returned, a broad smile cutting his usual devil-may-care expression. "Damn she's a gem, that pretty Miss Smithfield. I shall have to thank your future spouse for the introduction. I'm taking her driving tomorrow. Her Papa is as rich as Croesus. Perhaps it's time I considered a leg shackle too."

"You are rich yourself, you don't need her money." Drew shook his head at his friend's foolishness. He'd lay heavy odds Peter had no inclination to marry the girl.

"True, but when a woman is so ripe for the picking…"

Drew laughed. "Well, you can save your courtship until tomorrow. I vote we vacate and head for a club, the others are already playing cards I'll wager."

"It's not cards I am in the mood for. I'd rather search out more women."

"While my aim for tonight is spirits. I need a drink," Drew concluded.

Peter wrapped an arm about his shoulders. "My friend, a woman would ease your anxiety better…"

Chapter 9

Mary sat at her writing desk, her hand trembling so badly the quill tip scratched across the paper leaving a spider track instead of her usual neat hand.

John had business to attend to at his main country residence. He expected to be out of town for a couple of days. His house was within a day's travel from London and so her parents had chosen to accompany him, to give the children some fresh air.

Most families left their younger children at home during the London season but her parents never had.

Mary had told her mother she would stay with Emily's family. Of course she would not. Emily knew about the elopement. Mary had agreed her silence and then told her everything, knowing Emily would be too timid to judge or tell. The guilt of using a friend was another burden to add to her list.

Of course her parents assumed Mary would not lie and so they'd accepted an invitation Emily had written as proof and not questioned Emily's family. People would think it lapse when they discovered the truth, but it was not lapse it was love that made them trust her.

Even after her father had seen her speaking with Drew, he'd assumed Drew had approached her. He'd chastised her and warned her to cut Drew, repeating all the reasons why Lord Framlington was unsuitable.

He'd not for one moment considered she would choose to speak to Drew.

Heat had burned her cheeks as she'd listened and declared he'd done nothing wrong.

She knew Drew. Her father did not.

He'd be disappointed with her when he found her gone, and her mother would be distressed and her aunts and uncles and cousins – and John – would all judge her badly.

Tears filled her eyes as she finished the note but she would not change her mind. She had not seen Drew for over a week but he'd written, passing her letters through the stable lad. He'd said he'd not attended entertainments to stop her father suspecting.

She desperately wanted to see Drew. Her thoughts constantly hovered on him.

Folding the letter, she sealed it.

Her heart raced. The emotional pendulum inside her swinging from expectation and excitement to guilt.

This would tear a rift in her family.

She even felt guilty for feeling happy.

She loved her family, desperately. She did not want to hurt them, but she was old enough to make her own choices. They would not allow her to marry Drew. This was the only way.

Mary left the letter on her desk, rose and walked to the window. She looked down on the street. Life carried on as normal, people hurried past and carriages rolled over the cobbles, the sound of the horses' iron hooves ringing on stone, seeping through the glass.

It would be the same in five days when she had gone.

The world would not change – but her life would change.

She'd have a new home.

He'd said they'd live in his rooms until he received her dowry and then he would look for a property out of town.

She'd start a family with Drew.

Her arms folded over her chest and her vision clouded, then a tear escaped on to her lashes and ran down her cheek.

She was happy, it was just that so much would change.

She sighed wondering how his family would receive her. She had not even known he had a sister until the other night. Would they like her? The butterflies took flight in her stomach. She unfolded her arms and wiped away the tear.

A knock struck the door of her room, she'd left it ajar.

Mary turned to the desk and stood before it, to hide the letter. "Come in."

A maid entered, she bobbed a curtsy, then rose, "Miss Marlow, Lady Marlow asked if you would come down to the sitting room. Lady Barrington and Lady Wiltshire have called."

Two of Mary's aunts.

Mary nodded.

As the maid left, Mary turned to the desk. There would be no going back once she'd sent the letter. Drew would make the arrangements and in five days' time she'd leave her family and her home.

Her heart pounding, Mary reached for her shawl and wrapped it about her shoulders then concealed the letter beneath.

She took it to the stables before going to her mother.

* * *

Drew opened the door of his apartment and his gaze dropped to a letter lying at his feet. It must have been pushed beneath the door. He bent and picked it up.

Mary.

The stable boy must have delivered it.

Drew had spent the day with his friends, sparring in a boxing club, then they'd eaten luncheon at Whites, before going on to Tattersall's to look at horses.

The letter could have been lying here for hours.

He lifted his hat from his head and tossed it onto the cabinet by the door. Then broke the seal on the letter and read it as he walked across the room.

His heart thumped. *My parents are going away.* A chill swept over his skin even though the day was warm.

They'd be gone for two days and two nights – plenty of time to get her away and irreversibly change the course of both their lives. After that long in his company, her family would have to approve the match.

I have told my parents I will stay with Miss Smithfield, but I shall not go there, and Emily knows that. So you may send a carriage to collect me. I shall say it is from Mr Smithfield, and then we can leave in the morning, when my parents and John leave. Emily has promised me she will not say a word to anyone…

It was perfect. Her plan could not have come together better.

He folded the letter and slipped it into his inside pocket, his heart still beating hard, and a smile pulling at one corner of his lips.

His gaze caught on the pile of bills lying on the cabinet beside his hat. They would be paid soon. No more borrowing from his friends and dodging the duns. He would have money... and he would have Mary.

* * *

"Papa, I love you," Mary hugged her father as they stood in the hall.

Their luggage had been loaded on the four carriages standing before the house. One for John and Kate, their son and her eldest sisters. Mama and Papa were to travel in the second, with the boys and her youngest sisters, and the senior servants were to travel in the third.

The fourth was an unmarked hackney carriage Drew had sent. This was her final goodbye, although her family did not know it.

129

Tears filled her eyes as her father held her. "We will only be gone two days, sweetheart."

When she pulled away her tears clouded his reassuring smile.

He reached into his pocket for a handkerchief. She accepted it and dabbed at her tears, but her tears did not cease.

"Are you upset over Lord Farquhar? There will be other men, and one who is right for you."

She shook her head.

She'd not tried to convince them they were wrong about Lord Farquhar, it seemed easier to let them think her odd behaviour linked to that. "I am being silly, Papa. I'll miss you that is all. Robbie and Harry spend months at a time away at college and here I am crying over two days."

He hugged her firmly again. She pressed her cheek to his shoulder.

What if he despised her when he found out she'd lied?

Guilt cutting at her heart she drew away and kissed his cheek. He kissed hers too.

She turned to her mother.

Her mother's eyes shimmered with tears also, as though she knew this was really goodbye.

Mary embraced her.

"I know you're sad about Lord Farquhar but time will ease the pain, you'll see, be patient. You are young. There will be other men...."

"I know." Mary wiped her nose with her father's handkerchief. Her mother's palms framed Mary's face. Mary looked down, unable to hold her gaze.

"Sweetheart, one day you will be happy and settled, with your own family to care for."

Noise came from the stairs, the voices of Mary's younger siblings. She and her mother looked up, her mother's hands slipped away.

The children's governess appeared at the top of the stairs with a nursery maid who carried Mary's youngest sister.

The children were all excited.

"Mary."

Mary turned as John walked into the hall from the library.

"I'm sorry you're not joining us." He gave her a considerate smile.

She smiled too. John had been her hero from birth, despite his starchiness as he'd grown older.

She hugged him.

He'd be disgusted with her.

When she pulled away, she smiled brightly. "I'm sure you don't care a jot whether I am there or not, you have Paul and Kate to absorb what time you have to spare."

He laughed. "But Katherine does not chastise me as much as you do. You keep my feet firmly on the ground."

"John!" His gaze lifted to the stairs, to Kate, his eyes glowing with adoration.

Mary hoped one day Drew would look at her like that.

John's gaze returned to her. "Be careful, Mary."

"Goodbye, John."

When Kate reached the hall, Mary said goodbye to her, numbness setting in. Then in a daze she said farewell to her brothers and sisters before they were herded into the street to climb into the carriages.

Her father offered his arm. She took it.

When she stepped into the warm sunlight, her heartbeat raced.

She wished her eldest brothers, Robbie and Harry, had been at home too, so she could say goodbye, especially Robbie, the next in age to her. Robbie would never forgive her for keeping him in the dark.

What if her mother and father refused to let her into their home again?

That awful thought hit her as her foot touched the pavement.

She clung to her father's arm.

He walked her to the carriage Drew had sent, while the footmen helped her brothers and sisters up into their carriages and John helped Kate with Paul.

What will I do if they never speak to me again?

"Mary." Her father took her hand as they reached the carriage. "Are you sure you would not prefer to come with us? I'm sure Miss Smithfield would not—"

"No, Papa, I cannot let her down." It had become too easy to lie.

Love shone in his eyes, but it became clouded by the tears in hers.

She hugged him, then rose onto her toes and kissed his cheek, before saying, "I'll miss you."

"And I you, but we shall see you in two days."

She nodded.

His hand gripped hers tightly as she climbed up into the carriage.

When she sat, her hands settled over her reticule in her lap. Shaking. The metal lock securing the door clicked shut.

As she held her father's gaze through the window her heart jolted into a rapid rhythm.

This was it.

No going back.

She lifted her hand and waved as her carriage lurched into motion, the first to leave, leaving them behind.

Her father lifted his hand. Her mother and her elder sisters waved. Kate and John were looking the wrong way, but at the last moment John turned and lifted his hand. Then they were all out of sight, unless she leaned forward to look back. She did not.

Her heart pounded and tears spilled from her eyes as a sob left her throat.

This was too hard.

She wiped her eyes with her father's handkerchief, and then curled her fingers about it.

The horses pace picked up to a trot and the carriage turned into a side street. She could hear the strike, strike pattern of their stride.

Her heart thundered as the distance between herself and her

family grew.

When the carriage finally drew to a halt in St James, she looked from the window but she could not see Drew. The vehicle rocked as the driver climbed down, and her heart raced anew. Clutching at her dress she prepared to get out as the driver came to the door to set down the carriage step.

What if Drew was not here? But when the door opened she saw him move forward, smiling broadly.

Her stomach flipped, warmth flooding from her heart. She smiled reaching a hand out to him, but he did not take it, instead he gripped her waist, and lifted her from the step.

Once she was on the ground he gave her a hearty kiss.

Her nervousness erupted as a laugh when he pulled away.

It was done. The tears in her eyes became tears of joy. They would be married.

His hazel eyes danced with shifting colours of emotion as he gripped her hand, then he lifted it. His fingers had closed about the hand which bore her father's handkerchief. "You have been crying?"

"I'm sorry. I love my family, Drew. I will miss them…"

This was not the jubilation he'd pictured. Drew wished her joyful. But the girl was attached to her family, he knew it. The ability to love was one of the qualities he'd picked her for, so he could hardly chastise her for it. Yet it clawed into his skin, that she may love her family more than him. He wished to always be higher in her regard than her family. He could not bear to be second best to her, when she would be everything to him.

He took the handkerchief from her fingers. "You'll not need this now."

He saw uncertainty suddenly restrain her smile.

"We're taking my phaeton." He looked from her to the driver, and handed the man the other half of his payment.

The driver had left her bag on the pavement. Drew picked it up. This was it.

He looked back at Mary. Her lower lip had caught between her teeth.

Damn… He hoped she was not having second thoughts. "This is your chance to speak up if you have changed your mind?" Why the hell had he asked her that? He did not wish her to withdraw, it would rip him apart if she did. But perhaps it was better he had, at least then he'd know the truth and not forever wonder.

Her pale blue eyes shone, beautiful, even in the shadow of the narrow brim of her straw bonnet.

The bonnet had a large lavender bow tied at one side of her chin and her light spencer matched the shade of the ribbon, while her dress was a muslin three shades lighter.

She made his heart ache.

Her lip slipped from between her teeth and she smiled. "I have not changed my mind. I want to be your wife."

His free hand cupped her jaw. "Good, because, I want you for my wife."

She lifted to her toes and pressed a kiss on his lips. It was placation. It annoyed him, that she'd seen his weakness. He did not like it. He did not wish her to know he was a weak scarred man within. But no matter, as long as she did not change her mind.

He gripped her hand and led her to his phaeton, nodding at the groom who held the horses' heads. The man was from the mews where Drew stabled his horses.

Drew handed her up. The tall racing curricle was not designed with a lady's ascent in mind, and he saw a flash of a narrow stocking clad ankle as she climbed the steps. He would soon see it in the flesh.

When she sat, he looked up, a surge of need, to protect her, rushing in his blood. She had become his responsibility.

His heart thumped as he walked about the carriage.

He set her bag under the seat, then climbed up.

She held the carriage's frame with one hand and the other gripped her reticule.

Drew picked up the reins and the groom let the horses go on Drew's nod.

Drew flicked the reins.

He'd told the stables he'd be gone a couple of days and he'd borrowed money from Peter for the journey. He planned to take the main routes and ensure they were noticed at the toll gates, so Marlow could find them.

A smile pulled at his lips, he had her, and soon he'd no longer need to fear the duns taking his horses.

Mary didn't speak.

He didn't either. He had no idea what to say to her.

He concentrated on driving.

The sounds of tack, hoof beats and the roll of steel-rimmed wheels absorbed his thoughts. He'd lived in London for so long, and before that in cities abroad, these sounds were like a mother's heartbeat to an infant in the womb.

When they reached the outskirts, the traffic thinned, then they progressed into open countryside and the world expanded to distant horizons.

The only sound now was that of his carriage and horses, as they rocked and rolled along the track, the carriage springs creaking and the horses' hooves thudding on the dry mud track.

Drew raised the horses pace to a canter with a flick of the reins. He felt good.

"Do you like the countryside?" Mary asked, making drawing room conversation.

"I was a boy once, boys love trees to climb and rivers to swim or fish in. I loved the countryside then, but now I am a town gentleman I'm afraid. I cannot even recall the last time I left town."

"My parents have taken my brothers and sisters to Pembroke Place to enjoy the park. It's John's estate. It's not far from London. The children get so bored in town. I like London when we are here, I enjoy the season, but I prefer to be at home. My father's estate is in Berkshire. It's peaceful there."

He'd looked at the road as she spoke, yet he didn't need to see her face to know she was wistful and thinking of the things she'd left behind.

He felt awkward with her now. Clumsy. He could not speak of families. He could not imagine the things she was thinking. He didn't say anything.

"Where is your family's home?"

He glanced at her, a bitter smile catching his lips. He did not wish to speak of his family, but he answered none the less. "Shropshire, just south of Shrewsbury."

He looked back at the road.

"And your parents are there?"

He did not look at her this time. "Yes, they are there. My eldest brother lives with them. I do not visit."

"You don't?"

"No darling, so do not expect to go there. It was a lifetime ago that I promised myself I would never go back and said to hell with them."

Silence.

He glanced at her. She was looking at him. "Believe me, you do not wish to know them."

He faced the road again, avoiding the questions in her eyes. Of course she would not understand a family like his, any more than he understood her past.

"Do your parents always bring the whole family to town?" He only spoke to crack the ice that had formed over their conversation.

"Yes, always. They cannot abide leaving any of us behind. We used to stay at Uncle Robert's and that was bedlam because he has a large family too. We would all run riot all season. But since grandfather died and the title passed to John we stay with John."

"Is he happy about that?" He glanced at her again, genuinely surprised Pembroke took the children in. Drew could not imagine Pembroke abiding noisy children, he was so stiff-upper-lipped.

She smiled, but not at him, she was thinking about her brother.

136

"When he came home from Egypt, I think he was a little irritated by us all. But now he has Paul he plays as rough with the boys as Papa does, they are always play fighting."

Drew could not imagine it, not of Pembroke, or even her father for that matter. He'd never known a man play with children. When he and his brothers had fought, it had been for real and there had been bloody noses, black eyes, and bruised knuckles. The outcome had been a beating with a cane and several days' isolation in a locked room with bread and water for his pains.

Out of sight and out of mind had been his parents' policy for rearing their unwanted brats.

"My aunts and uncles bring their families to town too, and my cousins who are married are now beginning their families and bringing their young ones with them also. We are like a hoard when we gather at Pembroke Place, which is at some point in the summer and often over Christmas."

He looked at her again, for longer this time. He supposed she'd want him to take her there. He could let her go alone. That was if her family would still invite her. They may well simply turn their backs.

A sharp pain pierced his chest, like someone had stabbed him with a blade. She would be devastated if her family chose to cut her completely. He'd not really thought of this from her view.

"You know your family are not going to like this."

Her blue gaze shimmered with unshed tears and she nodded.

"It may mean—"

"I know they may not speak to me again, but I think they love me enough not to cut me." It was said with hope.

A smile pulled Drew's lips apart, and the same sensation of pride and joy cut across his heart. He wished to be first in her affections, and did that not say he was. She had taken the risk of leaving her family for him. But… "This is a gamble for you then," *and… Lord…* "What if you are wrong? Can you bear it?" He drew the horses to a halt suddenly. He wished her to be sure of this.

Why the hell did he keep giving her the chance to back out?

Because he did not wish to be hurt by her rejection if it came later, if her family turned her away, and then she turned against him… He needed to be sure that she was sure; that whatever they were building together would be on a firm foundation, one that could withstand the battle he knew would come soon.

He could not bear to give his heart to her completely and then be rejected.

Twisting about in the seat, to face him, her pale blue eyes looked intently into his as both her hands gripped her reticule. "Are you asking if I am sure again? Do you think I made this decision on a whim?"

He had; he'd thought it the outcome of their physical encounter. He did not anymore.

She constantly showed him new depths to her character.

"I will not change my mind, Drew. I will miss my family. I will be hurt if they cut me. I hope they do not. But we will have each other, and build our own family. God willing. I have made my choice."

Lord, what a speech. Drew turned to the road and flicked the reins.

She had chosen him, he should be smiling again, whooping with joy, yet suddenly the weight of such a notion settled on his shoulders. She did not know who he really was, inside. Who she had chosen. He did. A worthless barren soul – a man whose heart had been kicked so hard, so many times, he was unsure it knew how to function. He had no clue how to build a family. He'd no idea how to be a husband or a father. But he did wish to make her happy – to make her constant, and be constant – and he did care for her. He knew that.

Perhaps the country estate he intended to buy would be enough to make her happy. She had said she loved the country, she could make a home there, with any children they had, and perhaps the children would make her happy; even if the man she lived with ended up to be an inept husband.

She slid across the carriage seat and rested a hand on his thigh. The sensation did odd things to his stomach, but he did not look her way as he urged the horses into a faster motion.

After a moment her cheek rested on his shoulder, and her fingers gripped his upper arm.

Had she sensed his turmoil and offered comfort. He hoped she had not, he did not want her to know who he really was. She would definitely hate that weak, rejected man.

Then she kissed his cheek, and it jolted the world's axis.

God, he treasured this woman. He utterly adored her. Who else could look beyond all his faults and say they loved him regardless, and would commit themselves to him and leave a perfectly good life behind. Tomorrow, or perhaps the next day, or the one after that, but surely by then, she would be his wife.

His grip on the reins had become over tight. He loosened it. *I love you*. The words slipped through his thoughts as her head lay against his shoulder and the pressure of her slender fingers clutched about his arm.

Did he? *Am I capable of it then?*

Devil take it. But if this was love, it felt good, it felt right. Now she had come closer all his fears slid away.

He wanted her to be proud of him, as proud as she'd sounded when she spoke of her family. Lord he felt as though he must compete with them for her affections.

He sighed. In a few days she would be his wife, though, and then she would definitely be his, not theirs. But tonight she'd be his partner in the flesh.

They rode on in silence, she with her fingers about his arm, and her head against his shoulder.

He would make this night special. This would be their wedding for him.

Good God. Since when did I become a sentimental man?

Why the hell do I feel in bits over this woman? He could not

139

think straight with her next to him. No woman had sat like this with him.

Movement in a solitary tree at the edge of the road grasped his attention. A large buzzard landed on a branch and its sharp eyes surveyed the field beyond, searching for carrion. Its predatory nature visible.

Life held up a metaphorical mirror for him to see himself.

That was who he was – what he was. A hunter. An opportunist. A man who ruled the world about him, rather than let it rule him. He was not sentimental and Mary was his carrion; life's flotsam and jetsam thrown to his shore.

He pitied her.

No woman would be proud of him.

He was conjuring up dreams. It was her effect on him. He was not like her; not accepted in the world.

She would be humiliated, friendless, and family-less when she realised it. God help her. He should stop raising foolish expectations and be prepared to comfort her when her family turned their backs.

Yet he would do what he could to make their marriage good. He would strive to make her happy out of affection and gratitude, whether he had any finer feeling or not – gratitude, affection and admiration would be enough. He hoped.

God, he hoped.

Chapter 10

When Drew stopped at an inn for luncheon, after hours of travel, Mary's bottom and back were sore, her neck stiff, and mental exhaustion swept over her.

They'd shared that one brief conversation and then he'd been silent again.

She'd told him she was committing herself to him and he'd said nothing since.

The day was hot, but Mary felt cold. Her reticule dangling from her wrist, Mary clasped her arms, gripping her elbows as Drew spoke to the ostler taking care of the horses.

"You will treat them well. Let no strangers near them. Ensure they are fed…" Drew moved with assurance and strength. She doubted anyone would dare naysay him.

The ostler lifted his cap.

The muscle in Drew's jaw looked taut and his hazel eyes promised retribution if the man did anything wrong.

An ache clutched about her heart and her stomach teemed with butterflies.

He was handsome, tall, athletic – but vulnerable today too. His external severity seemed to protect and shelter whatever lay beneath. With crystal clear clarity she realised how little she knew the man she had committed herself to.

She'd thought she'd met the real man in the summerhouse. But he was not that man today and he'd been different among his friends too.

Drew checked the legs of the animals he'd chosen to replace his. Then glanced at her before looking at his horses as they were led into a stable. He said something to the groom before he turned back to her

When he approached her he had a look of determination setting his jaw, yet beneath it there was something sorrowful and grim.

Did he not wish to leave his horses? "They will look after them, I'm sure."

A smile touched his lips. "My horses are the most expensive thing I own, I don't leave them with any ease, Mary, darling. I'm sorry if I look troubled, I have my weaknesses, and my horses are one of them."

He offered his arm. She gripped his bicep through the cloth of his coat, rather than laying her fingers on his forearm and they turned towards the inn.

Gripping Drew's arm felt more intimate somehow; she walked with her father and John like this.

His arm lowered as they walked inside.

"What are the others?" she prompted.

"Others?" Awkwardness flooded the air between them as he glanced at her.

"Weaknesses…"

"Oh. I shall wait until we're wed to share them. I would hate to put you off." He said the words with humour.

A man in livery stood in the inn's hallway which was full of travelling cases. It was a posting inn.

"A private parlour, please, for myself and my wife." Drew reached into his pocket and withdrew a card, which he gave to the man. "We'll want luncheon, and I will take a tankard of ale. My wife, I assume, will want tea."

Mary nodded when Drew glanced at her, heat burning her skin.

She was not his wife yet, but in that case she should not be alone with him, and so he'd had to say something like that.

He smiled, as though sensing her insecurity but the smile twisted to a roguish lilt when he looked back at the man.

The man bowed, then bid them follow. He led them past the busy taproom to another door which opened into a small rectangular parlour. An armchair stood in each corner and in the middle a circular dark oak table with four chairs about it.

"Make yourself comfortable, my Lord, my Lady."

Once he'd bowed deeply again he shut the door and was gone.

Drew took off his hat and gloves, tossed both into one of the armchairs then smiled at her. "Please tell me you will take off your bonnet and your spencer, its sweltering out there. We can surely have a break from being baked like kippers when we are alone."

She smiled, though her stomach wobbled like aspic, and pulled loose the ribbons securing her bonnet with shaking fingers.

Leaving her bonnet, gloves and spencer in the chair with his articles, she turned back.

A dark heat burned in his gaze as he came towards her, and then his lips were on hers, brushing hers slowly.

Her hands lifted to his shoulders, as his rested on her back, urging her against him as his tongue dipped into her mouth.

A delicious curling sensation, twisted low in her stomach and slipped to pool between her legs.

A sharp knock rang on the parlour door and her arms fell as he stepped back. He caught her elbow, steadying her.

"Come!" Drew's voice sounded unsteady.

When the door opened Mary caught sight of herself in a mirror above the mantle. Her cheeks shone red and her lips were dark.

She turned her back on the maid and crossed to the window. It looked out upon a broad valley. She could see for miles. Her arms crossed over her chest as she absorbed the view and listened to the maid set the tea and ale down on the table.

Drew thanked the maid, then the door closed.

Mary heard and felt Drew move behind her, her senses tingling, then his arms came about her, clasping over hers. For a moment he just held her, and she rested back against the hard muscle of his chest.

His lips brushed her neck, and she shut her eyes as his hands fell to her hips.

Hers gripped over his.

She had been looking out the window at a new horizon, now she looked at an inner one. Her new life.

His head lifted and he pressed one last kiss behind her ear, before saying in a husky voice. "There was no need to blush, they think you are my wife. It will be true soon."

She opened her eyes, and turned, smiling. *It would be true soon.*

His lips pressed to hers and her fingers slipped through his hair as his gripped her bottom through her gown.

When another knock struck the door she had become breathless and her heartbeat raced.

The maid who carried the first tray glanced at them, but then her eyes turned to the task of unloading the tray. The second maid cast Mary a sly look, though, before setting down her tray.

Drew lifted Mary's hand and kissed the back of it. Denying the woman's judgement. Then he moved to pull out a chair.

Mary sat as the maids finished laying everything out.

The second maid looked at her again, then glanced at Mary's hands.

She wore no ring.

Mary slipped her hands to her lap, beneath the table, and gave the maid a hard condemning look, the same her deceased grandfather, the former duke, and now John, used if he was unhappy.

It made the woman blush at least.

Both maids bobbed curtsies then left and shut the door.

Drew laughed as he sat. "I did not know you could set a person in their place so easily, Mary."

"There are some things you cannot help but learn when you

live in the company of dukes." She smiled at him.

"Do I need to beware then? Are there other things I should know about you?"

She reached for the teapot. "You may be warned I am stubborn. Papa often complains I will never give in."

He grinned at her. The look speaking of pride as well as amusement. "So you are stubborn and I am wary. We have both discovered one thing new about each other."

"What do you wish for?" She indicated the food.

"I'll serve myself, I am quite capable. You select what you wish."

As he helped himself to a piece of rabbit pie, awkwardness descended again and Mary wondered when she would become used to being constantly in his company.

She cut herself a slice of bread, but when she lifted it to her plate her gaze caught with his. The roughish glint in his eyes said he was laughing at her. She saw the man he'd been among his friends.

"You are very bad, you do not care what anyone thinks do you?"

"And you adore me for it, it is what enchants you."

"I take bad back, you are devilish." It was a joke, but when he had that dangerous look in his eyes a part of her did fear he could be wicked.

Steel gripped at his jaw, as it had done when he'd parted from his horses. "I will take that as a compliment, all women love a rogue and the devil is one better."

"The devil is one worse." She wished she had not said it. It made his eyes even darker.

"I suppose you expect me to be an angel when we are wed?"

Why did his words sound bitter?

Turmoil racing inside Mary struggled to redeem the conversation. "Well, the devil is a fallen angel... Perhaps there is hope for you yet..." A strange look caught in his eyes. Pain? Reaching across the table she laid a hand over his. It jolted beneath her touch as if he did not care for comfort.

She looked away from him, cut some cheese and changed the

subject. "Tell me what you were like as a child?"

He laughed and she looked up. He was not looking at her as he lifted a slice of cold ham to his plate, but when he did his eyes glinted with an odd dismissive light. "Well there you have me..." He picked up his knife and fork, humour ringing in his voice. "When I was a child I behaved so badly the servants removed the 'an' from my name and cut it short with a capital 'D' for devil. To save them having to say, *'you devil Master Andrew'*, they just yelled D-rew, the nickname has stuck, even my mother uses it."

She did not find his story amusing at all, she found it sad.

"How many brothers and sisters do you have?" She skewered a piece of the pie with her fork.

"I have three brothers, and two sisters." He cut a mouthful of ham.

"Are they all married?"

"No, two of my brothers are not."

"But you are not close to them, you said…"

He set his knife and fork down. "No, Mary, I am not." He reached for bread.

"I cannot imagine it. I have always looked up to John. Our entire generation admire him, not just my brothers and sisters, but my cousins too, and Robbie is my closest brother, in age and friendship, he is eighteen months younger than I. We were thick as thieves when we were young until he went to school. When he hears I am married he will hate it that I did not write and tell him what I planned."

"Eighteen is an awkward age. It is good he's away. If you had told him he would have been torn between whether to tell your parents or tackle me himself, I doubt he would have been happy for you… Most young men have an unrealistic view of the world."

"Did you?"

His gaze met hers. "I was different, I had a very real view."

"Why?"

"Believe me, you do not wish to know." There was that hard

146

look in his eyes, again. It warned her away from the subject.

"Tell me what you do with your days in town."

His eyebrows lifted. "I thought by eloping I was avoiding an interview with your father…"

His words stung. "I am marrying you. I need to know more about you than the colour of your eyes and that you care for your horses."

"The colour of my eyes; you like them then?" His eyes lit up now, dancing with deviltry and humour.

The awkwardness returned. "Yes."

He smiled. "And I like yours. The blue is so pale your eyes shine like jewels. Your beauty kicks me in the gut each time I see you, Mary."

Embarrassment flooding her, Mary looked at her meal.

She'd never cared to be complimented on her looks, her entire family had the same appearance. Gentlemen always looked. She found their interest vulgar. She wished to be liked for who she was within, anything else was shallow.

His knife and fork hit his china plate. "I'm sorry. I forgot you do not care to be complimented on your appearance."

Her gaze lifted.

"You may compliment me." As long as he loved her for more than her appearance.

"Then I consider myself honoured. But believe me if any other man compliments you now I shall knock him down. You wished to know more about me, then this another thing – I will not be played."

"Played?" She did not understand.

"No games, Mary, no beaux, no flirting and no frolics. I will not be made a mockery of. I will not be cuckolded." His eyes were burning with dark heat now.

She was being warned.

Yet there was something else, something deeper in the jet at the heart of his eyes.

Fear? Pain?

"I would not—"

"I know you will not. I shall not allow it."

"I would never consider such a thing anyway." She picked up her tea, her hand shaking as she sipped from it, hiding her disquiet, no longer able to look at him. Beneath his mask of self-assurance, Drew was very different, vulnerable, but that was the man who'd come to the summerhouse. He was the one she'd agreed to marry. She wished he would let his guard down entirely.

She looked up, determination flooding her. "I will not call you Drew. I shall call you Andrew, your real name."

His eyes widened but he did not look displeased.

He was not a devil. He was a man, a man who could make mistakes, had faults and felt fear. He was Andrew beneath Drew's sharp edges; the rogue was simply a layer upon that, a layer that she hoped would disappear when they were wed.

Chapter 11

Drew did not force the horses but kept them at a steady pace. They had two days or more before her father would find them and he did not wish to get too far ahead. At each tollgate he struck up a conversation when he paid so they would be remembered and when they reached Banbury, Drew asked the man at the toll gate to recommend an inn. If Marlow caught up with them earlier than expected he wanted the man to know where they were.

When he pulled into the stable yard of the Black Bull, it was five in the evening. He could have driven for another three hours but there was little point.

A young lad ran out to take the horses heads. The animals whinnied.

Drew looped his reins over the vehicle's bar, then leapt down. An ostler came forward. He told the man they would be staying the night, and to stable the horses and his carriage. Then turned back to Mary.

She'd slid across to his seat. She was looking anxious again. They'd been mostly silent since luncheon, though she'd gripped his arm as he'd driven.

He should have spoken but he disliked the clinical dissection she'd made of him as they'd eaten.

He did not like remembering his childhood or looking inward.

He lived for now, and now he lived for her... She was all he wished to think of.

She climbed down, her slender fingers gripping his firmly to steady herself as her gaze clung to the cobbled floor of the inn's yard, as though she was too anxious to look at Drew.

When she reached the ground he tugged her close and kissed her lips. It was the only way he knew how to ease her anxiety.

She blushed, sucking in a sharp breath.

In a couple of hours they would be in bed...

Heat flared in his stomach and his breath caught in his lungs... The surge of emotion he was becoming used to, in her presence, ripped through him. Only today it was a dozen times stronger. Lust. Need. Responsibility. Caring. Hope. Fear.

Do I love her? His heart rate thundered.

Turning away, still holding her hand he drew her after him.

He ordered dinner served in their room and French wine to accompany it.

Their room was the first off the landing. It faced the street and the broad four poster dark aged-oak bed within it stood against the wall, its canopy and covers the colour of port.

He'd take her there.

Her hand slipped from his.

The uneven floor boards creaked as she walked over to the window and looked down at the street.

He smiled. He was avoiding her questions. She avoided the bed.

Two leather winged armchairs stood before the hearth, with a small table between them, and on it, a three arm candelabrum. Another unlit branch of candles stood on a chest beside the bed. Then against the wall there was a set of drawers, with a basin and a jug.

Drew's gaze drifted back to the bed. Then turning he lifted off his hat and walked over to the table to leave it there.

A knock struck the door. "Y'ur bags, m' lud." A man's voice breached the wood.

"Come!"

He tipped the man with coins from his pocket then shut the door behind him.

Drew pulled off his gloves and threw them down beside his hat.

There was another knock.

The wine.

The maid informed him it would be an hour until dinner.

When the door shut again, he stripped off his coat, watching Mary.

She'd not moved.

Noises permeated the glass of the window, voices, vehicles, horses, even birds. This was no solitary haven and yet it felt like a private island in a lake. Mary was his sanctuary.

She walked back across the room, stripping off her bonnet. She set it down beside his hat. His gaze was drawn to the curve of her nape, then dropped to the arch at the base of her spine. She had such a delicate feminine frame.

His heart thundered, as the turmoil of emotion gripped in his chest.

He turned to uncork the wine, poured a little and drank it.

It was hard to be patient and wait until after dinner. But she was a virgin. He could not hurry this. He'd heard women bled their first time, that a man had to tear a membrane within her body and it hurt the woman. He did not wish to hurt her.

He refilled his glass, and poured some for her.

He felt her behind him, it was a whisper passing through his senses the instant before she touched him.

Her small hands slipped about his waist, over his waistcoat, and her cheek pressed to his shoulder.

Whatever the emotion in his chest, it fisted and gripped harder. He wanted this woman physically, more than he had wanted any other. His mouth dried.

"Will we share the bed tonight?" she asked quietly.

"We will. Does the idea frighten you?" He stared at the wall. It was a stupid question, of course it must.

"A little." She let him go then moved past him to stand on the other side of the table. Her wide pale blue eyes watched him sip the wine.

God, I love her. He did not heed the thought. He was still unsure he knew what love was.

He held out her glass.

She took it. "How will it be?"

He swallowed another sip of wine. A bride's mother usually explained these things, he'd avoided an interview with her father but she'd lost the opportunity to ask questions of her mother.

"It will be beautiful, I hope. But I believe there will be some pain for you this time. I shall do my best to make the pain brief, and even if the first time is not good for you I will make it wonderful in the future."

Her glass touched her lips as she blushed but once she'd swallowed the wine, she said, "Wonderful? You have a high opinion of yourself, Andrew."

Lord. The way she spoke his name was as if her fingertips touched his innards.

He gave her a wicked grin. "It is not my opinion."

Damn… That had been the wrong thing to say, he should not have boasted, he saw in her eyes she was now thinking of him with others.

She was not like the other women he'd known, and he should remember that. They would have been thrilled by his boast.

He put down his glass, then took Mary's from her hand. "And now my skill is all for you."

His hand braced the curve of her nape and pulled her into a kiss.

Her fingers slid into his hair.

Within hours…

Impatience ripped through him as he pressed his tongue into her mouth and she accepted it. He did not wish to wait but he must. He needed to think of her and not himself.

It would be the first time he'd put anyone's needs before his own, except perhaps Caro's.

He broke the kiss, picked up her glass and gave it back to her. There was a tremor in her hand.

She wanted him too but she was afraid.

Remember it Drew!

* * *

The room span as Mary sipped her wine. She'd drunk four glasses through dinner. The conversation had been easier, though. They'd spoken of their friends, sharing stories, while Andrew continually refreshed her glass.

She'd drunk quickly, using the wine to calm her nerves, but she was sure she'd been babbling inanely for an hour.

She had not eaten much, her stomach had fluttered with too many butterflies and the bed had shouted its presence behind her.

He'd said it might hurt.

Her mother had not mentioned pain when Kate had given birth to Paul months ago, and they'd discussed such things. Her mother had said the marriage bed need not be unpleasant.

The things she and Andrew had done in the summerhouse had not been unpleasant.

"Mary?"

She'd let their conversation ebb.

The stem of her glass dangling through her fingers, she leaned back in her chair.

"Do you want any more to eat?"

She shook her head, her heartbeat thundering in her ears.

His plate was empty, hers was still full.

This was nothing to him.

Her palms were sweaty. "I am not really hungry."

"And nervous…" His gaze held hers.

"A little, can you blame me?"

153

"No, sweetheart, I do not blame you." He rose and something sliced through her middle cutting to the point between her legs, but he did not come towards her, he turned to the bell pull and rang for a maid.

Her mouth dried. She sipped more wine, her fingers gripping about the glass.

"I think you have had enough of that, I do not wish you unconscious." He lifted the glass from her fingers and set it on the table.

Her hand shook as it fell to her lap.

"When they clear the table I'll ask them to send up a maid to help you undress, and I shall go outside for a smoke to give you time to prepare."

To prepare?

His fingers touched her cheek. "Smile sweetheart, this is meant to be a happy thing."

She licked her dry lips, wanting the wine again.

His light brown eyes held the depth she'd seen in the summerhouse; Andrew's eyes, not Drew's. Her focus fell to his mouth. He smiled. The room span again.

A light knock struck the door.

Andrew turned and she stood, gripping the table as the floor swayed a little.

A maid entered and loaded a tray with the empty dishes and her leftovers.

"Could someone come and help my wife undress."

"Of course my Lord." The maid looked at Mary, "I will return to help you my Lady."

Mary's heart raced so hard she thought she might faint when the maid left.

"I shall go outside for a walk and give you time to undress," Drew stated before leaving her completely alone.

Mary did not move until the maid returned a little while later. After the maid had lit the candles and drawn the curtains, she helped Mary unbutton the back of her gown and undo her corset, then left.

Once Mary was in her nightgown, she could not decide whether to climb into the bed.

When Andrew returned she stood at the end of it – still undecided.

His gaze dropped to her naked toes peeping from beneath the hem of her nightgown, then rose again. Darkness had gathered in his eyes, a darkness implying deep unfathomable seas of emotion.

He turned and locked the door.

Her heartbeat raced. This was her wedding night, but not her wedding night.

The butterflies in her stomach flew so raucously it made her nauseous when he turned and began slipping the buttons of his evening coat free.

He slid it off and draped it over the back of a chair, then with his back to her he unbuttoned his waistcoat too.

When he sat down to remove his boots, her fingers gripped the carved oak bedpost.

He looked up and smiled at her, then stood again, his feet now bare but his shirt and trousers still on. But when he came towards her, he pulled his shirt from his waistband and lifted it up over his head stripping it off.

Her breath caught in her lungs. His chest was contoured with muscular ridges and hollows. He was beautiful. Her fingers gripped the bed post tighter.

His shirt fell on the floor behind him. Then he was there before her, and his hand was in her hair, pulling her mouth to his.

Her fingers left the bedpost and gripped his shoulders instead, clinging as fear swayed around like the room.

His tongue slipped into her mouth and his hand touched her waist over her nightgown, then slid upwards.

The touch was not intimate and yet it felt intimate because she had nothing on beneath the fine cotton.

He broke the kiss and smiled.

The candlelight from the candelabrum beside the bed reflected in his eyes.

He gripped her nightgown and drew it upwards.

Her breath trapped in her lungs.

"Don't be afraid, Mary, it will be good."

Was it possible for butterflies to stampede, if so that is what they did within her stomach as the cotton slid up across her thighs, and her body shook as she lifted her arms so he could slip her nightgown over her head.

The air in the room touched her skin and made her shiver.

His head bent as he dropped her nightgown on the floor, then he kissed her shoulder and her neck, his hands at her waist.

The trembling in her limbs slipped through her body to the place between her legs. She was afraid and yet she still ached for his touch there.

Her body arched towards him and her head tilted back as he continued kissing her neck and then across her chest.

Perhaps the wine had helped because with the room spinning, it was hard to be too conscious of anything but the sensations he stirred inside her.

His thumb brushed over her breast, teasing her nipple.

She sighed, the air leaving her lungs in a rush.

He straightened.

He looked hazy through her wine tinted gaze.

"Lay down…"

She nodded and sat back on the bed, then slid backward as he undid the buttons of his falls. At least she had seen that part of him before. But that did not stop the heat burning in her cheeks.

He slid off his trousers and underwear all in one go.

Her stomach tumbled over at the sight of his naked thighs and buttocks and *that* part of him. He was statuesque.

She swallowed, to clear the dryness from her throat.

"Lie back," he said, as he climbed onto the bed.

She swallowed again and did so, one knee bent upright, and

one knee slack, as her fingers clutched at the covers.

"Relax, sweetheart."

She nodded, though her muscles refused to.

He knelt above her, on hands and knees, just looking, his gaze skimming over her body. "You're perfect," he whispered.

Again she nodded, like a fool.

The candles beyond the bed flickered, as his head lowered and he kissed her breast. Tremors raced through her body, beneath her skin.

He sucked, then licked her nipple, without touching her anywhere else, his body hovering above her.

The feeling was exquisite, then his hand touched her breast and his fingers shook too.

"Andrew." Her hands came down on his head, then it lifted and he kissed her mouth.

It was the most beautiful feeling in the world as she sensed his naked body above her, and his hand massaged her breast.

She arched upwards.

His kiss left her lips and travelled over her face then touched her jaw and her neck, as the room span.

When his hand left her breast it slid to her hip, and his mouth followed, kissing down her middle to her stomach.

Her fear became lost in the spinning room and the warmth of his lips on her skin.

When his kiss touched her intimately between her legs, her fingernails dug into his shoulders, gripping hard. Sensation ripped through her. She laughed a little. Nervously. But he did not stop. His tongue swept out to taste her.

"Andrew!"

"Relax." The heat of his breath burned her there, before he licked again.

A part of her could not believe she was doing this, it must be the wine which made her allow it and not speak, she was too languid. He sucked her there too, like he had sucked her nipple, causing sharp sensations to spin up through her body.

"Andrew." His name came out on a tide of want.

Then his fingers were within her as they had been the other day, only now it was no slight invasion, it was a deep intrusion, a claiming, as his lips claimed her too.

"Ah."

His other hand still gripped her hip, gently.

Her head pressed back into the bed, and her body lifted to his touch as her fingers gripped in his hair. The sensation he had first taught her in the darkness, swelled.

"Please," she whispered at last, not even knowing what she was asking for. She was so hot. She just wanted to be completed.

"Not yet." His breath brushed against her. "Not until you have reached the little death."

Her vision glazed as though she looked through hazy glass as her fingers clung in his hair, holding on to sanity, to reality, while he continued trying to steal her away with his wickedness. Oh, but then… "Andrew…" There was that rush of intoxicating, overwhelming, sensation. It broke over her…

Sweat glimmered on Mary's skin and her nectar filled Drew's mouth as the spasm of her release pulled at his fingers and pulsed on the tip of his tongue.

Emotion gripped in the back of his throat and caught tight in his stomach.

He'd known she was beautiful, but… naked… she outshone any other woman, there was not a single blemish on her skin. Her body was truly like porcelain.

"Mary." He moved over her as her eyes tried to focus on his face. They were glazed by the wine and her limbs lay slack and moved awkwardly to accommodate him between her legs.

She was young and innocent, pure and beautiful – and any moment now she would be his. He would be the first. The very first. The only. He would marry and protect her, and keep her for

158

himself. The emotion he felt overwhelmed him. *I… love… her…*

He positioned himself carefully above her, feeling his tip at the moist juncture between her thighs.

Her blue eyes were wide and luminous and fear hung there again now, as it had earlier, but it was best to get this over with. He could not delay it in case her father discovered her absence earlier than they thought. He did not want to delay it anyway.

"It will hurt, just for a moment…" he whispered to reassure her, and then he plunged, hard and quick.

She cried out as his penetration pierced her barrier. A high gasp.

Buried inside her he held still, watching her bite her lip as he breathed hard and fought against the emotion damming in his throat.

Then he kissed her brow, her nose, her cheekbone. He wanted to take the pain from her. *I love her, I do* – he'd never felt this way about a woman or known anything so precious.

When her expression relaxed he withdrew slowly. He had not been with a woman for a year, a whole year, not since he'd decided Mary was his choice. He'd waited a long time for this moment.

God his friends would be laughing if they knew how important she'd become to him. They had no idea he'd entirely abstained. But he was committed to her, as he wished her to be to him.

He was the first man inside her body.

The only man who would ever be inside her body.

Pressing back in, he relished every sensation, preserving it to memory.

Her fingers released the covers and lifted to his back as her body relaxed a little.

Her eyes had shut.

He moved out and pressed in, cautiously, over and over again, trying not to hurt her any more than he had, but knowing the best cure for her pain was pleasure.

Every contour in her face and her body was beautiful. The candlelight flickered over her skin.

She opened her eyes and met his gaze after a while, and now the glaze looked more from desire than wine. But he could see she did not understand this.

Lord... He did not understand this. The emotion inside him made him feel like he would split in two as he held her gaze and swallowed back the lump in his throat.

"Mary." Her name was a supplication, a promise – he idolised her.

Her fingers gripped his shoulders.

She had such a gentle, caring touch.

"Come again for me, sweetheart," he urged her vocally as he moved. A flame burned inside him for her, drying his throat.

It had burned for a year.

The breath slipped from her mouth. Her blue irises shone like glass.

"I love you," he whispered, his throat constricting with the emotion he could no longer hold back. Maybe it was true. Maybe it was not. He thought it was. But it was what she wished to hear and he would give her anything she wished, his heart was brim-full of her.

"Mary, it will be right between us. Everything will be good"

She nodded, her eyes clouding with tears.

"I love you," he repeated.

"And I you," she answered pressing her hips up against his next invasion as her fingers slipped to his back.

Oh, God, she was beautiful.

"Mmm..." The sound escaped her lips and her heels pressed into the mattress.

If this was pain for her, it was heaven for him.

She licked her lips.

He worked determinedly, with more skill. "Does it feel good now?"

Her blue eyes looked at him through a cloak of dark eyelashes and she nodded.

The muscles in her thighs gripped his hips.

"Can you bear it if I go a little faster?"

She nodded. Her eyes closing completely.

He increased his intensity pushing deep, fast and hard, forgetting her virginity and seeking bliss for them both as her breasts rocked with the force of his thrusts.

Her breath came in pants and her fingernails clawed into his back as her thighs fell open wider for him. She sighed with a whimpering sound. Then…

"Andrew?" Her eyes opened and her gaze clung to his, terrified for an instant as he took her to the edge. She hid nothing as she broke, crying out, her fingers clawing, her body arching into pleasure as sweat glistened gold in the candlelight dancing over her skin.

Lord. Once, twice more, he thrust in hard losing all restraint and thought. A third time, and then… he came to pieces – a wave crashing over the shore, a burst of rolling power.

God in heaven. Sex had never been like this before. He held still, buried deep inside her as sensation ripped through him. He bit his tongue and shut his eyes. *God.*

When it was over, he laughed and tumbled to his back, pulling her over him. "Mary, you are my dream."

"I love you," she whispered to his neck as he drifted into sleep with her as his blanket.

Chapter 12

Ellen Marlow rolled over in the bed she shared with her husband Edward. It was still dark and Edward lay stretched out beside her, one of his hands beneath her hip. The other slid from her waist as she turned. They'd dined and retired early. She'd been glad of a break from the season's late hours.

A light knock rapped on the bedchamber door.

Ellen sat up unsure if she'd imagined it. It was surely nowhere near dawn.

"My Lord! My Lady!" Mr Finch, John's butler.

Ellen shook Edward's shoulder. "Something is wrong."

He rolled to his back, his eyes opening.

"Mr Finch is knocking."

When he did not immediately rise Ellen slid from the bed and picked up her nightgown from where Edward had thrown it to the floor when he'd stripped it off her earlier.

She slipped it over her head, letting it fall and sheath her body as she crossed to the door.

She opened it a little. "What is it Finch? Is it one of the children?"

He held out a folded sheet of paper. "No, Lady Marlow. This. A servant delivered it a few minutes ago, I'm told it is from Lady Eleanor."

"Eleanor?" *Her niece? Why?*

"So I was told."

Ellen took the letter.

"Were you told any more?" Edward's fingers touched Ellen's waist. She stepped aside and he opened the door a little wider. "Why would Eleanor send a message in the middle of the night?"

"I cannot say, Lord Marlow, I was not told."

Edward leaned past Ellen to light the single candle he'd collected from the bedside, touching the wick to the one Finch held.

Ellen turned, her shaking fingers opening the letter as Edward held the candle close. He had dressed in a loose silk robe which shone a ruby colour in the candlelight.

Dear Aunt Ellen,

I am only writing because I thought. Oh, there is no way to say this to you with any ease. But I thought, I am sure you told me, Mary was not going with you to Pembroke Place but staying in town with the Smithfields. Only I saw that family tonight at a ball and she was not with them. When I asked after Mary they looked at me as though I were mad, saying she was not staying with them and that there had been no intention for her to do so. I hope I was wrong. Did I mishear, or did Mary change her mind. Is she with you?

An ice cold sensation gripped in Ellen's chest. "No."

"What is it?" Edward asked.

She could not breathe.

She looked up. "What has she done?"

"Eleanor?"

"Mary?" Ellen breathed her daughter's name, as tears clouded the words of Eleanor's letter.

Edward took the letter.

"No."

Edward's heart pounded. Mary had hugged him and cried when she had said good-bye. She would not have done anything wrong.

"She must be at John's. There must be a misunderstanding. We will go back now."

"What about the children?"

"We will leave them with John and Kate. We can return tomorrow."

Ellen nodded, her eyes expressing the same emotion which gripped in his chest.

He turned to the bell pull and called for Ellen's maid, not even wishing to wait for Finch to fetch the woman. "If you dress, I'll go and tell John." He looked back at the half open door, where Finch still stood. "Have the grooms ready a carriage immediately; we wish to be gone as soon as we can."

Elopement. The word whispered through Edward's head but he refused to believe it. Yet there was the image in his mind of her speaking with Framlington only days ago.

Mary had said, "It was nothing, Papa. He stopped me that is all, and I argued with him and told him to stay away."

But there had been the day she'd said she'd seen him in the park too. The day she'd unusually disappeared for an early morning ride.

Yet Mary was sensible – level headed… She would not. *Lord, I pray…* She would not.

He walked along the hall to John's rooms, fear gripping at his stomach.

He knew elopement was Ellen's fear too. But Mary had been fixed on Lord Farquhar and hurt by him… hadn't she?

She would not have…

Or, was her distress caused by something else, someone else?

He knocked on the door of John's rooms.

Lord. "Mary what have you done?" Edward whispered in a bitter voice as he pictured his first child in his mind's eye as an infant in his arms.

"Come!" John called.

164

Mary believed Andrew loved her. He'd made physical love to her again in the darkness just before dawn, kissing her throughout, his pace excruciatingly slow, as he'd whispered endearments over her lips, saying "I love you," again and again.

But it was not just his words, it was the gentleness with which he touched her that had convinced her of his affection.

He'd been mindful of her soreness, and at the end he'd stroked her hair back from her forehead and said, "You are beautiful, Mary."

He had gone back to sleep but Mary had been unable to.

When he'd woken it had been full light and he'd got up, washed, dressed and then he'd helped her dress and kissed her nape while she'd pinned up her hair.

He'd said I love you again, against her skin, and she'd turned and said it to him too. Then they'd kissed for a long time before going down to breakfast.

She'd eaten lots, her stomach was calmer, and he'd teased her over her sudden appetite. But when he'd risen he had come about the table, kissed her hard and then licked the taste of bacon from her lips.

His vitality, beauty and tenderness had wrapped around her, but she felt as if it was made of glass and at any moment everything would break as she pressed her thigh to his and gripped his arm, while he drove the curricle on steadily through the greenery of England's landscape.

Perhaps it was because she could not quite forget that her parents did not even know she had gone yet. They would discover her deceit soon.

* * *

A tight pain bit hard in Edward's gut when the carriage drew to a halt before John's ostentatious townhouse.

If Mary was not here?

That was a question he had refused to consider.

Glancing back at John who'd chosen to accompany them, leaving Kate with the children, Edward opened the door to alight. One of John's footmen was already there, setting down the step.

Edward jumped down, then turned to take Ellen's hand. She descended hurriedly. John followed. Edward left them behind him, rushing towards the open door.

Dawn had broken as they'd travelled, flushing the sky pink. Now it was full light, and the sky an azure blue.

"Is my daughter here?" Edward thrust the words at the porter who'd opened the door. "Miss Mary. Is she here?"

The man looked blankly at him, as though Edward was a fool.

"Is she here!" She had to be.

"Miss Marlow left with you, my Lord, a day ago, she has not returned. I did not think she was expected."

The answer hit like a fist in Edward's stomach.

"She has not come back here!" Edward called across his shoulder to Ellen and John, a chasm opening in his chest.

Edward looked to the footman who held the coach door. "Have the stables saddle myself and His Grace horses, as quickly as they can." Perhaps Mary was at Smithfield's after all and Eleanor mistaken.

The footman had not moved. "Horses! Now! Run!"

The man did.

Edward looked at John. "We shall ride to Smithfield's. If she is not there perhaps his daughter will know where she is."

Ellen looked pale. "I will go to her room." She pushed past him. "Perhaps she has left a letter."

If Mary had left a letter it could only mean one thing – she had eloped.

Edward followed Ellen as she crossed the black and white chequered marble floor. Then he hurried up the stairs beside her, his hand at her back as she gripped her dress lifting her hem from

166

her feet, John followed behind them.

Edward walked through limbo – riven from reality. Someone had tied his hands so he could not reach out or do anything.

This was his precious daughter.

The child who had been a light in his life ever since her birth.

Moments illuminated his thoughts; the moment she had walked, the way as a baby she had rubbed his earlobe when she was tired. Her fingers gripping his leg to get his attention as she had grown. The beauty of her smile when she had come out. *Mary?*

There was no sign in her room that anything was amiss. Everything was still where it ought to be.

Two days ago he'd handed her up into a carriage, where the hell had it taken her.

"The writing desk?" John pointed.

Edward turned to look. He'd bought it for her, as a gift. It was mahogany and had a delicate inlaid pattern of roses carved from rosewood, walnut and apple woods.

Pain gripped about his heart when he opened the lid and saw a muddled pile of letters, some written by a hand he knew, but others…

The letter which lay on the top was the one Edward had seen from Smithfield's daughter, confirming her parents' agreement for Mary to stay. Was that a lie? Had he not even known his daughter? How many times had she lied?

John leaned past him and took out some letters.

Edward took a pile too and passed some on to Ellen. They all began scanning the words. Those that Edward read were inconsequential. These were letters from her female friends, young women's chatter. "There is nothing here."

"DF?" Ellen said.

Edward turned.

Her eyes shone with fear. "Mary received a letter. She said it was from Daniel. That is why I thought she had a liking for him. These are all love letters signed DF or D. Most are dated after

Daniel's engagement… Why would I disbelieve her? Mary never lied. Never…" Tears dripped on to the letters Ellen held.

Nausea gripped at Edward's stomach. "They are not from Daniel Farquhar…" *Damn*… would Mary really be so foolish.

"They speak of meeting her, Edward. Who has she been meeting? I thought her silence and distraction a symptom of a broken heart. These letters urge her to trust him. Why did she not speak of this to me?"

Edward cast the letters he held down on the desk behind him, and moved to comfort Ellen, though he felt no comfort himself. "Because they are from a man we told her to avoid…"

"Drew Framlington!" John growled. "She would not have been so foolish!"

"It looks as though she has been…" Cold fear raced beneath Edward's skin.

"They have been passing these letters through a stable boy." Ellen pulled away, anger in her voice now. "If we find who it was…"

John growled and turned away.

"She has eloped," Ellen said when John left the room. "We do not even know him, Edward. How could she? Why did she not at least try to persuade us? We have always told her she may choose her husband."

"Because both John and I would have told her no, Ellen. My guess is she feared that speaking would only alert us to the possibility. I would not have condoned this match. The man is a manipulator, he's charmed her. He will have told her not to speak to us."

"If he has hurt her—"

"I will kill him." Edward growled. What had Framlington said to her, done to her, to persuade her? Damn it. Edward wished he had challenged her harder the other day, he could have prevented this.

He held Ellen as she wept.

"Mama!" Edward turned as John came back. He held a young lad by the shoulder and the boy looked scared. "I found Mary's little messenger. Tell Lord and Lady Marlow, what you told me."

"I didn't do nothin' other than what m'lady told me to."

Edward glared at the boy. "Then tell us what she told you to do."

"She gave me letters an' said no one else should know. She made me swear."

"Where did you deliver the letters to, to whom?"

"I don't know the gent's name, m'lord, 'e was just some toff who lives in the Albany. I took letters there, an' 'e sends 'em back and one time 'e came 'ere."

A knife lanced into Edward's chest. "The man was here?" Had Mary lost her mind. What had happened then? What was happening now?

"Framlington lives in the Albany," John stated in a bitter pitch. "He has probably been playing her for weeks…"

"Damn." Edward could not look at Ellen. "We had better go there to begin our search. I saw her speaking with Lord Brooke and Framlington only days ago at a ball."

"Brooke is Framlington's best friend," John stated, "and he rarely goes to such things—"

"Well he has attended balls recently, twice, he danced with Mary," Ellen interjected. "Oliver had introduced one of his friends. I never thought to question…"

"And Oliver clearly never gave a damn," John growled.

"It hardly matters now," Edward stated. "What is done is done. Now we must simply find them…"

Chapter 13

Mary had no idea how many miles they'd travelled but it seemed a considerable distance, although they'd stopped at a busy posting inn for luncheon and he'd not hurried the horses. But her bottom was sore from being bounced about on the seat of his curricle over rutted tracks and due to the change in her status last night she ached in other places too.

Relief overrode every other emotion when they booked into another inn for the night.

Andrew had said it would take three or four more days to reach Gretna. But tomorrow her parents would discover her gone and follow. What had been done could not be undone, though. Her fate was fixed. She'd lain with Andrew.

Mama will be heartbroken.

Andrew's fingers clasped her elbow guiding her upstairs to their bedchamber.

They had eaten dinner in a parlour downstairs.

Papa will be hurt and angry and John will be disappointed.

She wished they'd find her before she reached Gretna, then they would be at her wedding. But she was not foolish enough to think anything could have been done differently. Papa and John would not have let her marry Andrew by choice.

The soft light of a vibrant sunset flooded the small room and it cast Andrew in gold, gilding his features.

He was so starkly handsome. Her heart melted a little more each time she looked at him.

"You're silent. A penny for them?" Andrew asked as he closed the bedroom door behind them and turned the key in the lock. His eyes gleamed with a dark honey colour. "What are you thinking, tell?"

Ah. Why must tears come? They burned in her eyes and her teeth caught her lip to stop them tumbling over, but failed.

"You are not regretting…" His expression twisted to pain. "Mary?" He caught her hand, and would have pulled her to him, but she pressed her other hand against his chest to stop him, before swiping away her tears.

"I am not regretting. I was thinking of my parents. They will know tomorrow."

His thumb, brushed another tear from her cheek, then he let her hand go and turned away; a bitter sigh escaping his lips as he moved to pour a glass of wine from a decanter by the bed. "Must we go back to this? Must you think of them now? I thought you were past leaving them; that we had left them behind where they belong." His voice rang with impatience and a note of anger. It was as though something had snapped inside, as he barked out his bitter words. "We have become something of our own, I thought."

He did not understand. He was not close to his own family and clearly he did not realize how much she cared for hers. Or because he did not understand he simply did not care. She did not try to explain or persuade him to understand. The emotion made finding the words too difficult.

Instead she went to him and hugged his waist, her fingers gripping across his stomach as she pressed her cheek to the fabric of his coat at his back.

He didn't touch her and his body was stiff; nothing in his stance yielded as she held him.

"I wish Papa to walk me up the aisle, and Mama to watch us, that is all…"

A condescending sound left his throat as he turned, forcing her to let him go and step back.

"Your father would drag you away from the aisle." Anger and annoyance echoed in his pitch.

She felt a frown crease her forehead. "I should have tried to persuade them to accept you…"

His eyes narrowed. "You could not have persuaded them. Nothing would have made them allow it."

Mary opened her mouth to speak, but no words came as he sipped from his wine glass, his hard gaze told her he did not wish to discuss her parents' point of view. After he'd drunk he held the wine glass to her lips and tilted it as if daring her to refuse to drink.

It was like he offered a poison chalice, or a potion – the devil in him shining in the black hearts of his eyes which had crowded out the honey colour.

When she had taken a sip, he put the glass down, and then his hands gripped her hips pushing her back against the wall as his lips came down hard on hers. The kiss felt like a brand burning into her – claiming her.

No one else would ever have been enough for her, no one else would have cared with the passion and intensity that he did.

When he broke the kiss, his hazel eyes were like treacle not honey, his pupils were so wide. Her bones were as weak as aspic.

"I love you. You know that." It did not sound like a statement, but a question.

"I know." Her words lacked breath. She believed him, but she knew he could not understand how much it hurt her to hurt her family. Yet it seemed as though when she spoke of caring for her family she hurt him.

He'd said in his letter, the day she had met him in the summer-house, he did not know love. He did not – but she would teach him what it meant, what it was. "I love you too, Andrew."

A guttural sound escaped his throat and then he kissed her, urgently. Then he spoke into her mouth. "I love you calling me

Andrew, no one else does..."

He kissed her again, and she kissed him back, her arms bracing his neck as her body remembered his touch.

Then she realised he was drawing up her dress.

She broke the kiss, her fingers gripping his shoulders and her gaze meeting his dark eyes, but before she could speak he threw her his rogue's lilting smile.

"Let me come into you now, here, no foreplay, no procrastination, let us make love now as we are."

Her lips trembled as her next breath faltered.

He gripped her hand taking it from his shoulder and pressing it against the column in his trousers. "See how ready I am."

He pressed a kiss against her temple, keeping the pressure on her hand, then he kissed her cheek.

She tilted her head as sensations of longing spiralled through her and she let him kiss her neck as he pressed the heel of her palm to his arousal. Then he let her hand go, and left her to touch him, as his hands returned to the task of raising her gown.

Yesterday he'd been tender; tonight he was being wicked. But his wickedness made something lurch low in her stomach as her body recalled how it had held him inside her.

In moments his fingers pulled at the bow securing her drawers and then he pushed the flimsy garment to the floor, and in another his fingers released the buttons of his flap. It was as if he'd touched a flame to tinder and they ignited as he lifted her feet from the floor, wrapped her legs about his waist and pushed into her.

There was heat, in flashes, and pain as he pulsed into her and her arms clung about his neck while her head and back hit the wall behind her over and over.

"Andrew?" she said, meeting his gaze as his fingers gripped even harder at her thighs.

"Am I hurting you?"

The urgency in his voice caught at her heart. He was, but it was pleasure as well as pain. He loved her passionately. It was the thing that made him so addictive. "No." She shook her head and bit her lip as he continued moving even harder and faster, the sounds releasing from his throat animal like growls and cries.

"Andrew!" When the ecstasy of their union struck, it was in a rush that knocked her senses to the floor, and it span through her nerves to her fingertips.

"Hush, darling," he growled in her ear as he carried on, and on... Her fingernails clawed into the back of his neck, and she panted out her breath, crying at the pleasure while her back hit the wall over and over, until suddenly he growled hard by her ear, and then he held still, as she felt her body tremble around him, and he pulsed with the pace of his heartbeat inside her.

"This is how I wanted you last night, just like this, quick and hard," he said over her lips before kissing her. She kissed him too; her arms about his neck. She felt as if he really needed her...

He broke the kiss, but he did not set her down as his forehead pressed against hers. "Say you love me."

Mary smiled, there were so many layers beneath his surface. "I love you."

"And I you, Mary. More than you can ever know," his husky voice seemed full of unspoken words. The grip on her thighs eased, then he set her down as if she was glass.

When her parents came she would make them understand and like him.

If she could see the good in him they must be able to see it too.

* * *

Drew could not sleep. She lay beside him, naked. But it was not only her body that was naked, it was her soul and her heart too and her openness and her innocence had cleansed him. Even the air drawing into his lungs felt different. Clean. He felt clean. He felt... blessed, and hopeful. He wanted to touch her. He did not, because he did not wish to wake her. The candle had burnt to a stub and the flickering light cast differing shadows across her face. She was more than beautiful. Her beauty was indescribable, because it was soul deep.

She was as clean and white as snow within.

But she was not innocent now. He had cut the first footprint, and he would keep walking with her, and cut the last too.

If the sensations within him were love, then love was possessive, and all consuming.

Her dark eyelashes flickered against her pale skin as her eyes moved beneath her eyelids, as if she was dreaming.

She had cried when they came upstairs after dinner. She missed her family. He'd feared she'd changed her mind when it was too late for that, but she had kissed him with all of herself still, and made love to him with every part of her being.

He had never known anyone do that before.

He did not wish to lose her. But the storm was coming. Soon.

Her father and brother would come. He knew they would. Then would come Mary's trial. He felt as though she still loved her family more. He wished for all of her to be his. Jealousy roared inside him.

He had sought to charm her with his body – to win her back, to hold on to her. The candle flickered one last time, then went out. The room was entirely dark, but he could still feel her breath on his skin, and imagine her face.

He was afraid that her father and Pembroke would turn her against him.

Now that he had this, her, he could not bear to lose her.

She would have to marry him, there was no doubt of that, but he did not want a hollow heartless marriage. He wished for a love match. A true love match. She could give him that, teach him how to live like that. Life would become the two of them together against the world, he would be her defender and she his... and this evening... when she had her second night with him to look forward to... she had cried for want of her family. He had been unable to dwell on what it meant. Yet he feared it had meant that despite leaving with him she still thought more of them.

He wanted her now.

He needed her now.

He only had hours to win her soul and keep it. *Please, Lord let her lean towards me for comfort and protection. Let me be who she cries her tears for…*

His hand reached out and touched her hip, then slid up her side and down again. Her skin was like silk.

He wished to be inside her, to claim her; to calm the fear in his head, and appease the possessiveness in his soul… He did not know how to be what she needed. He was terrified of failing her – of her rejection. Of failing himself. How could he win against the affection of her family, if she still cried for them, now?

She moved beneath his hand, rolling to her back. He gripped her breast, rose up and leant to kiss her shoulder.

This was all he knew, he knew how to please her in a bed, let that be enough… Let his physical love wrap around her heart and form a wall that would hold against her father and her brother when they came.

Chapter 14

Andrew had made love to her three more times through the night. The second time, like the first, had been rough and vigorous. She'd woken up as he'd touched her, arousing her, then he'd moved over her as she'd lain on her stomach, her fingers and toes gripping the sheet.

The third time, he'd pulled her over him, and moved her legs up so she'd knelt then bid her to rise up and lower over him. She'd felt uncomfortable and exposed, but then she'd fallen into ecstasy and forgotten her pride, her body hot and fluid like lava.

The fourth time she'd felt like an earthly Goddess half awake and half asleep as the first light of dawn had flooded the room. He'd made love to her with his lips, tongue and teeth, until she was panting and fighting to catch a breath, begging him to come into her. Then he'd settled between her thighs and ridden her deeply and slowly rocking into her with an adoration that made her mindless.

It was as if he wished to teach her everything about physical pleasure in one night.

She smiled when she woke again, blissfully happy, her muscles trembling from a night of adoration, ashes glowing warm beneath her skin.

His thigh lay over her legs, weighting her down and his broad palm rested on her stomach as she lay amidst tangled sheets.

The air was heavy with the scents of their bodies.

Shouts ran from the courtyard outside, urgent, angry masculine voices, along with a clatter of horseshoes.

Mary slid from Andrew's embrace and began sleepily gathering up her underwear and dressing as the commotion outside grew in intensity. People shouted.

Clothed in her drawers and chemise Mary turned to the window, but now the sound of the commotion came from within the inn, as heavy strides struck the stair-boards, reverberating through the internal walls.

Andrew woke stretching as the aggressive, hurrying, strides drew nearer. Then he sat up, no longer languid, and looked to the door then at her. He smiled but it was not his normal smile, it looked odd. It was like the smile tried to speak to her, it looked uncertain, and his eyes said something she could not read. Something she had never seen there before.

The footsteps stopped outside their door and someone banged a fist against it, making the wood jolt against the lock. "Mary!"

"Papa," she whispered towards Andrew, rushing to grab her clothes. Andrew's expression immediately changed, it became the expression of the man she had first met in London, the man of the ballrooms. The defiant rogue. "Andrew." She wished for him to get up.

The door jolted at another strike. "Framlington! I know you are here! Open this door!"

Mary feared the door would break as she clutched her clothes to her chest, her fingers shaking and her stomach nauseous with fear.

"A moment, Papa!" Mary shouted, as Andrew rose.

He was in his stupid arrogant mood; his movement was languid, again, and his lips twisted in a roguish smile, as if he did not care that they had been caught like this. But he did care; she had glimpsed the defiance in his eyes as he'd risen. It denied that he cared, and the fact he needed to deny it proved he did. What could be seen of Andrew never seemed to be what lay beneath. Yet this was not the moment for his roguery, or his devil to rebel.

"Let me in!" Her father roared.

Mary had never heard him sound so angry.

Her heart pounded as Andrew crossed the room and collected his shirt, then slid it over his head as her father hit the door again.

"Open up!"

Andrew walked to the door, wearing only his shirt, which hung open across his chest, without even looking back at her.

He would not open the door until he'd dressed... He—

He turned the key in the lock...

The door flew open and bounced back against the wall as Andrew stepped out of the way.

The air left her lungs as she stood motionless holding her clothes against her.

Her father's fist was already raised and he struck Andrew's jaw with a swift hard punch. Andrew stumbled back against the wall but he did not fall.

"Papa!" Dropping her clothes Mary ran across the room, to stop them fighting.

Her father's gaze did not even acknowledge her. "I will kill you!" he growled at Andrew. She moved between them.

She had never seen her father like this. "Please, Papa..."

He looked at her... His eyes accusing... "Why would you do this? You have hurt your mother! Do you know how terrified we were to find you gone?"

"Sorry." The word leaked from her throat on a torrent of pain.

"Mary?" John stood at the open door. His fingers curled to fists.

"Don't hurt him," Mary begged looking back at her father. "I love him, Papa."

"You love him?" Mary's father growled. "You fool, Mary!" Contempt and condemnation burned in his voice. "He's charmed you."

Drew looked at Mary without lifting his weight off the wall. *Hold by me.* He said it with his eyes, but she did not see, she was glaring at her father. Relief gripped in Drew's chest regardless, she was taking his side.

Marlow looked at Mary.

Drew had not expected her father to catch them for another day, but his timing was perfect; to arrive when they'd been in bed made the situation absolutely clear.

Mary caught hold of Drew's arm and pulled him away from the wall, then wrapped her arms about him as she stood at his side, in only her underwear, defending him.

Her hair brushed his chest, catching on his open shirt, as her chin tilted upward. "He loves me, too, Papa."

It was surely true, he'd lived under her spell for two days; he did not wish it broken.

Her father's sharp slate coloured eyes looked his accusation and judged Drew wicked.

Marlow had a hard edge when he wished to reveal it. But Drew was not cowed. He smiled in condemnation, pride burning like fire in his chest.

Mary had stood with him. Against them.

Her family could go to hell.

Marlow's fist lifted as though he would strike again.

"Papa, it is not his fault." Mary moved in front of Drew, acting like a shield.

"Whose fault is this then? Yours?" Marlow growled at her. "Who approached who? Was this elopement your idea? You love him because he wants you to love him! He's been playing with you! You've been seduced! You're innocent and he's manipulated your lack of understanding!" Marlow gripped Mary's wrist, to pull her away.

She pulled it free and turned to cling to Drew.

Marlow's palm hit Drew's shoulder with a hard shove.

The force knocked Drew back against the wall and Mary fell

with him. Drew's arms surrounded her and held steady. "How can you know? Have you ever spoken to me? You cannot know!" Drew spat the words at Marlow. He spoke lies. Marlow was wrong.

"I know you," Pembroke stated from behind his father, his silver eyes so like Mary's but without the softness, flashing blue fire. "I've seen you manipulate women. You are selfish and greedy! You bastard!"

The insult hit. It was the one insult that always hit, because it was true. Drew's hands fisted, but he did not strike out.

Pembroke did.

Drew pushed Mary out of the way. Pembroke's fist hit Drew's jaw.

His mouth filled with bitter blood.

Mary screamed and her father shouted.

Then Drew was slammed against the wall and Marlow's hand was at his neck. Marlow thrust a sharp punch to the side of his lower back. The air rushed from Drew's lungs. Her father threw another vicious punch.

Something snapped in Drew's side and a sudden lancing, excruciating pain had him bending forward and fighting to breathe.

"Stop!" Mary yelled.

Marlow let Drew go and stepped back, breathing hard.

Drew doubled over, falling on to his hands and knees. He spat the blood out of his mouth.

They would not have killed him. That would have left Mary in an impossible position; unmarried and possibly with child. He'd planned their flight as it was for a reason.

Getting control of his breathing and ignoring the pain which roared like a demon, Drew stood, one hand clutching his side, the other wiping the blood from his mouth onto the sleeve of his loose open shirt.

He glared at Marlow.

They had an audience in the hall now too, he saw faces looking in to watch and as Drew only wore a shirt the reason for this argument shouted itself from the room.

Pembroke slammed the door shut as Mary wrapped her arms around Drew. "We are to be married."

"But I see he could not wait until then." Her father accused glaring at Drew's nudity.

Drew smiled, disparaging her father's ill-judgement.

But then he felt Mary's tears against his chest. He had known there would be a fight for her ownership, yet he had not wished her upset by it. He was a naïve fool when it came to love – more naive than she was in other things, he had not considered what this scene would mean to her.

"Do you really think he intends taking you to Gretna?" Marlow snarled at Mary his gaze challenging her.

"He is." Her chin lifted, tears still streaking her cheeks as her hair brushed against his chest.

"He is not taking you to Gretna Green." Her brother responded in a bitter pitch. "He does not even have the money to get you there. The duns were at his apartment when we called there, they'd heard he'd disappeared."

"He is!"

Bless her, Mary still believed.

"He is not," her father said, his pitch falling, deflated. "Mary, listen to us, if he wished to reach Gretna and not be found, why are you still here at nearly eleven?" He withdrew Drew's card from his pocket and threw it so it spiralled to the floor at Mary's bare feet. "And why would he leave his calling card at the last inn and ensure you were noticed at every toll gate. He asked the last gate-keeper to recommend this inn so we would know where you were. He's been leaving a trail, he wanted us to follow. He cannot afford to keep you. He does not even have enough money to elope with you, he cannot have the funds to reach the border. He wants me to pay for your wedding, and simply wishes to obtain the funds he seeks." He said the last on a sigh.

Drew straightened denying the sharp pain in his side, preventing

182

him from breathing deeply. "Being without funds is no crime."

Marlow and Pembroke ignored him.

"Mary, he does not love you. He loves the wealth you will bring him." Her brother said. "He's used you."

Her hair swayed against Drew's chest catching on his open shirt, again, as she shook her head, but her confidence was failing, Drew felt it slipping away as she clung to him less aggressively.

She was like the hemp rope in a tug of war, they were pulling but Drew had a hold and he was not letting go. They could not pull her free anyway now, not fully, she had to become his wife.

"But it is pointless us arguing now. It is too late." Marlow looked at the tangled covers on the bed. "You have made your choice."

"He does love me," Mary stated in trembling defiance.

Her brother laughed, and the sound caught like a fist in Drew's gut. He hated Pembroke.

"I doubt he knows how to love," Pembroke mocked. "But he knows how to lie. I know how men like him work. He's no good, he asked Kate to bed him, the same night he danced with you last season…"

Damn Pembroke… Drew could not deny that. But Pembroke had cuckolded husbands too, he could hardly talk.

Mary's arms fell and she stepped away.

The pain in Drew's side sharpened for an instant, but another, different sought of pain, bit into his chest.

If Mary loved him, she ought to trust him… She should not judge him.

She looked at her brother, her arms limp at her sides. Then she looked at Drew. "Is that true?" Her voice held her confusion… her fear.

"It is true. Yet…" What? He would not explain before her brother and her father. "It occurred over a year ago. It meant nothing."

She turned away.

The devil take it… He would not demean himself and beg for her understanding. *Mary!*

Pembroke glared at Drew. "It would serve you well if I withheld her dowry. But I cannot leave her in poverty, which I presume you guessed." Pembroke looked at Mary. "That is why he's bedded you, to make sure we have no choice but to agree the match and pay him your dowry."

Mary's body was stiff, as she listened to Pembroke.

Pembroke came nearer and touched her arm. "Mary, you cannot trust him. I'm sure he's seduced you with kisses and words of love, but they are false. I'm sorry."

Drew's muscles stiffened. He wished to hit Pembroke, but there was no point in that, Marlow would join in and the two of them would knock him down. Yet, Mary was listening.

Damn her, why was she listening to this? She should be loyal to him! Drew's instinct was to reach out and grip her hand, to cling to her, but it would make him look weak before her.

"Mary, he chose you, because you were innocent, easily moulded and deceived. I warned you…"

She leant against her brother, seeking Pembroke's comfort and Pembroke's hold.

Mary! They are wrong. You know they are wrong! Drew closed his mouth on the words as a bitter anger flooded him. He wished to grab her back and shake her. But he had pride.

Her rejection stung even more as she sobbed against Pembroke's shoulder.

Drew turned away to pick up his underwear from the floor.

The pain in his side burned as he slipped them on. Already there was a dark red, almost black, bruise staining his side.

He looked at Marlow as he picked up his trousers and pulled them on. "You will want to obtain a special licence, or perhaps you'd prefer to wait for the bans and have a public wedding so that society believes this was not clandestine." He picked up his boots without looking at Mary, his eyes still on Marlow's expression which said, I'd like to kill you. "I'm sure you wish to protect her reputation. But remember a child may arrive early if we wait for the bans to be read." Drew punched them with his words; as they had punched him.

Marlow glared. But he had no choice.

"A license or bans," Drew stated in a mocking pitch as he sat to pull on his stockings and boots, "they are your choices." *Fuck them and their lies.*

"Choice?" Marlow growled. "She has no choice, you took that from her."

Drew could say, *I love her.* He could promise he'd protect and care for her. He did not. Why should he make promises to a man who'd no respect for him? Let Marlow sweat. Let him fear for his child. Let him believe what he liked.

Drew stood and tucked in his shirt.

"What do you wish for?" Marlow looked at Mary.

Drew looked at her too, as he picked up his waistcoat. Her pale gaze struck his as if she looked at a stranger. There was doubt in her eyes not love.

A sour taste filled his mouth. He was even more convinced he loved her, because his need for her was mindless. He wanted to be everything to her. She was all to him.

Anger and jealousy twisted inside him as his soul screamed out. *None of what they said is true! You ought to know that!* But he would not vocalise it still. He had never pleaded to anyone in his life, for anything. But God her rejection kicked.

Drew looked away and buttoned his waistcoat.

"Obtain a special licence, Papa."

"I'll hire a carriage here. A groom can drive your rig back, Framlington. I want you where I can see you. I will send up a maid to help you dress, Mary." Marlow left.

Drew picked up his coat. Pembroke hovered near the door his eyes on Mary. "You're a fool. None of us can help you now." Pembroke walked out then too, leaving them alone.

Mary sobbed her shoulders shaking as she turned to pick up

her clothes.

Their love was only days old and it had been ripped in two.

Damn it, when Drew had imagined this scene, he had not only not thought about how it would hurt her, he'd never imagined how her turning away would hurt him.

She did not bother trying to secure her corset, but instead stepped into her gown as tears streamed down her cheeks and her fingers shook.

He was still angry with her, he wished to growl at her. *Why side with your family? Why believe them and not me?* His anger screamed for him to yell and make her understand, but he refused to heed it. He would not plead. Yet her tears moved him... But what did he say to her... He was not sorry for anything he had done. He wanted her. He had chosen Mary the night he'd danced with Pembroke's wife. He loved Mary, and he needed her money. At least he would have that. *I am not sorry.* Everything he'd told her was true. Did she not love him now? Was love that fleeting? Only for him; because of who he was.

He sighed and went to her, then began securing the buttons at her back. She stood still, her body stiff. Last night it had been pliant.

When all the buttons were secure he turned away and moved to the washbowl to shave, tipping water from the jug into the bowl as in the mirror he watched Mary pull on her stockings. She did not look at him.

* * *

Mary's fingers shook as she packed everything back into her travelling bag. Her tears had dried but she felt morose and empty.

Had everything he'd said been false?

He'd not denied propositioning Kate... John had never told her that.

How many women had he been intimate with as they were last night?

186

The room was warm but she was cold. Her fingers rubbed her temple as more tears longed to escape and nausea threatened. They'd not eaten this morning, but she could not eat now.

Had this been a plan merely to obtain her dowry?

She glanced at Drew as he finished shaving, and then wiped his face. He looked as impenetrable as stone.

Yet, last night, she'd thought herself loved. He'd said I love you, numerous times. But the words were easily said.

He turned and looked at her. He was not saying them now.

Tears blurred his contours. *John is right. I am a fool.*

Within half an hour she sat in a hired carriage opposite her father, who'd not spoken to her beyond growls as he'd directed their departure. John had not even ridden in the carriage, he'd chosen to ride a horse.

Andrew sat beside her, his shoulders against the squabs and his arms crossed over his chest while one of his booted feet rested on the cushion opposite. He'd tilted his hat forward so it covered his eyes and stared out the window without speaking.

She looked out of the window beside her at the passing fields. How much further to London? How long before this agony was over?

But what if when they arrived Mama would not speak to her either.

Her gaze spun to her father as an ache gripped in her chest. "Do you not love me anymore, Papa, is there only hate now?" It was a childish question, but she did not care, she could not bear his silence.

His gaze met hers the slate blue depths unreadable. She loved her father so much. "I do not hate you, Mary, never that. I am angry, surely you can understand why." He leaned forward and gripped one of her hands as it rested in her lap. "I will always love you. But at this moment I am… furious." He glanced at Andrew, then back at her. "I am in no mood to talk." He sat back and looked from the window a muscle flickering in his cheek as if his jaw clenched.

Andrew had not turned to look at them. But she sensed irritation bristling from his body, as if he sulked, as if he had not liked her speaking to her father.

She folded her arms across her chest and looked back out the window.

She was angry too, and it seemed there was nothing to do but be silent.

Chapter 15

They'd travelled for a day and night, breaking only to change horses. She'd slept intermittently in the carriage, as had Andrew. But her father had not appeared to sleep at all.

She'd wished to speak to Andrew but not before her father.

She wished to ask if he did love her and if so why had he not told her father and she wanted to know why he had said what he'd said to Kate.

When London's skyline came into view relief flooded her.

"I'll take you to John's, Mary, to your mother. You may wait for us there while Lord Framlington and I obtain a licence."

"I'm not a child, Papa, you do not need to tell me to stay with Mama."

A note of humour rumbled in Andrew's chest as he sat upright and straightened his hat. Mary ignored it.

"I wish that I had done so these past weeks." her father growled, ignoring Andrew too.

Mary looked out the window as the carriage negotiated London's busy streets, watching the familiar scenes of town.

The carriage drew to halt outside John's house —*it is the same street, the same house, but I am not the same. I've made love with a man and this will not be my home.*

A footman opened the door and dropped the step. Mary did

not wait on the men to help her but stood and took the footman's hand. Her father descended in her wake and Andrew followed. Mary's gaze caught his. A half smile stirred his lips but it was condescending.

Why was he being horrible?

She turned and climbed the stairs to John's front door but before she reached it Andrew's fingers gripped her waist, in a loose embrace. The sensation made her jump.

"At least pretend you are happy to have me," he growled in her ear. "You wished me to touch you a day ago, as I recall."

Her father looked at them, but she did not think he'd heard, certainly Andrew had not intended him to.

"And I agree you are not a child. I know you are a woman. Besides, do not worry, within hours you'll have no need to listen to him barking orders."

Mary stiffened her spine against the warm sensation engendered by his gentle touch and ignored his churlish stabs.

John stood in the hall. He must have ridden ahead to have arrived before them. Her mother stood with him in the formation of a receiving line – cold and formal. John didn't even smile at her and her mother's face was set with pain, her eyes red rimmed from hours of tears. Mary wanted to hug her but she hesitated.

"I am sorry, Mama… I did not mean to—"

"Fall in love?" Andrew interjected.

When Mary looked back at him, he threw her a belligerent grin before looking at her mother.

"I am Lord Framlington, Lady Marlow." Andrew offered her mother a hand in a forceful gesture without waiting for an introduction from someone else. He had that look of deviltry in his eyes, and when her mother took his hand he lifted it and kissed the back of her fingers. Then he let her hand fall, glancing at Mary's father.

Mary saw her mother stiffen, she had a way of dressing herself in solid steel when she was angry.

A moment ago Mary had wished to hug her mother; she would not receive any comfort now Andrew had played rogue.

His arm reached about Mary's shoulders. The gesture was possessive not supportive.

Her father coughed, clearing his throat in disapproval.

Mary looked her apology, but her father no longer looked at her. He went to her mother and lifted her bare hand in his gloved one, then pressed it against his cheek. They often shared such gestures of affection and support.

Mary had always assumed she'd have the same with her husband...

"Has John told you," her father said to her mother, "we've agreed to obtain a special licence? I will take Lord Framlington now—"

"I've spoken to a minister," John interrupted. "He's agreed to undertake the ceremony. His church is in Whitechapel. Do you wish me to come with you?"

"Not unless you wish to, he's hardly likely to run." Her father spoke of Andrew as though he was not there. "He would not have her dowry, and we both know that is all he wants."

"Not all..." Andrew stated, throwing her father his rogue's grin and squeezing her shoulder. Mary blushed.

"We're leaving," her father barked, looking back at her mother with a conciliatory smile. "We will be back as soon as we can." Then he looked at John. "Have a coach prepared, one with no insignia."

John's answer was a growl of agreement.

Andrew's hand left her shoulder. Even though she knew he'd only held her to annoy her father she still regretted the loss of the assurance his touch gave. *But if he does not love me, I cannot trust in his surity.*

Andrew turned away.

Her father nodded. "We will not be long." Then they walked from the hall, out into the street.

"Why?" John said the moment the door shut. "Have you run mad?"

"I…" she began, but no explanation came. The hall of his town house always seemed cold, but today it was freezing.

"I suppose he lured you with a kiss or two. What else?"

"John." Her mother stopped him. "Mary has already learned her mistake, it will do no good rubbing salt into the wound. But, Oh, Mary, why did you not speak to me? I would not have judged. I would have helped you think this through."

Tears blurred Mary's vision as her mother touched her arm… Mary turned to her. "You would have told me not to speak to him again." Mary sobbed as her mother's arms came about her.

"For good reason!" John shouted.

Anger screamed inside her as she spun away from her mother's hold. "Except that you never told me the reason! You never said he'd asked Kate—"

"I didn't think I needed to spell it out to you! I thought you'd trust my word!"

"He was nice to me…" Mary's anger became pain.

"I'm sure he was," John growled, "but I do not wish to know how nice!"

"John," her mother challenged, "you will solve nothing by condemning her. It is too late for this. I just wish, I wish…" Her mother's voice broke and Mary turned to offer comfort, as much as to receive it.

"Mama, I'm sorry—"

"I'm not angry with you." Her mother swiped the tears away. "I'm sad because you will suffer from this choice, if Lord Framlington is as bad as John thinks." Her voice broke, her last words slipping out on a whisper. "It is not an easy choice to elope, I know – and I know you must love him. Just… does Lord Framlington love you, Mary?"

Mary's mother waved her hand before her face as if putting off the tears.

"Anyway, whatever the outcome, unlike when I eloped, you are not leaving your family. We are here. Come." With that she took

Mary's hand and began leading her upstairs.

A lump caught in Mary's throat and to hide her distress she looked back at John, as he followed "Is Kate not here?"

"No, she's at Pembroke Place with the children. We left in haste at night—"

"At night?" Her gaze spun to her mother.

"Eleanor sent word to me. She saw Miss Smithfield at a ball. She knew you were supposed to be with them and you were not…"

Mary sighed, "So they know. Does everyone know? Oh Emily will be in so much trouble…"

"I'm sure she shall, Mary. We have always trusted you. I am appalled by all these machinations. Why did you not trust us?"

"She was charmed, Mama. I would lay odds he told her not to speak."

Andrew had.

"I would also lay odds he used physical inducement, promised her devotion and claimed he loves her. It is very easy to say the words. It does not mean he feels them." John's words echoed about the stone stairs in the marble lined hall.

Andrew had done all of those things…

"Men like him lie, Mary. I suppose he said you were special and precious…"

He'd used such words when they'd made love.

"It was all lies."

She did not want to believe what John said but Andrew had been cold towards her, and angry, since her family had found them.

Drowning in emptiness when she reached the top of the stairs, she let go of her mother's hand. "I shall change. Will you call for a maid, Mama."

Chapter 16

When Andrew returned to Pembroke's house he stood in Pembroke's opulent Palladian hall, awed, but not by his future brother-in-law's home; by his future wife. She'd changed clothes and she outshone the gilded splendour of Pembroke's hall.

The girl is gorgeous, and mine.

She wore a pale dove-grey muslin dress, shot through with silver thread. It shimmered as it caught the daylight from the long window above the door. The dress made her appear ethereal – ghost like. The colour engaged with her eyes; and her pale skin and dark hair made a perfect frame for it.

A vision of her naked before him, with smooth, flawless, porcelain skin, made his throat dry. He knew the body beneath that dress now.

The bonnet she wore was a slightly darker grey, and at the edge of its brim were small white rose buds. She looked like a virginal bride. She was not that.

The air left his lungs, when she looked at him. A few ebony curls framed her face beneath the brim of her bonnet.

I love you, the thought spun through his head. He was certain of it now. The ground had shifted, tilted, beneath his feet when she'd faced him, his feelings were strong and no other word came to him to describe it but love.

Her gaze met his, but the look did not say, I love you too. It was cold.

Drew looked away, trying to swallow the knot tied in his throat.

"Are you ready?" Marlow asked his wife who'd followed Mary downstairs.

The man had given Drew a lecture on the way to the bishop's palace to obtain a licence to be wed without bans. The return journey had been threats. If Drew hurt her; if he did not look after her; if he treated her false; if Marlow heard that Drew was behaving inappropriately, setting up a mistress or having an affair… Marlow had found a hundred different reasons to threaten Drew, promising castration at least, murder at the most.

Unfortunately for Marlow, Drew did not care. The only thing he did care for was Mary, and sadly, judging by her stiffness and her look – she no longer cared for him. He felt as if she lanced his chest with a knife. He would not be able to bear it if she turned her back on him.

He sighed.

He'd informed Marlow it was a mistake to tell him no, because he was a contrary man. He'd also told Marlow that his daughter was equally contrary and that if Marlow had not warned her off she'd probably never have gone near him. Then ignoring the pain of his broken rib, he'd patted Marlow's shoulder with a smile and laughed. He refused to let these people ridicule him and set him down.

Marlow's hand had fisted, and Drew had readied himself not to flinch if the man hit him. But Marlow's arm had not swung, he'd gritted his teeth and growled, "You are not worth fighting."

Drew lifted his arm offering it for Mary to take. His rib hurt like hell but he did not show it, he did not wish to look weak.

Pembroke glowered as Mary laid her fingers on it.

Drew disregarded him, and focused his attention on Mary. "I suppose Pembroke has been cursing me again," he said to her quietly.

Her gaze flicked up to meet his, then darted away.

She was not admiring Drew's attractiveness; he sported a black eye and a bruised jaw. So Pembroke had been speaking of Drew and voicing more lies.

Damn it. Yesterday, he'd been everything to her, and he'd told her a dozen times how he felt, but clearly his words counted as nothing compared to Pembroke's. Her family still came first.

"And you've been lapping it up... Am I the villain now then?"

She looked at him but didn't answer. Her gaze saying, be quiet, as her fingers rested on his arm, light and unmoving, not really there at all, as though she'd rather not touch him.

Never tell me not to do something, it is like a red rag to a bull.

"What did he say then? Am I charged with something new or is it still seduction? Perhaps I should get a pistol and shoot him so he has a decent challenge to make. Or I could—"

"This is not a game, Andrew," she whispered harshly as they led the little wedding party out on to the street.

"Am I laughing?" he answered on a low growl before looking over his shoulder at Permbroke. "Have you the cheque?"

Mary flinched even though the hit was for Pembroke. It was the only way he could hit the man back. Pembroke would hate signing Mary's dowry over.

Drew held Mary back when they reached the carriage so the others could enter first. He did not wish to hurt her, but he did not know how to manage this, and she was hurting him.

A footman held the door of Pembroke's unmarked carriage and two grooms held the horses' heads. The coachman was already in his seat, while another two grooms hovered by the footplates at the rear of the glossy black beast. All were dressed in Pembroke's livery.

Hell, if this was the service Mary was used to she would find life sparse at the Albany. Drew had no staff.

Pembroke's pale impenetrable gaze was no more than a mirror as he looked at Drew before entering.

The man must be good at cards; no one would guess what was

in his hand. But Drew grinned, he knew the strike had hit. Let them think he was taking Mary just for their money. Let them hurt too.

After her mother and father had entered, Drew handed Mary up, then climbed in after her. She sat in the far corner. He sat beside her and slid up close, only because she'd sought to move away. He was not in the mood to let her shut him out.

He took her hand and wove his fingers through hers, before resting them on his thigh, in clear view of her father, mother and brother sitting opposite.

God, from their dire looks anyone would think she was heading to prison. Surely society did not think him that bad?

He looked out the window, as the door slammed shut and the lock clicked home.

But then society had tarnished him from birth with prophetic words and he'd never done anything to dispel their prophecy.

Why the hell should he? He only cared for the thoughts of those who really knew him – his friends.

The carriage pulled into movement and silence reigned.

Drew glanced at Marlow, he and Pembroke stared out the windows while Mary's mother looked at her daughter, a picture of concern.

Mary was also looking out the window – doing her utmost to pretend Drew did not exist.

She had known he existed the night before last. He rubbed his thumb across her wrist above her glove to remind her of his presence. She did not move, not even a single muscle in her face twitched. He supposed she'd learned that stony expression from her brother.

When the carriage reached Whitechapel, Drew looked beyond Mary to the narrow street as the stench of the city's less affluent area assaulted his nostrils. The houses became crowded and the buildings more crooked.

Drew supposed Marlow and Pembroke had brought them here to avoid the world believing Mary had been forced to marry him.

Yet the state of Drew's face was testimony of that.

Reputation was all in high society – but it never mattered what people did behind closed doors, just as long as no one actually saw.

When the coach pulled up before a small church, Drew sneered at Marlow, opened the door and leapt out before the footman could set down the step. Then he knocked down the step and helped Mary down.

When Marlow descended Drew said, "So, what do I call you once we are wed? Papa?" A vicious vane had cut through him today. He owned her now. Sod them and their lies.

Marlow scowled. "You may call me, Lord Marlow, and it will always be so."

Mary sent Drew a quelling look and whispered, "Please put down your stirring spoon?"

Drew shot her a smile, saying without words, do I have to. He was enjoying making Pembroke and Marlow uncomfortable. They deserved to feel bad after the things they had said of him.

She shook her head at him as her fingers slipped from his, then she turned to her father.

The rejection kicked Drew in the gut, making his ire burn harder. He hated rejection, he had endured enough of it in his life. In general, now, he did not give people a chance to do it. But this was Mary. *I love you, you foolish girl… Do you not care for me?*

She walked beneath the church's carved wooden lynch gate gripping her father's arm. Drew followed. Pembroke and her mother behind him.

Drew's hands slipped into the pockets of his trousers, his patience wearing thin.

The vicar appeared in the stone porch beckoning them in.

Drew took off his hat and gloves.

The dark glass in the church only let a little light in, wreathing it in shadows.

Their footsteps echoed on the glazed stone tiles as the vicar led them along the aisle to the altar.

The vicar bid Mary and her father, to stand on the left, and Pembroke and his mother to sit. Then looked at Drew, his eyes bearing disapproval. "Stand here, Lord Framlington."

Drew gritted his teeth and set his hat and gloves on the end of a pew. If he did not hit someone, or something, soon, he was liable to explode.

The vicar let his leather-bound book fall open where a red ribbon marked a page and held it in one hand. Then he looked from the book to Drew, then Mary, and began reciting words in a dirge-like voice.

Aggression hovered in the air as Marlow stood beside Mary on the other side and Pembroke threw daggers at Drew's back.

When they came to the point where Marlow had to hand Mary over to him and lay her hand on Drew's. Drew grinned at him. *Fuck you she is mine now.*

When it came to their vows Drew forgot her family, staring only at her, looking into her eyes, speaking to her face with a firm intonation. He wanted her to hear and believe.

She looked at the knot of his cravat, and when it was her turn to speak and mumbled the reply with no conviction.

It was no romantic memory to hold dear for the rest of his life.

"Have you a ring, Lord Framlington?" The Reverend asked.

Lifting his right hand to his mouth, Drew gripped the signet ring on his smallest finger between his teeth.

His mother, or rather his father, whoever he was, had given it to him. A thank you gift for a night's entertainment, and an unwanted son. The gift had become his compensation for his undesired life. *Fitting*, he thought.

He looked at his unwilling wife as he slid the ring off with his teeth. Then he took it from his mouth and polished it on his coat, before sliding it on her finger.

She did not lift her gaze even then.

This was not how he'd pictured his wedding. He'd thought her feelings for him would hold. He'd thought she would think more of him than her father and brother, because surely, love, which included the physical kind, was a greater bond.

Apparently not.

He sighed as her hand trembled in his, love lodging like a spear through his heart.

Finally she looked up.

He smiled, genuinely, offering reassurance as the vicar continued reciting words, then Drew echoed them holding her gaze. It was as though the hours which had passed since her father had entered that room at the inn slipped away – had never been. It was just the two of them in the church, her pale eyes shining with intensity as they had when they were alone.

Then the vicar said, "I now pronounce you man and wife. What God has united, let no man set asunder." His book snapped shut, and the echo of it bounced back off the stone walls.

Drew bent to kiss Mary. She looked away. His kiss fell on her cheek.

Straightening, Drew looked at the vicar, as Mary's fingers slid from his. No one said a word. You could have heard a bloody pin drop in the silence of their acclamations.

Turning to her family, he declared. "Is no one going to wish us happy?"

Her father grunted, Pembroke jeered, and her mother bit her lip and glared through glimmering moisture.

Lifting his fingers to his forelock, Drew tugged it and briefly bowed his head. "Ma'am."

"You are not amusing, Lord Framlington," Mary's mother stated, her eyes flashing with the fire he'd sometimes seen in Mary's.

"No, Ma'am, but I am your son-in-law."

"You need to sign the register." The vicar's voice cut through the hostile air. "If you'll come this way?"

Marlow moved past Drew and offered his arm to Mary, Drew instantly shifted and gripped her elbow, drawing her to his side, before turning and leaning to collect his hat and gloves.

Drew followed the vicar, with his hat and gloves in one hand and Mary in the other. She was his now, for good or ill. Marlow could go to hell.

"Must you keep stirring the pot? Why are you upsetting them?" she whispered.

He leaned to her ear and answered. "Are they not insulting me?" Why did she keep siding with them? It irked him. It hurt him. No one ever cared for *his* feelings.

They did not speak again, and her arm was stiff in his hold as he steered her into the vestry, where the large record book lay open on a chest. In silence they watched the vicar enter their names. When he asked for Drew's father's details, Drew looked to the ceiling and mumbled the Marquis's name, the man who'd been forced to claim him but had never been a father to him.

They both signed against the record of their marriage.

Her name was now Lady Andrew Framlington, Mary Rose Framlington. Warmth gripped in Drew's stomach.

Pembroke signed as a witness, along with Mary's mother, then the deed was done.

They donned hats and gloves, and climbed back into the carriage.

The next stop was Pembroke's business offices, where Drew discovered Mary knew Pembroke's man. Mister Philip Spencer was Pembroke's brother-in-law. That, had Drew's eyebrows lifting, he did not realise Pembroke had married a commoner.

Within a quarter hour the cheques from her father and brother were signed and in Drew's pocket. Joy had ripped through Drew as he took them. No more hardship, no more threats of debtors' jail. For the first time in his life he could do as he pleased.

A smile held on his lips as Drew walked from the offices several thousand richer, while Pembroke and Marlow aimed bitter looks at him.

He did not care what they thought, he'd never been influenced by conscience. Life had taught him the voice of conscience was a feeble thing. No one he had known had ever adhered to it.

Yet when they descended the steps to the street, Mary gripped Drew's arm with a gentle and uncertain hold... Devil take it.

It was her money.

He must remember that. No matter how much he hated the men in her family, he did not wish to hurt her. He needed her money, but he still needed her too. He did love her and there was a solid lump of heavy stone in his chest crying out for her to love him too.

At the foot of the steps he stopped and leaned to her ear. "Go back with your parents and pack your things. I'll come to collect you at five. My curricle should be back at the stables by then."

Her fingers gripped his arm tighter. "Where are you going?"

"I have things to do." He set his expression in a smile he knew turned female bones to aspic. He was too angry to be natural, and besides he did not wish her father or her brother to see the man beneath his mask. Let them think as they wished. He did not care for them.

"Things to do?" Her pretty eyebrows lifted.

"Duns to pay, Mary." He lifted her fingers off his arm, and tapped her under the chin. "As I said I will collect you at five."

"At five then." She nodded, her gaze wounded and suspicious. *Damn it.*

He thought about kissing her but remembered the church and did not attempt it. He had never had to force his kiss on a woman.

He walked away then, without a word to Pembroke or Marlow. *Let them stew.* But he glanced back to smile at Mary when he'd walked a few feet. She'd clasped the iron railing at the edge of the steps and watched him with a look of doubt.

He would not just pay the duns, he would go to his boxing club and beat the hell out of someone.

Chapter 17

Mary watched his tall figure walk away, his arms swinging in time with his long strides.

She gripped the iron railing tighter to stop her knees from giving-way. Within an hour of her taking his name, he'd taken her money and left. He'd said he would come back but how could she believe him when she was unsure of anything he said anymore.

"Where has he gone?" Her father's fingers touched her arm, offering consolation. When she turned she saw pity shining in his eyes.

"To fetch his curricle," she lied, but she could hardly tell her father he'd gone to pay off his debts with the money they'd given him moments before. "He said he will collect me from John's at five, once my things are packed."

Her father smiled. "Come then, let us get you home."

It is not my home anymore, Papa. Desolation cut through her middle. She had no idea where her new home was, she'd never asked Andrew where he lived.

Her father led her to the carriage, as her mother smiled sympathetically.

They were not angry anymore.

Everyone sat in silence during the journey home. There was nothing to say, nothing could be changed. Time could not be turned back.

As the streets passed the window Mary promised herself, she would be happy. *I will make the best of this.* Perhaps if she continued to love Andrew, he'd learn to love her back.

When they reached John's, her mother called for the maids to help, and then pandemonium erupted as they all began emptying wardrobes and drawers, and her mother and one of the maids hastily folded and layered ball-gowns, dresses, underwear and outerwear into trunks.

Mary gathered together her personal items and filled a bag. Opening each jewellery box as she did, remembering the moments each gift had been given to her, by her father or John.

She put her writing desk on top of one of the full trunks, tears clouding her gaze.

"Mary."

She turned to face her mother.

"When we return to Berkshire, I shall have the maids pack your winter clothes and send them to you too. But your pianoforte… shall I write and ask for that to be sent to you now?"

The tears brimmed over and rolled onto Mary's cheeks.

Her mother turned to the maids. "You may all go, we have nearly finished and I wish to speak with my daughter alone."

Once they'd gone she took Mary's hand and led her to the bed, then sat down and simply held her, offering physically comfort as she could not offer words. How could she, her mother knew nothing of Andrew, and he'd not given them any impression he cared.

Eventually, sniffing, and taking a handkerchief from her mother to blow her nose, Mary set aside her tears.

"I'm sorry. Please do not tell Papa, I cried? It will only make him worry…" She did not want either of them to know she regretted eloping, but at that moment she did.

Her image in the mirror across the room revealed her red, puffy eyes. Her father would know anyway.

"Let me ring for tea." Her mother rose from the bed. Once she'd pulled the cord to ring for a maid, she turned back.

"Do you wish to take one of the maids with you? I know your father would agree to it."

"No, Mama, I should leave such decisions to Andrew." And besides she had no idea where she was going – if there would be space for her own maid...

Her mother returned to sit on the bed, and held Mary's hands. "I suppose I must tell you all you should know... It is too late for your wedding night but I hope he has been kind to you and if you argue, then seek to resolve it, rather than let it run into another day, even if it sometimes means saying sorry when you do not think you are in the wrong.

"There will be disagreements, at first, arguments are natural for any couple as they come to know one another, and you should not let them upset you too much. Yet if you feel hurt or angry you must simply tell him how you feel because if you do not, how is he to know. Talking to one another is the best foundation for a marriage..."

Mary let the words pass over her. Her mother spoke about Papa. He was gentle, kind and thoughtful. But Andrew was bold, brash and independent. He was not the same.

A gentle knock tapped the door. "Your tea, Ma'am."

"Bring it in."

As they drank it her mother talked of more things Mary should know. About running a household, and managing staff, and marriage...

But then Mary heard horses whinnying outside.

She put down her cup, her heartbeat racing, and rose to look from the window.

Her fingers touched the glass as she watched Andrew climb down from his curricle.

"He's here."

Her mother's eyes welled with tears as she rose and turned to collect the bag of Mary's personal items.

Mary rushed from the room. Despite everything she felt… in love.

When she leaned over the banister, he looked up, and for a moment there was a glimmer of the looks they'd shared before her father had found them, as there had been at the church. But it was gone in a second.

Was that look a lie? It still felt real… She still saw an intensity of feeling in his eyes.

John and her father were already in the hall. Mary hurried downstairs. She supposed they'd planned this welcome reception. Her father bristled as John stood like a stone statue observing, and behind her, her mother sniffed, wiping away tears with a handkerchief.

When Mary reached Andrew, she longed to kiss him, to be reminded of the man who'd said he loved her, but she did not.

"Your things?"

"Papa will have them sent in a cart." She touched the bruise on his jaw. There was another about his eye. He leaned back, pulling away, giving her a look that said, do not.

Mary turned and took the bag from her mother, but then Andrew took it from her, before looking at her father. "I will leave my address with Pembroke's groom."

"Mary still has things at our estate to be sent…" her mother said. Andrew looked at her. "Perhaps you would come to dinner soon?"

"I am not sure we shall be free." Andrew gripped Mary's elbow to turn her away.

"But you will visit us in the country and stay for a while once the season is over. Mary, I doubt we will stay in town much longer now."

Mary looked back, hearing the unspoken words, *after this*. They had come here for her to find a husband…

Her mother took a breath, moisture glimmering in her eyes. "The children are much happier at home."

Marry nodded. "Let me know when you will leave?"

Andrew pulled her into motion. Tears threatened. She held them at bay ignoring the sharp pain in her throat.

Her mother moved forward, lifting her arms.

Mary pulled loose from Andrew's grip and turned to hug her. "Of course we shall," her mother whispered to her ear.

She and her mother cried as they hugged.

Mary's father came close, she let go of her mother and turned to hug him.

His arms came about her. "I will miss you," he whispered to her ear, "I wish I was losing you in better circumstances. But if he treats you ill and you need us, we are here."

She nodded as he pressed his handkerchief into her hand, just as he'd done the day she'd eloped.

When she looked up into his eyes tears glistened there. She hugged him hard.

"We need to go," Andrew stated, his voice cold.

Her father kissed her cheek before he let her go. Then he threw an angry look at Andrew.

There was no need to hurry. Andrew was merely prodding her father's ire again.

She sighed.

"You will always be my daughter, and you will always be welcome at home."

Mary lifted to her toes and kissed his cheek. "I know Papa, I love you." She looked at her mother. "I love you too, Mama." Mary hugged her mother once more, ignoring Andrew's impatience. Then she turned to John.

He'd stayed back watching with a look of disengagement. He came forward as Mary moved towards him. When she hugged him, his hand laid on her back and he whispered to her ear. "Kate and I will always be here for you too, we'll be in town, the House of Lords is sitting for another few weeks. I'll send for Kate and Paul tomorrow. If you need to come back, just come, you do not need to give us notice."

Mary thanked him, and kissed his cheek. John could be misunderstood, because he appeared so stone like, but she knew the man beneath his façade, her brother. His fingers touched her cheek, the pad of his thumb wiping away a tear.

Andrew coughed.

Mary swallowed back more tears and turned to Andrew. He gripped her arm.

"Marlow, Pembroke." Andrew looked from one to the other, then at her mother. "Lady Marlow." Then he drew Mary away.

She held her father's handkerchief tighter and looked back. "Mama. Papa. John. We will call on you soon." She hoped.

As she looked away Andrew's fingers slid down and gripped her hand, and his ring pressed into her finger beneath her glove. The ring was loose, it would probably fall off if she took off her glove.

She'd looked at it upstairs, it had the initials T R inscribed on it, not Andrew's. Perhaps he'd won it in a card game. That felt a little sordid – to have a wedding ring which meant so little. Like a marriage which meant little.

When they descended to the pavement, Mary looked back.

Her parents had come to the door. She kept looking back as Andrew let her hand go and lifted her bag to place it under the seat. Her mother smiled. Mary did too. Then Andrew was back at her side, and he took her hand to help her climb the awkward steps.

When he walked about the carriage to climb up into the driver's seat, she lifted her hand and waved goodbye, tears running down her cheeks.

John's groom stepped away from the horses' heads. Andrew lifted the reins and flicked them, setting the horses into motion.

Mary waved harder as her parents waved, and tears ran down her mother's cheeks.

"*You* may call, *we* will not. And I cannot see why you are weeping. Four days ago you chose to leave them and come to me. You look as if you've cried since I left you. I'm not sentencing you to life imprisonment. You may visit them."

She turned, pain and anger piercing her chest. "Where have you been?"

So the accusations began, barely five minutes from her parents' door. "I told you I had debts to pay."

He'd banked her brother's and her father's cheques and settled several of his most urgent debts with cheques of his own, including his rent, and after that he'd gone to his boxing club and beat the hell out of anyone daring to step into the ring with him, and the sharp pain in his side had only made him more bloody violent. He'd then washed and changed, retrieved his curricle and his horses, and come to fetch her.

She said no more, merely looked ahead.

He guided his horses on through the busy streets of Mayfair his curricle a focus of attention, or rather Mary. Open carriages passed them, Landau's and Barouches, and people within them stared at the sister to the Duke of Pembroke – niece to quarter of the House of Lords – and seated beside her, 'that bastard', Framlington, who sported a black eye.

Her father would not need to publish the announcement. It had been made.

One woman even leaned from the window of a carriage.

If Mary's parents went to any balls tonight they'd face a thousand questions.

That would stir up Marlow's and Pembroke's ire.

God, Drew was angry again. That damned scene in Pembroke's house had annoyed him, and why the hell was she crying again?

Because she believed them, not him.

He glanced at Mary, she sat straight backed, her fingers gripped together on her lap as she ignored the speculation.

He liked her backbone. Some men preferred meek and mild women, he thought them dull. Mary had fire and passion, but what he did not like was her weakness for the lies her family told.

Sighing, he looked back at his horses.

"Do you have a mistress?" Her question shocked him. It was spoken without emotion.

He did not look at her. "No, Mary. Even if I'd wanted one, I could not have afforded one."

"A man does not need to pay for a mistress, I'm not so naïve. You propositioned my sister-in-law, how many others?"

He did glance at her then. She looked ahead. No one would guess the subject of their conversation from her expression.

"I have not kept a tally. I do not notch my lovers up on my bedpost, as you will see when we get home. Men aren't usually celibate until they wed. I know your brother was not, he had an affair with my older sister. I made an indecent proposal to his wife, yes. It was tit-for-tat, if not exactly an eye-for-an-eye. Would you ask your brother, or your father, the same question? How many women?"

She looked at him and their gazes met and held for a moment, before he looked away.

"So am I a tooth-for-a-tooth?" she asked on a bitter note.

"You are nothing to do with that." *I have told you, Mary.* "It was long ago." *I have said I love you, and I have never said that to another woman.* He did not complete his sentences aloud, they were in the street.

She was silent for several yards, then she turned abruptly, shifting on the seat to face him, her body expressing her thoughts just as a Landau passed containing three matrons of high society. "What is it that you want from me?"

He was inclined to pullover and let the passing traffic stare if she wished to argue in public. Damn it she was making him angry again. He gritted his teeth, then breathed in. "I want nothing from you." That was the best lie he had ever told. *I want all from you, Mary, I want to be all to you. Yet you listen to your family over me...*

"Nothing but my dowry."

Lord, he needed someone to hit again. Why did she have to listen to them? He did not answer. They'd had this conversation, he was not returning to it, and damn her if she chose to believe her brother over him. Let her. He'd paid off half his debts today. He would pay the other half tomorrow. There would be no more duns knocking at his door with their threats. He wanted to feel happy. He had her…

He felt empty.

Chapter 18

When they reached the mews where he stabled his curricle and horses, the grooms came out to attend to the horses.

Drew tied off the reins, then jumped down and walked about the vehicle to help Mary.

Before he reached her she'd lifted her dress and was carefully climbing down alone.

He took her bag out from beneath the seat and set it at her feet, then moved to pet his horses, slapping the nearside animal's flank lightly.

It was good to have them back. He'd always found solace in his horses.

Moving to the animals' heads, he rubbed their cheeks as they nuzzled his shoulders, and then rested his forehead against the second mare's, whispering his gratitude.

He need not fear losing them anymore.

He smiled at the groom who began unharnessing them. The man tugged his forelock.

When Drew turned back to Mary, there was a sudden burst of feeling in his chest, but it was muted by a nervous sense… Her posture was stiff and she clutched her bag, fire glinting in her pale eyes.

He walked over and held out his hand for her bag.

"I'll carry it," she said.

He ought to let her, just to spite her, but instead he gripped the handle and pulled it from her hold. Fortunately she did not fight for it.

He offered his free arm to her.

Her fingers lay on it but in the dispassionate way they had at the church.

At the street corner they waited for a street sweep to clear a path and when they reached the other side Drew gave the boy a ha'penny.

"Good-day m'lud." The boy titled his cap. "An' dun't forget if y'ur needing y'ur boots cleaned. I'm y'ur man." He was not a man, he looked barely ten, but Drew had always liked these boys. He bought them bread when he could, and coffee when the weather was cold, and he'd stand and listen to their tall tales occasionally.

Drew tipped his hat and smiled. Mary's fingers slipped off his arm. "Good-day, Timmy, lad. When I have a task I'll let you know."

Mary stared.

God forbid she realised he was not the evil bastard her family had portrayed. He had never been a hunter of women, they had hunted him. He'd make a point of ignoring the boys in her presence in future. He had no wish to improve her ill-informed image of him.

The entrance to his apartment was a hundred yards from the corner. He knocked on the door, it opened almost immediately.

"Lord Framlington."

Drew nodded at the doorman who gave him a formal bow.

"This is my wife," Drew stated, looking from Joseph to Mary. "This is Mr Moore, Mary, our doorman. He's the man to call upon if you need anything."

"My Lady," Joseph hid his surprise and bowed deeply. "As his lordship says, if there is aught you need, ask."

Mary became the woman Drew had seen in the ballrooms, smiling and thanking the man with inherent grace. Drew turned to the staircase.

The hallway was narrow, tiled with red and black polished diamond shapes and the stairs simple oak.

Wide-eyed, Mary took in her coming down in life.

If she'd pictured his home, he doubted she'd pictured this.

He encouraged her to walk ahead. She did. It left him with a view of her swaying bottom as he followed three steps behind her.

She stopped at the top, waiting for him.

Passing her, he went to his front door, one door along, then put her bag down, withdrew the key from his pocket and unlocked it. The door swung open. He picked up her bag and let her enter before him.

She stopped, standing in the middle of the rug before the hearth, her gaze spinning about his parlour.

He had a table, set to one side, which seated six. The other half of the room contained five armchairs at various angles, a games table, and a couple of pieces of furniture, like his writing desk. The room was extremely sparse with Pembroke's house as comparison. There were no ornaments, or decorations. The walls were just green. Everything he owned was necessary, he had no frills.

Obviously she found it lacking.

He did not look at her, he did not wish to see disgust.

He carried her bag into his bedchamber, and put it on the bed. When he turned she'd followed.

"See, no notches." It was spiteful but he could not help it, defensiveness ran in his blood, her lack of belief was cutting at him.

He sighed.

She looked as if she'd been thrown into a lake and told to swim when she did not know how.

A wave of love washed over him…regardless of the feelings of betrayal warring in his chest.

He wished to take a hold of her and tell her not to be so foolish. Not to listen to their lies. But she had made him a coward now. He was too afraid of more of her rejection. Yet she was only believing

214

what she had been told – and this was all strange to her.

More sympathetically, he said, "The dressing room is through there. There is space there for one personal servant, but I have none. These are my rooms, the sitting room and this bedchamber. I buy in meals or eat out, at a friend's, or at my club." Of course she could not do that, it was gentlemen only. But then it was a gentleman's apartment block. The only females who usually called here were paid. Mary would probably die of mortification if she happened to see one of those women.

"There are people below-stairs who will do laundry and such like, and a maid who cleans weekly and attends to the grates in winter. I don't expect you to keep house for me, if you need anything, just ring." He pointed to the bell pull. "The kitchens here can bring hot water."

She looked at him, her skin very pale. "What will we do for dinner tonight?"

He smiled, "I'll send out for something, I know a place which sells magnificent pies."

"We purchased a picnic once from Gunter's, before John came back from Egypt, and took it to Green Park."

It was not a good sign that she'd been reduced to small talk. She was in shock.

He stared at her, his hands hanging by his sides – helpless and unworthy. They were not feelings he liked. He was equal to anyone. Circumstance did not define him. If she thought it did, he would like her less.

A knock hit the door. Glad of the excuse Drew walked away.

It was Joseph. "Lady Framlington's articles have arrived."

Behind Joseph a man in Pembroke's livery carried a small trunk. Behind him two more men bore a much larger one.

"There are another two trunks the size of the second, My Lord," Joseph said.

He'd recognised Mary's wealth, and also, that Drew's rooms were not large enough to accommodate it.

Drew grimaced. The doorman laughed.

Ignoring him, Drew stepped back, holding the door for Pembroke's men. When they entered, he pointed them to the open bedroom door. "Stack them in there, against the walls and the end of the bed, if you can."

Drew stayed by the door, as they brought up the rest, watching Mary in silence, as she came back into the sitting room and wondered around touching his furniture, as though she expected to miraculously discover something more than the poor man's home she saw.

He wanted to know what she thought but he would not ask; a part of him was afraid of the answer. *I have become a coward.*

The men did not look at him, nod, or show any deference. Mary must be well liked in Pembroke's household and Drew had become the villain.

A few choice words ran through Drew's head as he waited for the men who carried up the last trunk.

Mary looked out the window. It did not look onto the street, but down onto the courtyard at the rear of the house, where the maids hung the laundry. There were usually strings of sheets, shirts and men's underclothes out there – another embarrassment for her.

He said nothing as he stepped out of the way of the men bearing the last of her trunks. *Coward!*

Footsteps hit the stairs. David Martins came up, Drew's neighbour to the right. He grinned at Drew, looking into the room at Mary. "You have a guest?"

"I have a wife."

"Pretty..."

Drew did not like his neighbour's intrusive stare. He lifted an arm and braced his hand on the doorframe blocking David's view as Pembroke's men carried Mary's last trunk into the bedchamber.

"We're very happy," Drew answered a question which had not been asked.

"And very rich, I suppose," David answered. "I saw the trunks."

"Enough to get out of here," Drew responded, his pitch getting colder. "Now if you will excuse these men."

Drew stepped back to let Pembroke's men leave. David lifted his hat and smiled.

Drew shut the door.

A knock hit the door. Another of Pembroke's men stood there with a writing desk and a mirror. The writing desk Drew told the man to place on the table in the sitting room. The mirror, he had him put on the chest of drawers in the bedchamber.

Drew reached into his pocket to give the man sixpences for them all, but he looked at Drew as though the gift was an insult. "We do not want y'ur money, m'lud."

Was there any greater insult than to be snubbed by servants?

A measure of guilt stirred in Drew's gut. It was not normally an emotion he felt. It made it harder to know what to say to her when he shut the door.

When she did not turn he walked over to the window and stood behind her, bracing her waist.

Not a single muscle yielded to his touch. Instead her arms crossed over her chest.

"I love you. It will not always be like this," he whispered to her hair. "As I said, I will look for an estate as soon as I have the chance."

He kissed the curve of her neck where it turned to her shoulder, longing for her to say I love you, back.

Her muscle flinched, and then she spun to face him, her eyes saying, *do not touch me.*

His anger flared. "You were happy for my hands to be all over you the night before last, Mary! You said you loved me! I love you!" He glared at her. He'd never been good at holding his anger back. He wanted her to love him. That was all he asked.

Damn it, his anger would not achieve it. "But if I am nothing to you, then I want nothing from you…"

He turned away, refusing to shout anymore, or be judged ill anymore, and caught up his hat and gloves. "I'm going out." he

217

stated on a growl, walking from the room before slamming the door behind him.

Chapter 19

When the clock on the mantel chimed eight times, Mary rose from the armchair she'd occupied for hours. Andrew obviously had no intention of returning to dine with her. She may as well retire.

Her stomach growled in complaint. She had not eaten. She could have asked the doorman to send out for something, but she was too nauseous to eat.

In the bedchamber she searched through her trunks for a night-gown and then undressed, struggling to reach behind her back to loosen the laces of her corset.

There was nowhere to store her clothes beyond the trunks, the one chest of drawers was full of his clothes. So she put the clothes she removed in the trunks. Her clothes would have to stay in them.

"You said you loved me. I love you," he had yelled before he left her. Was that true then? That he loved her. It was the first time he'd said he loved her since her father had found them.

How was she to know now?

When she climbed into his bed she was not sure which side to sleep.

This was nothing like the marriage she'd imagined, everything felt wrong, it was a nightmare.

The sheets were cold, and she lay there weeping into the pillow.

When she heard the front door open, she threw back the covers to get up and greet him, but then she heard voices echoing about the sitting room – his friends, who'd danced with her.

She lay back down and pulled the covers up over her shoulder.

They were laughing. While she'd been crying.

Her heart hammered hard as she heard Lord Brooke say, "So where is your hard won bride hiding, I've only come back with you for the pleasure of seeing our trophy. After all, we all played a part in your victory. Her dowry will be the making of you Drew."

"Wait a moment, I'll fetch her," Drew answered. She heard the sound of his boots on the floorboards. "She must be here…" His voice didn't sound certain though.

It would have served him right if she'd left.

She shut her eyes as the door-handle turned and candlelight spilled into the room. She held her breath, pretending to be asleep.

He stopped still.

Drew's heart had skipped a beat when he entered the sitting room and Mary was not there. As he walked towards the bedchamber it hammered cold fear through his veins.

She would not have left, surely…

Apprehension tingled in his nerves.

He opened the door and in the shaft of golden candlelight saw her dark hair splayed across the pillow he usually slept on. He could not breathe, he felt like weeping, and as if he'd been kicked in the chest. His bedchamber smelt of her.

He lifted the brace of candles, casting more light into the room.

Her arm half covered her face, but he could see her closed eyes were puffy. She'd been crying again, then, because of him, and she'd not eaten, there were no remnants of her dinner in the sitting room. She'd ordered nothing in.

He could have at least ordered it before he left, and not have stayed away so long, but once he was with his friends it was hard to get away.

He should not have gone out at all.

Yet at the time it had seemed the best thing to do. He did not want her to know how deeply she'd hurt him, how much it cut when she rejected him, and he also did not wish his anger to hurt her.

It had...

He'd decided to say sorry before he'd even reached his club. But that had not turned him back, because he'd needed normality, the sanity of his friends, to get over a day of Pembroke's and Marlow's ill-judgement.

He'd planned his apology while his friends talked. But cowardice still haunted him. He should have come home, instead he'd eaten at the club and played a hand of cards. He was not used to thinking of anyone beyond himself.

Even when he'd finally decided to return, when his friends had proposed returning with him, he'd agreed when he should not have done.

He'd left her alone, in an unfamiliar place, on the back of an argument. She would not welcome him bringing back his friends. He'd brought them as a shield for her wrath. His new found cowardice running deeper.

Yet this was Mary. Good, kind, Mary. There was no wrath in her, only hurt, hurt which he bore the guilt for.

Devil take it! His conscience no longer whispered, it yelled. Nausea stirred as guilt smote him with a double edged sword.

"My, my," Peter said looking over Drew's shoulder.

Drew shut the door. He did not want his friends ogling her.

Turning to Peter, Drew set a devil-may-care grin on his face, he did not wish them knowing how important she was to him.

"She's a prize." Peter laughed. "I like to think it was my prose which won her for you."

"You're not the only who contributed to those words," Harry called from across the room helping himself to a glass of Drew's brandy, which Peter had bought. "You cannot claim all of Drew's success for yourself."

"Ah, but it is the prose that women love, and the prose was all mine," Peter answered.

Drew said nothing, crossing the room to poor himself a drink too as the conversation carried on and they all fought over whose words had been the best, quoting their various contributions.

"Well if you helped Drew win the fair Miss Marlow," Peter said eventually. "Then you can help me with Miss Smithfield. I am not getting very far, since Drew stole her pretty friend away, her parents will not consent to her driving with me."

The others laughed.

Drew turned and watched them, as they began developing a plan of attack, as they'd done with Mary. He sipped his brandy, wishing to be drunk, but for some reason the alcohol failed him tonight. He could not reach uncaring oblivion.

It was about two after midnight when his friends took their leave. He bid them goodnight, extinguished the candles and slipped into the bedchamber as quietly as he could, his heart thumping.

He stripped off in the darkness, leaving only his shirt on, before climbing into the bed beside her.

She did not move, or make any sound beyond that of her slow shallow breathing.

Sighing he rolled to his side and let sleep claim him too.

* * *

Mary woke the next morning, having finally fallen asleep at some point after he'd slipped into the bed beside her, to find Andrew looking down at her, his light brown gaze soft and intense; his eyes were honey today.

He lay on his side next to her, his head cradled on his palm, supported by his bent arm, while the fingers of his free hand played with a lock of her hair. The linen shirt he wore hung open at the chest.

She said nothing. Her heart breaking.

"I'm sorry." He said the words as though they could stitch her heart back together.

She'd heard his friends speaking about the letters and she'd heard them plotting to seduce Emily as they must have planned to seduce her.

It was as John had said. Drew was false and everything he'd said was false.

"I should not have left you alone last night," he continued. "It was wrong of me. I was angry at your brother and your father and I took it out on you. I'm sorry. Do you forgive me?"

She said nothing.

He smiled, it looked genuinely apologetic. Yet she'd thought him genuine that day in the summerhouse, when she'd read the heartfelt words in his last letter. It had all been lies.

She closed her eyes. His breath caressed her neck, then his lips brushed her skin. A stir of desire clasped at the juncture of her thighs.

A sound left her lips, it was grief, yet he must have heard it as pleasure as his fingers began to draw up her nightgown.

The memory of his touch whispered in ripples across her skin, and despite her broken heart and the knowledge that he was false, she still wanted him physically. She still loved him.

His kisses brushed the skin of her neck and she ached for him inside turning her head away as his fingers touched her inner thigh.

Her arms lifted above her head as he touched her gently, as he'd touched her the first night.

When her lips parted on a sigh, which was pleasure, his fingers stroked more deeply, more intently, and then his lips touched the corner of her mouth, calling her to turn and kiss him back. She felt like weeping as she did, so physically happy, and yet so heart sore. She was his, no matter that he would never wholly be hers.

He moved over her and his flesh became her flesh as they joined. His palms pressed into the bed beside her.

The cloth of her night gown caressed her breasts as he moved, while the tails of his shirt, brushed against her stomach and her thighs.

"I love you," he whispered. "I swear that I do. With all my heart, I love you."

Lies. She clasped his shoulders and prayed for it to end – or begin – to reach the escape of ecstasy.

The way he moved and touched her felt like love.

It was just another lie.

Just physical.

Guilt pressed its little knife into her heart because she still enjoyed it, and she fought her pleasure at first, but it was too hard. He was all to her.

He'd accused her of wanting nothing of him now. He was wrong. She wanted everything from him.

She opened her eyes.

He watched her. It looked like tenderness and devotion in his eyes.

She wanted to believe in it, she desperately wanted to believe.

But he had lied.

His hand cupped her breast over her night gown. "I adore you, Mary. You're so beautiful, I will forever worship you."

Lies.

Her fingers gripped his hips, and the lean muscle that played beneath his skin. He enchanted her, entering and withdrawing. She broke in half, body and soul separating, as her senses soared and burst, trembling in release.

Her wet heat surrounded Drew, and her inner muscle contracted, grasping for his seed. He broke straight after her. It was becoming a pattern of their encounters, and his muscle locked as he shut his eyes and let pleasure sweep over him, its intensity burned like lit brandy in his blood the flame flickering through his nerves. It even stole the pain away from his broken rib, which had clawed at his side while he'd moved

They were made for one another. Sex had never been like this with any other woman.

He opened his eyes, only to see that a tear had slipped from hers. Her lower lip quivered before she caught it between her teeth.

He could not breathe. She was crying. The mist of sexual lust left him, and cold emptiness replaced it, as the emotion evaporated.

She'd been enjoying it, hadn't she? She'd reached the little death.

He withdrew from her, turning away, not knowing what to say. He said the only thing he knew, glancing back at her, as he moved to get up. "I love you, Mary." But he heard uncertainty in his voice.

She sat up, gripping the sheet to her chest, her pale blue eyes starkly cold, like ice. "Liar."

They'd just shared something blissful…What?

"You do not love me. I doubt you love anyone bar yourself."

My God. "I do love you. I know your family told you otherwise, but they are wrong."

She let the sheet fall, slipping off the bed, going to one of her trunks. "You cannot lie anymore, I heard you last night."

She'd been asleep.

She lifted the lid of a trunk. "I heard your friends joking about how they helped seduce me with their words in those letters."

Damn it all to hell! He turned and crossed the room.

The lid of her trunk banged down as it slipped from her hand and she nearly fell in an attempt to avoid him.

She had feared he would hit her. He would never do that, but it cut him hard to know she'd believe he could.

He lifted his hands, palm outward, as the pain in his side roared from his rib being jarred. "Mary…" Her eyes flashed fire at him again. "You were pretending to sleep…" God he was an ass.

"You never wrote those letters. Your friends did. They were laughing at me. I'm glad I amuse you all—"

"Mary—"

"I shall not let them do the same to Emily, I am going to call on her and tell her not trust Lord Brooke."

225

"Mary, darling, come on, they were jesting…"

Tears suddenly sparkled in her eyes, and then one tumbled over. She sniffed and wiped it away. "It was unkind of you. You should have left me alone."

They were not words of accusation, but those of a desperately unhappy young woman. A wave of love rolled in on top of him, crashing over him, a sensation he was becoming used to now. He stepped forward, he wished to comfort her. "Mary… Honestly, darling."

She pushed his hands away.

Devil take it. "Mary?"

She turned her back and bent to open her trunk again, her voice weighted by tears. "What is done cannot be undone. Will you help me dress?"

"Of course I shall. But I only asked them to help with the letters because you would not meet me again, I am not good with words, it does not make the sentiment within them and my feelings untrue." He turned to dress himself. "I would have done anything to win you."

"Anything?"

He turned back. She stood with a dress clasped to her chest.

"So you would tell me lies for my dowry. Words are easily said, Andrew, and I foolishly believed them."

"They are true. I love you." Anger and frustration had begun to sizzle inside him. Why must she make him so angry?

"I don't believe you."

Damn her. He turned away. He was tired, still half asleep and a little drugged by the aftermath of sex.

He picked out his clothes and tossed them on the bed then looked back at her. "I do not know how to convince you, Mary."

"You cannot, it would be better if you simply did not lie."

"I am not lying but clearly you value your family's word more than mine. I suppose you do not love me now?" It was a childish question. But Drew was out of his depth.

"I do not trust you…" she answered.

He turned away, disgusted with himself as much as her. Perhaps if he had not made such a mull of things yesterday and become angry, she would still have believed. "I will dress and then I am going out for a ride. I usually take one of the horses out before breakfast." He was running away from her again, coward that he was. But he didn't know what else to do.

He turned to the basin and tipped in some water from the jug, it splashed into the bowl. She kept her back to him, searching through her trunks, while he washed and dressed.

Once dressed, he looked back at her. She'd laid her clothes out on the bed. He supposed she missed having a maid to do such tasks. He ought to find them better accommodation as soon as he could, with space for staff.

He sighed. "I'll leave you. What do you want for breakfast?"

She looked at him as though he was a monster with two heads.

He did not wait for her answer. "I'll have some bread and cheese sent up."

He left.

When he returned an hour and a half later the sitting room was empty, and the untouched loaf of bread and cheese stood on the table.

The door of the bedroom was open, but she was not in there.

Fear beat its drum in his heart. Had she left him?

He'd ridden his horse hard and fast across the open lawns of Hyde Park, burning off his anger and frustration, willing himself to work out how to convince her that he loved her. He'd found no answers, but he could not keep hiding and so he'd returned. Too late?

Her things were in the room though. Hairpins, her hairbrush and the mirror stood on his chest of drawers. She'd not left him.

Her corset had been thrown on the bed.

Damn, she'd asked him to help her dress. He had not.

He returned to the sitting room. A sheet of paper rested on top of her writing desk. *I have gone home to fetch some things.*

Home. The word cut him as deeply as her accusations this morning. Here, should be her home now, where he was, not there, where her family was.

Hell. She must have walked alone, she had no one to accompany her.

He should find a maid, to come during the day. He looked at his watch. How long ago had she left? Perhaps he ought to go after her. But as the bread was untouched she'd probably left early and would already be there.

This was a statement to him; that she would not be tied down by him. He heard it loud and clear.

He could follow, but he did not wish to call at her brother's house, he'd no intention of subjecting himself to her male relatives' spite. He could go out himself of course, again, and pretend he did not care that she'd gone. Or he could wait here for her return. He chose the last, slipping off his coat as he walked to the window. Today the fine weather had broken, the sky was hidden behind grey clouds… What if she was caught in rain?

She would not be, though, Pembroke would send her back in his carriage, and curse Drew.

His selfish side wished her family had cut her. But that was a stupid thought, because he had always known they would not exclude a child, and that was to their credit.

Drew cut himself some bread, trying to learn a new skill – patience.

She returned after three tedious hours in which he'd played a boring game of chess against himself. The minute the door handle turned, he stood, feeling like the child who'd craved the attention he never received.

Her cheeks were flushed and her eyes bright beneath the brim of her straw bonnet. She wore a pale pink walking dress, the cloth decorated with cream flowers. The ribbon on her bonnet was cream too. She looked beautiful, as she always did.

She stood back and let Pembroke's footman pass her, pointing to the table on which the half eaten loaf rested. "Put them there please Tom."

The young man moved to the table, not even looking at Drew, and set down the pile of books he carried. There was a small bag on his arm, which he set there too. "Miss Marlow, if that is all."

"It is thank you, Tom. But if you would call for me at two tomorrow, I'd be very grateful."

It appeared she'd resolved the issue of accompaniment herself.

Drew's hands slipped into his pockets as she shut the door.

She turned and looked at him, her fingers lifting to untie the bow of her bonnet.

"Mary." He sucked in a breath. "You went to Pembroke's for the books I take it—"

"And my embroidery and threads." Her sweet voice echoed about his room. It denied the fact they'd argued this morning.

Lifting his hands out of his pockets he walked towards her. "You should not have gone alone."

"I did not." She looked at him as she lifted off her bonnet. "Joseph had one of the maids from below stairs accompany me there, and as you saw Tom walked me back." She turned away and put her bonnet down, then drew off her gloves.

His contrary nature admired her for defying any need to rely on him. "You should have eaten though. You did not eat last night I know."

"I ate at home. Breakfast was still being served when I arrived." She walked past him, avoiding him, going to the pile of books.

"It is not your home anymore." The word had kicked him.

Her fingers resting on the books, she looked back. "Mama and Papa are going to a musical evening tonight, at the Everetts', Mama asked if we wished to join them."

He sighed.

She continued, holding his gaze. "They will call for us."

He did not want to let her go and yet, as things stood, what would they do if they stayed here together? Argue… Hurt one another… "You may go if you wish. I'll pass if you do not mind."

Her gaze fell away, looking at the floorboards at his feet. "I'm sorry I took so long." She turned back to the table and looked at the books. "My sister-in-law arrived with my nephew and my brothers and sisters. I could not just walk out again."

"I'm glad you had opportunity to see them. Shall I send down for coffee or tea, or is there something else you'd like?"

"No, nothing." She glanced at him like he was an anomaly.

"Well, I want some. I'll send down." He rang the bell, then turned back, watching her in silence as she lifted an embroidery frame from the bag. It was the strangest feeling having her feminine things in his rooms, with her perfume lingering in the air.

It was not just her things though which changed the atmosphere, but her, her warm nature, and internal beauty. She made the place a home and yet she did not think it so.

Sighing, he ignored the urge to bite at her, hanging on to his patience and keeping his voice temperate. It was not the outcome he had hoped for with her. But for now at least if they could be companionable, better that than nothing. "I am sorry about this morning. But you were wrong. I do have feelings for you. Yes, my friends came up with the words in those letters, but that is the only part they played. Everything that I have said to you is the truth, Mary. I've been playing an unfulfilling game of chess against myself. Do you play?"

She looked at him, suspicion in her eyes. "I play, yes."

"Then would you play a game with me?" She still looked suspicious, but she nodded.

He returned to the armchair he'd been sitting in and moved the table bearing the chessboard, so it stood between the two most comfortable chairs. Looking up he encouraged her to sit. She did, as he began resetting the game, moving the pieces back into their starting positions.

Chapter 20

Mary watched Andrew as he stood before his mirror, tying his cravat.

He'd laced her corset and now she waited with her back turned so he could button up her dress.

"I shall be only a moment." She watched him look at his reflection as he secured the knot, and set it just so. Then he turned to her.

His fingers brushed against her bottom and then her corset as he slotted each little ivory button into place.

They'd spent a quiet afternoon over the chessboard.

It was easier to believe they could form some sort of an acceptable marriage from this mess when he behaved like this. She had pulled herself together after he'd left this morning. Whether he loved her or not, he was her husband. She had made this choice, she had no option but to live with him, and therefore she must make their marriage work.

"There you are."

As he finished Mary caught sight of her image in his mirror. She'd been unable to do anymore with her hair than she'd done earlier. She'd merely twisted it into a knot.

She turned to the small bag in which she'd put her personal items and jewellery. She searched out a pretty silver comb and looked in her mirror to position it in her hair, to make it look more ornamental. Then she found out a necklace with a small silver cross which her father had bought for her.

"Here, let me." Drew took it and looked at it for a moment before setting it about her neck.

The loose ring on her finger called its presence, she had kept her finger curled a little all afternoon so it would not slip off, but then earlier Andrew had tied a thin band of leather about it so it did not slip.

"Are you ready?"

"Yes, apart from my shawl."

It lay on the bed. He turned to pick it up, then set it about her shoulders. At the same moment Mary heard a knock strike the door downstairs.

"That will be my parents and John."

"Perfect timing then."

"Yes." She was about to hurry away.

"Mary." He lifted his arm. "Let me walk you down. What time will you return?"

"I am not sure, possibly midnight, or perhaps after..."

"Then I shall come home before midnight. I shall be here when you return."

She felt as though he liked her at least. She knew he liked her body, but she thought he liked her company too.

A vast chasm stretched between like and love though.

They walked down the stairs in silence.

One of John's footmen waited at the door. He stepped aside as Andrew gripped her arm and led her out.

A footmen held the carriage door open, waiting to help her, and within she could see both her father and John watching Andrew, with accusing eyes. Andrew stiffened, his fingers gripping her arm a little more firmly, before sliding to hold her hand instead, to steady her, as she climbed the step into the carriage.

"Goodbye. I hope you enjoy your evening."

She glanced back at Andrew and saw a genuine look of good will.

He did like her. She was sure of that at least.

She smiled. "Goodbye."

He bowed his head, as she settled into the seat beside Kate. Then the carriage door shut, and Andrew walked away.

Mary felt as if her marriage was a game she played. She'd stepped back into her old world this morning, and now again, and her mind could not merge the two.

"Why is he not coming?" John asked.

"It's not Andrew's sort of entertainment." This morning she'd said he'd attended a business meeting and weaved a web of white lies about their evening together. She wished her parents to think her happy, otherwise they'd hate Andrew more and it would make everything worse.

"And what is his favoured entertainment?" Her father growled.

Mary looked out the window. She didn't know where he'd gone. He had not said.

Kate's fingers touched her arm, "It was good of him to walk you out. I'm sure in future he may be persuaded to join us."

"I hope not. I do not wish him anywhere near you, Katherine." John sighed.

"He is Mary's husband," Kate answered.

"Kate is right, John," Mary's mother agreed. "We must make the best of this now for Mary's sake."

"But I cannot stand him either," her father responded.

Mary looked at them all. "Please, do not argue… and must you keep glaring so horribly at him. I was silly to let him persuade me but I am married to him now and–"

"And you love him," Kate finished for her, squeezing her arm. "Otherwise you would not have chosen to elope with him. You should remember that, John…"

"I do not blame Mary," John leaned forward and touched her hand.

Her father sat in the far corner. "You love him, still? Even knowing he lied to you?"

"I cannot choose to love or not, Papa. I cannot simply stop, and he is not all bad. He is still saying he loves me too."

John made a disparaging sound and her father said, "I shall give him a chance to prove himself worthy of you, and you may tell him so. But as I told him yesterday if he does one thing to hurt you…" The threat was left to hang in the air.

Mary wondered what else her father had said to Andrew yesterday.

Was that the cause of Andrew's anger, and why he had stormed off when she'd taken her father's side?

He'd said when he'd apologised this morning that he'd been angry at John and her father and taken it out on her.

Perhaps her father's threats were one reason why.

* * *

At half past the hour of ten in the evening, Drew sauntered into the Everetts'. Conveniently it was the supper hour.

Mary's absence had tugged at him like the pull of a magnet all night. He wanted to be near her, no matter that he'd have to endure the presence of her brother, and her father. He'd decided to brave it for the benefit of his beautiful young wife's company. Of course society would observe the bruise on his chin and his flourishing black eye, but it would be Pembroke and Marlow who'd bear the embarrassment of that, and half of them had seen it yesterday anyway.

It had been easy persuading his friends to provide him with some cover when he'd advised them that Miss Smithfield would be there. They walked in, in their usual pack, wolves on the hunt. But once they'd entered he separated from them instantly, leaving them as they decided to head for the drinks table.

It took Mary all of seconds to spot him, and her mouth dropped open a little as she did so, unable to hide her shock.

He smiled at her. It did not look as if he was an unwelcome

234

shock.

She turned away from her usual knot of friends as he neared, and when he reached her he caught up her hand, bowed over it and kissed her knuckles, then tipped over her hand and also kissed her wrist above her glove.

When he straightened, he said, "Wife."

"I did not expect you." She sounded stunned.

"I did not intend coming, but I missed you, so I changed my mind."

A blush flared on her pale cheeks but if his arrival embarrassed her she hid it well and turned to introduce him to her friends. He'd watched her with these young people for a year. They were barely younger than him but they all seemed so naïve, it was as if he had a dozen years on them not four or five.

As they stared at him as if he was an oddity, he forced himself to be polite, while Mary's fingers gripped his arm.

He felt as though her fingers clasped his heart.

When the introductions were complete, he turned to her. "Have you eaten?"

"No."

"Then may I escort you to fetch some supper before the performance recommences."

"Thank you, yes." She smiled, and then turned to excuse herself from her dull friends.

Drew's world flooded with a light only Mary could bring to it.

He helped her fill a plate, ignoring his friends, who were clustered in a corner about poor Miss Smithfield and another young woman, positioning himself so Mary could not see.

They sat at an empty table, but within minutes it filled up, mainly with her family. Firstly her cousin arrived, Lady Eleanor and her husband Lord Harry Nettleton. Drew knew Lord Nettleton, although not well. Mary's mother and her aunt, Lady Wiltshire, then also orientated in their direction. So, therefore, did Mary's father, and Lord Wiltshire, the Duke of Arundel, her uncle. He gave Drew a measuring stare as he held out a chair for his wife.

When Pembroke saw Drew seated at the table, though, he turned to another, gripping the Duchess's elbow.

The final seats were taken by another aunt and uncle, the Duke of Bradford and his wife.

When the time for introductions came, Drew cringed internally; his instincts prickling with a desire to run. This was an endurance test, but his determination set. He'd survive it for Mary.

Her father watched, hawk-like, as Drew answered questions and participated in the conversation as best he could, while Mary glowed beside him, like the sun, burning bright and keeping him warm. It was novel indeed to have watched her seated among her family like this, as an outsider looking in, and now to be within.

He actually enjoyed himself as Lord Nettleton shared a joke and the table broke into laughter. Then the bell rang, indicating the performance was about to recommence.

He'd never attended a musical evening. He'd expected to be bored.

He rose and offered his arm to Mary, then led her back into the hall among her family. Mary's father sat on the other side of her, and Drew had her sister-in-law, the Duchess of Pembroke, beside him. The lady he'd propositioned once.

She kept her distance, leaning against Pembroke's shoulder, her fingers clasped about Pembroke's as they rested on his thigh. The man must have some redeeming qualities because she still looked in love with Pembroke.

Drew lifted his right leg, his body jolting a little as his broken rib jarred, and set his ankle on the opposite knee. Then he reached for Mary's hand and wove his fingers through hers, leaving their joined hands in her lap.

"I did not think you were attending," Pembroke whispered in Drew's direction.

Drew turned, lifting one eyebrow. He was here to be with Mary, he'd no intention of making the place a battleground. "I changed my mind."

"John," Pembroke's wife dug an elbow in her husband's ribs.

Smirking, Drew looked away. At least Pembroke's wife was sensible. Mary squeezed Drew's hand. Drew looked to see the same tone he'd heard in the Duchess's voice, reflected in Mary's eyes. He smiled, determined to restrain himself. He'd come here to continue making peace with her, not start another fight.

He looked forward as a harpist began to strum. Mary's shoulder touched his arm, her delicate weight leaning upon him.

That tight restriction clenched about his heart. It hurt that she did not believe he loved her, that she thought him a rogue, a wastrel, and a fortune-hunter. He'd come to prove those things were not who he really was.

He wanted her to trust him, to rely on him, to lean upon him emotionally. The fact that she leaned upon him physically gave him hope that one day she'd do more.

When the harpist sang, the music actually reeled him in. Perhaps his awakening emotions gave him new ears. Music had never touched him before. The woman's voice was haunting. A piano concerto followed, and then the night's entertainment was closed by a soprano, who again was outstanding.

Letting go of Mary's hand, he applauded the performers with the rest, before everyone stood to leave.

Drew possessively rested his hand at Mary's waist as they filed from the row, and noticed Marlow look down at his hand, then up to Drew's face, but her father said nothing.

"Will you ride home with us, Lord Framlington?" The Duchess of Pembroke's voice rose behind him. "We were to take Mary, we could take you both?"

Her words were an olive branch. He was willing to accept it but he wished Mary to be reliant on him not her family. He turned, smiled and bowed to Pembroke's wife. "Your Grace, thank you, but I shall take my wife home. We can hire a hansom."

Pembroke eyed Drew hard.

Drew turned to Mary. "I'll take my leave of my friends, then we'll go, if you'll excuse me a moment."

Her eyes opened wider at the mention of his friends but she did not deter him, merely nodded and turned to her father.

Drew could not see them in the room, and Miss Smithfield stood with her parents. He presumed they were in the card-room then and headed there.

"I cannot believe Mary would take a man like Framlington willingly. Do you think he forced her?"

Looking sideways, Drew sought the owner of that voice. It came from a group of young people, Mary's friends. They'd not noticed him.

"Emily said she ran away with him, and now Mary told her not to trust any of his friends, or even Lord Framlington himself."

"Have you seen his black eye? It's a beaut. I heard Marlow did it. He caught them up, knocked the hell out of him and forced him to wed her there and then." The last came from a tall young gentleman – one of Farquhar's boys. Drew knew the family, far too well. His mother was a friend of Drew's mother.

The woman clutching Farquhar's arm caught Drew's eye and her mouth dropped open.

"Do you think he even intended marrying her?"

"Of course he did, at some point," Farquhar answered. "He was after her fortune."

His companion pulled on Farquhar's arm.

Half of Drew wanted to laugh, the other half…

The first woman who'd spoken, squealed, her hand covering her mouth as she saw Drew approach, and Farquhar, turned scarlet.

"Your voices are carrying," Drew stated in a hard measured voice. "If you malign a man have the guts to do so to his face and not behind his back. And if you'd care to observe what you risk, you may meet me at Manton's practice range on the morrow, Farquhar, to see how well I shoot. Or, you may prefer, to simply not speak ill of myself or my wife—"

"We were not—" one of the young women began.

"My dear, I heard…" Drew stared at her, "and I'll not have it repeated." His glare travelled about the group. They were all cowed.

And these are her friends. Drew turned away and walked on.

"Can you believe he—"

"He is still in earshot Bethany, and even if he were not, I do not fancy giving him cause to call me out." Farquhar at least had received the message clearly.

Drew saw his friends walking from the card-room.

"Gentlemen!" Drew called as he grew closer to them. "A goodnight?"

"A very good one for me," Mark answered patting his pocket.

"A not so good one for Peter," said Harry.

Drew looked at his best friend. "Ah, well, you can afford it at least."

"I played ill, I am out of sorts. Your wife has shattered my hopes of the fair Miss Smithfield."

Drew laughed. "Did you have any honest, decent hopes, you scoundrel."

"I do not recall even mentioning decent or honest, but whatever my intent, my hopes are dashed, your wife warned her off…"

"Ah. I can explain that. She was not asleep last night, she heard you talking. I'm afraid you shot your own foot."

"Bloody hell!" Peter barked with a laugh, drawing eyes from about the room.

"Bloody hell indeed. I took a battering for not being the author of those letters too…"

"Then we must apologise in person," Harry stated with bravado.

"Yes," Peter agreed, "you have to let us speak with her, you cannot hide her from us forever. Or are you ashamed of us now you are rich."

"I am still not as rich as you," Drew responded, "and therefore why would I have reason to cut you. Come, I'll let you speak with her, as long as you behave."

"I'm wounded," Peter said, pressing his hand to his heart over his evening coat, "Do I not always behave."

"No," Drew answered, looking at them all, "we do not, but I have to start behaving now, I am married. So you must respect my wife when you speak to her, understood."

They laughed, not taking him seriously in the least.

Sighing he turned, wondering if he'd just cast his marriage a death sentence. But these were his friends, who were more like brothers to him than his brothers had ever been. They were, and always would be, a part of his life. Mary had to accept that, it was not negotiable.

Her eyebrows lifted at him as she saw them coming. She blushed. Clearly she did not wish to meet them but there was a point to be made here. He'd do much for her, but he would not reject his friends.

The Dukes of Bradford and Arundel stared as Drew and his friends neared Mary's family; wolves approaching the pride of lions.

Drew beckoned Mary, to bring her away from them. He did not fancy a full blown war beginning in the Everetts' ballroom.

She came, although she looked nervous, but obviously his turning up here had gone some way in building bridges as opposed to hurdles.

He hoped this did not knock them down.

"Sweetheart," he stated as she came over, "my friends wish to apologise, they did not mean to offend you last night." She blushed harder as he took her elbow and turned her to the others.

"Lady Framlington. Felicitations on your marriage," Peter stated with a brief bow.

"Lord Brooke." She bobbed a slight curtsy. "Thank you."

Drew doubted she was thankful at all.

"I'm very pleased the prose worked." Peter claimed one of her hands, and lifted it to his lips, "and glad you deemed our dear friend worthy."

Discomfort rippled through Drew's nerves; he did not like another man touching her.

Mary withdrew her fingers before Peter could kiss them. "Your prose was very good Lord Brooke but I have told you before, I do not value false flattery."

"But my dear it was never false." Peter flirted. The hairs on the back of Drew's neck stood up. "Now if you would simply unsay whatever it is you said to your friend—"

"Miss Smithfield," Harry inserted. "Congratulations by-the-by, Lady Framlington."

"You have my good wishes too. Congratulations," Mark stated, vying for her attention as he and Harry bowed and reached for her hand. Mark claimed it first and pressed a kiss on the back of it, before passing it to Harry.

"And Miss Smithfield…" Peter prodded.

"Will have nothing more to do with you I'm afraid, Lord Brooke, if she is sensible."

"And from that I conclude you think yourself, not sensible…" Peter's eyebrows lifted as he glanced Drew's direction. "So all is not roses in heaven then, Fram." Peter slapped Drew's shoulder. "But you are still rich…"

Drew shrugged, he would not discuss his issues with them. "But not as rich as you." He quipped, to hide his unease.

"May we call on you at Drew's?" Mark asked Mary.

"You have such lovely eyes," Harry complimented.

Drew stepped closer to her. "No one is to call unless invited. Mary will not wish to be hounded by you reprobates."

"And if you do call, she is likely to be out!" The deep pitch came from behind Drew.

Marlow.

Drew turned.

The Dukes of Arundel and Bradford stood at Marlow's right and left shoulder.

Once again Mary became the rope in a tug of war.

Drew should have stayed away.

At least his friends recognised the moment to bow out. They withdrew, rather than begin a brawl, laughing, presumable at Marlow and his in-laws.

"Why would you subject my daughter to their lechery?" Marlow accused when Peter, Harry and Mark were barely beyond hearing.

"Papa…" Mary gripped her father's arm.

Marlow removed her grip and instead held her hand, as both Arundel and Bradford flanked him.

What do they think I will do?

"Mary." Drew held out his hand. This was the moment when she had to make her choice. He was all, or he was nothing to her. "I will take you home."

To his irritation she hesitated. Drew's jaw clenched as her father's grip tightened about her hand.

"You're my wife." Drew lifted his hand higher. She had taken a vow to obey him but he wanted her to come because she wished to.

Her pale blue gaze met his, just as Pembroke joined the altercation. Then she let her father's hand go.

"I will go home with Andrew, Papa. John." She looked at them both. "I'll call on you tomorrow."

When she took Drew's hand, he gripped hers tightly, emotion wrapping about his heart, stealing his breath.

"Good evening, Marlow, Your Graces," Drew said. Then he turned away and pulled Mary with him.

He strode from room with a brisk stride, meaning Mary had to grasp at her dress and raise her hem from the floor to keep up.

They were watched by the entire room the full length of their flight and when they reached the door, he could not help himself, he looked back and glared at everyone who still stared.

The men of her family had huddled together in the centre of the room, forming a conference, undoubtedly planning what to do about him.

Fuck them.

He obtained Mary's shawl and his hat and had a footman call for a hansom. The same man held the door of it as Drew handed Mary in.

When he climbed in beside her, she had pressed herself into the far corner of the small two-seater carriage, her gaze focused out the window.

The carriage lurched into motion a moment after the door shut.

There was nothing to see in the darkness of the cloudy night, but still Mary looked.

The ground he'd gained earlier had been lost.

"Why did they come? To play their games with Emily?" she said to the darkness. "Could you not have stopped them?"

He sighed.

She turned to face him, her voice growing in strength. "I was pleased to see you until you said they had come with you. How can you condone their behaviour?"

Her condemnation of them was condemnation of him, and she knew it. "Lord Brooke is not such a bad catch, he is remarkably wealthy."

"But we both know he's not thinking of marriage, is he?"

"If she is properly chaperoned, what does that matter? You never know, he might fall for her." The last was a quip at his own expense, which of course she would not understand, as she did not believe he had fallen.

"But we both know that chaperones can be avoided." Her pitch had soured "I suppose you've all played these games a hundred times."

Drew turned to face her, one knee lifting onto the seat, his arm stretching across the squabs behind her. His body jolted with the damn pain from his rib. "So we are back to how many are we? Well, for your information, you are the first woman I have courted, and the first woman I have known who had any need of chaperones, and for all Peter may play around and act the fool, he's never courted a virgin before either. Judge them how you like, but at

243

least my friends are loyal. I caught yours gossiping about you..."

How did she have the power to make him feel like a belligerent child? Because he loved her. That was what love did. It made you weak and vulnerable. But he was not giving in yet, he was fighting for her.

Her gaze struck his in the lantern light of the carriage. "I suppose you frightened my friends into silence."

"Do I frighten you, then?"

"Yes. Sometimes. Like now, when you feel threatened, and become angry with me."

Her admission shocked him and his anger fled instantly. *Lord.* "I'm sorry. I did not mean to make you afraid of me."

His hand lifted.

Without him even urging, she moved, rising and turning to sit sideways on his lap, her arms reaching about his neck as a little sob came from her throat.

Damn it. He gripped her chin and lifted her face so she looked at him. Tears sparkled on her cheeks as her long slender fingers slipped to his lapel. "How else do I make you feel?"

"Sad... I wonder if you will ever love me, or I will ever understand you, or if we can be happy."

"I do love you," he answered, his gaze dropping to her lips an instant before he kissed them.

Her arms came about his neck and she kissed him back, her tongue dancing with his.

He broke the kiss and met her gaze. Their lives were worlds apart. She could never walk into his but he could walk into hers. He should try. The onus to make their marriage work lay on him. "When you go to Pembroke's house tomorrow, I'll come too."

If nothing else it would stop her family influencing her while he was not there.

"Do you think it wise? Papa is not very happy with you at the moment."

"That is the reason I should go." The familiar surge of love for her raced through his blood.

She smiled, then her fingers slipped into his hair and brought his mouth back to hers.

When the carriage pulled to a halt, they were only prevented from being thrown onto the floor by Drew bracing his feet hard and holding onto her.

He moved her from his lap as the hatch below the driver's seat slid open. "We're here m'lud."

Drew freed the lock and pushed the door open. His hand slipped into his pocket as he climbed out seeking money for the driver.

He paid the man then held out his hand to help Mary descend.

He kept a hold of her hand as they crossed to the door. A night porter opened it when Drew knocked, and the light from the lantern in the hall spilled out onto Mary, illuminating her face.

Awe and emotion gripped him.

He could not quite believe she was here.

A lopsided smile titling his lips he bent and caught her up in his arms. She gripped his shoulders. "Andrew!"

"I omitted to do this before, didn't I? It was remiss of me. A bridegroom should carry his wife across their threshold."

The doorman grunted his amusement, stepping aside.

Damn the pain in his rib, despite Marlow and his bitter words and violence, Drew was going to make her happy. He would prove them wrong and make Mary love him more.

Chapter 21

Mary laughed, smiling at Andrew, looking into his eyes which were dark in the low light. He was a day late, but the gesture touched her heart. She could still not believe he'd come tonight, although she was unsure why he had. Yet even if he'd come only because Lord Brooke wished to chase after Emily, Andrew had sat with her, not his friends.

In the two seasons she'd spent in town she'd never seen him at such an event. He'd even eaten among her family. But then it had all gone wrong. She wished he'd not brought his friends to speak to her, then her father would not have become angry, and she wished his friends would leave Emily alone.

Yet Andrew was right, Emily would be safe, she was chaperoned – as long as she did not fall for Lord Brooke's charm, as Mary had fallen for Andrew's.

That charm flowed about her as he carried her upstairs.

When they'd played chess and dressed together today, she'd glimpsed how their marriage may be, and tonight she'd felt one of a couple. Now…

She watched his face as he carried her. His eyes reflected the light of the lanterns in the hall.

Her husband was a complex man. "You value your friends, don't you?" she said, as they reached the landing.

He glanced at her. "I value them yes, they are like brothers."

"How long have you known them?"

"Since school, we were boys together." He withdrew a key from his pocket and opened the door, balancing her on his knee and his forearm.

"Kate, my sister-in-law's, brother was John's best friend at school."

"Your brother's man of business? I didn't know he'd been Pembroke's friend." Andrew carried her in, over their real threshold. A maid must have been into the room. A single oil lamp had been left burning by the door.

"Kate played with John and Philip. I was too young."

"What exactly are you saying?" He laughed, as he let her legs swing gently to the floor.

She faced him.

A tender smile pulled at his lips. It spoke of love. Was it a lie?

"Do you like my friends now, or are you thinking about liking them?"

"I am thinking about getting to know them and judging them for myself."

"A suspended sentence, then."

He could be fun when he wished to be, and sweet, and kind... and he'd no reason to be false now, he had her money... She did not understand him.

"And my judgement, Mary? Where do I stand?" His light brown eyes looked at her.

She turned away slipping off her shawl, setting some distance between them. She would not admit she loved him when she was not sure what he felt. "You are my husband..." She laid her shawl over the back of a chair and looked back. "Do you want me to pour you a drink?"

He still stood by the door, looking as though he tried to solve a puzzle. "That is a very wifely offer. Yes, I will have a drink."

"Brandy?" she asked, as she walked to the decanters.

"Yes, please."

She heard him remove his hat, gloves and then his evening coat. She did not look back.

His hands slipped about her waist and his lips kissed her shoulder. The decanter wobbled as she set it down.

"Do you want me to ring for some water for tea?" His breath touched her ear.

She turned, forcing him to step back as she held out his drink. "No, the maids will be in bed, I would not wish to wake them. I'm not thirsty."

His gaze travelled over her expression as he took the glass. "Have I taken you from heaven Mary and brought you to hell, to live with me?"

Sometimes he said the strangest things, but the words proved that he was leagues deep. Her fingertips touched the dark purple bruise about his eye. "Does it hurt?"

"A little." He took her hand from his face and drew her towards a chair, a roguish smile playing on his lips.

Once he'd set his drink down he sat and drew her down onto his lap. Then he reclaimed his drink and sipped from the glass.

She touched his bruised eye, again and then pressed a kiss beside it.

His smile broadened as he moved her hand to his jaw. "It hurts here too."

She leaned to kiss his jaw. "Did Papa and John hurt you much when they hit you?"

"Now she asks…" His voice rang deep. "I'm sure you do not care if they did. I believe the word is comeuppance."

"You were a day late in carrying me over the threshold. I am a couple of days late in asking if you were hurt. We're even…"

He brushed strands of her hair back from her face, while he took another sip of brandy.

"You did not hit them…" She began unpicking the puzzle. Why had she not noticed that?

"That would have been unjust, don't you think?" He looked down and stared into the amber liquid in his raised glass. "If I was your Papa, or your brother, I'd have punched me too." Her gaze lifted again. "In fact if anyone took you from me now I would reap carnage just as they did."

Her fingers pressed against his midriff, as she moved to get up. "Ow! God."

She stopped moving. "What is it?" Her palm still rested against his side.

"Your dear Papa, broke my rib, Mary."

She slid off his lap and stood. "You did not say."

He sipped his drink, before saying, "When was the moment to mention it? I can take a punch. I'm not complaining. I did seduce you, after all…" He watched her as he spoke, as though judging her response.

Her fingers clasped at her waist.

Deviltry flashed in his eyes as he drained his glass, then set it down. "I seduced you because I wanted you, Mary. I am guilty of that. I should have asked for your father's consent, but we both know I would not have received it, so I planned to elope. I did plan it, from the first. They were right... But at some point along that path I fell in love with you, and I did not even lie to you and say I love you until I did.

"Yes, I urged you to choose me. But you knew that. I did not lie to you, and you came with me by choice…" He lifted his hand. "Come back, sit down, you were keeping me warm."

"I'll hurt your rib."

"I'll worry about my rib. Come on, sweetheart, sit and talk to me."

"We are talking, but I do not think it's what you wish to do."

His smile tilted sideward, turning her stomach to fluid. "Ah, you got me. Come and give me a kiss, then."

His presence pulled her physically. It was hopeless pretending she did not want to be with him; she loved him. She'd told Emily to learn from her mistakes, yet *she* had not learned from them. He'd just admitted seducing her, and she was letting him do it again.

Yet his words were true. He'd urged her to marry him from the start, and she had known he sought her money as well as her...

She longed for some control.

She did not know where she stood.

Who to believe.

Whether to trust...

How much of her heart to give...

How much of herself.

But she knew a way to take control of him.

Catching up her dress she raised it. His smile turned predatory as he realised what she meant to do. He shifted in his seat, so her knees could fit beside his hips, as she straddled him, her raised dress spilling about them.

"You can get rid of these for a start," he said, catching a hold of her hand then tugging off her glove.

It felt very intimate, to sit astride him, as his fingers worked her gloves free, and she remembered the feel of his fingers inside her. She shivered at the memory.

He smiled slyly, a moment before slipping one of her fingers into his mouth, then he sucked it gently.

She did not wish to be submissive, this time. She did not want to be seduced. She would rather seduce him. She wished him to know he could not keep controlling her.

Pulling her finger from his lips she leaned forward and kissed him, gripping his nape, as he liked to do to her, dominating him. It felt like doling out exquisite justice.

She slipped the buttons of his waistcoat loose, freeing them quickly, and then she tugged his shirt from his waistband and slid her hands underneath over his skin.

He flinched.

She stopped, pulling away. She'd forgotten his broken rib.

He smiled. "Don't stop, just be careful."

"Let me see?" She pushed his waistcoat off his shoulders. He let her take it off, and his shirt too.

The dark purple, almost black, bruise, stained half his side. Her fingers ran over it.

"You should have asked me to bandage it for you."

"You would not have done it at that inn. Not after your father and brother convinced you I am evil." It was petulantly said.

"You're not evil. But you do have a devil in you that likes to kick out, Andrew?" She met his gaze. He'd not fought back against them physically, he had not even fought against their accusations. But he had been angry with them and jabbed back at them with words.

He laughed. "Yes, I suppose. But perhaps that is because people hit out at me." Then in a deeper tone, he said, "Enough talking." His hand gripped her nape.

"Your rib, Andrew."

"Darling, physical intimacy is the best painkiller ever. Forget my rib. I'm half naked beneath you…"

She shook her head, pulling away and rising, if she could not gain the upper hand in that way, she knew there was another. She had contemplated this when he'd used his mouth and teeth on her. It would completely claim him, as he'd claimed her and make it clear that she had the power to seduce him too.

If her marriage was to work, it would be with her as an equal, and she knew exactly how to make her husband pay attention. He would view her differently, hear her differently, if she took control of him physically.

He looked disappointed.

"I have a better idea." She dropped to her knees and his gaze burned bright, gleaming in the lamplight. This would win his attention and change everything between them.

Drew forgot pain – forgot about anything but her – this beautiful woman, whom he loved, his wife, as she undid his flap. *Hell*. This was Mary. The prim Miss Marlow. His fingernails dug into the arms of the chair. But she was not Miss Marlow any more, she was Lady Framlington. Perhaps his name had tainted her. *God*, his arousal was agony.

Her dark ebony hair was a vivid contrast against his skin as he watched her.

This morning she'd cried when he'd made love to her, this evening...

"You do not have to do this." His voice only came out on a whisper as her lips encompassed him, and he gritted his teeth and hung on. *God in heaven.*

She did not stop, and she did not answer. *Lord.*

He slipped the comb out of her hair, set it aside and then pulled out the pins.

Her hair fell down her back and his fingers slipped through it.

"Mary, darling," he groaned.

She focused on what she did, ignoring his noises and his attention.

Lord. It was like he didn't know how to breathe anymore.

"Mary..."

His hips took up her rhythm – claiming what she gave.

Hell and the devil.

"Mary." If she did not stop, he was going to come undone. His fingers gripped her arms, to urge her up, but she didn't stop, ignoring his insistence.

He could not bear it. His fingers gripped the arms of the chair again and he shut is eyes and gritted his teeth, hanging on, fighting... *Lord... Damn.* "*Mary!*"

He came into her mouth on an overwhelming rush, and could not believe he'd done it. She'd been respectable, an innocent women, until a couple of days ago. He sucked a deep breath into his lungs, his fingers clasping in her hair as he waited for sanity to return. When it did she was already moving away, standing up.

"Now you know how it feels to be seduced," she said, leaving him in the chair, hot and drained, and *fucking hell*... She could seduce him anytime.

"Mary." He wanted to rise and follow her but his limbs refused to move.

She did not come back.

Damn. Had that been a lesson? If so he had not learned it.

After a moment, he rose, holding his trousers up with one hand, as he followed.

She was undressing in the bedchamber. "Mary, I love–"

"Don't spoil it," she answered bluntly, glancing at him.

He moved across the room, caught her arm and made her look at him. "Mary, I do love you."

Tears glistened in her eyes as she looked at him. "You do not have to lie to me, anymore, Andrew, you have my money. I know you like me, that is enough."

"I'm not lying!" *God*, how could she have done what she'd done, then act like it meant nothing. Other woman had done the same of course, but it had never felt like that.

She stared at him.

He let her go and she turned away.

He wanted normality, happiness, he'd hoped to have it with her, yet she knew him for who he was – worthless.

She'd found him out, and found him lacking.

Who was he trying to fool? He could not be happy with her. He did not know how to love her. A part of him wanted to go out and find the others. They would still be in the clubs, and he could do with a bloody good drink and a few laughs.

She sniffed as she let her dress fall to the floor and began awkwardly trying to unlace her corset.

She was crying.

Damn. He secured his trousers as he moved to hold her. He could not leave her alone. Doing that would prove her right. But she was wrong – he did love her.

One hand brushed through her hair, while his other stroked her back. She was his alpha and omega, his first and last, no matter what else. "It will be right between us, Mary. It will. I promise."

Her arms gripped about his midriff, holding him too tightly and jarring his broken rib.

"Let us get into bed," he said over her hair. If she would not accept his words of love, then he would show her with his body, he had to find some way to make her believe.

Chapter 22

When Drew woke the next day, Mary slept. He rose, washed and shaved quietly, in the dressing room, and then once he was clothed he ordered breakfast.

He ordered bread, eggs, fried bacon, coffee and chocolate, and when it arrived his rooms became full of appetite stirring scents.

The bed chamber door opened and Mary stood there, her hair mussed, her eyes sleepy and her cheeks strawberry and cream.

He ignored the impulse to take her straight back to bed, that would be crass.

Smiling he encouraged her to come and eat instead, even though she was still in her nightgown. He poured her chocolate while she buttered bread, her bare feet resting on the rung of the chair, while her ebony hair spilled about her shoulders over her cotton nightgown.

He swallowed back another lustful itch as he passed her the drink. How had this beautiful girl become his wife... How the hell had a scoundrel, an unwanted bastard like him, won her.

They ate in silence for a moment but then her eyes lifted, and her pale translucent gaze fixed on him.

The food in his mouth lost its flavour.

Her gaze asked questions he knew he would not want to answer...

Her gaze caught on Drew's. He was different when they were alone. What she'd done last night, to teach him a lesson, had made him think. She knew afterwards when he'd made love to her, in bed, that there had been repentance in his tenderness.

But it had made her think too. She'd thought about how happy John and Kate were; how happy all her married cousins were with their husbands. That is what she'd wanted for herself.

But what she'd said last night was true. He might not love her, but he did care, he was seeking to make her happy today, and he had yesterday.

His cheeks darkened with a blush, then his gaze dropped to his food.

"Will you ride this morning?"

He glanced at her, throwing her a smile, then shook his head. "It's raining."

She looked out the window. It was only drizzling. She looked back at him. "That is not rain. You cannot even call it a shower. It is falling dew. I've been riding before in a deluge with Robbie. Riding in the rain is fun. Can we not go together? I have my habit in my trunks."

"And when I take you to your Papa's later and you've caught a chill, it will be me he'll blame."

"Papa knows me well enough to realise who to blame, and I have a far better constitution than to catch a chill from a pathetic attempt at rainfall such as that."

His eyes shone with amusement. "I ride my carriage horses, I've no others; they're spirited, Mary."

"I can handle a spirited horse. I'd be bored by a tame animal."

He laughed. "Well that explains much."

"Can we ride then?"

"Yes, we will ride."

Oh, she felt happy for the first time in days. It would be wonderful to do something normal. Rising and leaning over she hugged him and kissed his cheek. Then whispered, "Thank you."

Before letting him go and saying, "I'll go and get ready, will you help me?"

"Yes. You find out your clothes, I'll be there in a moment."

Their ride was exhilarating, the fine rain only served to keep her cool, although it dampened her hair and habit. Yet due to the rain, they had Hyde Park virtually to themselves so they rode across the lawns at pace, laughing and shouting without a care for what others thought. She felt as good as she always did when she rode at home with Robbie.

Andrew's horses were fast, she'd no need for a whip to make them run, they'd wonderful temperaments too. That was because he spoiled them with affection. He had petted them and whispered to them, when he'd greeted them in the stables. No wonder he'd been moody when he'd had to leave them at the inn. The animals seemed as important to him as his friends.

She glanced at him as they rode back from the park, at a trot, side by side, his eyes were gleaming and his damp hair was plastered to his head beneath the brim of his hat, while his wet riding coat moulded his body.

He sat a horse well, his strong slender thighs and calves gripping at the animals flanks, while his posture held straight.

If she saw him from a distance across a field, she would think him handsome, without even seeing his face. He oozed untamed strength and masculinity. It seemed she liked spirited men, as much as spirited horses.

When they reached the stables, he swung down from his horse, dropping easily and then came to help her.

"I understand another fragment of you Andrew Framlington," she said, gripping his shoulders as he took her weight.

"Do you," he smiled, lifting her down. "Should I be concerned?"

"You are an escapist." They faced one another, her hands on his shoulders, his at her waist.

"Am I?"

"You are. I've found you out, my lord. This is why you've hunted an heiress, rather than settle to a trade, you'd rather escape for an hour's ride, than work…"

He smiled still. "I suppose that is not a compliment, but you can hardly judge, you are the same. I'd guess you'd much rather be out riding than sewing or reading…"

"Guilty." She laughed. But then she sobered as he let her go and turned to pet the horse she'd ridden. "I understand something else about you too; you are not as uncaring as you want people think?"

His gaze met hers, and his smile twisted as he patted the animal's rump, when a groom led it away. "Pray do not tell a soul."

He gripped her arm then. "Come, let's eat luncheon before we go to your brother's."

* * *

When he arrived at the Duke of Pembroke's town house two hours later, Drew felt like a king as he stood on the doorstep, solely because Mary was in charity with him.

They'd walked as the rain had ceased and they both liked exercise, and she'd donned a bright indigo blue day dress, beneath a navy pelisse. Her bonnet was also navy, and sported a small clutch of bluebells above her right ear. She looked charming, and he was not the only one who thought so, many men had noticed her as they'd walked. It had not dampened his mood. It felt good owning something so prized. He'd told her his horses were the most valuable thing he owned, they were not now, she was priceless.

The large door opened. Drew faced Pembroke's imperious butler.

"Mr Finch," Mary acknowledged, stepping inside as the man stepped back. She clung to Drew's arm and took him with her. "Is everyone in the upstairs sitting-room?"

Drew's discomfort rose like mercury in heat. He did not want to be here, and he doubted he'd be welcome. He was here for Mary's sake.

258

The butler bowed, aiming his supplication at Mary. "Yes, my Lady. They are. Shall I show you up?"

She laughed. "I cannot get used to being my Lady... Don't worry Finch, we can take ourselves up."

The stiff-looking butler gave Mary a hint of a smile, then glared at Drew. Drew's devil-may-care side shifted into place, and he answered with a nonchalant smile. *Think what you will...*

"May I take your outdoor garments, my Lady?" the butler offered, ignoring Drew. Mary let go of Drew's arm and pulled the ribbons of her bonnet loose. Drew took it, and her pelisse, and handed both to the butler, along with his hat and gloves. Let the man know his place.

A moment later they climbed the stairs; she eager, he reluctant but enduring.

He'd gone no farther than the hall, the other day. The landing was lined by two dozen intimidating portraits, Mary's ancestors, and artefacts gathered on grand tours. Some he guessed Pembroke had brought back from Egypt.

Voices reached them from further along the hall and Mary's pace quickened.

A drowning sensation took hold. He was tempted to stop and refuse to go further. Why had he said he would come?

You are an escapist – he heard her words. Or a coward...

Instead of running, he set his jaw and walked on beside her, as her fingers clasped his arm. He was here for her.

"Papa!" When they entered the drawing room she let go of Drew and rushed to her father.

He'd been ambushed. Not only her mother and father and her brother and his wife, but her aunts and uncles were here; the Duke and Duchess of Arundel and Bradford, and the Earl of Barrington, Marlow's brother, and his wife. There were others too, her cousins.

He'd been thrown to the Pembroke lions.

Looks were cast across the room, aimed at him, all judgemental and accusing.

His jaw set and his lips pressed together. Mary came back and pulled him towards a woman he'd not yet been introduced to. It was then he noticed the children in the room too, a couple of dozen of them, seated on the floor playing games, laughing and talking, and younger ones settled on the knees of their mothers, or beside them in chairs.

His heart clenched.

Family life like this was a thing of books – a fairytale.

A group of boys captured his attention. They sat crossed legged on the floor in the corner of the room playing cards, and it was hard to tell which child belonged to whom, so many of them bore the Pembroke's dark hair and pale eyed colouring.

Mary completed an introduction. Drew had not listened.

But he knew the woman, it was Arundel's Duchess. She bid two of the girls to move from a sofa and make room for him and Mary to sit together. Then she offered him tea.

The whole occasion felt surreal. He could not recall ever in his lifetime attending an afternoon tea.

He had been confined to the nursery as a child, out of sight and mind, and as an adult, well he'd never been invited to take tea.

Mary's family laughed and chatted around him. He accepted a cup from her mother, but could not force any words of gratitude from his throat.

Lifting the cup to his mouth he did not drink, as he watched the girl who'd moved to let him sit bring an embroidery hoop to Mary and ask advice on some stitches. The child was her sister…

The women sat in the chairs all talking, the children playing about them. Drew felt as if he looked in on them through glass.

When Mary finished speaking to her sister, the girl glanced at him, like he was some oddity, before swiftly turning away. A much smaller girl ran up to them. A ragdoll dangled from her hand.

"You're my new brother aren't you?" Her small hand rested on his thigh.

"Jemima," Mary caught the little girl up onto her knee. "Every

260

one of us is new to Lord Framlington; I think he is a little overwhelmed."

Drew looked at Mary. His cup had been balanced before his lips for an age, and he'd not sipped from it. He did so, then set the cup and saucer down on a table.

He didn't know what to say, or do. A lump swelled in his throat, blocking off the air.

The little girl began telling Mary all about her doll.

Mary's fingers brushed his thigh, as though she understood. But she could not understand his childhood. It would be as inconceivable to her as this was to him.

A deep masculine laugh rang from a group of men in the corner behind Drew. He stiffened, wondering if their laughter was directed at him. He was sure he made a fine sight, sat in Pembroke's parlour, with the women, drinking tea. God, Harry would laugh his head off if he knew, and Peter and Mark would have him sentenced to a madhouse in a week.

Drew cleared his throat, trying to shift the lump within it.

"Jemima," Marlow's voice called from across the room.

Drew looked up. The men had split up and were joining their wives.

The girl on Mary's lap slid off and ran to Marlow, with a bright smile. "Papa."

Despite the fact her name had been barked she did not seem scared. When she reached him, she clutched Marlow's thigh, then he bent and picked her up. She lifted her doll up to show him, and he answered her, whispering to her ear.

Drew looked away. He'd glimpsed a bond that must hold between Mary and her father too – years ago it would have been Mary in his arms. No wonder Marlow had not liked Drew taking her away without a by-your-leave.

Mary had turned to talk to the women. Drew glanced about the room and met the Duchess of Pembroke's gaze. She sat in a chair near them. She had probably been watching him. She had reason to dislike him. What she made of his marriage to Mary he didn't wish to contemplate.

"Helen, dear," she said, looking away, at one of the girls. "Please pass about the plates and offer people some of the cakes, would you."

The girl, one of Marlow's Drew would guess, and therefore another of Mary's sisters, did as she was asked.

"Helen is the perfect helpmate," the Duchess said turning to look at him, offering another olive branch.

He nodded, like a fool.

"I'm pleased you came today. You mustn't let my father-in-law or John put you off, they will mellow to you, if you prove your loyalty to Mary."

Drew fought to choose the right words. She was the one he needed to make peace with; he had insulted her. "Your Grace, I appreciate your…" *What?* He began again. "I ought to… that is… I'm sor—"

"That is past, Lord Framlington." She rose, and moved away.

Devil take it, he'd upset her. His gaze tracked her as she went to Pembroke, who talked with the Earl of Barrington, the only other member of Mary's family Drew knew to have had a less than savoury reputation at one stage in his life. Barrington's hand clasped his wife's as he talked, and a good number of the brood here seemed to be his.

Pembroke's arm settled about the Duchess's shoulders as she spoke to the others. Then Pembroke whispered something to her ear. She nodded, and then Pembroke looked at Drew, his eyes firm with judgement.

Drew looked away, anger and hostility stirring, only to see Marlow deposit his young daughter on his wife's lap, and kiss first the child then his wife. When he straightened, as if sensing Drew's observation he turned and caught Drew's gaze. His expression stiffened then and he looked at Mary.

"Mary, may I speak with you a moment," *alone*. He did not say the last word but his voice did, and Mary heard because pressing her palm on Drew's thigh she rose and went to her father.

Marlow clasped her elbow and led her to a window seat on the far side of the room.

Drew watched feeling cut off and isolated – just as he'd done as a child – knowing Mary was about to be coerced with more condemning words.

"So, Lord Framlington, whereabouts did you grow up?"

Drew looked at the woman who sat in the seat Mary had vacated. She had unusual emerald eyes.

"I am Mary's aunt Jane, Lord Barrington's wife."

He knew.

Drew saw Marlow's fingers lift and touch a small bruise on Mary's throat, left by Drew's over ardent kisses as they'd made love last night.

"Mary is precious to us, Lord Framlington." Lady Barrington said, as Marlow's hand clasped Mary's. "Her marriage shocked us all."

He turned to look at Lady Barrington. "Mary is a grown woman and capable of making choices."

"She is, but she is also very kind and loving. We just wish she'd chosen the right man. A man who could give that back to her."

"The right man? Not me then." His pitch shifted to defiance, and in defiance he gave her a what-do-I-care smile.

So this was the plot they'd been hatching in the corner, send the women in to get at him. Mary would not spot their ploy and he'd feel unable to defend himself too aggressively. Clever.

"It could be you," she answered, "we will have to wait and see, we hope it is you, for Mary's sake."

"Not mine…"

"At the moment Lord Framlington, you have gained everything and Mary nothing. I think you have enough."

His instinct was to leave and to take Mary with him, but her family were important to her and the woman was right, he'd gained

263

much from marrying Mary, the least he could do in return was sit among her family and drink their damned tea. "Mary has gained one thing, Lady Barrington. She has gained me. I'm aware you all think me lacking, but Mary does not."

God, he hoped Mary did not find him lacking. The thought took his gaze back to Marlow, who still sat with her, gripping her hands.

Lady Barrington's fingers touched Drew's arm. "I hope you prove us all wrong. Again, for Mary's sake…" With that she rose and left him seated.

Anger kicked his gut. No one had ever wished him happy. Was it any wonder he'd grown into a selfish, bitter man?

Mary's sister Helen offered him a slice of cake from a plate. He did not take one, he did not feel hungry. Then one of her young brothers, who Drew had a suspicion had been dared, came forward holding out a pack of cards to show Drew a trick he knew.

The next half an hour was spent with the boys, as one by one, they came closer, asking questions about horses and carriages and boyish things.

Mary stayed silent when they walked home, her fingers clasping his forearm, her arm tucked under his.

He did not ask her what Marlow had said. He had a feeling he would not want to know and he had to face them again in a day and half, because before leaving he'd agreed to accompany Mary to a ball her family were attending.

When they reached his rooms he asked Joseph to order them a good dinner from Gunter's. Then led her upstairs, suggesting they spend the evening playing cards or chess. Perhaps their marriage might work after all, if he could just cope with continually facing her family.

Chapter 23

Mary watched Andrew move the bishop across the board and take her knight.

She'd discovered a few small elements of him, yet there seemed dozens more. He was so complex. He could be kind and tolerant, but most of the time he was stubborn and defensive, and foolhardy with his friends.

Her father thought Andrew selfish, although pig-headed was the word he'd used, and he'd sought assurances from her, asking if Andrew let his friends come to the apartments when she was there and if they acted inappropriately towards her. Then he'd touched her neck, where Andrew had sucked her skin and left a bruise, and asked if Andrew was too rough with her.

She'd answered no, to every question, and sworn that Andrew was gentle, and respectful. She'd not told her father Andrew had stormed out and left her twice. She did not wish to give him cause to doubt her other words. She'd tried telling him about their ride in the park, only to make her father annoyed that Andrew had taken her riding in the rain. He'd called Andrew irresponsible for letting her gallop when the grass was damp.

She sighed. She was not quite sure what had happened to Andrew this afternoon, but something had. He'd appeared confused, as he'd sat in silence watching her family with an intent but abstract look. It was like he simply did not know what to do amongst them.

Perhaps he did not.

Since the day they'd eloped Andrew had not spoken of his family.

But they must know he'd married; the announcement had been made in the paper yesterday.

"Have you spoken to your parents?" She lifted her bishop, moving it from the path of his.

His gaze lifted and focused on hers, and she saw the muscle in his jaw tighten. "My parents?" His pitch was bitter, but as he spoke he leaned across and grasped the neck of the bottle of champagne he'd had delivered with their meal, then topped up her glass.

It was as though he sought to distract her from her question.

"Do they know we are married? Have you arranged to introduce me?"

His attention returned to the game and he slid a castle across the board so it faced her king. "Mate. No, Mary, and I do not plan to introduce you. Our marriage is nothing to do with my parents. Are you going to make your move?" He looked away, and took a sip from his glass.

She moved her bishop to defend her king.

He also made a defensive move.

"I'd like to meet your parents."

"You would not." He leaned back, sipping his champagne.

"Let me decide." She moved her queen in between two pawns, then looked up. "I do not want to bump into them and not have been introduced, it would be embarrassing. Are you ashamed of me?"

"Ashamed of you…" His eyebrows lifted.

"Well, why else would you not wish to introduce me?" His light brown eyes which had been bright and glowing all evening were now guarded. "If we are to make this work, Andrew, you cannot hold me at a distance from your family."

He was no longer looking at her but looking at the board,

ignoring her, as he awaited her next move and sipped his champagne.

Her fingers which had been toying with her king, lifted it off the board, and to her lips, so that his gaze followed it. "Are they in town?"

His gaze lifted to meet hers, with a look that said he thought her wrongheaded.

"Andrew."

They were in town, he'd seen them at the one of the balls he'd attended pursuing her, but Drew was not taking her to meet them. He moved another piece, not really even trying to read the game anymore

"I want to meet them."

He ignored her, sipping his champagne and looking at the board, wishing she would give this up. They'd had a good evening together until now, until she'd broached the untouchable subject of his parents.

"Andrew," she said again, prodding at him for an answer.

He sighed, then answered. "It's your move." Without looking at her.

She moved her pawn from the line of his king and suddenly he realised she'd trapped him in checkmate. *Damn*, that was the end of any distraction.

Conceding, he tipped his king over and looked up as she rose from her seat. The fabric of her dress rustled as she came to stand beside him, and then her gentle fingers touched his cheek and lifted his gaze to hers.

She smiled, her eyes gently pleading. "Please, Andrew, let me meet your parents? They must want to meet me."

"They will not." He doubted they'd have even lifted an eyebrow at the announcement in the paper. "Nor will they wish to see me. So, no, we will not go."

"Did you argue with them?" Her fingers slipped away from his cheek, and she picked up her glass.

"Mary, I do not want to discuss this." His temper increased by notches. He wished she would understand that no, meant no.

She stood silent for a moment, as if working out another way to ask to persuade him.

He sighed, then drained his glass, and stood. Well, if she needed something else to occupy her mind...

An hour later, lying naked beside her in bed, and feeling satisfied, he let his fingers drift across her shoulder, as he remembered her seduction the night before. "Your skin looks like porcelain, and you seem so fragile, Mary, yet you are not breakable at all, are you? There is steel beneath your skin."

Her eyes asked questions, which she didn't ask, instead she said, "I can be hurt, Andrew, but probably not broken. I have my family to support me."

Her answer kicked him in the chest. Her family were still her stronghold. Not him.

As he'd made love to her he'd felt his soul join hers, yet now again, when it was over, she did not believe in him.

He rolled to his back and she moved to rest a palm on his chest, and her head on his shoulder, then whispered to his chin. "Introduce me to your parents, I want to meet them." *Damn*, she had not forgotten that conversation either. But, *God*, if it would convince her to finally believe in him, was it not worth the risk. As soon as she met them she would know why he had not offered to take her. She would not ask again.

"Yes." This was the worst thing she could ever ask of him. Once it was over it could be forgotten and things would be normal between them again. They had been building bridges and a future together until she'd raised it.

Perhaps afterwards she may understand him better, and believe he spoke only the truth – his family would have no desire to see him, and she would see that.

Chapter 24

Over breakfast Mary watched Andrew. He was silent and moody. But last night she'd begun believing he loved her. He'd not said it, not once, but she'd felt it when he'd made love to her. His touch had been reverent. She didn't really know him yet, but she thought she was more to him than money.

She hoped meeting his family, who he claimed did not care about him, and who he said he did not care for, would help her understand him more.

Perhaps knowing his family would explain things – like why he'd felt so uncomfortable yesterday and why he was so fiercely self-reliant. She would always seek the support of her family. He sought support from no one.

"May we ride again this morning," she asked, the day was cloudy but it was not raining.

He looked up, "Yes, I suppose."

"Then I thought we ought to call on your parents before luncheon, I would not wish to call when they may be expecting others, if they do not like me—"

"I did not say they'd dislike you, I said they would not be inter-ested in you." His pitch was cold as he added sugar to his coffee.

She did not respond. He did not wish to take her to see his parents – he was doing it for her, because she'd been persistent.

269

That was surely another sign he thought more than nothing for her.

She sighed, and then made a face at him, because he was not looking. But he looked up and caught the tail end of her expression.

His eyebrows lifted. "Mary, are you sure you wish me to take you? I'll warn you only once more, it is a bad idea."

That was not true.

He warned her another time as they rode to the park, trying to persuade her against it. Then after they'd given the horses their heads for a while and pulled up, he warned her again, as though it had been on his mind through the whole gallop. Then he warned her as he lifted her down from her horse in the stable yard, continuing as he walked her over the road. He even ignored the street-sweep who he always stopped and spoke to.

His warnings became adamant as he helped her change into her day-dress, and finally he warned her over and over again as they rode in a handsome carriage towards his parents' home. But in all these warnings not once did he say why he did not wish to take her.

When they reached the town house, which was a tall, wide building in Cavendish Square, Drew took her hand to help her down the carriage's step.

His hand trembled as it held hers.

She glanced at his face. He'd paled. He really did not wish to be here.

He looked up at the house.

Yesterday he'd been hesitant when they'd reached John's, but here, it was more than hesitance – he looked afraid – and trapped inside himself.

She wrapped her fingers about his arm, every muscle in his body felt stiff, like iron.

He looked at her, and coughed to clear his throat as though it was dry.

She should change her mind. She should not have made him come.

The front door opened and the carriage pulled away.

Oh, it was too late...

"Come on." He moved forward.

He'd turned so pale it looked as though he led them to their deaths.

"Andrew?"

He gave her a stiff lipped smile, then said, "Remember, I warned you. Do not blame me."

This area of London was old money, his family, therefore, had held a place in society for generations. Of course she could have looked Andrew up in *The Peerage* at John's house. She'd not because she thought it disloyal to research him rather than ask him.

"Is the Marquis at home, Mr Potts," Andrew questioned as they entered. "And my Lady mother?"

"Indeed, Master Drew."

She remembered Drew saying it was the servants who'd first shortened his name.

"Shall I ask if you may be received?"

Mary just stopped her jaw from dropping. Why on earth would the butler seek Drew's parents' permission? He was their son.

"That would be the point of me standing here, Potts. You may wish to explain to them that I'm here because my wife wishes to be introduced to them."

"Your wife? Ah, forgive me." He turned to Mary then and bowed with perfect formality. "Lady Framlington." Then he said to Andrew, "Please wait, I will ask if it is convenient."

Andrew stood stiffly. His chin lifted as the man walked away.

Being asked to wait in the hall was clearly not odd to him. Nor was it any surprise to him that the butler had not known he was married. It meant his parents, if they'd seen the announcement, had not spoken of it in the house. If they'd done so, the servants would have heard.

It was five minutes or more before Mr Potts returned baring the news that they "may" attend upon the Marquis, and then he

271

showed them upstairs, striding ahead of them as though Andrew would not be able to find his way about his parents' home.

Andrew had established the look of nonchalance he favoured, he looked as though he did not care, but she knew he cared.

Her fingers lay on his arm, and she would have reached to hold his hand except that it was held away from her, over his midriff, giving her the impression he would not welcome the gesture. He was utterly insular, just as he'd been yesterday at John's and during their carriage ride back to London after they'd eloped.

She glanced sideways as they reached the drawing room and saw his eyes bore that devil-may-care glint which always came before some argument.

"Lord and Lady Framlington, my Lord," the butler intoned within the room.

"Yes, yes, bring him in then," an impatient woman's voice called.

Looking at Mary, Andrew whispered, "You owe me for this." Then he led her into the room.

He stopped just inside. An older woman, she presumed to be his mother, sat in a chair across the room near the hearth. She had a generous, curvaceous figure and wore an emerald taffeta morning-dress and a matching turban. A fire burned in the hearth even though it was summer.

A stately looking gentleman sat opposite. He had a large crooked nose. Andrew's father, she assumed, although there was no resemblance, either in his face or his build.

Two young men were also lounging in chairs about the room, their legs sprawled over the arms; neither moved to stand or even sit straight. While a tall very slender gentleman, who had a nose similar to Andrew's father, sat beside a woman, a book open on his lap. The woman was a few years older than Mary. She was working on embroidery and Mary noted the glint of a wedding ring.

Not one of them acknowledged Andrew, or her. They simply did not move, and his father did not even look up.

"Sir," Andrew bowed. "Mother." He bowed again. "I've brought my wife to meet you, at her wish. She did not want to embarrass you in a public meeting. She wished to be introduced."

"Yes, yes, Drew, Potts told us your reason for being here, get on with it," Andrew's mother said, while his father's gaze lifted.

He looked first at Andrew, as though Andrew was something abhorrent, and then at Mary, as though she was… Well, she felt like Andrew's mistress, not his wife, the way she was being visually assessed.

She saw Andrew swallow back what she knew was an insulting retort, which he would have spoken to her father or John. Then he looked at her, his eyes cold and dark, but fathoms deep within burned ire. "Mary, allow me to introduce you to Lord Framlington, the Marquis of Philkins, and my mother Lady Framlington."

Mary dropped a deep curtsy to them both, ignoring the pitch of his voice, which said I told you, you would not wish to meet them. Then he progressed, "My eldest brother the Earl of Alder and his wife." Again Mary curtsied. Then Andrew introduced the two younger men. "And my brothers Lord Jack, and Lord Mark Framlington." Mary bobbed a less eloquent curtsy in their direction as neither of them had risen for her.

The room fell into silence.

Then the Marquis cleared his throat and stared at Andrew. "I cannot see why you have brought this damned woman here. She is naught to do with me, is she?"

Mary heard Andrew take a deep breath.

She'd made an error, urging him to bring her here. They should not have come.

"No sir," he said at length. "However as we are here, perhaps you could offer Mary tea, Mother?" Andrew had become belligerent. She heard his anger and arrogance slipping into his pitch. Mary blushed. She could never have imagined that he'd need to beg for their hospitality, how could she have foreseen this?

"She's a prize beauty," Andrew's brother Jack stated, as though Mary was not in the room, while he swung one leg from the arm of the chair lounging with his elbow on the other arm. "But God be damned, how the devil did you win her, she's Marlow's is she not?"

They had heard of Andrew's marriage… But they obviously had not cared.

Mary saw the muscle in Andrew's cheek tighten even more, if that were possible, and she could not believe that his mother said nothing to reprimand the rudeness of his brother. But it appeared, here, it was not deemed insulting for a man to swear in female company. Her father and mother would have gone mad.

"I suppose she's bloody rich as well, knowing your luck, Drew." The other of his younger brothers stated.

Mary gripped Andrew's arm, awkwardness rattling through her nerves. They had not even been asked to sit, and his mother had neither confirmed nor denied the offer of refreshment.

"*She*, is my wife," Andrew answered, "and therefore Lady Framlington, and *she* is also the sister of the Duke of Pembroke, and niece to a quarter of the House of Lords so if you do not wish to offend the better half of society you'd best mind your words…" Andrew glared at the two young men.

His family merely stared back at him, the Marquis's gaze piercing.

"Edward Marlow would not have given his permission for this." The Marquis stated.

Andrew's older brother stood. "I'm sure he did not. Drew has merely been up to his usual mischief."

Mary looked at Andrew, expecting some retort, but there was none. Instead he watched his brother move to pour a drink from a decanter. He did not offer Andrew one, even as he turned and offered their father one.

Mary had a sudden desire to get Andrew out of the house. *I should not have pleaded with him to bring me here.* The atmosphere was poisonous.

"If you wish for refreshment, Drew, you must tug the bell pull," his mother said. "There is no point standing there thinking

274

someone will serve you."

Mary's cheeks burned with a blush – on his behalf – at his mother's inconsiderate words. But in response, letting go of his arm, she turned and walked across to pull it and call for a servant herself. Her mother would never expect a visitor to do such a thing.

"She's got a hell of a fine figure on her ain't she?" Mary heard Jack say. "You're a damned lucky bastard, Drew, I bet… fu—"

Mary heard the sudden movement and a strangled sound as she spun back.

Andrew leaned over his brother, one hand gripping Jack's cravat. "You will speak to my wife with respect. Do you hear me?"

Mary saw Andrew's hand twist, tightening the fashionable neck cloth, like a noose.

"Drew!" His mother was on her feet.

The Marquis rose too. "Out!" He pointed a finger at Andrew. "You are not welcome here. You never were, and you never will be. You are not my son and I regret the day I let you have my name. Now go!"

Andrew thrust his brother back into the chair with a hard shove, let go, and straightened.

Mary stood still, unsure what to do, as he glared about the room.

He looked at his mother with scorn and then glared in his defiant way at the Marquis.

If she could only turn back time, and have listened to him this morning. But how could she have imagined this. They had disowned him. What had he done to deserve that?

"Get out!" the Marquis roared at Andrew again, his finger thrusting like a spear.

Andrew bent a little, giving only an impression of a bow. "Sir." The single word was cold and condemning.

He threw his mother one of his devil-may-care grins. "Forgive me for reminding you of my existence, Mother."

Then he turned towards Mary, and began striding across the room, his movement stiff with anger. "Mary!" He gripped her arm tightly, painfully, as he reached her and turned her away from them.

She did not try to free her arm, but let him pull her along, lifting her dress a little so she could keep up.

Looking back across her shoulder she said, "Good-day." Feeling a need to be polite, even if his family were not. No one answered as they left the room.

But as Andrew's hard strides resonated along the hall she heard his father say, "Good riddance."

The butler met them mid-flight. "Master Drew." was all he said, as he turned to walk with them.

Andrew cast a look of thunder upon him. "I'm quite capable of showing myself out without thieving, Potts. I do not wish for anything from this damned house or its occupants anyway." He was striding on along the hallway with both Mary and the butler hurrying to keep up with him.

"Andrew," she whispered, in an attempt to slow him down. He did not slow. But when they reached the stairs he let go of her arm, and jogged down ahead of her.

If he could have sprouted wings and flown from the house, she thought he would have done.

When he reached the hall he strode to the door and opened it himself, leaving it open for her to follow.

Her heart pounded as she stepped outside and saw him waiting on the pavement below, reaching into an inside pocket of his coat. By the time she was beside him, he held a thin cigar and matches.

Squatting down he struck a match on the pavement, then rose up and lit the cigar, drawing on it. He looked upward and blew the smoke out, then looked at her. "Are you ready then?" His voice sounded emotionless. "We'll walk home, if you don't mind. I cannot smoke in a hansom and it will take several streets to find one anyway, we'll be halfway home by then."

He lifted his free arm, offering it to her.

His actions dismissed what had happened only moments ago – denying it, as if he did not care. He did care. She had seen his anger. She knew he cared. But she accepted his arm and began walking, unsure what to do.

For ten minutes he spoke of the weather, commented on passers-by and carriages without any mention of his family.

The muscle in his arm beneath her fingers had relaxed, and he spoke animatedly, occasionally sucking on his cigar, and then blowing the smoke out over his shoulder, away from her.

He'd shut what had happened out of his mind, like sweeping dirt beneath a carpet.

But it would not be gone. It would be there to find later. She did not think it good...

When arguments exploded among her brothers, her brother Robbie would never fight. Instead he would let any disagreement fester. Andrew reminded her of Robbie. She wondered how long this particular argument had been festering.

Perhaps, if she knew how it had started she could help. Maybe if he apologised to his father, then he could lay some new foundations with his parents and build up a relationship with them again.

As they walked, and he talked nonsense, her mind began planning, what to say, how to help him establish a truce with his family. There must be a way.

When they reached his rooms, as he closed the door and her fingers lifted to untie the ribbons of her bonnet, she asked, "Why did you fall out with them?"

She had her back to him when she asked the question, but she knew, he knew, which them she meant, as he growled behind her.

She turned to see him crossing to the decanters. She pulled the ribbons loose. "What did you do to upset them?"

"What did I do?" he growled, turning back suddenly, and glaring at her as he had done at his father.

The look said he thought her opinion worthless.

Her lip caught between her teeth for a second, but she wished to speak... She could not bear to think of him at odds with his family, she could not stand to be in that position. "You can tell me. I shan't judge you. But perhaps I can help you heal the rift."

Drew's anger reignited, it had been like glowing coals since he'd left the Marquis and now she had blown upon it and made it flare. "The rift?" Was she not there… "Were you not in the room, Mary?"

What did she want, for him to spell it out for her? He'd no intention of doing so. He was an unwanted, unloved, worthless bastard. Did she want him to explain that to her.

She came towards him, all sweet innocent charm and quiet voice.

"Andrew, what harm would it do to tell me what you did? It must have happened years ago anyway."

It cut that she laid the blame on him.

He'd thought that in the last day or two her opinion of him had begun to change. It had not. She judged him by the view of her brother and her father, still.

But God, this mess was not her fault. He tamped his temper – his urge to yell at her. "It's not a rift," he said to the decanters, "it is a damned canyon a mile wide and there are no bridges to cross it, Mary. Let it rest."

"But apologies can make amends, and—"

"I have nothing to apologise for." He lifted a stopper from a decanter.

"I know that it often seems that way…" she said, as he half-filled a glass with brandy. "But sometimes if you apologise even if you do not feel in the wrong…"

Was he to apologise for his birth? He swallowed back his anger and lifted the glass to his lips.

Her fingers slipped about his middle pressing over his stomach for a moment as she rested her cheek against his shoulder, at his back. She was offering comfort, but he had a feeling she sought to appease him too.

She let him go and he sensed her step back.

He turned. She was twisting his ring around on the third finger of her left hand, and she glanced down at it.

His breath stuck in his lungs as he sensed the question coming.

She looked up, her pale blue crystal like eyes staring into him. "Why T R, I'd thought it must be your family ring, but the initials do not link with anything?"

Could the woman not work it out for herself? He sipped his liquor once more.

"I'm sorry, I suppose you won it in a game of cards, or…"

Good God, Drew felt his anger sore. *Or?* Was she accusing him of stealing it?

"Or what? Mary." His pitch was low, but he could hear the threat hanging in it as his temper slipped out of his control. "Say it!" Leaning forwards he growled the last in her face.

She stepped back, grasping the back of a chair to stop herself from falling. "Or, nothing…" He could see the confusion in her eyes that asked, what had she said wrong, but he could not get a grip on his anger. She had accused him!

"Nothing? Mary…" He felt as though she had unleashed his devil. He glared at her. But damn her! "Not that it may be stolen? From whom would I steal it? Why would I give you something of so little meaning?"

"I did not mean—" she stuttered.

"To call me a villain? To assume I must be in the wrong and them in the right? You did mean, Mary. You meant every damned word. Well, I am sick of knowing you condemn me. I don't give a damn anymore! Not a single grain of sand, for what you think." He turned away, then said with his back to her as he walked away. "Think what you damn well wish."

He had to get away from her.

"Andrew…" She followed. "I meant nothing. I just… I do not understand why it is T R…"

He'd reached the table where the chessboard was. The pieces on it had been reset since the game they'd played last night. He turned back, lifting a hand to warn her from coming close. "I told you

I did not wish to go, but you insisted. Are you happy, now?" He felt like she'd pulled a loose thread and he was fraying at the ends.

T R, how the hell am I to know what T R stands for, whomever he is, he is only my damned father! Would you have me beg my parents' forgiveness for my mother's lechery, and my birth?

A fire of pain and anger burned bright within him, and then he saw pity in her eyes. "Do not pity me, damn you!"

"Andrew, please..." She tried to grip his arm, but he stepped sideways.

"Please what? Befriend my damned family, who have always hated me, and regret my existence. Hell no, Mary!" With that he bent and struck the chess-pieces from the board, sending them flying with a satisfactory crash, and then for good measure he lifted the table, tipping the marble board to follow its players.

When he stormed from the room his heart thumped, pulsing blood into his veins.

Chapter 25

Mary paced the sitting room for the thousandth time. There was still no thud of her errant husband's footsteps on the stairs.

Her stomach churned with anxiety. Of course it was empty, she'd not eaten luncheon, or dinner, but she'd hoped to eat supper at the ball…

It appeared now they would not be going, it was getting too late.

She'd dressed over an hour ago in the hope he'd come back, although she'd not been able to lace her stays, so she'd left them off.

Looking at the clock, as she'd done every five minutes, she saw it was now ten. She'd would have to lie to her father again tomorrow when he asked why they had not come.

She heard footsteps. They weren't Andrew's, she'd learned the sound of his step.

Dropping into a chair she clasped her fingers together over her stomach. Where is he?

The footsteps travelled along the hall outside then stopped at the door. A knock hit the wood.

Wonderful, now he had a caller.

"Drew, old devil, are you in?"

It was Lord Brooke's voice.

"Drew! Come on. Stop closeting yourself away with that wife of yours and let an old friend in."

Mary had assumed Andrew was with his friends. Clearly she'd assumed wrong. But if Lord Brooke was here, where was Andrew. She rose and opened the door.

A blush heated her cheeks. "L-L-Lord Brooke. A-A-Andrew is not at home, I th-thought he was with you..."

One of his hands gripped the doorframe. "I have not seen him."

"Oh." She stepped back, feeling uncomfortable. He took it as an invitation to enter, and walked past her, heading for Andrew's decanters.

"I'll wait for him if I may."

"Andrew had to go out, unexpectedly. I cannot say how long he will be." Uncertain what to do, she closed the door. She'd never been alone in a room with any man other than her family, or Andrew.

He helped himself to a drink. "No matter," he said, turning back. "But I see you've dressed for the evening, so I assume you are expecting him back."

"As I said, I am not sure. I thought I would dress in case... We were going to a ball." Mary kept her distance, leaning against the door, her fingers still on the handle. His dark brown eyes danced with humour.

"But you're not now?" he said, before sipping his brandy.

Mary shrugged. "I was to meet my parents, but—"

"Now, he's left you at home, a damsel in distress." Lord Brooke's smile softened then he glanced about the room. His gaze stopped on the chess set.

Mary had righted the table, placed the board back on it and reset the pieces, but the board was broken in two and that was obvious.

His eyes came back to her. "Where were you going?"

Her gaze lifted from the broken chessboard and met his. "To the Caldecotts." She let go of the door handle and instead clasped her hands at her waist.

His gaze followed the movement.

When it lifted he smiled, before drinking the last of his brandy. Then he set the glass down and bowed sharply. "Lady Framlington, as Drew's friend I believe it is my duty, and it shall also be my pleasure, to see you safely to the Caldecotts'. If you will allow it?"

Mary's thoughts spun like a top. If she went with Lord Brooke her father would be less likely to think something was amiss.

But what about Andrew?

He knew she'd agreed to meet her parents, though – he could find her.

"Yes, thank you, Lord Brooke. I'd be grateful for your escort, if it will not overly disrupt your night."

"It will not. My carriage is here and I shall stay with you at the Caldecotts' until Drew arrives."

"If he arrives, I really have no idea how long he will be. I'll fetch my cloak." She turned away, hurrying, her heart thumping. Perhaps it was madness accepting the escort of Lord Brooke, a man she barely knew, yet he was Andrew's friend. Andrew trusted him, so surely she could.

Her cloak lay over one of her trunks in the bedchamber. She picked it up and turned to return to the sitting room, only to see Lord Brooke at the bedchamber door. "Let me," he said, entering and taking the cloak from her hands.

She turned so he might set it on her shoulders. But immediately after he'd done so, her hands lifted to secure the buttons, to ensure he would not. Her fingers shook though.

When she looked up he gave her a broad roguish grin. It reminded her of Andrew and made her heart lurch. *Where is he?* If only the thought would bring him home, but it would not, and waiting here would only make her more maudlin.

No. Better to go out and pretend all was well.

After all he'd left her here; so he could hardly complain about her going.

Lord Brooke offered his arm. She nervously laid her fingers on it. "Thank you, Lord Brooke."

"Peter, my dear, if we're to be friends; which I hope we are." He patted her hand.

She smiled, a little easier. "Call me, Mary, then, Peter." He was flirting, but it was not threatening.

Awkwardness hung over her during the carriage ride, alone with him in the confined space, but he kept her talking, as though he sensed her fear.

When they reached the Caldecotts', the carriage rocked as Lord Brooke's footman jumped from his post at the rear. The door opened.

Lord Brooke climbed out and lifted a hand to help her.

Her fingers shook furiously when they were announced to the receiving line, which was about to break up. Lady Caldecott's eyebrows lifted, an unspoken question burning in her eyes.

Mary ignored it, smiling. Just a few more yards and she would reach normality – her family.

Lord Brooke turned her to the room and began walking her in their direction.

She would have to quell her father's concerns first.

Why was everyone staring at them?

Mary focused on her father. He turned, saw her and frowned.

She let go of Lord Brooke's arm and took the last five or so steps alone. "Papa." She pre-empted the barrage of words in his eyes, "Andrew was not able to come; something urgent arose to detain him. Lord Brooke kindly offered to escort me so I could attend."

Mary looked back at Lord Brooke, her heart pounding. "Thank you, Peter, it is very kind of you to volunteer." He bowed graciously, and she hoped, ungraciously, he would go away.

She'd deliberately not said Andrew was unaware of the arrangement. Her father's eyebrows lifted, in criticism of Andrew for leaving her with Lord Brooke. But it was better Andrew was ill-judged for that, than for an ill-temper.

The orchestra struck up the tune of a waltz. Instantly Peter bowed at her side. "Mary, my dear, will you do me the honour?"

Nausea tumbled through Mary's stomach.

His gallantry was sweet. *But her father…* To refuse would look odd to everyone around them and she wished her father to think her comfortable with Lord Brooke.

"Thank you, Lord Brooke." She had not even said good-evening to her mother. It did not feel right.

His hand gripped hers and then his other laid on her back. Why must the dance be a waltz? It felt too intimate.

I want Andrew.

A painful emptiness ran through her.

* * *

At just past ten o'clock Drew ran up the stairs to his apartments. Late. He'd been walking off his irritation for hours. None of it was really Mary's fault. She was not responsible for the situation of his birth.

But at least now she'd probably dismissed the stupid idea of him apologizing to his family out of her head.

She had her own, she did not need his.

He'd not realised how late it was until he'd finally heard a church clock strike somewhere in bow. He'd walked miles.

Shame hitting him he'd turned around and rushed back. He'd left Mary alone... He'd promised to take her out... They'd be late.

The door was locked. Mary must have given up on him and gone to bed. Guilt grasping in his gut, he opened it. Damn, he hoped she had not left him? His heart pounded.

The chessboard had been set back on the table and put to rights, but it was broken and two used glasses stood with the decanters. One had been the one he had drunk from before leaving. The other... Something gripped in his gut like cold stone.

What? "Mary?"

He went into the bedchamber, she was not there but her things were.

But where the hell was she?

With her family.

Common-sense spoke the answer.

She'd have sent word to her father and they'd have called and collected her. She'd be at the ball. Drew would meet her there.

The smell of her perfume hovered in his rooms as he put on his evening dress. Arriving late was better than not arriving at all.

It took him little more than half an hour to dress and reach the Caldecotts'. The receiving line had broken up but the footman informed him that Lady Framlington was indeed in the ballroom.

Stiffening his spine and straightening his shoulders, preparing for the animosity from her family, Andrew stepped into the ballroom.

His gaze passed about the hall's glittering mirrors, chandeliers and people, society in full splendour, displaying its feathers like a peacock. Marlow and Pembroke were easy to spot, like him they were a head above most of the women and some of the men. He moved towards them without thought, drawn like metal to a loadstone. *Mary?* His spirit cried for her.

She was not with them though.

His gaze spun around the room skimming over the heads of those dancing, stopping at every dark one. He noticed the exact shade of ebony secured in a high knot by a silver comb that had lain on his dresser.

His feet stopped moving, weighted with lead, and his blood turned to ice.

She was waltzing with Peter! Her slender figure gripped in his hands. A red flood swamped Drew. *What the hell!* The glass in his room. Peter had been in his rooms, with Mary! And now here!

The thread she'd pulled loose, unravelled at a rate knots. He could see nothing but red. His teeth clenched and his hands balled into fists.

My best friend! Why my best friend?

He did not hear any music, nor the buzz of conversation. No one existed but the two of them.

She'd ripped his heart out!

He walked across the floor, through the dancers. People stumbled, moving out of the way and shouting at him. Then the music ceased and the couples broke apart.

Peter's hands fell and she stepped back smiling, her colour high and her eyes bright.

Drew's stride lengthened.

Mary looked his way, and opened her mouth to speak – she did not.

Peter turned too, at the moment Drew reached them.

Drew shoved the heel of his palm into Peter's chest. Peter stumbled back and Drew thrust a satisfying punch. The impact reverberated up his arm as it hit Peter's jawbone, knocking him off his feet.

A chorus of screams rang about Drew along with disapproving masculine tones.

Peter moved to rise. Drew struck his shoulder with his heel of his shoe. "You bastard!" The words echoed in the almost silent ballroom.

Mary's fingers gripped his arm. "Andrew stop! Please stop!"

Peter lay sprawled on the floor leaning on one elbow.

Drew was not done with this. "Leave my wife alone! Do you hear?"

Drew dropped to one knee, to throw another punch, but Peter caught his wrist.

"I was doing you a favour," Peter growled in a disgusted voice, his other hand lifting to wipe blood from his mouth.

"I don't care what you were doing! Don't touch her! I told you not to call on her. She's mine, do you understand?"

"Bloody hell, Drew! I only danced with her."

"Do you understand?"

"For God sake Drew, don't be ridiculous!"

Drew's vision flared red. He gripped Peter's cravat in his fist and twisted it as his knee came down on Peter's chest, and his other hand on Peter's shoulder.

"Enough! I say enough!" A yell rang behind Drew. Marlow. Someone gripped Drew's arm and pulled.

Drew's grip on Peter's cravat lifted Peter a little, then Drew shoved him back and let go.

"You've made fools out of both of us." Peter growled as Marlow dragged Drew up onto his feet.

The Duke of Wiltshire helped Peter up.

"More importantly you've embarrassed my daughter." Marlow, growled in Drew's ear in a low pitch. "What the hell is this, Framlington?"

Gripping Drew's arm, Marlow started walking him away from the scene. "The show is over," he growled at the crowd who watched them.

Drew yanked his arm from Marlow's grip.

"Have someone send for our carriage, Ellen."

Drew turned. Mary's mother had her arm about Mary's waist but Mary had not turned to her mother. She looked at him her skin so pale it was grey, and one hand rested over her stomach the other over her mouth as though she would be sick.

Hell and the devil. He'd done it now – she'd lost all feeling for him.

But she'd let another man escort her... and dance with her... Peter had been in Drew's rooms with her! Drew's whole being revolted at the thought.

"We are going, anyway." he said in a low voice, looking at Mary, denying Marlow's order.

She said nothing.

Drew did not apologize, not to Peter, nor to Marlow. He would not apologize for who he was! They could like him or not! He did not care!

He only cared for his friends... Damn!

But he still had Harry and Mark, didn't he? And if he did not, so what? He had Mary, she could not leave him.

He held his hand out to her, saying he wanted her.

Her hand slotted into his, in that perfect fit he'd become accustomed to.

A tight vice like pain clenched about his heart as in his head he saw Peter's hand on her back resting between her shoulders, and the empty brandy glass which stood on the side in his rooms.

Drew forced a path through the people, elbowing them out of his way if necessary and pulling Mary with him.

Reaching the hall, he growled at a footman to find her cloak, quickly.

He turned at the sound of a masculine stride behind them, echoing on the tiles.

Marlow, and his wife hurried behind them, Lady Marlow's dress was clasped in her hand lifted a little to enable it.

"Framlington!" Marlow's voice echoed about the stone trappings in the hall.

Mary's loyalty was to be tested again. Marlow was going to begin another tug of war.

"What the hell did you think you were doing? Do you know what people are saying now?" Marlow's strides ate up the distance between them.

"Let them say it!" Drew snarled. "What do I care?"

"I care!" Marlow growled, stopping three feet away from Drew, his gaze challenging. Then his voice dropped to a low threatening pitch. "And Mary cares. You will have her ostracised. You've hurt my daughter." The wind blew out from the sails of Marlow's anger as he looked at Mary.

Drew gripped her hand harder, this was it, another moment of choice, her family or him.

"Mary," Marlow's voice cut through the air between them soft and understanding, "come home with us, we should not have let this happen. Just come home now. This is enough. We can protect you from this—"

From this? From Drew!

"Let us weather this storm together. Ignore others' judgement,

Mary. You need not continue this…"

Drew's jaw locked hard.

Her hand gripped his more firmly. "No, Papa, I'll go home with Andrew. Do not worry. I'll call on you tomorrow. We can discuss things then. But not now."

The feeling that raced beneath his skin, through blood and bone and flesh, was relief, but it was hard and cold as ice. It was too late for her to cling to him now! She'd taken his heart and torn it in two, it was not beating anymore, not for her, not for anyone. He was stone inside.

Her father sighed.

"Mary." Her mother came forward at the same time a footman brought Mary's cloak. Her mother took it and set it on Mary's shoulders, while Drew kept a hold of her hand as if the girl was driftwood in a swelling sea. The pain in his chest ate at him. Excruciating. Unbearable. He could barely breathe as they turned to the door.

"Tomorrow," her father stated, as though he intended to persuade her to leave tomorrow.

Somehow Drew knew she would not. She would be like his mother, stay but be unfaithful. He could not be good-enough for her – he was worthless and unlovable. She would turn to other men, men who knew how to love her without running mad with jealousy. Men who knew how to cope amongst her family.

Men like Peter.

A cold shiver ran his spine as they walked the length of the street, until they found a handsome carriage waiting on the corner. Drew called up their destination to the driver and opened the door for Mary.

He did not speak as he climbed in.

Her hands rested in her lap.

He did not touch her. He did not think that he could ever bring himself to touch her again. It would only break his heart more when inevitably she let him down with someone else.

Chapter 26

The carriage rumbled and bounced over the uneven cobbled streets, the horses iron shoes ringing on the London stone, echoing in the silent air between them.

She had nothing to say to him, what could she say? He'd stormed out of their rooms hours before and then hit the Caldecotts' ballroom with the full force of a hurricane, now they were in the eye of the storm. He'd neither spoken nor moved.

Without moving her head, Mary glanced towards him, hoping he would not see. He sat in the far corner, the ankle of one leg resting on the other knee, his elbow on the shallow ledge of the small window and his forearm and fingers lying back against the window.

Rain began falling outside the carriage, striking the hide roof in a hard pitter-patter.

He still did not move a single muscle, just stared from the carriage, his eyes focusing on nothing.

He looked in turmoil, and pain, not simply angry.

She should never have made him go to that house. She should have listened to him. Now she understood his complexity; the hidden fragments were broken pieces. He'd said once, in the beginning, in a letter, the second, which had won her soul, her heart having been given to him a year before. *I cannot say I love you, not*

291

yet, I do not even know what on earth love is, but I do know that I cannot sleep for thinking of you, or dreaming of you. I think of you and I lose my breath, I see you and my heart begins to pound, I hear you and my spirit wants to sing. I am yours, Mary.

She'd read that letter again this afternoon, a dozen times, although his words had already been etched on her heart. But, oh, she understood it now, he had really not known love, because he'd never been loved. How could he know? How could he see that she gave it? Yet he had not written those words, his friends had written them.

But she believed the essence of those words were his. He did not know love.

She sighed, and his sharp gaze turned to her.

Mary looked out of the window, while his observation made her spine tingle. The first time she had met him, he'd carried a sense of mystery, holding dangerous secrets in his eyes. But the truth behind his secrets was pain, loneliness and longing. She saw through him now.

'Don't pity me, damn you!' His last words before he'd stormed out this afternoon, she did not want to pity him, she just wanted to love him and be loved in return. But the darkness outside the carriage window was endless and the silence between them was a wall she did not know how to scale. His pain was a fortress she had no idea how to conquer. She would simply have to wait until his defences fell again.

He said nothing as he walked behind her up to their rooms.

In their bedchamber she tried to undo her dress. He came to her and began releasing the buttons, but he still did not speak, and then when she slipped out of her chemise he walked from the room into the sitting room.

She heard him pour a drink as she slid her nightgown over her head.

Then she heard a glass shatter against the hearth.

She knew it was the one Peter had drunk from.

She climbed into bed, her stomach growling with hunger. She'd still not eaten but she was not hungry, and nor could she sleep. She lay facing the door, watching the candlelight flicker in the other room and listening to him walking about.

He came to bed an hour later and undressed in the dark. His weight made the mattress sag as he lay down. He did not speak or touch her.

When she woke the next morning, it was to the smell of fried bacon, fresh bread, coffee and chocolate.

Her stomach rumbled loudly and she felt physically sick with hunger as she slipped from beneath the covers and searched out her dressing gown. Andrew sat in an armchair, a broadsheet paper open before him. He'd already eaten.

"Good morning," she ventured.

Without looking up from the paper he answered, "I've ordered breakfast, luncheon and dinner, whether you or I are here or not, seeing as you'll not order for yourself. I am going to Tattersall's today to buy a carriage. I'll employ a driver at the stables. I'll buy another pair to pull it too. It will be yours, Mary, you can then go wherever you like, whenever you please."

"So I will have no need of an escort…"

"Quite so." His voice was deep and bitter. He was still angry. Still full of pain.

Mary sat down to cut a slice of bread. She had no idea how to respond, or what to do.

"I will also employ a lady's maid to come in the morning and evening, to help you dress."

"And to undress?" Mary's voice left her throat with quiet uncertainty. Was he saying he would have nothing more to do with her?

"She will await your return."

Did he not wish to touch her anymore? Did he not love her anymore? Mary stood again, her hand gripping the top of the chair. "It was just a waltz, Andrew. He only took me because you were not at home."

He stood too, but he did not look at her, he folded the paper and tossed it onto the table where the broken chessboard stood. "I'm going riding."

Mary hurried forward and gripped his arm. "Wait, I'll dress and come with you."

His hazel eyes were empty and cold – lacklustre. "That is not necessary."

"Not necessary or do you not want me to?"

"Both, Mary. I'll have your carriage by tomorrow, you may do what you like then, ride your brother's horses. Or Peter has some good ones, perhaps he'd oblige…"

"Do not be ridiculous. It was one waltz!"

His look narrowed. "We both know I am not good enough for you, so find someone else. It's what you'll do eventually anyway. I'm going out."

"Andrew, stop it." She followed him into their bedchamber. He did not stop but pulled on his long riding coat. "You cannot shut me out over one waltz!"

"It does not matter." He picked up his gloves. "That is not the issue."

She knew that. "The issue is your parents." Stepping back she opened her arms wide across the door frame so he could not leave her. "I'm not responsible for them."

His gaze met hers. His dark eyes desolate.

"Andrew." Her fingers touched the shadow of the bruise on his cheek.

"Let me go, Mary."

"To where?"

"*I'm going riding.* I'll come back at midday, take you to your parents and then go to Tat's to find you a carriage and horses."

Tears burned in Mary's eyes, but she refused to let him see. "You can be cruel!"

"You wished to be introduced to my parents! You accepted Peter's escort!"

294

"And they are sins?"

"It does not matter. Just let me go, and stop making a childish scene."

"As you did last night?"

"I will not argue with you. I do not care about it. Just get out of the way and let me go! I am only going riding!"

But it did not feel like that, it felt as if he was leaving, as though he'd left.

"Andrew?"

He merely stood, staring at her, his hat in his hand.

Mary's hands fell to her sides and she stepped out of the way. There was no point in arguing, he was unreachable in this mood.

* * *

When Drew returned from his ride it was to find Pembroke's carriage standing in the street before his apartment. Two grooms held the horses' heads at the front of four glossy blacks. The coach itself was a shining black beast of a thing with Pembroke's coat of arms emblazoned on the side, picked out in gilt, and a polished brass trim gleamed along its edges. *Devil take it.* What did Pembroke want? No doubt Drew was to be threatened again. If so his patience, currently paper thin, would rip, and he'd likely slam Pembroke up against a wall.

But when Drew reached his rooms it was only women's voices he heard.

He entered without knocking. They were his rooms.

Three women looked at him, Mary, her mother and an aunt, the Duchess of Wiltshire.

So Marlow had sent the women in to do battle again, they were surveying the ground. It was extremely early to be calling, perhaps they'd hoped to catch him out. Perhaps they thought he would not have unchained Mary by this hour. They were obviously seeking to know how well he kept her.

295

The remains of their breakfast was left on the table. Mary had at least eaten. He may be angry with her, he may wish to hold her at arms' length, so she could not hurt him, but he still cared for her. The girl would make herself ill if she did not eat.

Taking off his hat, he bowed to them, although not formally. He was family whether they liked it or not.

Her mother stood and stepped forward. "Lord Framlington, we are about to leave, we thought we might miss you. I'm glad you've arrived. We have asked Mary to accompany us to the Duchess of Bradford's garden party this afternoon."

Her aunt stood then. "We were passing, as I am visiting Margaret, so we thought it would be nice to call rather than send a message via the servants."

That was nonsense, Mary's cousin lived streets away and Drew's apartment was not on route.

"We had letters for Mary too," her mother concluded.

But most importantly you wished to spy.

Drew looked at Mary wondering what she'd told them. That he was an ignorant monster, probably; incapable of loving her and unable to be loved.

But he was not ashamed of his rooms. She did not have extravagance and excess here, but Mary had everything she needed. They could not fault him on that. Or rather she had all she needed if she would deem to take care of herself, which she did not.

He'd been angry when Joseph told him this morning she'd eaten neither luncheon nor dinner the day before. That was the moment he'd decided to take control of her life, although it also eased his conscience, employing servants to manage her meant he could withdraw without feeling guilt.

"Does my home meet your expectations, Lady Marlow?" He asked of her, ignoring her little speech.

"It is not my expectations you have to meet, is it, my Lord?" her answer was sharp and shrewish.

"No, it is Mary's, and she has everything she wants." *Except a man she can love.*

"Except a husband who can apply restraint, Lord Framlington."

"Mama!" Mary stood and came to stand beside him. As though he needed her to defend him. As though he cared. He did not care what her mother thought. But obviously Mary had not been honest with them, she'd not told them he was a hell-born bastard who no one could ever love.

"Your mother is right," her aunt looked at Mary, then at Drew, just the way he imagined she would look at a street-sweep, with disdain. "Your behaviour last night, Lord Framlington, was unforgivable."

Mary's chin lifted in defiance. Drew sighed, he did not wish her to argue with her family on his behalf anymore, the time for that had passed. She needed her family, *he did not need her,* he'd told himself that a hundred times already. "You're quite right, Your Grace, Lady Marlow. Obviously I'm sorry I spoiled the evening, but it is water under the bridge today and as you can see, I do not keep Mary in a prison cell or feed her gruel, you may report back that all is well here."

Both women stared, their matching eyes – the spit of Mary's – narrowing. Those pale blue eyes could be sharp as a pin prick.

"You are not amusing, Lord Framlington," her mother stated.

"Yes, I think you told me that before, Lady Marlow. I shall try to remember in future that you do not appreciate my humour." Mary's fingers gripped his arm.

"Mary, do you wish us to collect you?" her aunt asked.

"I can deliver her to where she needs to be." Her aunt's and mother's eyebrows rose. "But have no fear I'll not stay. I take it I am not invited—"

"I'll meet you there," Mary answered.

"Very well," her mother accepted, but she showed no sign of going.

Drew turned, "Mary, did you offer our visitors tea, I can call down," and then he looked back to her mother, "Or something stronger, perhaps a brandy to suffer my company a little longer."

"There is no need for spite, Lord Framlington." the Duchess of Wiltshire stated.

"My sentiments exactly."

Mary's fingers gripped his arm so tightly her fingernails began to bite through the fabric of his coat.

"Very well ladies, you clearly do not wish me here, and so I shall withdraw and leave you with Mary. I need to go out again anyway. Your servant." He bowed to one then the other, then turned away. Mary's fingers slipped from his arm uncertainly. He did not look back as he left.

He had not planned to go to Tats for a couple of hours though, and so in fact he had nothing to do, but he crossed back over to the stables and told the grooms to prepare the curricle for three hours' time. Then leaned against the wall and watched about the corner with his arms folded over his chest waiting for the women to leave.

But before they got back into Pembroke's grand carriage, the Duchess called over young Timmy and gave him a coin or two, dolling out her largesse.

Drew was lower than a street-sweep in her opinion then.

I don't care.

When the carriage pulled away he walked back across the street and knocked off Timmy's hat to make him laugh, passing a wry comment on the Duchess's gift.

Mary was seated in an armchair opening the letters her mother must have brought, there were half a dozen or more.

"Who are they from?" She jumped when he spoke, having not heard the door. Then stood. He held up a hand. "Read your letters, you do not have to tell me."

"They're from family, those who aren't in town. This…" She held up the letter she'd just opened, "is from my younger brother Robbie." Her face lit up as she said her brother's name.

It was impossible not to love her. But he had to stop, because he could not bear to watch her with another man, and the time would come. He knew it would.

When she sat back down, he crossed the room to collect the paper, but as he passed he looked over her shoulder.

I cannot believe you fixed on a man so suddenly, and Framlington, a man with a renowned reputation. Good heavens, what has become of my sister!

It was more condemnation.

Drew put his hat and gloves down on a chest, then took off his riding coat, and threw it over the back of a chair. Picking up the paper he dropped into the seat beside hers, only to realise Mary had stopped reading letters and was currently reading him.

He looked at her. She was extremely pretty in the dusky pink muslin she'd chosen today. It had embroidered rose buds at the hems.

"You did not have to be rude to my mother."

"She came here to spy."

"She came to see if I was well. Which I was, until yesterday."

Until she'd met his parents, and known him for who he really was, a worthless bastard. He would not wish to be married to himself. He shrugged and opened up the paper, deliberately covering his face.

"And now you hide from me."

Coward. "Persist and I will go out," he responded from behind the paper.

"Again?"

"If I wish to, yes. I can do as I please, Mary, as can you."

He heard her rise, and then the paper was crushed down before his eyes and she leaned down, her blue eyes sharp and flashing with fire like her mother's and her aunt's earlier. "So that is it. You do not love me anymore."

Oh, I love you, but I know you cannot love me. "No."

She rose up to full height, hands on hips, eyes flashing, his little fire cracker. *Not his, some other man's.* God it hurt to think it, but he had to think it.

"And if I love you?"

"You have no business doing so," he held her gaze, schooling his to be cold. He had to shut her out. "Your father and brother are right. I am a bastard, Mary. I'm sorry to disappoint you."

"And you discovered this yesterday?" God the woman could be clever when she wished.

"I discovered it last night."

"Because I let your friend who only the night before you told me I should trust, escort me to a ball in your stead and dance one dance with him! And that means you will not even pretend to love me."

He threw the paper aside standing as he did so. She took a step back. He wanted to hurt her as she'd hurt him. "I *was* only ever pretending, I see no point in keeping on. I will go out then, seeing as you are determined to pursue an argument."

He walked about her.

Coward. Bastard.

"You have a letter too, Joseph brought it up!"

As he turned back she threw the thing at him. Better paper than pottery.

Having donned his coat he bent and picked it up. It was from Caro, his younger sister's hasty handwriting formed his name in sharp strokes. It had no seal. Gripping it in one hand his other collected his hat and gloves and then he left.

In the street he stopped to read the letter. Kilbride had beaten her again, she'd lost his child, for the third time.

Drew was never sure which came first, the beatings or a child's loss.

He sighed.

He'd never been in a position to help her, but he could help her now and as he seemed unable to help himself it would be good for one of them to have a happy end.

He gave Timmy another ha'penny when he crossed the road

and told him to give it to his younger brother seeing as he'd had the Duchess's largesse.

Chapter 27

Two weeks later Drew wandered down an aisle in the House of Millard, a warehouse in Cheapside, which sold Bengal Muslins and flannels. His sister gripped his arm. Despite the obscurity of their meeting place she wore a fine gauze veil over her face. Although it could be to cover bruises.

Kilbride had banned her from maintaining bonds with her rakehell brother, but when she asked, they met, even if only for minutes.

He'd been her shoulder to cry on and an ear to listen since they'd been children. She was illegitimate too and had been excluded and ill-treated in their childhood; he'd comforted her then, as he did now.

The Marquis, the man whose name they'd been given, had sold Caro off to the highest bidder as soon as she'd reached six and ten, disposing of his second embarrassment.

None of their family acknowledged her in public, or even in private. She was ostracized like Drew.

But Caro was in a worse state, she had no friends. Kilbride forbade it.

But then Drew had no friends either, now; since he'd hit Peter none of them had been in contact.

And *Damn it*, the thing that cut most was the fact his family had seen him punch Peter. He hated the possibility that they knew how much they'd dislodged his self-control or rather his self-worth. That was what they'd wished. They'd succeeded. He had no wife to turn to now either.

Pain gripped tight around his heart. He'd been living with an invisible metal band wrapped about his chest since he'd punched Peter.

He leaned to his sister's ear. "I have found a house for you. You are leaving him."

"I cannot, Drew, you know I cannot."

Drew stopped and sucked in a breath, trying to dispel the tension in his chest. He could not let her stay with Kilbride, the man would kill her. "You can, Caro. The house is in Maidstone, it is not far from London. I'll visit you frequently. It's small, only a cottage, but I will employ a woman to manage it, cook and clean and such. You can be out of Kilbride's reach in hours."

"What if he finds me?"

"Why should he, he has no reason to go to Maidstone and you may change your name."

She gripped his arm as two women walked past them.

"Sorry you will not be able to take much—"

"I cannot, Drew."

His fingers lifted her chin. "Caro, if you do not I will call Kilbride out and then where will we be."

"With us both dead..." Her forehead tipped to his shoulder.

She was a tiny slender woman, fragile but not weak, he'd always admired her bravery she had never fought against her fate, merely coped. But they had both learned stamina and endurance as children.

He patted her shoulder. "How can I let you know the date?"

She lifted her head and he could see her smile through the gauze veil and a slight flinch as it touched a swelling on her lip. "I'll send word to you, when I can."

She glanced along the aisle as though she expected Kilbride to

303

appear. "I have to go. I need to get back."

He nodded once, took her hand and squeezed it gently.

"And your wife, Mary? I've not even asked how you are? How is she?"

"Miserable." A roguish grin caught at his lips, although it was not at all amusing. *You're not amusing, Lord Framlington.* No I am human wreckage, and I must either laugh or… He shrugged. "The poor girl married me and I am a bitter, twisted bastard. As you know."

She hugged him. "No. I know you are not." She pulled away. "Do not spoil what you have, make it good, Drew."

"Too late I'm afraid, I've ruined it. You were at the Caldecotts' so you know, you saw. How much worse can it get?"

"A lot worse, Drew. Do not lose her, she is from a good family, they are good people."

"Exactly why I can never fit with her."

"You should not have married her then," Caro whispered.

Women always saw the woman's side. But she was right, he knew that now.

"But it has paid my debts and it will allow me to help you. The deed is done. She'll find happiness some other way, without me."

"You're going to let her go?" Caro's brow furrowed.

He sighed, he'd thought about it, he'd sat up the last two nights thinking about it, but he could not do it, not yet, he'd not worked up the courage. He could not bear never to see her again. Not yet. He needed more time. More time to set her in his memory and keep her there, but evict her from his worthless heart. He forced a smile, giving Caro no answer.

"Drew, do not. She is good for you."

"No, Caro. Mary is bad for me, and I am very bad for her. She makes me lose control." *She makes me face who I am and hate myself. I care too much about what she thinks.*

"Have you apologised to Peter?"

"I have not seen Peter to be able to…"

"Are you avoiding him? Drew stop running. I am grateful that you're helping me but do not destroy your own life in return. I will never forgive you if you do."

He laughed. "You will simply have to join the crowd already calling for my blood then. Which is our own family, and now every kin of Mary's and my friends. Oh and let us not forget the whole of society who have always disliked me."

Her fingers touched the nearly faded bruise by his eye. "Bruises heal." *The outer ones.*

"You had better go, Caro. You are wasting time worrying over me, save your concern for yourself. Contact me as soon as you can and promise me you will not renege."

She nodded. "I promise," she said, quietly. He had waited years to hear those words – to hear her agree to flee that monster. Thank God he need no longer worry about her soon.

She smiled before pressing a kiss on his cheek, then she turned and left him.

Drew saw the two women in a far aisle looking. He didn't recognise them, their faces were covered by wide brimmed bonnets. But Caro's veil had been so heavy he doubted they could have recognised her.

Chapter 28

"Mary, show me where the stitches should go…" Jennifer leaned closer holding out her embroidery.

"She is reading me a story," Jemima complained.

"I can do both," Mary took the cloth and quickly pointed out the next stitches to Jennifer, then passed it back and recommenced the story, her fingers rubbing at her temple.

She had the headache. They had been a frequent complaint ever since Andrew had withdrawn from her.

He'd been true to his word she had a carriage, a driver and groom, a lady's maid who came in daily – and a husband who did not love her, and did not touch her, nor speak to her, nor even look at her.

He avoided her when he could, and when he could not he acted as though she was not in the room. If he spoke to her it was only to say, "I am going out."

So she now spent her days with her parents, living much as she'd done before they were wed, apart from the fact she returned to sleep in Drew's bed. He did not lay in it. He had been sleeping in a chair.

She would even change at her parents to join them at evening entertainments and then in the early hours of the morning they would drop her at Drew's door, and her father would walk her up to his rooms.

Sometimes when she got home Andrew would be there and sometimes not.

She had no idea what he did with his days, he never spoke.

She did, she shared a continual inane chatter as she called for the woman to help her undress. But then she would disappear into the room while the woman helped her, and when she climbed into bed there would be only silence.

She never spoke of Andrew to her family, and they never asked.

In the beginning when she'd called more frequently and gradually lengthened her stays she'd told her father that Andrew was busy finding a property for them. She did not actually know if he had even looked. Her father had not asked since. She thought he was simply content that Andrew was excluded. She was not.

Her heart was breaking and she did not know what to do.

She hung on to the cliff of her marriage by her fingernails, about to fall.

She'd been tired and listless for days as well as nauseous. She had barely eaten and she could not sleep. She longed for home, but neither here with her family, nor Andrew's rooms, felt like home anymore and so often when she was here she hid. Like now. A large group of her aunts, uncles and cousins had gathered downstairs, so Mary had come up to the nursery with some of the children.

"Mary."

She jumped, startled as her aunt Jane pressed a hand on her shoulder.

Jemima had fallen asleep and Mary had not even noticed, although she'd stopped reading... lost in thought.

"The others are still downstairs, don't worry, but there is something I need to tell you." Her aunt's green eyes were bright with concern. She bent and then lifted Jemima from Mary's lap. She looked to one of the nursery maids. "Please put Miss Jemima to bed." Then she looked at Jennifer and the other children who were there. "Why do you not go down, there is tea and cake being served..."

Jennifer smiled, and stood, leaving her embroidery on the sofa while the boys deserted a game of soldiers they'd been playing on the floor and ran out.

"Thank you for your help, Mary." Jennifer said before curtsying to their aunt. Then she left too.

A tingle of apprehension – wariness – ran through Mary; whatever her aunt wished to say, was clearly not for the ears of the children.

Jane moved the embroidery frame and took the seat Jennifer had vacated as the maids tidied up.

She said in a quiet voice, "I wish I did not have to tell you. I knew a few days ago but I have been warring with myself over whether or not to speak. Yet, you should know." She sighed, looking at a maid. "I would never forgive myself if you hear it from someone else." She looked back at Mary. "But let us go out into the garden, to the summerhouse, to talk."

Mary's hands shook as she rose. She swiped them over her dress to hide it, pretending to clear the creases. It could not be good news, and Mary guessed it was about Andrew.

Butterflies took flight in her stomach, a million of them.

Her aunt kept looking back as Mary followed her through the house.

Mary wished she could just disappear.

When they stepped out on to the terrace, the sunshine touched her face.

Jane slipped her arm about Mary's and led her down the steps and on through the arbour.

Mary had a painful memory of walking with Andrew here, and when they reached the summerhouse the pain constricted like a vice about Mary's heart.

She had stopped believing Andrew would come about and like her again, days ago. He would not. He'd shut her out. He had not loved her. What had happened here and after – had been lies.

Jane drew her to a cushioned seat beside the one on which she'd first lain with Andrew, and let him truly touch her.

Jane took one of Mary's hands in both of hers and held it on her lap as Mary focused on the current time, on the truth, and met Jane's emerald gaze. "Mary, there is no easy way to tell you this, but…"

Just tell me. Please tell me? How worse can things be?

"A friend of mine, a good friend, Violet, Lady Sparks, who you know and would trust as well as I, saw Lord Framlington last week. He was with a young woman who was veiled. Violet said they were whispering and they looked… affectionate… Violet is no gossip, you know that, she only told me because she felt you should know. We have told no one else, not even Robert because he would tell your father.

"Violet was with her sister-in-law but she believed her sister-in-law was out of town when the announcement of your marriage was published. She saw Lord Framlington but did not appear to make any connection to you and of course you are never seen together. If Violet is right, this woman is—"

Mary lifted her head. She'd listened in silence, numb… She'd thought the distance between them was her fault because she'd insisted he visit his parents, because she'd accepted Lord Brooke's kindness. *But there is someone else.* "A mistress…" she said on a pain-filled breath.

Jane squeezed her hand and went on. "If this woman is his mistress, and they were in a draper's, Mary, so it is very likely that she is, then the story will break at some point, there are too many people in society who hold a grievance with Lord Framlington, they will dine on the news.

Mary, wanted to press her palms over her ears. But she could not hide.

Tears gathered in her eyes, clouding her view of the garden. "Funded by my dowry…"

He'd said he could not afford a mistress before.

He'd loved her for less than one month.

"It's up to you what you do, of course it is, and there's no definite evidence she is his mistress. But perhaps your father, or Robert, or John, would have him followed? If you wait too long then the rumours may begin and if they do it will be far worse for you, I know."

Mary met her aunt's gaze. "You think I should leave him."

"It is your choice. But you are not happy with him. We can all see it. You barely spend an hour at his rooms. Your home is here. There is no shame in it, Mary. The family will protect you, the whole family. You may sue for divorce, you will have grounds."

But it was not that easy, not now.

"I need to think. Do not tell anyone, please."

Jane gave her a warm sympathetic smile.

'*Don't pity me!*' Andrew had yelled.

Why, because she ought to pity herself? Her entire family did. Everyone looked at her with grief in their eyes.

"Aunt Jane, would you take me home." *Home?* Had she been that silly girl who laid down with him here?

"Will he be there?"

"I doubt it." At least now she knew where he went.

"Will you pack today?" Jane urged.

Mary lifted her gaze, which had fallen to their joined hands. "I need to think. I don't know what to do. What do I do when I love him, but he does not love me?"

"Oh, my dear." Jane held her, and Mary longed for the tears which had clouded her vision earlier to fall, but now they would not come. There was too much pain.

"I was not at all sure of your uncle's love when we met again after years of separation, I'd lost him when I was very young. But fate will always run its course. Someone will love you as you deserve, Mary. The right man will come along."

Mary, let go of her aunt. "But I love Andrew. I do not want anyone else."

"Oh, sweetheart, come, I will take you home. Do you wish me to tell everyone you're unwell."

"No, I will say goodbye, Mama will know something is wrong if I do not."

When they arrived at Andrew's rooms an hour later, he was not there, and the luncheon he'd had delivered for her stood on the table uneaten.

Jane had insisted on coming up with her, probably to ensure Mary was safe, proving again how much her family feared for her.

Jane looked about the sitting room. "Your mother told me he joked that he keeps you locked up."

"He likes to annoy Mama and Papa."

Jane sighed. "Would you like me to stay with you awhile?"

"He really does not chain me up, Aunt Jane." Mary laughed at the foolishness of it, although it was a dry sad sound.

Jane did not laugh.

"But nor does he make you smile..." Her aunt noticed the broken chessboard and her gaze stayed on it.

"If you must know, if you promise to say nothing to anyone else, things were good between us until the day of the Caldecotts' ball. I insisted he take me to meet his parents. He did not wish to go, he said they would not want to see him, or me, but I persuaded him to take me. He was right of course, he knows his own family.

"When we returned he went into a rage. I think it humiliated him to be turned away in front of me. That is when he broke the chessboard. He knocked the table over, just in case you think he threw it at me; he did not.

"He went out then, and did not come back in time to escort me, but his friend, Lord Brooke called and offered to take me. That too was a nail in my coffin.

"I have not been forgiven for allowing Lord Brooke to escort me. Andrew is polite. He is not ill-treating me. He's paid for a lady's maid and a carriage since then. He has meals sent up, even though I am not here to eat. But he does not share the bed with me. He will not touch me, and he does not speak to me, or spend time with me..." Her words dried, as pain cut deep, but she forced them out.

"And now there is another woman, and I suppose it never really was fine at all, and Papa and John were always right, and I was just another silly young woman, with my head in the clouds." Mary crumpled into a chair, her head pressed into her hands, the headache throbbing in her temples.

She'd forced herself to smile through the false goodbyes.

She could not smile anymore.

Her aunt rubbed her shoulder. "Oh Mary, we all so wanted a happy-ever-after for you. My first marriage was not a good one; it was arranged and I had no family to fall back on, I could only endure it. You do not have to. Do not spend your life tied up in a mistake. Walk away, with your head high. You can come and live with Robert and I in Yorkshire; if you wish to escape. He would not mind at all, you know he would not."

"What is this?"

Mary stood, she had not heard Andrew open the door.

"A witches' coven… But there are only two of you. You need three to turn me into a toad." He pulled his gloves off. "I presume, *I* am the mistake." His dark gaze penetrated her as he gripped his gloves in a fisted hand. "Are you leaving me then?" Anger and accusation made his pitch heavy. "Did you realise you had not quite shut the door. Were you intending to tell the whole building you're leaving me before you do?"

"Lord Framlington." Her aunt stood, going into battle.

Mary did not move. She hurt too much. Let him rant, he'd already found another woman.

"If Mary leaves, it is because you are selfish and heartless."

His lips twisted and his hand gripped his gloves tighter. He wanted to argue. She recognised the signs of his growing anger. If she let this go on it was not going to be short.

"My niece is loved by her family! We will not let her suffer like this!"

Andrew's gaze turned to Mary, and the fight seemed to suddenly drop out of him.

Mary stood. This was enough, her head hurt too much to listen to them argue.

"I know—" her aunt began.

Mary gripped her arm. If anyone confronted him about his mistress it would be her. "Aunt Jane, thank you for bringing me home. I will speak to you tomorrow."

Jane's green eyes were alight. "If you are sure?"

"I am." Mary's voice held little conviction, she was too tired. All she needed now was sleep, her head hurt so much.

Jane hugged her, and kissed her cheek, then left without another word to Andrew.

"Good-day Lady Barrington, it was good of you to call and beg my wife to leave me!" He said before the door shut in her wake.

"So are you?" Andrew turned to her once the door had shut.

"I hate you, when you're like this." Mary turned away and sought peace and silence in their bedchamber.

"You are then... you're leaving me!" He followed her.

"You seem very keen. I suppose this is what you hoped for?" Her speech slurred a little as her vision became a screen of shifting zigzag patterns. Her hand clasped the doorframe. She'd not had the headache like this for years, not since she'd been a child.

"Hoped for?"

"You have pushed me away from the moment we wed." Her vision was so confused now she could see nothing beyond a muddle of shifting colours.

Her arm stretched out, searching for the bedpost as she crossed the room, nausea rolling over in her stomach, and heat racing over her skin. If she could just reach the bed and lie down.

"So they still think I was only after your money. I suppose that is what she said."

"Were you not, then?" Anger and bitterness burned her throat.

313

He had another woman! Her fingers touched the bedpost. Then the floor tilted suddenly and the colours faded to black as a hot sweat raked over her skin, and she went down heavily, falling into the darkness.

She must have fainted. He was lifting her on to the bed. "I do not feel well." Mary gripped his arm as the colours danced before her eyes. "Andrew, I am going to be sick."

The mattress was a soft comfort, and then she heard him place the chamber pot on the chest beside the bed, but she could not see it to reach for it.

"I cannot see!" The desperate sob escaped her lips.

The chamber pot was pressed into her hands.

She was horribly sick, before a man who did not love her and did not care about her, who did not even like her. She could not be more humiliated. Could one cry and vomit all at once. Yes.

He gave her a towel. She wiped her mouth, holding on to it as he moved the chamber pot.

She lay down and shut her eyes, longing for sleep, for escape from the pain.

Tears rolled onto her cheeks. She sniffed, pressing the towel to her nose and her mouth, and curled her knees up, wrapping herself up small. Papa had always said she slept like a dormouse when she'd been a child.

Andrew's weight dipped the mattress beside her.

"What is it? Do you need me to fetch a doctor?"

"I would not worry, you never know, you may kill me off and be rid of me more easily." Cruel, instinctive defence sliced through her pitch. She hated him – *and loved him.*

"Mary?"

But being angry would only make the headache worse – and her like him. She refused to be bitter like him. "I'm sorry. You need not worry. Thank you for helping me, but you can leave me now, I just need to sleep. It is only the headache. I always seem to have one now. Please leave me alone."

"Let me call for a doctor." His palm pressed to her forehead. It was the most intimate contact she'd had with him for weeks.

More tears spilled over.

"You feel hot."

"I just need to sleep. I do not want a doctor. Please leave me alone now."

He got up, and the sound of his footsteps walked a path from the room.

Tears ran in streams down her cheeks as she cried audibly and rolled over so she lay on his side of the bed. His scent rose from the pillow.

Then he was there again, his hand on her shoulder. "I really do not think I ought to leave you like this, sweetheart."

Oh lord, I hurt, I hurt so much. "Don't call me, sweetheart, please do not. Please leave me alone." Mary covered her ears. She could not bear to hear soft words from him now she knew for certain they were false.

But the nausea rose up again and, clutching at his wrist, she groaned, "I am going to be ill again."

A clean chamber pot was placed before her and Mary retched painfully, while his hand stroked her shoulder and he whispered kind words, caring words. *Lies all lies!*

"I'll not go out tonight, I cannot leave you like this," he stated when she'd stopped retching, and he'd set the chamber pot aside.

She did not argue anymore, it felt as though a farrier was banging out a horseshoe on an anvil in her head and she was too weak, too tired to fight with him.

But then he began releasing the buttons of her dress.

"Leave me alone!" She could not bear his touch.

"Mary, darling, just lie still, if I undress you, and loosen your stays, you will be more comfortable and the maid cannot do it, she is not due for hours. You'll sleep easier if I do."

She cried, pitifully, as he worked the buttons free and then pulled loose the lacing of her stays. Then his hands slid beneath

315

the fabric and he stripped her garments off.

Her stomach clenched at the intimacy, her body remembered his touch. She would not know it ever again. Misery hollowed out her soul.

He bid her lift her hips and slid her dress from beneath her, before drawing off her stays. When she was clothed in only her chemise, he drew the covers out from under her then tucked her beneath them.

But he didn't leave her then. He sat beside her on the bed, and pulled her head on to his thigh while his fingers took the pins out of her hair.

Her headache began to ease, but her heartache did not, and tears ran from her eyes onto his leg.

She wept for everything she'd hoped for as a child and lost.

* * *

Drew left Mary in the bedchamber to sleep and walked into the sitting room, leaving the door ajar in case she was ill once more. He leaned on a cabinet on which the decanter stood; his head bowed and his heart a heavy lump of cold marble.

He'd hurt her and he sensed he'd hurt her irrevocably.

She'd been stalwart, ignoring his disengagement, simply spending less and less time at home to avoid him.

Although it was not her avoiding him was it? He'd started this, deliberately shutting her out. She was simply surviving it, as Caro survived her husband's violence.

She is going to leave… He'd succeeded, he'd pushed her away completely. Or certainly her aunt had been urging her to leave.

I cannot bear for her to go.

Standing straight his fingers gripped his nape and his head tipped back.

It hurt too much, and if it hurt for him, how much was it hurting her.

He had a feeling her illness today was his fault.

She was not normally home at this hour.

He thought she would have stayed with her parents as she felt ill. The fact she did not implied she had sought to escape their urging.

This game of tug-of-war with her family was tearing her apart.

She'd told him half a dozen times, "leave me alone", and told him not to call her sweetheart.

Ah God.

All he'd done by shutting her out was to convince her he'd *never* loved her. Of course she believed it; he'd treated her horribly over the last weeks. Even told her he had lied about his love. He'd deliberately been the evil bastard people thought him.

Because that is who I am and she would see it in the end anyway. She will go now or she will go later. All he'd done was bring forward the inevitable.

But, *Devil take it. I cannot lose her. I cannot let her go. I will not! I'll make her stay.*

When the maid arrived at six, Andrew sent her away and ate his dinner alone, quietly, so he did not wake Mary. Afterwards he settled into a chair with the bottle of red wine that had been sent up with dinner, beside the broken chessboard.

He picked up a pawn and toyed with it in his fingers. Then leant back and wondered what the hell he'd done with his life before he'd known Mary. But of course, he'd had friends then.

Now he sauntered his way about gambling dens alone, not gambling because he refused to waste Mary's money but he did waste hours until he knew Mary would be in bed.

He'd been wasting the time he could have spent with her.

"Drew, stop running," Caro had said. She had need to run. What the hell was he running from – the chance of a perfect life.

The deeds to Caro's cottage would be signed over to him in a week and then he planned to move her. She would be free, but he doubted she would be happy.

And himself? "Do not spoil what you have, make it good, Drew."

Was he capable of making it good? It was probably already too late.

She'll find happiness some other way, without me.

Yet he was not so sure she would anymore.

She was deeply distressed, not happy, and he was a heartless bastard, who'd stolen happiness and contentment from her, and brought her into his world of misery.

Heaven to hell, he'd said to her once.

What am I doing? Neither of us are happy.

Perhaps it was not too late to make it work? To try.

He could not lose her. He was not willing to let her go.

He would try.

He drank the wine in his glass setting down the pawn on the broken chessboard one place forward, just as a knock struck the door.

What were the odds it was Marlow or Pembroke prepared to call him out? He stood, a malicious grin on his lips.

But it was the other man who had good reason to call him out. "Peter."

Peter's eyebrows lifted. "Are you going to ask me in, or am I no longer welcome?"

"You may come in," Drew stepped back, holding the door.

"But am I welcome?" Peter's hands slipped into his pockets as he walked in.

Drew did not answer, he was unsure how he felt. "Would you like some wine, or brandy?"

Peter sighed. "Brandy. I need it. I thought you'd send me an apology but you are clearly too pig-headed to send it, so I have come here to have it from your lips."

Drew turned with a full glass in either hand. Peter stood beside him. He took one, meeting Drew's gaze.

Peter had been Drew's best friend since school, but the image of Peter's gloved fingers resting on Mary's back hovered in Drew's head. Even now the thought made him nauseous.

Peter's eyebrows lifted, as though he read Drew's thoughts. "It was a waltz. Before three hundred or more people. It meant no insult. None ought to have been taken." His free hand rubbed his jaw. "Remind me to keep you off my face at Jackson's, your right hook is a demon. I prefer you on my side as you were at school. So does it warrant an apology or am I still to be cut."

"I am hardly cutting you, I poured you a drink." Drew moved away and dropped into a seat.

"But you are still angry with me…" Peter sat down too. "As I thought; seeing as you've not been near the club. Harry and Mark blame me. They think I broke some unwritten law they've invented about touching each other's wives. I personally think if we are to stay friends when, and if we settle, we ought to make friends of our friends' wives, which is what I'd intended. Clearly you think her beneath my friendship."

"Hardly that," Drew's gaze lifted to meet Peter's then fell back to his glass.

"You could have said you were marrying for love of the girl, as much as money. We would not have judged you for it." Drew met Peter's penetrating gaze.

It was a bloody joke, a rake of his reputation falling head over heels for a debutante. But that was just the thing, his reputation had never really been earned and Peter knew it.

Peter sighed and leaned forward, drinking some of his brandy, then resting his elbows on his knees.

He looked at Drew.

"Drew, seriously, you are my friend. I would do nothing to take her from you. She was anxious, pacing about the room. I merely offered to escort her to a ball to meet her family. It was no more than that."

"So she said."

"But you did not believe her?"

"Of course I believed her. It was just a bad day. I did not have a clear head. You became caught up in it. I'm sorry I hit you."

"Ah, at last, the apology." His friend lifted his glass in the form of a toast. "So we are still friends then. And your wife?"

Drew lifted his hand and let it slide across his face, then grimaced. "Hates me... She's asleep in there." His hand indicated the bedchamber.

"I've seen her a lot about town. With her family," Peter added pointedly. "And before you ask, or think it, I've not spoken to her. I was looking for you. Your absence has been noted you know. Society thinks your marriage already on the rocks."

"It's no one's business."

"I am merely saying what I've heard. It's not my opinion. I only came tonight because I thought she'd be out and hoped you'd be here, seeing as I have not seen you anywhere else."

"Mary's unwell. That is the only reason she is here."

"Unwell? And you? Where have you been?"

A bitter sound of amusement broke from Drew's throat. "Here, there and nowhere, and tonight I am here because my conscience has kicked. She is leaving me, I think. I overheard her aunt persuading her to go."

"You will let that happen... Have you been spending any time with her? Or have you been hanging on to this damned grudge against the both of us, for dancing one dance. I know how stubborn you are."

Drew's hand ran through his hair, then fell. "It is not that."

Peter drank his brandy, then stood and walked over to collect the decanter. He brought it back and filled Drew's glass then his own. "You love the woman, does she not know?"

"She does not believe it. I have a certain reputation you see..." Drew lifted his glass in a salute and gave Peter a wry grin.

"And you have a certain temper, and a streak of pig-headedness as strong as iron." Peter set his drink down and then caught Drew out; leaning a hand on either arm of the chair Drew sat in, his face hovered before Drew's. "What do you think of Kilbride?"

"What?" Drew looked into his friend's dark brown eyes with bewilderment.

"Do you agree with the way he treats Caro?"

"Of course not. You know I do not."

"Then what the hell are you doing?

"What?" Drew had no idea what Peter was speaking of.

"How frequently have you spoken to your wife since the night you caused that fracas?"

Drew did not answer.

"Have you taken her out once? No one has seen you together since then, yet she has been out."

Drew took a breath, but he was not explaining to Peter how unlovable he felt himself.

Peter pushed off the chair with a growl, and straightened, then stood staring down at Drew. "You said she is unwell, could that not be due to your silence and your distance?"

It was no more than he had feared himself… But his conscience kicked too hard for him to admit it. "She has her family."

"While enduring your iron will, and your will when it is against a person is not a pleasant thing, Drew. You more than most should know how painful silence and being disregarded are. As painful as violence, perhaps… I have watched it create and change who you are. Do you think me blind? You have hidden who you are within, but I know."

Drew would have stood, but Peter leaned and gripped his shoulder to push him back. "Have no fear, I have no desire to fight with you again. I am not touching the subject you hate. But I wish you to know, that I know. I have seen the impact of such bitterness on you. Do not emulate what happened to you and destroy what you have with this girl… She is in love with you too. It screamed from her the night I came here. She was afraid for you. Making excuses for you, when I presume you had charged off in some rage…" Peter lifted an eyebrow.

Drew did not deny it. It was true.

Did she love him?

I hate you, when you're like this. I suppose this is what you hoped for? You have pushed me away from the moment we wed. We will not let her suffer like this. Everything Peter said was endorsed by the words Mary and her aunt had thrown at him earlier.

"I know." Drew replied simply, "I have become very aware of the mess I have made of things today. Mary made it clear – I was sitting here digesting it when you arrived." Drew looked up at his friend. The person who had been his sole supporter for many years of his life.

Silence was equal to violence… had he been that dreadful a husband…

Peter emptied his glass, his adam's apple shifting as he drank.

Drew drank down his brandy too. Its fiery heat burnt his throat in a satisfying penance. Peter reached for the decanter and filled his and Drew's glass again.

He set the decanter down beside the broken chessboard and retook his seat. "Anyway, I have said my piece, but just beware, if you have treated her with distrust and pushed her away, I am not surprised the girl is thinking of deserting you."

Drew smiled at his friend, his lips stiff, accepting the advice for what it was… "and yet you have never deserted me…"

They both laughed, because they both knew there had been numerous times when Drew's anger and stubbornness had tested their friendship.

But then Drew's mind turned to his sister. She knew the truth of rough handling.

"I've seen Caro too," Peter said.

Obviously the link with Caro was clear to Peter too. There was desirable roughness that women enjoyed in a bed, and then there was cruel brutality. The second his sister had in droves.

"I've bought a house for her. I'm moving her in there next week. But say nothing, I cannot risk it getting out. At least some good has come of my marriage, Mary's money has let me do it. Whether Mary stays or not I'll have Caro settled."

322

Male laughter rang from the sitting room as Mary opened her eyes and sat up. The bedchamber was dark but a line of light spilled in through a crack where the door had been left ajar.

The pain in her head had eased, but her limbs were shaky.

The laughter died.

"I've seen Caro too."

Lord Brooke. Andrew must have reconciled with his friend at some point.

"I've bought a house for her. I'm moving her in there next week. But say nothing, I cannot risk it getting out…" *It's true. He has a mistress.* "At least some good has come of my marriage, Mary's money has let me do it. Whether Mary stays or not I'll have Caro settled." Nausea gripped at Mary's empty stomach, but her heart was empty and sick too.

She lay back down and pulled the covers over her shoulder. She did not cry, the well of her sorrow was dry. She could not continue crying for him. She *would* leave. She could not stay. Tomorrow when he went out to ride she'd go, and then it would be over.

The men's voices continued in more bland conversation on clubs and horses, and eventually the sound lulled her back to sleep.

* * *

"Goodnight."

"Goodnight; your wife will come about. You should simply let her see how you feel for her, and do not ignore her, and hold your temper and there you have it."

Drew smiled. "Goodnight."

"May Cupid be with you, my friend." Peter turned away and walked along the hall. Drew shut the door. His hand stayed on the handle and his forehead pressed against the wood.

He thought of the day her father had found them in the inn.

Of lying awake and watching Mary the night before her father had come. That had been how it ought to be, the two of them. Wholly and entirely together. Melded. She had been made for him, he was still the first few footprints in her snow…

He thought of Caro, lying in the snow as a child making snow angels and making him laugh.

Instead of fighting with Mary's family, and trying to pull her away from her family, to keep her to himself, he and Mary should have been lying in the bloody crisp fresh snow of their life and making damned snow angels, completely claiming the ground.

But it was the wrong time of year for snow… Hay then, they ought to be in fields crushing the damned hay.

He smiled, a twisted smile. Solely for himself.

He would repair this. He would make it right. He would try harder. He would be what she needed, who she needed… if it damned well killed him.

She would have to show him how to be that man, but she was capable of that.

He let go of the door handle and turned to the bedroom. The first thing to do was share her bed again.

He sighed out his breath, then began unbuttoning his evening coat. He did not go into the room. He slipped it off and draped it over the back of a chair, then undressed until he only wore his shirt. He walked about the room quietly snuffing out the candles. The last one, he picked up and carried into their bedchamber. She was facing toward the door, on the side of the bed he had always slept until she had come into his life.

She had taken it over – his bed, his life. His body. His mind. His heart.

He'd made mistakes. He was going to correct them…

He would ensure she knew how he felt every day of her life from this day forward. He turned the sheet back, put the candle down on the chest beside the bed and then slipped beneath the covers beside her.

His heart ached. Terribly. It hurt as much as when Marlow had first broken his rib. No. It was even more aggressive than physical pain.

Her dark hair spilled across his pillows and the sheet, not plaited.

He turned and blew out the candle, wrapping them in darkness.

His fingers reached out and touched her hair, he let it run through his hand a couple of times, as he listened to her breathing. Then he moved closer to her, and rested a palm on her hip.

It had been far too long since he had loved her physically. He'd pretended he did not love her with his heart, because of the pain he was in now, and yet if she left him, he would be in even greater pain. He did not wish her to leave. In the morning he would show himself to her – naked in body and heart and soul, as she had shown him how to be, and he had rejected, because the idea scared him to death... It still did, but losing her scared him more.

He wished her to be happy; to be able to rely on him. He had been so insistent that she only rely on him before... but that had been about fear... possessiveness had torn him apart. Now things would be different. She knew who he was, exactly who he was, she had seen all his faults. If she loved him, if he could win her back, then, there could be no weakness, he need not fear, just love. He would just love her.

He fell asleep thinking of hay fields, and snow, and Mary, and what they would do in them when they found a property for themselves.

Chapter 29

When Mary woke in the early light of dawn, it was as if she was dreaming. She had dreamt of this so many times.

Andrew lay flush against her back, and his hands were beneath her chemise, splayed across her stomach and kneading her breast as his erection rubbed against her bottom in shallow stokes.

She was aroused. He'd aroused her body while she'd slept. The short and shallow rhythm of her breaths filled the room, and her skin burned hot, she glowed under his spell. She had missed this so much. This had always worked between them, and like this she could believe he loved her.

Desire swelled in the place between her legs as she let it continue, half awake, and half in a blissful dream.

His hand slid down across her stomach.

A moan slipped from her throat. She'd longed to feel adored, to feel wanted and treasured again, and yet the moan was part bitter pain.

He does not love me.

His teeth nipped at her neck as he drew her bottom more firmly back against him. His erection pressing between her buttocks.

"I love you," he whispered against her neck. "I'm sorry. I have been a fool. Let me show you, that I love you again. Let me prove that I can be the man you need. I want to be inside you again.

I've missed you, sweetheart. Oh God, I've missed you."

Lies, all lies.

Mary shut her eyes. She should tell him to stop, but she could not. The need inside her burned to know his love making just one last time before she left. She would never experience this again.

I love him even if he does not love me.

She could claim this moment from him – let him give and just take. What harm in that? The harm was already done.

She'd never love another man. This was her last chance to feel like this.

What harm in grasping one last memory, even if it was a lie, it would be precious to her.

His fingers slipped between her legs and into her. He must know she was aroused, she was soaking wet for him.

She let him roll her to her back and he stripped off his shirt then took off her chemise. The smell of last night's brandy carried on his breath, and his own personal musky cologne hung in the air. Lust spiralled in her abdomen with a tight longing and her arms slid above her head as he kissed a path down between her breasts and across her stomach. She shut her eyes tight, she did not want to see his face, or his eyes, and know the lies they carried.

He took his pleasure caressing the place between her thighs with his tongue and teeth, and she came for him, the little death swirling over her, shattering into bright lights and spinning pieces. Her arms fell and her fingers gripped his soft hair.

She absorbed every sense and sound to preserve it to memory, for all the years she would be alone.

When he opened her legs with his, and slid into her, the moan that came from her throat was half sob.

He withdrew and pressed back in, coupling with her in an enchanting intimate dance.

"Open your eyes for me, Mary, darling." His whisper brushed her cheek.

She swallowed back the urge to cry and did – looking at the

dark amber and honey shades in his eyes – one last time.

She could not see lies there. She saw love, as he withdrew from her and gently slid back in, weaving an excruciating bliss into her blood.

"I love you," he whispered, withdrawing and re-entering.

You do not!

"God Mary, I am such a fool. Can you forgive me? I will be a better a man, I swear it to you. No more games. We will work things out between us."

Mary shut her eyes. She could not bear looking at the lies in his anymore.

Blissful sensations danced beneath her skin.

They made her forget his deceit and betrayal.

For this moment, suspended in time, she let him love her and believed – and expressed her love for him.

Her desire reached a fever pitch and she gripped his shoulders as release washed through her errant senses and her inner muscle clenched and gripped at his invasion.

Beneath her fingers his muscle locked hard and a deep long sound of relief ripped from his throat as his body trembled between her thighs.

His forehead fell to her shoulder for a moment, and his weight settled more heavily on her hips and her stomach.

She dropped from hot sunshine into a cold icy sea.

It was over. She would never know this again.

He withdrew and tumbled on to his back, pulling her with him, holding her close.

Her head fell on his chest, in the position she had once thought heaven.

"I know I've hurt you," his voice rumbled in his chest, as his hand ran over her hair. "I'm sorry, Mary. It will not happen again. I cannot lose you, sweetheart. I promise I shall be different now."

Ah, so that was the reason for these new lies. He fought to make her stay. A public separation and divorce would embarrass him.

She no longer cared. She'd go back to her parents' estate to hide and lick her wounds and never come back to London.

But for now… she clung to him her fingers gripping at his bare chest, as his fingers stroked through her hair, and she pretended to her heart that he did love her back.

He whispered false promises of love, of finding a home for them and settling down somewhere quiet in the country.

She did not even think he noticed that she'd not said a word.

But when he rolled her to her back and leaned over her as though he would make love again, she knew the time had come to stop dreaming and face what was real.

"I'm hungry, Andrew. I need to eat."

He smiled. His caring smile – not the roguish one. "I am being selfish, keeping you in bed. See, I have a lot to learn. But I shall learn, Mary. I'll get your breakfast. Stay here."

He got up, gloriously naked, his body so beautiful, and plumped the pillows making her sit upright, before setting them at her back. Then he disappeared and came back with a plate of buttered bread and sliced ham, as well as a cup of chocolate.

"Did you wish to ride with me today?" he asked, when he returned with a full plate for himself and sat at the end of the bed, one knee raised so he faced her.

She shook her head.

He looked so normal, so casual, as though he'd never told a lie in his life.

"No, thank you. You go. Milly will help me dress while you are gone." *And help me leave.*

"Would you rather I stayed here?"

"No." He had to go out, because she had to leave, if she did not she might begin believing his lies again.

He set down his plate, leant forward and brushed a finger down her cheek. "I will make you happy, sweetheart. I'll dress and go riding. I will be back all the sooner then, and then you and I will call on your family and tell them all to go to hell with their good

329

advice. We're not separating."

A sharp pain pierced her breast, but she did not speak.

When he left half-an-hour later she got up as soon as the door shut, dressing herself without stays, and when the maid arrived she sent her to bring a groom from the stables at Pembroke House to bring a cart to take her trunks. There was hardly anything to pack. Everything was still in the trunks and boxes anyway.

The maid carried down Mary's writing desk and mirror and the four grooms who had arrived lifted her trunks out to the cart. In less than an half an hour the cart had been loaded.

She looked at Andrew's rooms, and the bed, one last time, and the note she had left balanced between the chess pieces on the broken board. She had said very little beyond goodbye.

Chapter 30

Smiling at Timmy, Drew handed the boy an iced bun he'd bought at the bakers, instead of a coin, and the young street-sweep grinned his thanks.

The sun seemed brighter today, the sky bluer and the grass greener, and Drew was hopelessly in love with his wife.

Loving her this morning had been divine.

He was a new man, a man who would love her as she deserved. As she loved him.

She did. Still. It had been in her eyes this morning when she'd opened them and looked at him, he'd seen her breaking heart.

But she'd forgiven him. They'd made heavenly love. They'd survived this rift.

He would apologise to her family. He needed them on his side, if he was to make this work, Mary loved them. He loved her. He could not separate her from them.

Perhaps I ought to do it publicly. He tipped his hat to Joshua who was speaking with another resident.

Perhaps he ought to call them to silence and stand up in the bloody lions' den – Pembroke's sitting room – and tell them all they were wrong, that he did love Mary and it had never just been because of her money.

That would give them something to talk about behind his back.

He laughed, as he ran upstairs, and swung around the banister onto the landing. His boot heels rung on the floorboards as he strode along the hall.

The world was a good place with Mary in it. Caro would be proud of him.

He turned the door handle but the door did not give.

His fingers on the door he pushed it, but it was locked.

A shiver ran up his spine.

No.

We made love this morning. She would not have...

He pulled the key from the pocket of his riding coat, and his hand trembling, he slotted it into the lock and turned it.

The door opened.

He forced himself to be calm.

She would not have left.

A dozen curses ran through his head. Her writing desk had gone. *Hell.*

He turned to the bedchamber, one hand gripping the doorframe, everything of hers had gone, as if she'd never been here – but a dent still hollowed the pillow where she'd slept – where he'd made love to her scant hours ago.

Why did she let me do it?

He walked to the bed, and picked up her pillow to smell the scent of her hair. She'd gone.

He cast the thing aside, his hands shaking, and walked back in to the sitting room. He stopped. There was nothing he could do. It was over.

She has left me.

He went to the decanters and poured a drink, numb. The neck of the decanter rattled against the rim of the glass.

He drank the first glass and poured a second as nausea twisted in his gut.

What had this morning been about? Goodbye?

He cursed, out loud, and drank the second glass. Then poured a third and turned to face the room.

A folded sheet of paper, stood amongst the chess pieces.

His heart dropped like a stone as he crossed the room to pick it up.

Pembroke's men must have come to help her move everything out so quickly. It must have all been arranged.

Then why the hell had she let him touch her this morning?

He was only worth two lines of hurried script.

I cannot stay. I have lied to my parents for you since I met you. I cannot carry on living with any more lies.

Had this morning been a lie? She'd clung to him and come for him... Had that been a lie? Had he forced her? Had she not wanted him?

Hell! He was an ass. His soul writhed in pain.

But a broken heart did not kill you. It only made you bitter. And hurt...

He crumpled the paper in his fist and tossed it into the empty hearth. Then dropped into a chair with a sigh.

He swore, falling back and lifting a knee up on to the arm.

There would be no happy ending.

"It is your own fault, you bastard." He saluted himself with the brandy and drank his third glass. "You should have left her alone. You should not have taken her from happiness. You are poisonous! Let her be now, for God sake."

He'd done enough harm.

Tears flooded his eyes and spilled onto his cheeks. He'd never cried in his life. His head tipped back against the chair and he looked up, trying to control the pain writhing in his chest.

Now he knew how she had felt for the last weeks. No wonder she had gone.

He lifted his knee from the arm of the chair and leaned forward, leaving his glass on the floor, then stood up and wiped the tears away on his sleeve.

Devil take it, crying for her would change nothing.

But he knew what he would do. He'd sell the carriage and the blacks he'd bought for her, then he'd go to the bank.

Chapter 31

Kate, John's wife, sat on the edge of the bed beside Mary. "I've brought you some lemonade and biscuits. Would you like me to stay with you for a while?"

Mary was sitting with her knees bent up and her body curled over them; too agitated to lay down. "Thank you, Kate. But I would rather be alone."

"You've been closeted away all day, Mary. Your mother is worried. Why don't you come down to dinner?"

Mary wiped her nose on the handkerchief she gripped, then clasped her bent knees. Her hands still shook.

Her mother, aunts and cousins, Eleanor and Margaret, had spoken to her too; all offering comfort and setting aside the marriage they'd predicted would fail.

Aunt Jane had told everyone he'd been seen with a woman.

Her father had hugged her tightly when she'd come home, and told her he'd protect her. Tomorrow he said he would publish a notice in the paper, announcing the separation, so the gossip would be fact and not fiction and she would no longer be tied to Andrew's reputation.

She did not care.

She'd no intention of ever stepping out in public again, she'd told her father so, but he'd just held her hand and said, "You will in time. Time will heal."

She did not think she'd ever heal. Andrew had loved her this morning, and his scent was still on her skin. Time would take that away, and her memories would fade, but her love would never ebb…

Her forehead dropped on to her knees as silent tears spilled from her eyes.

All she'd done since she'd reached here was cry.

Her mother had sat beside her for the first hour, until Mary had asked to be left alone. But her family had been unable to stay away, every half hour someone came up to see how she fared, each of them bringing fresh words of reassurance.

But their words could not sooth the pain. She missed Andrew – and he'd betrayed her so badly. Why had he made love to her today? Why had his eyes glowed with affection? How could he lie so easily, so physically?

The words he'd whispered as she'd lain on his chest listening to the rumble of his voice, held more weight in her heart than any her family said.

He'd promised to be different, to love her, to make a home with her, away from London as she wished… and yet the night before she'd heard him say, "I've bought a house for her. I'm moving her in there next week… Whether Mary stays or not I'll have Caro…"

Kate's fingers touched Mary's shoulder. "Drink a little lemonade and eat, Mary, we can all see you've lost weight these last weeks."

Like a clockwork toy, Mary lifted her head, accepted the glass and sipped, she was too numb to argue.

Kate's fingers brushed Mary's hair back from her brow again as Mary drank. "What will you do?"

"I asked Papa to take me home, but he said he cannot for a little while as he has business he needs to settle in town."

"Are you sure what Jane said is correct?"

Mary smiled weakly. Trust Kate not to jump to conclusions, her sister-in-law had a tender heart. She did not judge people without

336

giving them a chance. She'd saved John from himself, with her refusal to accept him at face value.

"I know it's true. I heard him talking of his mistress last night. He's bought a house for her. She is moving in to it next week." Mary met Kate's gaze.

"He made love to me this morning, as though there was nothing wrong... He has not touched me since he hit Lord Brooke. He's slept in the sitting room. He said he loved me this morning. But yesterday he heard Aunt Jane telling me to leave. I suppose he wished to avoid the embarrassment and make me stay... He is not here, begging me to come back, is he? He has not even written. He lied. He does not love me. He can go to his mistress and not have to bother pretending he does love me now."

"Have you told your mother this?" Concern and affection weighted Kate's voice, and softened her gaze.

"No, and do not, Papa or John would attack him. It's bad enough as it is."

Kate's fingers covered Mary's hand for a moment before slipping away.

"He is so believable," Mary whispered. "Even his eyes look as though he loves me, and when he touches me it feels real, it feels as though he treasures me. I thought he loved me when I ran away with him. He said he did, like he did this morning. But he is angry and bitter, Kate. He hates Papa and John, but then they hate him, and yet he said that he'd have been as angry as them if I'd been his daughter, so they had a right to hate him.

"Did you see how he was when he came here that afternoon? He looked lost among the children and the family. That day I asked to meet his family and even though he did not wish to, he took me there. They were horrible to him. They asked why he thought they'd wish to meet me, then threw us out as though he was nothing to them. That was the day he hit Lord Brooke. He hated me after that, and he stopped pretending to love me and stopped touching me. But then this morning he changed again.

337

"I do not understand him. I thought he was just bruised by his life. But I love him. I'd have helped him. But he does not want my help, does he, just my money? Do you think there was always someone else, do you think he loves this other woman?"

Kate's fingers pressed on Mary's knee, offering comfort, "How can we know, Mary?"

"I still love him. I will always love him."

Kate's fingers gripped Mary's knee a little tighter and Mary sipped the lemonade, fresh tears slipping from her eyes, and agony clutching at her heart.

When Kate's fingers slid away Mary leant to set the glass down, looking at her sister-in-law.

She'd told no one this. "And I am carrying his child. Please do not tell Mama and Papa, not yet, I need time to get used to the idea."

"Oh, Mary."

Kate hugged her close, as tears slid down Mary's cheeks in rivers.

"All will be well. You have us all to help you."

Mary did not answer, she could not, she just held on to Kate.

She had not only taken herself away from Andrew, but his child too. A child who she did not want to know its father. She did not want anyone to know. This was her pain, her secret – that she had created a child with a man who did not love her. But she would not be able to hide it forever. She could hide herself, though, and that's what she wished to do, hide away and pretend this had never happened.

Kate's hand brushed over Mary's hair, then she pulled away. "John and I told lies too. After the party he held in Ashford, while you were at the end of your mourning for your grandfather, we made love. I went to him because I loved him. He did not love me then, but I fell pregnant and John did the honourable thing. He loves me now, Mary."

"Of course, he loves you," Mary whispered, clutching Kate's hand, she had not known that. "I see it in his eyes every time he looks at you."

Kate smiled. "I know. I did not tell you because I needed reassurance. I said it so you'd know things are not always straightforward. Perhaps things aren't as they seem. Perhaps things will work out for you too."

"He has a mistress, Kate."

"And you are carrying a child which you have both made. At some point you have to tell him, you cannot keep the child a secret when it is born. It would be wrong to stop the child knowing its father. I'd intended to keep my child a secret from John, but you've seen how he adores Paul, it would have been cruel."

Mary sighed. Kate's mother took her own life, Kate knew what it would be like for a child not to know its parent.

But if Mary told Andrew he could take the child from her, and then her only option would be to go back. But what if he then refused to take her back?

The situation only seemed to worsen.

"Why not come home to Pembroke Place with John and I? You will be left alone to think things over and heal a little, without the noise of all the children. We can go to tomorrow. John can still travel into town to attend the House of Lords and your parents will agree I'm sure. Then when you feel more able you can tell them and Andrew about the child."

"I'd prefer to be away from the others. I know it's selfish…"

"It is not selfish, Mary. The children cannot understand, and your parents must share out their time among you all. But you know they love you…"

Mary smiled, "Yes."

"Now eat, though. You must think of the child, and not only yourself and I had better go and tell John that we're leaving tomorrow."

"Will he mind?"

"You know he will not. He'd do anything for you, he loves you dearly, and it's no trouble to him to travel back when he needs to. He prefers being on the estate anyway, he'll be glad of an excuse to go."

Catching Kate's hand before she turned away, Mary said, "Thank you."

"You need not thank me. You are my sister."

"Would you send Mama to me, and I'll tell her I will leave with you?"

Chapter 32

It took two weeks to get the deeds signed over and organise a date, time, and place, to get Caro away. But now the day had come to move her.

Drew met her in Mayfair, in Madame Duval's, the modiste's, to make it look to Kilbride's staff as though she was simply shopping.

Drew turned as she slipped out of the back of the shop. "Caro." He leant and kissed her cheek, gripping her hands. They were shaking. "Come." Keeping a hold of one he pulled her on through the shop yard.

"Did they query your exit?"

"No, I asked the modiste if I might use her closet, but there is a footman waiting for me in the shop."

"Then we had best hurry." Drew Pulled her through the back gate, and then began to run at a slow jog, forcing Caro to do the same. "There is a hired carriage at the end of the alley, I ordered it in a false name, and we will change carriages once we are out of London, and go the opposite way, and then change again. No one will be able to trace you. Where was Kilbride when you left?"

"I waited until he'd left for the House of Lords, he will be there hours before he knows I am gone. He cannot abide being interrupted while he is in The House."

Drew had left the carriage door ajar so they could ascend

quickly, he handed her in, and climbed in behind her. "Go!" he yelled up to the driver as he shut the door. The carriage jolted forward. He fell into the seat beside Caro, then pulled the blinds down to hide them from view.

Caro breathed heavily her hands shaking even more as she pulled a folded silk handkerchief from her reticule. "I have brought something to help. I cannot allow you to support me entirely, Drew." Gold and jewels glinted in the low light of the carriage as she opened the handkerchief. "They are all gifts he has given me, they were mine to take, earbobs, hair slides, bracelets and necklaces."

Drew smiled awkwardly, he had not expected her to bring anything, but if she sold these, they would help her live better. He had not told her his circumstances had changed. He'd thought if he did, she would change her mind and refuse to leave.

Drew leaned to the window, and looked about the blind at Kilbride's carriage as they passed the shop front. There were no panicked servants surrounding it. The footmen must still be waiting patiently inside.

The journey out of London was fast and easy, and when they arrived in Maidstone the housekeeper he'd hired was waiting at the cottage to settle Caro in.

The cottage was small, there were two rooms downstairs, a kitchen and a parlour, and two upstairs, with an attic for the housekeeper. He'd had the housekeeper stock it with clothing and everything Caro needed, furniture, food and other provisions.

Knowing Caro was anxious and afraid of what was to come, he stayed with her for a couple of hours and drank tea with her in the sitting room.

He thought of Mary, as Caro talked with the housekeeper.

He'd not thought of Mary for most of the day, because his thoughts had been absorbed by helping Caro... but now... as they sat in the cramped little parlour he remembered all the moments he'd shared with Mary that had been commonplace like this. The afternoon they'd played chess. He wished for more. He longed for her. For quiet peaceful moments with her. Even to sit in her brother's damned drawing room and drink tea with her.

"Drew…"

But his hope of Mary had passed. The sunny drawing room of their own small house in the country would only ever be a figment of his imagination. He smiled at Caro. To reassure her. "Sorry, I rose early, I am tired, and wool gathering…" The truth was he had barely slept since Mary had left, but he lay no blame on her. All the blame was his. He had made a very large mess of his marriage.

Caro leaned forward and gripped his hand for an instant. It was laughable… the two of them… When he'd eloped with Mary he had deemed her life's flotsam. No. She had not been. She was protected and loved by the numerous members of her family. He and Caro were flotsam. Two lost souls searching for what they thought ought to be theirs by right, with no capacity to find it, because they were too damaged by their years adrift.

"I should leave you." Drew stood. Kilbride would guess he'd been involved with helping Caro if he did not get back to London. He had to return to town to quell the rumours and cover any potential tracks.

"Caro, you know I cannot return for a while, Kilbride will have people watching me for weeks, we both know it. Do not write either, it is not worth taking the risk. I will come as soon as I can but in the meantime, simply live quietly here."

She nodded. But then she lifted to her toes and hugged him. Crying.

"You must be brave, Caro, stay calm and stay strong and sit it out here. He will not find you, I promise."

She nodded again.

"I'm very grateful, Drew. I cannot tell you how grateful."

He smiled.

* * *

343

Several hours later Drew climbed the steps of Sheffield's town house with Brooke by his side to attend Sheffield's ball. He was here as a deliberate bluff, for Caro's sake. He knew Kilbride would be looking for him, and he was here to send a silent message – you will not find her.

But truthfully that was not the only reason he was here – he hoped for a glimpse of Mary. He and Peter had attended several balls so he might be able to see her, to ease his soul and know she was well.

The last time he had seen her had been the day she'd left – the day he'd loved her and she'd loved him back.

God that moment haunted him. Why the hell had she let him do it?

Yet he would not speak to her if he saw her. The emotion inside him pulled for him to go to her brother's and win her back. But he refused to act on it. She was better off without him. They were too different.

A deep sigh left Drew's lips as the footman stepped aside to let them in and Peter looked over his shoulder. "I doubt she's here."

"I doubt it too; it does not stop me wishing, though…"

Peter gripped Drew's shoulder as they walked through the hall towards the music and voices. "I told you to write to her. I'm sure Marlow would pass it on."

"More likely he'd burn it and if he did not, then Mary probably would."

Peter's hand fell away. "You were an ass, my friend. But I still do not understand why you sent the bloody money back."

"It seemed wrong to keep it. It was her money."

"Not legally."

"Who cares about legality? I just wish I'd had it all to give back, but I'd already paid my debts and I need money to support Caro." He had some in a trust fund.

"Still I bet it had the man shocked."

"I doubt it. I think my name is a swear word in Pembroke's

344

house. But regardless I am glad of your help. I'd rather work for you than borrow from you again. I need to do something with my life. If she wants a divorce I'll let her have it but I'll not marry again. I'm done with the parson's noose and I'm done with women. I shall happily bury myself in the country with your horses."

"You've an eye for them and a skill. I am doing myself a favour not you, Fram. When you take over the stud, I'll have the best racers out there."

"Your faith may be misplaced,"

"Let me be the judge of that," Peter whispered their final aside as they crossed the threshold into the bright light of the ballroom.

Drew surveyed the room, looking for Marlow but only to find Mary. They were not there. But the Wiltshires, the Bradfords and the Barringtons were. He'd seen them all twice before. He'd not seen Pembroke or Marlow at all.

The Duke of Wiltshire gave Drew a bitter stare.

Drew's gut turned over. What had Mary said to them?

They'd hated him before. They must despise him now. If any of them carried daggers, they'd be in his back.

Wiltshire turned his back, in a cutting gesture. It was nothing to a man whose own mother refused to acknowledge his existence.

Speaking of that, she was here too, with the Marquis and Drew's eldest brother and his wife. They probably credited his ill-fate to themselves for making Mary see that he was a pathetic, worthless bastard.

"Not here," Peter said. Drew knew he meant Mary. "But Kilbride is," Peter concluded. "And so is my sister, come on, she'll tell us any rumours that are circulating."

Even though Wiltshire had turned his back, Drew sensed the man's gaze follow him. He was getting used it.

"Hayley," Peter kissed his sister's cheek. "Spill, what are we missing, what is going on tonight?"

She held out her hand to Drew. He'd known her since she was a child. Drew gripped her fingers and bowed over them, then lifted them to his lips for an instant. She smiled as he straightened. "You are the gossip, Drew. Since that announcement. I believe your wife has left town. Certainly both Pembroke and Marlow have gone. You men, you do as you like and leave us women to suffer."

"She left me." Belligerence burned in Drew's voice. He had not expected them to announce the separation. "I thought their announcement made that clear." He schooled his voice, he did not want the world to know how hurt he was.

Hayley's fan tapped at his upper arm. "And you are entirely innocent I suppose, she left you for no reason at all..."

"None that I can think of." His tone was dry now.

Hayley's gaze passed over his shoulder and her eyes widened. Her fingers gripped at his sleeve. "Have you some grievance with the Marquis of Kilbride? He is coming this way with a look of thunder on his face."

"The jig is already up then." Peter said.

"Lord Framlington!" the Marquis of Kilbride's bellow rang about the high ceilinged hall, bouncing off the mirrors and the glass, echoing over the music which played on, and the conversation which then ceased.

Damn it, Drew had known this scene would come, but he'd thought Kilbride would challenge him in private; he had not expected him to do so at a ball, and certainly not before Mary's kin. This would add even more fuel to their fire.

Setting a twisted be-damned smile on his lips, Drew turned. Perhaps having this out in public was preferential. In private Kilbride would have brought his thugs and probably dumped Drew's broken body in a back alley. Still he'd made a will in case and left everything to Caro, so even if Kilbride did get him, he would not win. She would have her cottage, and all she needed to survive.

Guilt hit him.

Mary's money had bought the cottage; if he died, it ought to go to Mary but he could not leave Caro unprotected.

As Kilbride neared, Drew stiffened his spine, stretching up the two inches he had over his brother-in-law. "Is there something you wish to say to me?"

"You know there is!" Kilbride bellowed at full pitch as though he was speaking to the House of Lords, even though he now stood immediately before Drew.

"Forgive me, but, no. You have me at a disadvantage…" Drew let the smirk on his lips slide into his voice and took pleasure in watching Kilbride's anger rise.

Let him hit a man for a change, it would give Drew the chance to hit him back.

"I know you have her! You have stolen my wife! You have been bedding her for years. You incestuous bastard!" Kilbride's words echoed and now even the music had stopped.

Drew's fists balled and his vision tainted red.

"It is no wonder your wife has deserted you! She knew you for a wretch! She caught you in bed with my wife, your sister!"

Drew's control cracked, his anger flaring into rage. He lunged at Kilbride, grabbing his lapel and striking with a fist. He hit bone, probably breaking his brother-in-law's nose.

The noise about him was a vague sound as his fist struck again, hitting Kilbride's jaw. Kilbride threw a fist in return, but Drew dodged so it merely struck his shoulder with no weight.

One voice rose above the others, speaking into his ear, "You'll kill him and it will be you who hangs." Peter gripped his arm.

The words pulled Drew back to his senses and the red mist faded. He thrust Kilbride away so he fell to the floor.

"I'll see you swing for this and I'll find her!" Kilbride growled.

Drew dropped to his haunches, and gripped Kilbride's arm, as if to help him up but instead he held him down. "Do it, and I'll find a dozen witnesses who'll swear they've seen you beat her. Then everyone will know the truth, and you'll make yourself look the fool."

Drew stood up and yanked Kilbride to his feet too. "Do it if you dare!" A hundred faces swum about him as Drew let Kilbride's arm go and turned away.

Women came forward to console Kilbride, while men with clenched fists glared at Drew, and at the front of them, Wiltshire, and beside him Barrington and Bradford.

Drew cursed aloud and then a woman actually spat at him.

His eyes caught those of his mother's among the crowd. She turned away. While his brother was looking down his nose as though he smelt horse dung.

"Incestuous." Drew heard the outraged word on someone's lips. It repeated on a wave of sound, rippling through the crowd.

The music and dancing had ceased. He'd become the entertainment.

"For God sake move, get out of here," Peter whispered, his hand gripping Drew's arm.

Drew's other arm was grasped in a harder hold. Wiltshire. "You've shamed my niece. If this is true…God help me… I will kill you myself if you've entangled Mary in this."

Drew pulled his arms loose.

"Let us have music!" Barrington shouted from beyond Wiltshire, gesturing to the orchestra as Bradford spoke with Kilbride, No doubt Kilbride was pouring poison into Bradford's ear. *Devil take it*… Why did Mary's family association have to be so broad?

"Go back to your dancing!" Barrington shouted at the observers who hovered.

Drew could see himself accused and found guilty in Wiltshire's eyes. Mary would know of this by the morning. But he'd lost her days ago anyway.

"Go to hell, Wiltshire," Drew hissed through his teeth in a low cutting voice, and then he spun on his heel and walked out with a lengthened stride.

Peter followed. "Expect to be called out by a dozen men in the morning. I would not go anywhere near White's or any of the clubs…" People moved out of their way, looking at Drew as though he really was the devil, before turning their backs.

"It'll do no good," Drew answered as they reached the hall. "They know where I live."

"Then for God sake, leave London." There was a lack of humour in Peter's voice.

A footman opened the door and they stepped out into the night, a lynch mob had not yet formed. But Peter was probably right, it would come tomorrow, when they'd had time to plan.

Drew glanced at Peter "They may do what they like. I have a will."

"So now you have a death wish."

Drew did not answer as they descended the steps and turned to look for Peter's carriage among the line of those waiting.

"Drew?"

Drew cast Peter a devil may care grin. It hardly mattered what the outcome was. If Mary's family wanted to have their revenge and call him out, he would not fight; he'd delope and fire into the air.

If they shot him, if Kilbride shot him, they would do him a favour. He could not imagine living the rest of his life bearing this much inner pain.

He'd freed Caroline, she was secure. What happened to him did not matter.

Peter's hand settled on Drew's shoulder. "I'm not ready to part with you, my friend. Do not do anything foolish, and tonight I would suggest you get very drunk, and as your best friend I'm willing to help you achieve it. Let us find Mark and Harry, they'll willingly help you too, and then you're sleeping at mine. I'm not letting anyone shoot you. And believe me I shall be telling everyone tomorrow you are not an incestuous man."

"You think they will believe you…" Drew laughed, but it was a broken sound.

Chapter 33

"Good God. That bastard!"

Mary and Kate both looked up at John's words.

"John," Kate whispered a rebuff for his foul language.

He was reading his letters at the breakfast table.

Setting her chocolate down, Mary met John's hard gaze as it shifted from the letter he was reading to her. Something had made him angry – something to do with her…

His gaze changed to a look of regret, "I'm sorry, Mary."

She had only suffered a slight nausea in the mornings, she had never been physically ill, but now she felt as if she would be sick.

John's gaze span around the footmen waiting about the table. "Leave us, please." They bowed deeply then filed out. "You too, Finch." John prompted the butler, in a dry voice.

Mary had never known him send the servants from the room.

A hand pressed to her stomach, a sense of panic flaring. John stood.

She did too. "Do not tell me, I do not wish to know if he's been seen with her. Don't tell me. Please."

"Mary," John breathed walking closer. "You have to know this. The letter is from Richard. You must hear it from me, or you'll hear it by another route. It's worse than that, far worse."

Fingers touched Mary's arm.

Kate's.

"Sit down again," John said gently.

Mary must have paled. She did sit, her thoughts scrambling in a ball of mixed up threads. What had happened? What could be so bad?

"John, please simply speak?" Even Kate's voice shook.

John's gaze softened. "There's no easy way to tell you this. Richard saw Lord Framlington at Sheffield's ball last night. Uncle Robert was there too and Uncle James. Lord Framlington was involved in another brawl and an accusation was thrown, which everyone heard."

"Over this woman? Is she married?" One of Mary's hands pressed over her stomach.

"She is." He looked sorrowful as he sat in the seat beside her. "It is the Duchess of Kilbride, his sister Caroline. He's been accused of incest by his brother-in-law and his sister has disappeared. It is said that he's keeping her. That they've been having an affair for years."

"Good Lord." Kate's fingers gripped Mary's shoulder.

But it was not true. *It is not true...*

"No," Mary shook her head. Her throat had dried. She felt as though someone had stripped out every nerve from her body she was so numb. "John, it is not true. He would not."

Kate's fingers pressed Mary's shoulder more firmly. "You told me his family have cut him. They also cut the Duchess of Kilbride. This would explain it, Mary. If their family knew..."

Mary looked up to Kate, as John gripped Mary's hands.

"It is not true! He would not do such a thing. I saw him speaking with the Duchess of Kilbride once, before we wed. It was when Papa saw me approach him, they'd been outside."

"Is that not added proof," John said in quiet understanding, as though he thought she simply did not wish to hear the truth.

Her gaze swung back and caught John's. "No." Her voice grew in strength. "Andrew told me Kilbride beat her, and all he could do was offer comfort. He was the only person she trusted. I saw bruises on her neck once after that; with my own eyes, and they looked like finger marks."

Mary looked back up at Kate. Suddenly everything made sense. "Oh Kate! The woman in the draper's was her!"

Mary stood. The breakfast room spinning about her. She gripped Kate's hands. "What I heard that night. He'd bought a house for her. He said, Caro. His sister. I did not make the connection. He did not have a mistress. Oh Kate, he made love to me and said he was sorry, that he would try to prove himself to me, and I left him. He was not lying."

Mary turned to John, who was now standing again too. She clutched his morning coat. "John, you have to take me back. I must go to him. Please?"

John's gaze became uncertain. "You cannot, Mary. There are a dozen men all prepared to kill him. Kilbride wants him hanged. Although as far as I know there's no charge against him yet. But he's disappeared."

She shook her head. "He won't hide from them, that is not Andrew. He won't run. If they've accused him he'll look them in the eye and tell them all to go to hell…rather than hide."

John's lips twitched at one corner. "That is, apparently, what he said to Uncle Richard."

"Then Mary is right, John, if she knows him so well." Kate pressed. "Yet if Mary cannot go to him, then we ought to bring him here. If he loves Mary he'll come and they will have time away from these rumours to resolve the rift between them, while the gossip dies."

Kate's gaze caught Mary's. "There is something else you ought to know, which I believe now indicates Lord Framlington's innocence. John and I discussed it and we thought it better not to tell you before, but now… Your father and your mother know this too and agreed with us. But Mary…" Her fingers gripped Mary's tightly. "When you came back to us, the same day John received a cheque from Lord Framlington. He returned most of your dowry, with a

352

letter that stated he could not keep it if he did not have you. He said it would only be a bitter reminder of what he'd lost. John thought it just a ploy to win you back, and yet we were not sure because he asked John not to tell you. At the time it made your father and John doubt their judgement and yet knowing he had a mistress, we thought it would just confuse things for you—"

"Were we wrong, Mary?" John touched her arm.

"Yes." She hugged him hard for a moment then let go. He understood at last, his voice and his eyes said so. "Andrew never argued against the things you said, John. I think he thought it lowering to have to defend himself. Yet he told me a dozen times that he loved me, but I did not always believe him, because you told me he was just saying it to win my dowry. If it was not for my dowry, John?"

"Then it was because he loves you." Kate concluded, "What you saw and felt was real, Mary, you said he was believable, it was believable because it is true." She looked a John. "We must bring him here."

"I'll have them ready a carriage."

Chapter 34

Peter threw a paper on to Drew's lap. "Pembroke is back in town. Apparently he's turning over every stone in search of you."

Drew had not slept, he'd merely sat in Peter's town house in Mayfair, since two in the morning, figuratively kicking his heels.

He'd drunk himself sober last night and then Peter had insisted Drew stay and sent a servant to collect some of his belongings so Drew could pass a few days here.

This morning Peter had gone scouting for news of how things stood about the clubs. While Drew had little more to occupy his mind than twiddling his thumbs. He'd tried playing a game of solitaire with a pack of cards but his mind kept slipping in to thoughts of Mary. What would she think when she heard this latest rumour?

Incest.

It was no small accusation. It was immoral and illegal.

If she believed it… He denied the thought as too unbearable. She was the only one whose good opinion he cared for.

"Pembroke is on a war path. He's called at every club and every single haunt you favour." Peter walked over to the decanters, his back turned to Drew. "He's been demanding to know where you are and if anyone has seen you. While Kilbride has a man, without any livery, standing outside your rooms waiting to inform him if you return, and Wiltshire has put a sum on your head to have you found, he wants you charged. Kilbride, I believe, just wants you dead."

"They can hang me if they wish. I really don't give a damn. Caro is safe, they will not find her." Even Peter did not know where Caro was, no one knew. Drew had not taken a single risk.

"I know you don't care," Peter turned, holding the neck of a decanter in his hand, lifting it to ask if Drew wished for a glass, "but the rest of us do. I'm not going to let it happen." He turned to pour their drinks. "I've already made it public in White's that I, who happen to know you very well indeed, believe the whole story is a pile of horse dung. My brother-in-law is speaking for you in Brooke's and Harry has raised it in Watier's. Our version will circulate."

"Your version?" Drew stood and tossed the paper aside, he did not care to see the slander in there anyway. "You have not said there is any truth in the fact I have her. I do not want Kilbride to know he's right; let him stew and wonder."

A glass in both hands, Peter walked across the room. "We've not said anything other than that it's nonsense. But we've more subtly begun the rumour that Kilbride was beating his wife. It will grow like a snowball. People will have guessed it previously but will have been too cowed by Kilbride to say. Wait and see. The truth will out now."

"But that is not illegal." Drew took his drink. *Damn it all to hell*, there was naught he could do bar sit here and wait it out.

"Do you want luncheon? Harry and Mark said they'll call in later."

"And how long before people guess I'm here?"

"I'll go out this evening and leave one of the others to keep you company. That will throw people off the scent. The fact that I've already been abroad has not made them think of it yet. I've let people think I'm looking for you too."

This was a hell of a muddle.

"My Lords" Drew and Peter turned to the butler who stood in the open door. *Damn it*, Drew hoped he had not heard them speaking of Caro… "There is a woman downstairs Lord Brooke, who wishes to speak with you, she's come to the servants' door with a letter for you, but she will not pass it on to anyone but yourself, my Lord."

Beyond Brooke's butler they heard light quick steps. The woman was no longer downstairs at all, but rushing past the butler into the room, swamped in a voluminous cloak, despite the heat of the summer day. She threw the hood back.

Pembroke's wife.

Drew set down his glass, preparing to defend himself verbally – but then there was always a possibility she hid a pistol beneath the cloak. Her hand drew from beneath the folds. Peter moved towards her, ready to catch her arm and make her drop it if she did.

The thing in her hand was paper.

A letter.

Her eyes darted from one to the other of them. "I am not here to cause harm, Lord Framlington. Mary has told us the truth of this ridiculous tale. John and I have been searching for you all morning. We wish you to come back with us. You'll be safer away from London and Mary wishes you to come. She would have come to London herself but John and I refused to let her join us. We have promised to bring you back. If you'll come? Will you come with us?"

Drew stared at her. The Duchess of Pembroke had come through the servants' entrance to offer him help.

She had no cause to help him.

"This letter is from Mary. Read it if you do not believe me…" She held it out further.

Hell and the devil. He did not know what to think, but walking forward, he reached out for the letter and took it from her fingers.

His heart hammered.

Dearest Andrew,

I am sorry I did not believe you. I believe you now. Come, come quickly, John will take you out of London and bring you here, where you will be safe.

Mary, your devoted wife.
Will you forgive me for my lack of faith?

He looked up at Pembroke's wife, something tight gripping about his heart. "Where is she?"

"At Pembroke Place, not far from London, it is John's principal estate. No one will be able to get near you there. The house and grounds are extensive. You will have both privacy and security. You'll have time and opportunity to resolve these things with Mary."

"Is Lord Marlow there also?"

"No, Lord and Lady Marlow have gone to their own estate."

Mary, your devoted wife.

Did she love him still?

His hand covered his mouth.

"Mary will be distraught if you do not return with us, Lord Framlington. I promised I would bring you."

She believed Mary but she was still not certain of him – and yet she was standing in Brooke's house having forced her way in and determination glinted in her eyes.

"Where is the Duke?" Drew's fingers creased the paper Mary had written upon, he clung to it so tightly. "Why have you come and not him?"

"He is waiting a hundred yards away, in an unmarked carriage. John has asked for you everywhere. I realised no one would tell him, because they know he is against you. Therefore I thought if you stayed with Lord Brooke I had more chance of getting in."

"I am not going out there to receive a bullet in my chest, then?"

The Duchess looked at the letter in his hand. "They are Mary's words. Would she lie to you? Certainly we would not lie to her. I've told you the truth, Lord Framlington; John and I wish you to come for Mary's sake. Mary left you because she overheard a conversation between you and Lord Brooke, about a property you'd purchased for another woman, a lady. John's aunt believed you were seen with her in a draper's.

"Mary now understands that was your sister. If you are guilty of anything, it is not telling Mary what you have been doing. She did not leave you for lack of love. She has been desolate and inconsolable these past weeks. Is that not reason enough for you to come."

Drew looked at Peter.

"Go, I'll not hold you here. This is what you want; to have her back..."

Drew looked at the Duchess. "I'll fetch my things. I haven't much."

An hour later, his bag stored in the box, Pembroke seated beside him, with the Duchess seated opposite, they were barrelling along the main road out of London and into Kent. The same road he'd travelled with Caro. Drew lounged in his seat, the sole of one boot resting on the far seat, the other on the floor, to prevent him rocking and sliding with each bump in the road.

His arms were folded over his chest and the brim of his hat tipped low to hide his eyes.

Apart from acknowledging Drew as he'd handed the Duchess up into the carriage, Pembroke had not said a word. He'd sat there studying Drew as though he was an absurd anomaly, while Drew resisted an urge to stare back.

Mary had used to look at him like that sometimes, when she was seeking to unravel him. He did not wish Pembroke doing it, thus he'd tilted the rim of his hat and Pembroke had looked away. God. Hope was breathing in Drew, again, as they travelled, that silent quiet beast. Was it resolved? Did she love him... Damn, I love her.

His whole body was tense with longing to see her again. To

wrap his arms around her again.

The Duchess had attempted a few words, on bland subjects such as, "I hope you are comfortable?" "At least the weather has held," 'It will only take a couple of hours to reach Pembroke Place," "The parkland there is beautiful," and then her well of obsequious conversation ran dry.

Pembroke coughed. It was an odd sound, half cough, half humour. "Mary knows you fairly well, does she not, Framlington?"

Drew's fingers lifted and tilted up his hat a little, as he turned his head. "In what way, Your Grace?"

"In that she said, when I told her our uncle's account of the incident last night that you would not run but would rather tell them all to go to hell. I had not told her yet that you'd said those words to our uncle. Are you sitting there wishing me to hell too?"

Drew held Pembroke's sharp, penetrating blue gaze. His eyes were so like Mary's. "I am doing my best not to, Your Grace." He was thinking solely of Mary; his heart thumped hard in his chest as mental images of her flooded his head. "After all Pembroke, this is a kindness on your part. I'd be a fool to be ungrateful, wouldn't I?"

Pembroke gave him a closed lip smile. Drew had not known the man could smile. "Have I got you wrong, Lord Framlington?"

"I'll let you to be the judge of that, Your Grace." Drew tipped his hat back down and turned to look out the window.

"Mary also said you will not defend yourself."

Mary ought to keep her mouth shut. Drew did not answer, or look back, but he heard a humorous sound leave Pembroke's throat.

Drew shut his eyes and pretended to sleep.

The devil take it, he didn't wish to argue with Pembroke. Yet too often he could not help himself. Since childhood it had become his nature to be defensive.

Another fault. His faults were legion. If he was to win Mary back he must do more than say the word sorry. She would have to help him fix his faults. Her smile came into his thoughts.

He felt like hope slept inside him. He dare not quite let it wake

359

until he saw her.

Pembroke tapped his shoulder. "We are here, Framlington."

Drew must have fallen asleep.

Dropping his other foot to the floor he sat upright and looked from the carriage window, his heart thumping as hope awakened without his bidding.

They were sweeping along a broad avenue, and as the avenue turned to the right Drew saw his first glimpse of Pembroke's principle estate.

He swore within his thoughts, the Palladian property was sitting like a beast on a ridge in the landscape, a manmade master dominating the land about it.

He'd known Pembroke was wealthy, but he had not imagined this. Drew had housed Mary in a two room apartment in St James. He would lay odds on the fact her bedchamber here was the size of his whole apartment.

The horses' hooves and the carriage wheels crunched in the gravel as the carriage pulled up in front of the ostentatious mansion.

Drew's stomach dropped and his heartbeat became erratic as the air in the carriage evaporated.

A dozen men in Pembroke's livery stood before the broad stone columns, fronting the property and the right side of the giant double doors stood open. They must have seen the carriage coming from a distance.

Drew saw a flutter of pink muslin up by the house. "Mary."

He pushed the door open before a footman could and jumped down. She was flying down the shallow steps, her dress gripped high in one hand, pulling her hem up to her calves, all decorum forgotten as she raced at him.

He raced to her and caught her midway.

She flung her arms about his neck with a fierce cry of joy.

Ah, God. He hugged her hard. It hurt so much, having her in his arms. Relief. He'd thought he would never know her feel or her smell again. His cheek pressed against her hair as her embrace gripped about his soul.

"I'm sorry, Andrew," she said against his neck. She was crying and she'd lost weight, he could feel her spine and her ribs beneath her gown.

His fingers splayed within her hair. "You have nothing to be sorry for. I pushed you away. It is I who am sorry, I could not bear for you to see the real me, I thought you must hate me; that you could never truly love me, and so I pushed you away to avoid future pain. But then I regretted it. I thought I'd lost you, Mary." He pressed a kiss on her hair as the feel of her soaked back into his blood.

Pulling away from him, tears running down her cheeks, her fingers framed his face. He smiled as tears clouded his vision too.

"You are not hurt."

"No."

Her fingers slid down across his chest looking for wounds regardless of his words, followed by her gaze.

His fingers lifted her chin. "Mary, I'm fine, sweetheart. No holes." He wiped the tears from her cheeks with his thumbs.

He could no longer doubt how much he meant to her. "I am here now. I was an ass. Caro told me so too. But I was too stubborn to listen," He held Mary again, absorbing the scent in her hair. Roses. Clinging to her, ignorant of the world beyond her.

He pressed a kiss on her hair, then looked up and met Pembroke's gaze. He stood a few feet away, watching with a hint of a smile on his lips.

Drew sucked air into his lungs. It was not going to be easy letting her family have an insight into him. He did not want people knowing him at all. It would make him vulnerable. Yet, he had to. Mary's family were import to her and she was important to him, he had to trust in that.

Hadn't her sister-in-law, Pembroke's Duchess, said something similar earlier, "our loyalty is to her, she believes you innocent…"

That loyalty must work both ways. They were letting him in for her benefit, trusting him. It would be crass of him not to trust them back.

He drew Mary to his side, leaving one arm about her shoulders and nodded at Pembroke, ignoring the discomfort flooding his veins.

The Duchess walked up to Pembroke, slipped her arms about his midriff, then pressed her head to his shoulder, he bent and kissed her temple. When she looked up they shared a brief kiss.

Drew saw a man he did not know. He had never expected to see Pembroke be so openly affectionate. He'd feared Pembroke would judge his and Mary's display.

"Are you coming in?" Pembroke said to Mary, a smile pulling his lips apart.

Mary looked up and Drew looked down as her arm wrapped about his waist. She smiled broadly. "I do not want to go in. Shall we walk out here for a while so we can talk?"

"If that's what you want, sweetheart."

"We'll have dinner served for six, Mary. You do not need to dress. It is just the four of us," the Duchess advised.

When Drew looked at her, she smiled warmly.

Mary slipped from beneath his arm and caught hold of his fingers.

God, he loved her, it was a physical presence in his blood. A surge of warmth. A rush of feeling.

"We'll walk down to the lake, come on." She pulled on his hand, but then stopped, came closer and lifted off his hat. "Here." She turned to look at a footman. "Take this, and Lord Framlington's gloves inside."

Smiling, Drew pulled off his gloves and handed them over.

Mary gripped his hand again, skin against skin, and she pulled him towards the vast open lawns, oblivious to any damage to her complexion; leaving Pembroke and his multitude of servants behind.

Weaving his fingers between hers, Drew glanced back. Pembroke and his wife were watching them, holding hands too as half-a-dozen footmen hung about them.

"Is this where you grew up?" He asked, as he looked back at Mary.

"No, my father has his own estate, near Uncle Richard's but it's nothing like this. Papa's property is a small manor house with farmlands. But he ran Uncle Robert's property for years, until Uncle Robert came home from the continent and Papa met Mama. John was ten then. But we came here once or twice a year to stay when grandfather was alive, but never for long because Papa didn't like him. He suffered him for Mama's sake, so that she could see my grandmother. But since John has owned it we've come often. I love the grounds. In the summer when all the family are here it's wonderful.

"How is your sister?" she breathed then, looking up at him.

He'd doubted her belief in him from the moment when Marlow had found them; thought her incapable of knowing the man trapped beneath the hard shell he'd set by experience; he'd thought she could only see the man carved by rumour.

Yet when rumour had him at his lowest – incestuous – without any moral fibre at all; Mary believed him innocent without knowing the truth.

Drew glanced back up at the house. Pembroke and his staff had gone.

They were out here alone unobserved.

Tugging their joined hands, he stopped, smiling as he pulled her closer, and then he kissed her. A long deep kiss, weighted with feeling. Love gripped at his heart as he ended it.

He tugged her hand to start them walking again.

Her smile widened.

"Caro is a little shaken and afraid. It took her courage to do it. It will take her considerable time, I think, to feel safe and settled. She's scared Kilbride will find her. If he ever did, I'd be frightened for her. He'd beaten her this time because she miscarried his child. It is not the first time."

"Where is she?"

She'd asked in all innocence. He smiled, *trust her Drew*. "If I tell you, it puts you in danger. Kilbride's cronies could push you for the information."

"You think I would tell…" She looked hurt.

"No, Mary. But I do not want to endanger you anymore than I'd risk him finding Caro. But if you must know, she's not far from here."

"I'd like to see her."

"Not any time soon, sweetheart, I'm not going near her for a long while, just to be safe. Kilbride is like your brother, he has money and men everywhere."

She looked away, and for a moment the only sound was the swish of the long grass giving away beneath their feet as they walked on.

Her fingers squeezed his.

The hill swept down to an ornamental lake in the distance.

"I'm sorry," Mary said to the horizon, "I overheard you talking to Lord Brooke. I thought you had a mistress. You had not been coming to bed and…"

They kept walking.

Drew did not care to think of the agony she must have felt. He'd been cut by her just dancing with Peter… and she'd thought… He squeezed her fingers. "So the Duchess told me. She said your aunt told you someone saw me with Caro. I do not blame you for thinking it, Mary, I should have told you."

She glanced in his direction. "You were not talking to me."

"No, as I said. I am an ass."

"You are friends with Peter again…"

"He called that night, he knows my tendency to sulk and stew. He also knows my dislike of admitting my mistakes. He probably knew I'd never go to him. Your sister-in-law found me at Peter's."

They didn't talk then, for a while, walking hand in hand, his fingers woven through hers, gripping tight, for fear of losing her again.

The heads of clover amongst the grass sent sweet perfume into the air, as they walked, and bumble bees buzzed about them.

Love for her sank deep into Drew's bones.

When they reached the lake, they walked along the shore a little way.

The water was still, like glass, a mirror reflecting back the summer sky, until a pair of swans with trailing signets glided across it, sending out fans of ripples on the surface.

"I feel like I've walked from a nightmare into a dream." He looked at Mary. "Are you real? Or did I fall asleep at Peter's. Am I dreaming?"

She stopped and turned to him, then lifted their joined hands and pressed a kiss on the back of his.

Drew remembered their last morning with painful guilt. "Why did you let me make love to you that morning? I thought…" A lump constricted his throat at the memory of her beautiful face as he'd made love to her barely an hour before she'd left.

He coughed and began again, as her smile fell. "I thought you had forgiven me, and understood, and wished to…stay… then…" Her eyes were bright with a confusing mix of love and uncertainty. "I did not like myself when I found you gone. I thought… I dreaded… Did you feel forced? That was my fear, Mary." His fingers, touched her cheek. "You broke my heart."

"My heart broke too." She turned away, her fingers slipping from his as she walked on. "I loved you. I love you. Just one last time I wanted to pretend you loved me too."

"You stupid girl." He rushed her, to break the sudden melancholy, grasping her from behind, trapping her in his arms and lifting her off her feet. "If I am an ass, you are a fool, I was not pretending. I adore you woman, you may get that into your silly head if you please."

He set her down. She laughed breathlessly.

"Let's sit for a while." He began unbuttoning his morning coat. She smiled, then bent and snapped off the head of a buttercup, spinning the stem in her fingers as he shrugged off his coat and then laid it on the ground for her to sit on, ignoring the fact he had no valet to repair any damage.

She swept her dress beneath her and sat amongst the long grass – a portrait.

Drew dropped to his knees, and then stretched out beside her, lying on his side, his head supported on his palm, in a nonchalant pose, denying the raging melee of emotions in his chest.

"Why were you so angry after we visited your parents?" She asked the question of the lake as she looked at the view and not him.

His view was her perfect profile, etched against the blue sky. "That is an untouchable subject. Even Brooke knows I will not converse on it."

She looked at him. "Andrew?"

"Mary." He broke off a stem of long grass and brushed the tip across her nose. She made a face at him, which said, speak.

"So you insist I go there, again, even though I have said I hate the subject."

She dropped the buttercup then her arms wrapped about her knees, her vulnerability showing through, as she lay her cheek on top of one knee, looking at him. "Are we going to argue, when we have only just been reunited? If you tell me, then I no longer need to ask and we need not argue."

Drew held her gaze. If she met Caro, Caro would tell her. Yet he did not like people knowing. His parents had never made it public, but they hardly hid it… He'd faced censure in all his years at school and from then on – ill-judgement.

He cared nothing for what others thought.

But he cared about her opinion.

Emotionally naked, he took her left hand from its grip about her knees and held it up between them, his fingers gripping the third finger that bore his ring, with the little leather cord wrapped about it to hold it on her finger. "You asked about this…" He pressed her ring finger up. "T R, whoever he is, Mary, is my father, not the Marquis. Caro and I are products of affairs my mother would like to pretend never occurred; however when a wailing child arrives nine months later they are rather hard to hide. I am named Framlington on my birth certificate, but my blood is not his. You see when I said I was an evil bastard, I truly am. Sins of the parents and all that…

"It is understandable therefore, I suppose, that the Marquis hates me. What I've never been able to accept is that my mother hates me with equal wrath. I am a constant reminder of her shame, an embarrassment, nothing more, as is Caro. Their manner of resolving that issue is to ignore our existence."

"Oh, Andrew." Mary unravelled from her self-protective pose and lay beside him, mimicking his posture as her free hand settled at his waist.

He shut his eyes rather than look at her. "If I see pity in your eyes, you will make me intensely angry again." Her fingertips touched his cheek.

"What about love? Can I look at you with love? It's not pity I'm offering. I love you, so I care about you. If you are hurting, I hurt. Is care allowed?"

Opening one eye, Drew gave her a crooked smile. Her eyes shone bright with concern, but mirth caught there too. He opened his other eye, and she laughed.

"Very well, I will accept care, and raise it. I admit, I want to hate her, and I tell myself I hate her, and the rest of them – but I still desperately want to belong among them – and now you know I am not an evil bastard but a bitter unwanted child."

"Not unwanted…"

Damn it. Her eyes glittered with pity. It pricked like a thorn in his side.

No. It is not pity. It is care.

God someone cares for me. Warmth stirred in his chest, not anger.

Mary clasped his hand, which still held the strand of grass. "You are very much wanted." She leaned forward and kissed the corner of his lips briefly, then rolled to her back. Looking up at the sky.

She was so beautiful. He brushed the tip of the grass he held about her cheek and down her neck. "But not by them; it is a hard lesson, well learned, I'm afraid. I steel myself by saying I do not give a damn for their opinion, or anyone else's for that matter. But then I met you. I care for yours. You wished to meet them, and for some ridiculous reason I thought perhaps, just perhaps, my mother would like you and be proud of me. I should not have taken you there."

"You should have said why you did not wish to go. Had you said I would not have persisted. The moment we walked in the door I knew it was wrong. But how could I have imagined that—"

"When your family all adore you." He brushed the tip of the grass over her bodice following it with his gaze. "The Pembroke clan are like lions, prowling and protecting, preventing scandal or harm attacking their pride. Did you realise that your womenfolk have even been busy waging a subtle war against me, while your men glare and prowl."

She smiled. "You do not expect me to pity you for that I hope? You chose to take them on."

"And I have had my money's worth."

"It was my money and if you did not wish to battle them you should not have fought. Instead of making friends with them, you made them enemies."

He dipped the tip of the grass into her cleavage, smiling. Pink stained her skin from her bodice upward. She was modest even now. A Pembroke to the heart. She would never cuckold him.

"Old habits die hard, darling. I do not trust people, especially families. I am judged by my birth and my family's reputation, when I am responsible for neither, and if the issue is their ignorance, why should I defend myself?"

368

"Ah, and now we are at the crux." Her gaze gripped his. "You do not like to be rejected, so you say you do not care what others think. Yet it is simply a mask. Avoiding that, says you care anyway, Andrew."

Drew ignored the proclamation, his gaze breaking free and lifting to a bobbing head of clover. He broke its stem, and its sweet perfume carried on the air. He drew a line down her cheek and neck with the flower, then trailed it along the neck of her bodice. "I made up my mind, the afternoon you were ill and I saw how much I had hurt you, that I was going to go to your brother's with you, stand up in the lions' den and declare my love for you."

She laughed. "If they did not believe it, then you would have then told them all to go to hell."

Drew laughed too. "Yes, I suppose so…" He smiled wryly.

"Then my father would have told you to go to hell too,"

"Careful, if you get a taste for foul language I will divorce you. You may like your men spirited. I like my women staid." His gaze fell to the smile hovering on her lips as he slid the stem of the clover into her bodice and left the flower there.

His gaze returned to the beautiful pale blue. "I do love you."

Her answer was in her eyes vivid and bright for him to read, *I love you more than anything*. How long had it been there and he'd not seen, hurting her regardless. He was an ass – a bastard. He did not want to be either anymore.

His gaze skimmed down to the flower he'd tucked in between her breasts then back up. *Ah, God*. Love pierced his soul. He had her back. He leaned over, his leg sliding between hers over her dress, and his hand cupped her breast over her bodice then he kissed her…

Her tongue played with his as her fingers gripped his hair.

He longed to take her here, in the long grass, lift her dress and have their pleasure, and it would be blissful. But this was about building better foundations for them – they'd never had a problem with their physical bond.

He pulled away, his mouth hovering just over hers. "Things will be different now."

Chapter 35

Painfully happy, but wary, Mary held on to the one thing he did not know. It made it so much more important that they resolved his issues. He'd said he did not like to admit he'd been at fault, even to Lord Brooke, and yet he'd said sorry after being so silent and cold during their journey back to London and he'd said sorry the morning she had left… He'd said sorry to her now. She hoped it was a sign he was changing.

But he was right, she liked his wildness, his freedom from restraints without those things he would be dull, and not Andrew.

"I know you returned my dowry to John."

His hazel eyes lost their rich amber depth and turned to shallow gold mirrors before he rolled away to lie on his back, one leg bent, his foot flat on the crushed grass as one arm slotted behind his head.

"I'm sorry it was not more." He looked up at the sky.

Mary rolled to her side, balancing her head on her palm and looking down at him.

"I had to spend some on Caro, and I'd paid my debts of course." His brown eyes looked to her saying, *damn the consequences.* "I am sorry it was done with your money, but I do not regret rescuing Caro from that marriage."

"I did not ask you to regret it; I would guess neither John nor

Papa would either. They will think it heroic of you." Her palm fell on his chest over the fabric of his waistcoat, where his heartbeat beneath.

He made an uncomplimentary sound in the back of his throat. "They will think me a sop. A man has a legal right to beat his wife if he chooses too, and it was their money, they gave it to me to protect your security, not Caro's. That is why I gave it back, you were no longer mine to keep secure…"

"I think your returning it jolted John's opinion of you. He thought you without conscience or the ability to care, and then you did something that made him doubt that. Protecting your sister proves you can care. You have pulled a rug out from beneath any argument he may have to dislike you."

"Except that I did once proposition his wife…" He smiled, wry amusement in his eyes.

Laughter rose from within Mary's chest. "Ah, yes, I forgot. That is rather undeniable evidence is it not, except that you told me why, perhaps you could tell him. But that would mean admitting you care for his opinion, and that, in your opinion, is a terrible thing…"

His smile parted his lips. "Are you mocking me?"

"Perhaps." Mary smiled too. "Why did you choose me over anyone else? If you married me for money, why did you give it back?"

His eyebrows lifted at the question and his smile fell. "Mary, I have told you. The first time I danced with you I knew you were the most beautiful creature—"

A bitter taste in her mouth, Mary's hand slid down over his waistcoat to rest on his stomach.

"But I remember you do not like to be appreciated for your looks. Yet you wished for honesty from me, and your beauty played a part. It was more than that though. You danced with me and smiled at me and talked as though I was any other man, because you had no idea I was untouchable, a hell born bastard. You charmed me. Perhaps I was even in love with you then. Perhaps I fell at first sight." His fingers snapped. "I wanted you. The impulse was immediate and instinctive."

"Except that during the waltz after that you asked Kate to share a bed with you. No more lies. I asked because I want to know the truth. Even if your answer is ugly, and merely because you liked my looks and my money, I would know the truth. I know it is not what you think now."

His arm moved from behind his head and his hand gripped hers where it lay on his stomach. "It is the truth, Mary. I asked your sister-in-law out of spite. I told you so. Not that I am proud of it. It is another of my faults, if people expect me to behave badly I have an incontrollable itch to infuriate them. I did not know I'd fallen in love moments before because I have never known love. All I knew was, I was mesmerised by you. When I saw you after that, a strange emptiness always gripped my stomach. I procrastinated, for a whole season. I needed money, you had it, and yet you seemed beyond any hope. But you kept glancing at me and you gave me hope.

"This season I watched you, and those same feelings were there. My bumping into you at that garden party was deliberate, and when we met in that dark glasshouse my stomach was queasy," he moved her hand, "just here, with anticipation and longing, and here," he slid their joined hands back up to cover his heart, "there was pain. It is the same when I look at you, when I hear your voice, and… when I make love to you it hits me like a flood of emotion brimming up and over. Am I right, is it love?" His eyes shone light brown, gilded with gold in the sunlight.

"It is. It is how I feel too." Mary pressed her fingers more firmly against his chest.

"But I should tell you the whole truth, I suppose…"

A frown crushed Mary's brow.

"Since I danced with you the first night I met you, I've not bedded another woman."

"That was a year ago—"

"I know. I have never really been a rake, Mary, just a little wild and misled, and I shall admit too that your sister-in-law's refusal only piqued my interest more. I did not only watch you, but I watched your family. They all seemed to have monogamous marriages; love-matches I suppose. A thing my family are incapable of. That is the one thing I longed for in a wife. It seemed to me that if the women of your family were faithful, you would be faithful."

She slid her fingers out from beneath his and touched his cheek. She'd seen how vulnerable he was after they'd called on his parents, but now she saw how deep it ran.

He may have learned to love her, but he did not love himself because no one had loved or cared for him as a child. He did not think himself loveable.

He would call himself a fool, she would call him wounded – but not aloud, he'd take it as pity. "And I chose to go out alone with your friend…"

His eyebrows lifted.

"I suppose your conclusions were instinctive…"

"That was crass of me." He caught hold of her fingertips and kissed them. "I knew it then, but I saw his hand on you and… it cut. It was wrong of me. I judged you by others, just as people do to me."

"In future may we always be honest with one another? I loved you too from that first night. You were the only man there whenever you entered a room. You fascinated me. I wish you had come forward and dealt openly with my father and told him the things you've just told me, he would not have kept us apart. He always promised me my husband would be my choice. It is why John added to my dowry so my choice need not be restricted by a lack of money."

"Your father would not have wanted a bastard for a son-in-law, especially not one with a rake's reputation."

"My father will not care if you tell him you love me. He only wishes me happy – and you make me happy."

His brown eyes held her gaze and he kissed her fingers again, then his breath hot on her fingertips he said, "I'll tell him, and I promise not to be so sour."

"You are not sour. You are handsome," she leant and kissed his cheek, "and kind," she pressed a kiss on his brow, "and good – when you wish to be." She smiled. "Yet most importantly you are mine. I care for you, I love you, and I'll not let you go, nor share you, Andrew."

"When I took you away, when your father and your brother came to get you, I hated that they had a greater claim on you, that your affection was for them, that you believed them and not me. I was jealous. I want to be all to you."

"You have been all to me since the day you came into John's garden when my parents were away from home. I was hurt by what they said, because I love you. I did not want to believe it, because I love you, but you would not say a single word to argue your case."

"My faults are legion." His fingers squeezed hers. "I will no longer be an ass and I shall apologise to your father."

Mary lowered her head and kissed his lips, then holding his gaze whispered over them, "I love you."

His fingers cupped her scalp and he kissed her back for a long time.

When they drew apart, she rested her head on his shoulder, and rolled to her back, listening to the bees gathering honey from the clover.

But then she remembered, she had not been wholly honest with him yet… "Andrew. There is something I have to tell you."

"What, Mary?" He turned, rising. Mary's head slipped on to the grass.

Concern shone in his eyes.

She gripped his hand and pulled it to her stomach. "It is this. You are to be a father. I am carrying."

He sucked in a hard sharp breath and his hand lifted, as though the contact had burnt him, while his gaze dropped to her stomach.

God in heaven! A child! His gaze lifted back to her pale blue eyes; they shone like diamonds. A child?

Hell, she'd left with his child in her.

"Would you have told me if we were apart?" The words were a little bitter.

But Mary simply smiled. "Yes. Kate is illegitimate too. That is her story to tell, but Kate brought me here so I might adjust to the knowledge, but she made me promise I would tell you. Although I would not have spoken with joy. But now we can be happy, and our child will be happy."

"Our child…" His palm settled on her stomach. There was no change, but inside her a new life had been created. It was being nurtured, by a woman who would love it.

Emotion overwhelmed him and moisture clouded his gaze.

He turned away, sitting up with his knees bent, looking out at the lake.

A child. A son or a daughter. His. His wife. His family.

It felt as if the ground rocked underneath him.

He'd always been unworthy and unwanted, but his child would be wholly worthy and wholly wanted. Mary would love it, and he would love it.

She sat up too, and her arms came about his midriff as she pressed her cheek to his shoulder.

Something broke inside him, something hard, dark and cold and it became warm and light as he leant his cheek against her hair. It smelt beautiful. Roses. Love played about in his heart, and his soul, dancing.

He wiped his cheeks, *devil take it* he would not have any one see him being so unmanly. *Lord* his friends would laugh themselves stupid if they could see him now.

When she lifted her head, there were tear stains on her cheeks too. He wiped them away with his thumbs, and then his palms pressing against her cheeks, he kissed her fiercely.

A gong rang out announcing dinner.

She pulled away. "Oh goodness, do you think they have been waiting for us." She stood. "Do I look a state? Have I grass in my hair?"

"You look beautiful." She looked flushed, happy and bright eyed. He stood and offered her his hand.

She took it and rose. "You cannot wear your coat…" She turned and bent to pick it up. "It is too creased. You will have to give it to John's valet to see if he can repair it."

"I'll live without it." He took it from her hand.

"It is only John and Kate who know I am with child. Neither my father nor my mother and nor anyone else within my family know…"

He smiled and hugged her hard. Then when he released her, captured her hand and wove his fingers through hers. They walked back up to the house thus.

Chapter 36

Drew walked down to the breakfast room, feeling like a different man to the hollow one who had stayed at Brooke's the day before.

That other man was a stranger.

Drew had gone for a walk and a smoke before breakfast, leaving Mary in bed. He'd wandered down to the lake. It was so ridiculously quiet here. Calm. Peaceful.

When he'd returned, Mary had risen, and already gone down to break her fast. He was on his way to join her, but not looking forward to another meal with Pembroke.

Dinner last night had been strained. They had made polite conversation to avoid uncomfortable silence and the Duchess had worked hard to draw him into it, but he had not really known what to say.

As soon as the meal was over he'd grasped the opportunity to escape with Mary.

They had retired to her rooms, which were as large as he'd guessed, and then they'd held one another, and talked again. There had been no lust then.

But he'd woken in the night, at her urging, as she'd kissed his lips. He'd kissed her back, thoroughly, with an urgent desire to be inside her.

They'd made love in utter darkness, the call of night owls

reaching them through an open window, the warm breeze brushing across his skin and the smell of clean, fresh grass and clover scented air flooding the room. He had made love to her slowly, adoring every inch of her body, and afterwards he'd tucked her beneath his arm and slept, knowing to the very depths of his marrow she was entirely his, and always would be.

He had not dared to think of the child.

"Framlington? Are you sure, Mary?"

Drew stopped as his foot left the staircase, and Pembroke's voice echoed about the hall.

People who overheard conversations about themselves never heard anything good. And yet… he could not help it, he wanted to know what she said behind his back. Drew crossed the hall as quietly as he could.

"He does love me, John." The doors of the breakfast room were a little ajar, Drew could see the Duchess was not there, and nor were there any footmen, even in the hall. So the conversation had grown private.

Her brother looked at her, his gaze assessing.

All Drew could see of Mary was her back.

"We watched you yesterday for a while, Katherine and I, as you lay in the meadow, talking; his behaviour certainly suggested he has feelings for you."

"If you knew him –"

"He is not a man to be easily known."

"Only because he closes himself off. It does not make him bad, it just means he is wary, because he is vulnerable, as I said."

Her brother's gaze showed something Drew would have not even recognised two months ago – care. He cared immensely for his sister. "You were vulnerable too..."

"That is different, and not why I fell in love with him."

She was vulnerable?

"You wished to be special to someone. No doubt he made you feel it. It is not always easy growing up in a large family is it?

379

Even if that family is full of love, one becomes another member of a crowd, and loses any individuality." Pembroke smiled in a way Drew would not have thought him capable. Pembroke was different at home.

"No," she admitted. "I have longed for a few years to have someone to love and love me in return with their whole heart and not just a piece of it."

Her brother drank the last of his coffee and rose then walked about the table to rest a hand on her shoulder. "I felt the same. I shut you all out rather than admit the truth. Katherine was my answer. I think perhaps you have found yours too. I did wonder when he turned up at that musical evening and came that afternoon. But he is good at masquerading. He makes it appear he has no interest at all."

She looked up at her brother. "He will be different now. He's promised to be different."

"I hope he is for your sake, but I do believe that he has feelings for you. I hope he loves you. I wish you happy, as does Katherine."

Pembroke leant and kissed Mary's cheek.

Drew took a breath and walked into the room. Now was his moment to prove Mary's words true. "As do I."

Pembroke straightened, suspicion in his eyes, obviously wondering how much Drew had heard.

Enough.

Mary stood.

Drew walked to her side, and settled his arm about her shoulders. "I love your sister, Pembroke, she will be happy, there is no if."

Mary turned and embraced his midriff, pressing her cheek to his shoulder, as though they'd been separated for days, not less than an hour.

He kissed the crown of her head, love tugging inside him, and looked at Pembroke, expecting outrage over their show of affection.

Pembroke smiled, with the mellow look Drew had only just discovered Pembroke possessed.

"I shall leave you to your breakfast." He nodded at Drew, then walked out.

When Pembroke was gone, Mary slipped free, smiling. "He approves. I told you, all they wish for is my happiness. If you make me happy. Papa will approve too."

Drew's hand gripped her nape and pulled her back, then he kissed her, hard.

* * *

Mary chose to rest in the afternoon and Drew was at a loose end. He'd explored the grounds with her on horseback before luncheon, but after they'd eaten, she claimed her condition made her tired.

Drew also thought it might be because she'd not been eating enough. He'd sat beside her at luncheon to ensure that changed, and filled her plate, ignoring any complaint.

Not wanting to disturb her sleep, he'd left her alone, avoiding temptation.

He walked along the upper hall to go back outdoors for a smoke.

"Steady now, a step at a time..." Pembroke's deep tone had a low sing-song pitch. A gurgling, gleeful sound followed. Pembroke walked forward from the other direction, doubled over, his forefingers gripped by an infant's chubby little hands. The child toddled before Pembroke on unsteady feet, rocking and swaying, but grinning and laughing.

A sharp lancing pain struck Drew's chest.

He had eavesdropped this morning, but now he felt as if he looked in through a window and had seen something personal – and precious.

Pembroke looked up, and smiled. "You have not yet met my son have you?"

Pembroke gripped the child's waist, and picked the boy up, tossed him in the air and caught him. The child squealed with excitement.

381

Then Pembroke balanced the boy on one arm while the other protected him from toppling.

Drew took two more steps towards them, feeling as he had done in Pembroke's drawing room that day – out of place – bemused.

"Katherine is lying down too, she is also expecting. I thought I would give Paul some air. He likes crawling on the grass, or rather he likes the endless space where there is nothing to make me say, no. Are you going outside?"

"Yes."

"Then we may keep each other company, if you wish?"

Drew nodded, then followed Pembroke as he turned to the stairs.

Pembroke crooned at the boy, while Drew fought to imagine himself with a child. He could not.

When they reached the downstairs hall Pembroke ordered lemonade and cake to be served in the garden. They did not go out the front, but to the back, to the terrace, where the sprawling building gave some shade from the sun's rays.

Pembroke descended the flight of steps on to the cut grass and set the chid down. The boy instantly sped off on hands and knees.

Pembroke rose up and set his hands on his hips, watching. "It takes some time adjusting to it, yet fatherhood is a wonderful thing. I shall never cease to wonder at the miracle of it. But you will know it for yourself soon enough." Pembroke glanced back at Drew.

He understood. He knew Drew was out of his depth and treading water hard not to suddenly sink.

"You may practice on my son, if you wish, or you may just wish to dive in to the deep when your own arrives." Pembroke was laughing at him, without actually laughing, but there was humour in his eyes. "I was like you once, Framlington. I assure you, the instinct to love will fill you, in droves."

Easy for a man to say when he had been loved and not hated by his mother and abandoned by his father. The instinct to love had not come to Drew's parents.

"If what you said, and what Mary has said, is true, and you love each other, you will love the child."

Damn it, was Pembroke reading his mind?

"I doubted my own capability. Edward, Lord Marlow, was a father to me from the age of ten, before that my uncles and grandfather had been it to me in various ways, my childhood had distorted my view of love. When you knew me in Paris I was as self-destructive as you. I sentenced myself to exile for a while until my grandfather died and then I came home. Katherine was my saving grace. My son is our completion."

Drew's hand lifted to comb through his hair. His hand shook.

The servants delivered the lemonade and Pembroke ran to fetch his crawling, wayward child.

Pembroke picked up the boy and returned to the terrace, then sat and fed the child small pieces of cake and sips of lemonade.

Drew watched mesmerized. Nothing in his life would have let him imagine this...

Yet he wanted to learn to do the same, he would not treat his child as he had been treated as a boy. He would love – no, more than that – he would cherish his child as Pembroke did his son.

When the lad was crawling across the grass again, Pembroke sat on the steps to watch.

Further along the terrace Drew leaned on the balustrade, watching them both and lit a cigar.

"I have a property you may be interested in." Pembroke said in the direction of his son.

"A property?" Drew straightened and moved closer.

Pembroke looked at him, "It's some miles away, so you would not literally be on my doorstep, but it is a small manor that adjoins my lands, I bought it recently when it was for sale because it did so. There are rents from two farms which belong to it and a home farm." Pembroke stood up.

"Of course I shall give you Mary's dowry back and I would be prepared to sell that property to you at a fair rate. Or if you preferred I would lease it to you and you could manage it, have the rents, but in that case you would not have the chance to pass it on to your son, and his son in future years."

"And you want us close, so you may keep an eye on Mary, because you do not trust me..."

Pembroke held Drew's gaze, but there was no fierceness or challenge in Pembroke's eyes.

"I do not wish you close, but I wish Mary happy and settled. The property is ideal. You and I were acquaintances once, perhaps if you let down your guard, we could be friends. Certainly Mary would like to have Kate and I near."

And Mary was the most important thing to them all.

"You may show me it, and I will consider it"

"Then we'll ride over there tomorrow."

Chapter 37

Andrew had been solicitous for days. He'd barely left her side, and they'd talked and walked.

In the morning they always rode out together, about John's estate, and in the evening they spent time with Kate and John playing cards. Andrew had even sat beside her as she'd played the pianoforte and sung, turning the music for her, and he'd read to her several times in the afternoon.

He was purchasing a property nearby. He'd taken her to see it the day after he'd been there with John. It was halfway down a hill which dropped into the river valley. It was a Tudor manor. Its wooden beams formed a skeleton, running through red bricks.

When they'd ridden down there the front of the house had caught the morning sun, as if it cast a blessing on their chosen home.

It was not overly large, but it was charming, nestling in woodland which surrounded it at either side.

Andrew was pleased with the prospect of building a home for them. It had become his favourite topic, and he'd begun learning estate management from John.

One afternoon, while she'd rested, he'd even ridden out with John, and John's steward, to the farms that would be Drew's, to meet the tenants and labourers and look over the fields and herds.

He and John seemed on good terms, and although Andrew claimed that living close to Kate and John would benefit her and that was why he'd agreed to John's proposal, she knew he would benefit from John's presence too. This was all new to Andrew, and John would be there to ask questions of, and provide assurance.

They had been together here for six days, and already so much had changed. Mary truly believed things would be good. They could become a true family and be happy.

"A carriage is approaching, Your Grace."

John had Paul on his knee. He looked at the footman. "Is there a coat of arms?"

"There is, Your Grace."

John stood. "Well it appears we have a guest. Would you prepare the kitchen…"

Andrew stood too. They were all still wary of Lord Kilbride's threats.

"I had better go down." John passed Paul to Kate.

"I shall join you." Drew rose.

Mary stood. "Then I shall come also."

Kate rose too as they left the room.

The carriage was pulled by four glossy blacks, and as it pulled up before the portico, they all descended the stairs. Mary recognised the insignia. Her uncle Richard's.

Mary moved forward with John, leaving Andrew behind. John's footman put down the step and the door opened.

"John." Richard's voice rang deep with formality. He looked back at Andrew.

Mary turned back and gripped Andrew's hand, as Richard looked at John.

"How fair you?"

"Well." John answered.

"And how are things?"

"Things are fine, Your Grace." Andrew answered, as though he knew the question was code for, *and how do you find Framlington…*

"Have you come all this way to ask that?"

John glanced back across his shoulder, clearly asking Andrew for restraint, then he faced Richard again. "Things are fine, if a certain person knew when to restrain his bravado. What has brought you here?"

"Lord Framlington." Richard stepped forward. "May I speak with you? May we go inside?"

Mary knew that John had written to Richard and told him Andrew was here and that they believed him innocent, but Richard had not replied, and his eyes said he did not trust that judgement.

Andrew's fingers gripped hers harder. Mary gripped his arm with her other hand. She would willingly protect him.

"Go up to the family drawing room," Kate said, from behind them. "Finch will send up a tea tray." The butler beside her bowed, acknowledging the request.

Richard lifted a hand, "There is no need for refreshment on my account." Finch bowed again, and Richard's hand encouraged Andrew to lead.

Mary's heart pounded.

What was this?

What new disaster?

She took a seat in the drawing, her legs suddenly wobbly. Andrew stood beside the chair, his fingers on her shoulder.

Richard did not sit, neither did John, and Kate hovered at John's side, her fingers laced through his. She must have passed Paul to one of the servant's to take up to the nursery.

"What is it?" Andrew asked, his voice an ominous deep pitch. "What charge have you against me now?"

"This is not my charge. It is a formal charge against you – of incest. I have come to take you back to London. If the story you've told Mary and John is true, then you must tell it to a magistrate. Your only other option is to flee the country, and I will not have that for Mary's sake. You should ask your sister to speak for you too."

"I'll not give Kilbride a chance to find Caro, but I will come with you and state my case."

"You would face one man's word against another, then, Framlington. When all evidence points to one conclusion. You will risk hanging, if your sister will not speak for you."

Andrew sighed. "I will risk hanging anyway; her word may count for nothing as I am sure you know, and I will not risk her."

Mary stood and faced him. "Andrew." Her voice begged as his gaze met hers.

He looked past her to Richard. "No, I cannot do it. I'm all she has. If they do not believe either of us Kilbride will have her back and he will kill her. I cannot risk her safety. I have hidden her alone, she has no one to protect her. No. I'll go, but I will not betray Caro. She is safe only as long as no one knows where she is."

"Lady Kilbride may come here," John spoke. "If you go to London, I shall fetch her. She may live here for as long as she wishes so you know she is safe. You have seen how many servants I have, no one can reach her here without me knowing."

Mary looked at John then Andrew; he hesitated. He did not trust John enough.

"It is a good idea," Richard added, "Your sister will be safe here whatever the outcome, remember this allegation is raised against her also."

Mary wished to scream when Andrew still did not speak.

She turned and took hold of both his hands. His eyes were pale amber and honey as they looked at her. "You trust me. Let me fetch her with John and bring her here. I promise she will be safe. Then she can speak for you."

"Very well, bring her here but I will not ask her to speak. I will not have her return to London, Kilbride's thugs would steal her away. I will give you the address and a letter from me. She will know she is safe with you, Mary." He looked at John. "But do not ask her to leave your lands, Pembroke. She would be in danger then."

He looked back at Mary, gripping her hands hard, as though he wished to promise he'd return, and promise all would be well

– he could not promise, it was not within his power, but his gaze held hope.

She withdrew her hands from his, denying her urge to cling to him, and turned to a desk in the corner of the room, hiding the tears in her eyes as she searched for ink, a quill and paper.

When he sat down to write she watched his fingers form the familiar script, which she had seen in his love letters; even if the words on the page had not been his, they had been in his hand.

When he finished, he blotted the letter, folded it and handed it to her. "It is addressed and carries nothing private."

He gripped her free hand as he turned back to face the others. "I'm ready, Wiltshire. I'd rather get this settled." Andrew squeezed her fingers again offering reassurance – he could not give it.

"Framlington." Her uncle nodded at Andrew with an intense light in his eyes.

Ten minutes later, Mary said, "Goodbye," crying, her tears now unrestrained. She had only just found happiness with him.

He wiped away her tears with his thumbs, and then bent to kiss her fiercely. "I am coming back," he whispered as he pulled away. "I would not have dragged you into this muddle for anything, but I cannot regret helping Caro."

"I know."

They stood on the steps beneath the massive stone portico, their foreheads resting together. John and Kate stood to one side of the waiting carriage, the same that Richard had arrived in, with fresh horses in the straps, Richard stood beside the open carriage door.

"It is not your fault. I do not blame you. I love you."

"I love you too," he whispered, back, and with that he kissed her again and then he was gone.

A few moments later she stood on the steps beside John watching as the carriage rattled off along the drive, the horses' hooves striking at a canter.

"We had best fetch Lady Kilbride immediately."

John looked at Finch, who nodded to confirm a carriage would be prepared.

"I need my bonnet." Mary turned and hurried inside, glad for a focus to prevent her crumbling entirely. She could help Andrew by helping his sister.

She returned to the hall within a quarter hour, tying the ribbons of her bonnet in a bow beneath her chin.

Andrew's letter was tucked in her bodice against her skin, beneath her day dress and spencer.

John looked ducal as he offered his arm. "We will be as quick as we can, Katherine, you must not worry."

John's unmarked carriage stood waiting on the drive, and his grooms and footmen were no longer dressed in the Pembroke livery. When they drove off Pembroke land, it left by the rear exit from the park. "Just in case Kilbride has someone watching the gates," John said quietly.

When the carriage reached Maidstone they stopped at a coaching inn. "Where are we to go then, Mary?"

Her fingers shaking Mary slipped the letter out from her bodice, and showed John the address.

"Come then."

One of John's footmen opened the carriage door, bowing with a little less gravity than was normal.

John must have told them to act as if he was not a duke.

Mary gripped John's arm as they walked past the Bishop's Palace, and the ford beside it, to find the row of terraced cottages Andrew had described to her.

Most of the narrow front gardens were planted with vegetables, apart from one; Caroline's was planted with a mass of flowers, hollyhocks and delphiniums, and beautiful frail little flowers which looked like tiny bonnets.

"I think it is best you wait here," Mary said to John as they neared. "Lady Kilbride may not open the door if she sees a gentleman calling."

John nodded, stopping.

Mary's fingers slipped from his arm, and she bent to open the low gate. It led onto a narrow, paved pathway.

The aged oak door was wide but just as squat as the thatched cottage.

Lady Kilbride must be very aware of her fall in circumstance. Previously she must have lived in properties almost as grand as John's.

Mary dropped the knocker against the door four times. The low thuds vibrated through the wood.

There was no answer.

But beyond the door Mary heard whispers. She waited.

"Who is there?" It was an older woman's voice.

"It is Lady Framlington." Mary leant a little towards the door, so her voice would not carry on the air. "Your brother sent me, he could not come himself."

Another hushed, urgent conversation ensued.

Then finally the sound of a bolt shifting breached the door.

A woman Mary presumed to be a housekeeper opened it. She wore a black dress, dusted with flour; as though she had been interrupted at work in the kitchen, and stripped off an apron a moment ago.

She bobbed a curtsy.

Beyond her, Mary saw Lady Kilbride. She stood in the shadows further back, with a brown woollen shawl wrapped tightly about her. Her dress beneath it looked plain, homely, and her hair was simply coiled and pinned in a knot.

"May I come in? My brother is with me."

Lady Kilbride's gaze reached past Mary, instantly afraid.

Mary entered, holding out the letter as the serving woman stepped aside. "I have this from Andrew, so you know that what I say is true."

Lady Kilbride took it, her hand shaking.

Mary turned to the door, and beckoned John.

When she turned back Lady Kilbride had paled. "He has accused

Drew of being my lover." She looked at Mary. "Incest is a crime. I never thought… *Oh God.*" She suddenly turned from pale to a sickly white.

Mary hurried forward and gripped her arm, as John entered behind her, removing his hat and bending his head to pass beneath the low lintel.

He could not even stand straight in the hall.

"This way Ma'am," the serving woman directed them to a parlour.

"You must sit," Mary whispered, guiding Lady Kilbride. There were two armchairs in the room; Mary helped Lady Kilbride to one and bid John take the other, as he could not stand comfortably.

"Drew will regret helping me," Lady Kilbride said quietly, her fingers gripping Andrew's letter so hard it crumpled.

"He does not. In fact the last thing he said to me, was that he could not regret it."

"Your Grace." Lady Kilbride moved to stand suddenly, when John sat, but Mary pressed a hand on her shoulder to keep her seated.

"Forgive me, I would continue to stand but it is a little awkward," John said "and I would rather you felt able to be informal in my presence… besides it is far easier to converse, with us both seated."

Lady Kilbride's hands trembled as they rested in her lap, the letter quivering in her fingers.

"I have promised to protect you," John continued. Ignoring her discomfort. "You will be far safer at Pembroke Place, no one can come within miles of the house without being seen, and my wife, Katherine, and Mary and I, will be there to keep you company. Of course the house and grounds will be at your disposal. You may mix with the family, or avoid us entirely if you wish. But there is a music room and a library to entertain you also. It need not be confinement as this must feel, and you need not live in fear, Lady Kilbride?"

"Why would you help me?" She looked from John to Mary.

Mary remembered Andrew's poisonous family. They had been Lady Kilbride's family too. "Because you are my sister now..." Mary dropped to her haunches and gripped one of Lady Kilbride's hands.

"You are together again?" Her light brown eyes were like Andrew's. Like their mother's Mary supposed.

"Yes."

Lady Kilbride's other hand gripped their joined ones. "He deserves to be happy and I knew you would make him so. But he is a stubborn man."

"And a good one."

"Yes, and a good one." Lady Kilbride smiled. "I owe him much."

"The two of you are not alone anymore. Will you come with us?" John asked, his baritone cutting the stillness in the room.

Lady Kilbride glanced at him, but then her gaze found Mary's. "I will come."

"Then we should go directly." Mary stood. "John can send a cart back for your possessions."

Chapter 38

As Drew stood before the magistrate, accounting for his actions, the Duke of Wiltshire sat nearby watching.

The pompous ass who quizzed Drew merely grunted at his answers, and glowered, as a clerk scribbled every word on paper.

Every expression said the man did not believe Drew innocent. The world believed too deeply in the façade rumour and his family had cast.

But incest... That was a hideous crime. Drew's stomach rolled.

His only counter evidence was that he had been protecting Caro. But there was no law against a man beating his wife – and how the hell did a man prove he'd not had intercourse with his sister.

Nausea spun in his blood again.

How could people think him so low? Where were his mother and his brothers to deny such a thing?

Hatred burned in his veins as he walked from the court to await an intermediate verdict on his fate.

Wiltshire sat on the hard wooden bench outside the court rooms, beside Drew, in silence.

Drew leant forward, his hands gripping his brow.

The fear biting at his innards was not for his own fate, his thoughts were for Mary – and Caro... Where was Caro now? What would this mean for her?

"Lord Framlington!" His name echoed about the stone hall.

As he stood, he met Wiltshire's gaze. The man did not look as though he believed Drew's fate would be positive.

In the wood panelled, dark court room, he faced the magistrate. "You will be held in custody until I have spoken with Lady Kilbride,"

Drew bit his tongue, he would not tell them where she was.

Kilbride had influenced this. He would use it to find Caro – and regardless the evidence of a rogue against the evidence of a Marquis would not count.

"You will tell the clerk Lady Kilbride's address. Lord Kilbride has assured me that you know it, and remember Lord Framlington, fleeing from London at the point you were accused does not imply innocence."

No words from him would solve this. He was being found guilty by the bias of society, who judged the person they had painted, not the truth.

When he left the court he looked at the clerk. "If you think I will give my sister back into Kilbride's hands, you may—"

"Lord Framlington!" Wiltshire gripped Drew's arm. "Have sense. Unless you wish a noose about your neck then you must agree, and I do not wish to see my niece a widow when she is barely wed." Then he leaned to Drew's ear and whispered harshly. "Lady Kilbride is safe with John. Tell them."

Damn it.

"I shall agree to it if the magistrate will go to her, and if His Grace, the Duke of Wiltshire may accompany him and be present while she is questioned."

"I will make sure of it." Wiltshire agreed. But it was not his decision. Yet the weight of a Duke's voice exceeded any, bar royalty, and Wiltshire was a principled man.

Wiltshire paid for Drew to have a solitary cell, sheets on his bed, and hot meals.

"Your Grace, I am grateful. But please tell Mary—"

"I will tell her that I am doing my utmost to get you home to her."

Drew held Wiltshire's gaze. He had done nothing to deserve this man's help, and yet he was helping.

He was helping because he valued Mary.

"Tell her I love her too, and tell Pembroke to make sure she eats, she has a habit of not eating when she is distressed and she has lost enough weight recently, she must think of the child."

"The child?" Wiltshire's eyebrows rose.

Andrew just looked at him in answer, what was there to say.

Wiltshire's hand rested on Drew's shoulder. "We will get you out of this."

When he left, the key turned in the cell door locking Drew in and leaving him in gloomy silence.

He hated silence and solitude. It encouraged introspection and he had always avoided that.

He lay down on the narrow bunk, with its uncomfortable straw mattress, and shut is eyes. He could not sleep, though.

* * *

Drew paced the length of the small cell, then sat for a while and then paced again. He would hear nothing today, they would be out at Pembroke's speaking with Caro.

At midday, Drew heard the jangle of keys.

He went to the small square of bars in the door and strained to look along the hall. The guard was trailed by Brooke. Gripping the bars, Drew's forehead pressed to the cold metal, he smiled, as Peter did. But Drew's smile had a bitter twist as he stepped back so the guard could open the door.

Confinement was torture.

Brooke threw a paper and a packet of cigars on to Drew's narrow mattress.

Drew sat down, as the guard shut and locked the door.

Hands in his pockets Brooke looked down.

"Feel free to claim a seat…" Drew offered.

"If it has fleas I might decline."

A humorous sound broke from the back of Drew's throat. "If it has fleas then I do."

"Mark and Harry came with me, but they would only let one of us up here."

Drew looked up and met Peter's gaze. "It is a sorry ending, is it not?"

"I doubt it is the end," Peter moved the paper aside and sat among the fleas. "You are a part of Pembroke's clan now, my friend. They are like a damned army, sweeping through every ballroom and salon dispelling the rumours. Someone mentions your name and one of them is there, putting them straight. Uncles, aunts, cousins, cousins of cousins… They have influence across three quarters of the society. You are in the fold and being looked after. Marrying that girl was probably the best thing you could have done."

Drew looked at Peter. "It was." But not for that reason.

Peter slapped a hand on his shoulder. "When you get out of here, you will no longer wish to know your old friends now you have such new and powerful ones."

"You will always be my friend."

"Mary, may not like that."

"Mary will not mind. Things are good between us again."

"I am glad for you then."

"I'm to be a father."

"I'll be damned, although I suppose it was inevitable. Poor child."

Drew smiled. "If I get out of here, just for your humour, and because I could not have you as my groom's man, I shall make you godfather, and if I do not get out of here, you must tell Mary it is what I wished. The child will be in the cradle of her family, but my child ought to have some memory of me."

"You wish me to share tales of how many cups you can drink and still stand…" When Drew did not laugh Brooke's hand settled on his shoulder. "You have Pembroke's and Wiltshire's influence you will get out."

"I hope so but I am not certain. Kilbride has influence too."

"Enough!" The guard shouted through the square opening in the door, announcing that Peter's allotted minutes were up.

* * *

Mary leaned against the drawing room door, her palms, and her ear, pressed to the wood trying to listen, but they were too far away, and Caroline spoke too quietly.

She pulled away and turned to look at John. "I cannot hear."

"You should not be listening."

"I know but what if they do not believe her."

"Then they are idiots. It is obviously not true."

Mary had been stalwart since they'd fetched Caroline, suppressing her fear, because tears would do Andrew no good. She'd ordered tea for the Magistrate and Richard when they had arrived because Kate was in bed, and acted hostess… Yet…

"Mary…" John held her as the tears suddenly flowed.

"I cannot bear it…I cannot think of what may happen. I cannot…"

John's hand stroked over her back. "I can make no promises, but Richard is trying to solve this."

She sobbed against his lapel.

"I sent a letter to Mama, I asked them to come. Mary, I think you need Mama here."

She cried even harder. She'd been brave for two days, she did not wish to be brave anymore. She wished to be with Andrew. She lifted her head, tears streaming down her cheeks. "Do you think Richard will take me back with him so I can see Andrew?"

John's hands framed her face. "No. It is better you stay away, let Richard manage it, and I doubt, with the amount of pride your husband has, he would thank us for letting you see him in such a situation. Stay here and support Lady Kilbride. That is how you may help. She needs you; you are the only person Lady Kilbride trusts."

Mary swallowed back her tears. She knew everything John said was true and yet she could not bear the pain. She had thought she'd lost Andrew, and mourned here, and cried for days, and then she'd discovered her thoughts the lie, and he'd been restored to her, and now… "What am I going to do?"

"You are going to remain calm, that is what is best for the child, and you are going to feel confident and trust Richard to return Drew to you."

A sob broke form Mary's throat. "What if he cannot?"

"Do not think about it. For now simply believe that he will come back, Mary."

She held John again and sobbed against the front of his coat.

"I am sorry." John said gently.

But no words were going to bring Andrew back. No that was a lie, perhaps the words Caroline was speaking beyond the door would bring him back.

The door handle turned.

Mary pulled away from John, wiping her eyes, as the door opened. It was Richard.

He looked from Mary to John. "We are finished. I believe Lady Kilbride would appreciate your company, Mary. John, may I stay with you and dine here before I return to town?"

"Of course," John answered.

Mary brushed past him to speak with Caroline, hurrying across the room, ignoring the magistrate. Let John play the obsequious role to try and influence the man; she had nothing to say to anyone who could think Andrew guilty. Caroline had risen from the chair, but she was shaking terribly.

Mary gripped Caroline's hands. They were cold and within one she gripped a handkerchief one of the men must have given her during her interview. "I am sorry you had to endure this."

"Better that than for Drew to suffer because of me."

A tear escaped her eye, and then more fell, Mary leaned to hold her, but instead of simply comforting Caroline, she cried too, and then they clung to each other.

Caroline broke their embrace, first. She looked embarrassed as she wiped her eyes. "I am sorry."

Mary wiped her eyes with the sleeve of her dress. "You have no cause to be sorry."

"I do, this is my fault."

"It is not…" Mary breathed. "It is no one's fault, and we are going to remain calm, that is what is best for Andrew, and we are going to feel confident and trust Richard to return him to us." Mary regurgitated John's words. She had to believe them. She would be unable to keep breathing if she did not.

"The magistrate did not believe me, not wholly. He is going to speak with one of my lady's maids to ask her to confirm what I have said, the whole thing is mortifying… and then I think of Drew in a cell, alone. When he has done nothing to deserve it."

Mary gripped Caroline's hand again. "I know. I know you are both innocent. I know you have both been through so much. But that is over now. We will have faith."

Caroline gave her a tentative smile. "Thank you. Thank you for your concern. But most of all thank you for loving Drew, he needed a woman like you—"

"And I need him—" Mary smiled, but a tear escaped.

Caroline wiped it away with the handkerchief she held. "I am glad for you both."

A light knock struck the door, which had been left ajar. "Come!" Mary called.

"Sorry to interrupt." It was Kate. "It is just, I wished to let you know we are serving dinner, your uncle is staying with us to dine Mary, and he sent me to fetch you to ensure you came to the table."

Mary nodded. She wished to speak to him, she wished to ask him how Andrew was.

"Will you dine with us, Lady Kilbride?" Kate looked to Caroline.

Mary looked at her too.

Caroline shook her head.

"I will leave you then. Come when you are ready, Mary," Kate said.

Mary looked back and nodded, then Kate left them.

"I'm sorry," Caroline whispered. "I feel as though they must think I am rude, and disrespectful of their hospitality, but I... I cannot tell you how... how I feel. I... do not like to be in company, not any more. Do you think the Duchess would send my dinner to my room?"

"Of course she will, you must not feel pressed."

"Thank you, Mary. I will retire then."

"Yes. But send a maid to fetch me if you need me."

Caroline nodded.

They left the room together, then while Caroline moved to the stairs Mary turned toward the dining room her heart racing. Caroline was not well. She had been damaged by her family and damaged by her marriage, and she was becoming more withdrawn by the day. She needed her brother here. He should not be locked away accused of something that was a monstrous lie.

* * *

At dusk another visitor arrived, and again Drew stood as the keys jangled.

The door opened.

Wiltshire entered. He did not smile.

The door shut. "There is no news yet."

Drew sat, because there was too little room for them both to stand. Wiltshire remained on his feet.

"Lady Kilbride has confirmed everything you said, but of course it could just be a ploy the two of you have agreed—"

"It is not—"

"I have not finished." Wiltshire lifted a staying hand. Drew leant forward resting his elbows on his knees with a sigh and his head bowed as he listened. "The magistrate intends to speak with a former ladies maid, who may provide evidence on whether or not the beatings took place. If she confirms that she saw the beatings and the bruises, then the Magistrate has said he is willing to accept the charge is not true…"

Drew looked up. "Did you see Mary? How is she? How is Caro?"

"I saw Mary and I myself watched her eat. John has promised to ensure she does so from now on. She is worried, and she sends her affection to you but she is a strong girl, she will cope."

Cope with what? His death?

"She has us, Framlington, we will not see her suffer. Your sister, however, is insecure and frightened; she did not wish to tell her story but she did so to help you. She is as frightened for you, now, as she was for herself. But she is safe with John, and I promise you whatever happens she will receive the same support as Mary. We will not see her harmed or left."

"Thank you."

"I also took the liberty of speaking to your father…"

Drew stood up, astonished and instantly irate, his hands curling to fists. "You did not, Your Grace. I have no idea who the hell he is."

"So I discovered." Wiltshire answered, not reacting yet not regretful. "*Is* Lady Kilbride your sister?"

Drew's eyes narrowed. "If you hope to get me off on those grounds, you cannot, Caro and I share a mother, but the Marquis is not our father."

"I see."

He did not see, he would have no concept of it, no more of a concept than Mary had had. But now he knew just how low a match his niece had made. "You could of course leave me to hang. You would be rid of me then."

Wiltshire's eyebrows lifted. "You think I think less of you because of your parentage. I do not judge a man by his birth, I judge him by his actions, Framlington. I judged you ill when you ran off with my niece. I judged you even worse when you chose to brawl over her with Lord Brooke in a public place, and I admit, when I heard this accusation I thought you the lowest of scum.

"But now I know the truth. You helped your sister, not harmed her, and I have seen how Brooke respects you despite that brawl, but most importantly I know of your true affections for my niece. I judge facts, Framlington, and so now I know the truth I am doing my utmost to get you out of this mess and I will continue to do so. But I can tell you, neither you nor Lady Kilbride will have any help from your family."

"Pray tell me something I do not know."

Wiltshire's hand gripped Drew's shoulder. "It is of no matter now, you have Mary's. *We* are your family."

Devil take it… Emotion caught in Drew's throat, and punched him in the chest. This was what he'd craved when he'd watched Mary – to be a part of a family like Mary's. He had hoped to steal her away and make their own, he had never considered that he might become a part of hers. "I am grateful, Your Grace." No more words would come without the emotion inside him spilling over.

"Not Your Grace, just Richard," Wiltshire's grip on Drew's shoulder firmed. "You are my nephew now."

"Enough!" The shout echoed from beyond the door.

When the door shut behind Wiltshire. Drew sat back down, his head gripped in his hands as images of Mary swayed around in his head.

He had felt uncomfortable on the peripheries of Mary's family, now he seemed to be being dragged right into the heart of it. There were benefits, *obvious* benefits, but hell he did not fit, he would not fit

Chapter 39

The dawn light crept across the grey stone in the cell, shining through a small, square, barred window.

Drew sighed.

He was extremely bored of lying on an uncomfortable mattress, staring at the same four walls.

How people survived years in prisons he had no clue. The hours of the day were marked only by the jangle of keys.

The first came when a lump of dry bread was handed through the bars.

The second came an hour after that... Too early for luncheon.

Drew stood, gripping the bars and trying to peer along the hall through the small, square opening.

Peter smiled at him from beyond the jailor's shoulder.

Drew stepped back.

This was damn degrading, to be so reliant on others – but he had always, in some way, been reliant on Peter, even at school Peter had been his fighting partner to keep the bullies at bay.

"You will not believe this..." Brooke began when the jailor closed the door. "Wiltshire confronted Kilbride last night. It was deliberately done to be a spectacle. He challenged him in the middle of Devonshire's ballroom, raising his voice so all could hear and denouncing Kilbride's claims as an utter lie and when Kilbride argued, he turned to the crowd and told them they would hear the truth in the morning."

"Those were bold words," Drew rubbed his unshaven jaw. "I am not so convinced. It is still the word of a bastard against the word of a nobleman."

Sitting, Peter risked the fleas again. "Ah, but not now. Now it is the word of twenty nobleman and one bastard, against one single man. They were all there, Pembroke's uncles and cousins, gathered together and standing behind Wiltshire, ready to defend, and when Wiltshire was done, then the room was abuzz with women claiming you must be the wounded party. Now Harry and Mark plan to attend every event, to brag about being your friend."

"To win women."

"To win women." Peter laughed.

Drew shook his head, smiling.

"Your parents were there. They walked out."

"Please tell me Wiltshire did not threaten them too?"

"No, he merely glared." Peter laughed again.

Drew grimaced. "I have had enough of this place."

"I'm sure by the end of the day you will be out."

"I wish I was sure."

Peter grasped him in a masculine grip, and struck a palm against his back then let him go. "I am sure. That is enough. Tomorrow you shall be at Pembroke's. Do you think he will mind if I call on you there?"

"I doubt he would turn you away."

"Good enough. I will call on you in a day or two."

"Enough!"

"I am sick of that man's voice ordering my day..." Drew whispered bitterly.

"It will be over soon. I shall see you again at Pembroke's."

The door shut behind Peter.

Drew sat down to resume staring at the damned walls.

405

When the keys jangled for the fourth time Drew did not get up, it would be the evening meal, and surely then too late for any word from the Magistrate…

Devil take it…

"Stand up, Framlington." It was not the guard, but a different man.

Drew's heart pounded. But then beyond the man he saw Wiltshire, and Wiltshire smiled.

"I am here with word from the Magistrate, you are cleared of the charge and free to go."

The stranger held out a rolled parchment, which Drew presumed confirmed the Magistrate's acceptance of his innocence. "Here."

Drew grasped it, not that he needed a piece of paper to tell him he had done nothing wrong.

Wiltshire held out a hand.

The air rushed into Drew's lungs as he accepted it. Wiltshire's grip clasped about his. *I am clear*. Wiltshire let go. *And welcome in Mary's family…*

Drew jogged down the stone steps ahead of Wiltshire, eager to get out.

God he never thought he would feel so happy to see sunlight.

"You may stay with me tonight, so you can shave and such. I will run you out to Pembroke Place in the morning or we could make it tonight, before dusk, if we leave now."

Drew looked back. "I wish to see Mary."

"Then we leave now. You will find that the numbers have grown there, though, the family has been gathering."

Drew's heart pounded hard. He wanted to see Mary but he did not welcome the trial of meeting her entire family again. Had he not endured enough? It seemed he was not to have a reprieve after all.

One of Wiltshire's footmen held the carriage door.

They drove through London during the fashionable hour. It made their journey slow as carriages crowded the streets to enable the elite to be seen... When they peered at Drew, he pulled down the blind.

Wiltshire laughed.

Drew's natural impatience rose. He itched to leap from the carriage and run to Pembroke's, not that that was even possible, or would get him to Mary any faster.

Wiltshire gripped Drew's arm. "We'll get there lad, however long it takes. Cool your temper and learn to consider the consequences before you let it rise."

Drew moved his arm. "I am grateful for all you have done, Richard, but do not tell me what I should do, you've no right."

"I think that is your lack, from what I've seen, you've had no one to guide you. Remember you will have your own family soon. I cannot order you but I can and will advise you. You may choose whether to listen."

Drew sneered, but even so... "You may call me Drew..."

"Yet Mary calls you Andrew."

"Because I was fool enough to tell her it was my given name, and she now insists upon it to recognise all that I am, and not simply the man people see."

"I am getting to know you, Drew. You are aggressive only when you feel vulnerable, and now I think you're nervous of facing the others. Yet if you let them near, they will welcome you. Set up your guard and it will take thrice as long for you to be accepted." He looked out of the window on the far side, leaving Drew to his own musing.

Drew pulled down the brim of his hat and slid down in the seat, resting his boot heel on the far side.

Mary's uncle laughed again.

Drew smiled and shook his head.

* * *

Mary hovered in the hall on the first floor, her fingers on the banister as she looked along the statues, busts, portraits and numerous ancient things her brother and her grandfather had thought of interest and acquired. It all seemed so meaningless, so hollow.

Laughter rang from the drawing room echoing along the marble figures and the plaster sculpting the ceiling. The house was full of people. John had sent for her mother and father, which of course had meant her sisters and brothers came too, but now the whole family had travelled out of London to stay with John.

There had been a scene in town last night. Uncle Richard had challenged the Marquis of Kilbride and accused him of lying about Andrew and Caroline and of beating his wife. Poor Caroline had been mortified when Mary had told her. She had not come out of her room since everyone had arrived, she did not even wish for Mary's company…

Mary sighed.

She wished for company, and yet she did not want to go into the drawing room where everyone had gathered to discuss the part they'd played last night and how exciting it had been to see the true villain cringe and stumble for words. Everyone, apart from her mother and father and John and Kate, had been there to support the principle of Andrew's heroic act – helping his sister escape.

Everyone now believed him innocent, and everyone had told her how happy they were that Lord Framlington was not the man they'd thought him.

But all the well-wishing and self-congratulation was irrelevant. *He is not here!*

She had been told that Richard believed whole-heartedly Andrew would be freed today.

Yet…

There was no surety.

She could not sit, or even stand in the drawing room listening to their chatter and their laughter. It would make her want to scream.

Yet nor could she go to her room, her room would be too silent. Sitting in her room would leave her head running free with fear, and her thoughts could not be distracted with books or sewing or anything quiet.

Another round of laughter echoed from the room along the hall, and then one of her uncles began recounting another element of the scene from last night.

Mary turned away and hurried downstairs.

She would walk out in to the grounds. The air and the sunshine and the space would do her more good than anything within the house.

When she reached the hall she said to the footman who appeared. "If anyone asks where I am please tell them I am merely out walking in the park."

She slipped out the front door, not stopping to pick up a cloak or a shawl or anything, but it was not cold.

She did not go towards the lake though, or even towards the gardens at the rear of the house, her feet led her from the gravel at the front of the house on to the drive, pace by pace. Her arms clutched across her chest.

She hoped her family were right – that Andrew would come home today.

She walked past the stables. It was nearly six of the clock when she had left the house, surely if Andrew was to come today he would come soon.

Her arms uncrossed and fell to her sides, as her pace increased, and they swung in time with her strides.

Perhaps he was already on his way.

Perhaps he was already near.

She gripped her dress, lifted the hem, then ran.

It was with desperation. With a desire to be with him. To fly to him. If she could have grown wings…

She raced along the drive for a long way, her heart pounding and her hope crying out for speed, as if simply by her belief in his return he would come back. But then she became too tired and out of breath, and a stitch of pain caught in her side so she had to slow, yet she did not stop, she continued, walking instead of running, her arms swinging at her sides again as she still tried to hurry.

Are you coming? I'm here.

Speaking to him, even though he could not hear, helped ease her mind, holding back her fear and restraining her roaring hope.

"Andrew!" she cried aloud as she began to run once more.

John's drive went on forever, she could not see the entrance gate, it was probably still two miles away.

She walked again when she became tired, determined to keep going, unmindful of the distance growing between her and the house. All she thought of was Andrew, of the chance that at this moment he could be sitting in a carriage, racing towards her. She ran again. The thought of him urging her on.

Soon. Perhaps. Soon she would see him.

She had no idea how far she'd walked and run. The avenue lining the drive was too similar to identify at what point you were along it. But she had been unable to see the house for a while. She still did not stop, though, she could not have stopped now. She wanted to see him, and she felt as though stopping, returning to the house, would be to admit she did not believe, and she wanted to believe.

She saw the gates. They stood open, the gate house beside them.

She stopped. If she approached the gate house, the gatekeeper would wish to know what she was doing this far out from the house, with no cloak, no bonnet and no gloves. But it was like coming to a halt at the edge of the earth. It was as though Andrew was in an underworld from Greek mythology a place she could not reach, she had run as far as she could, and now...

She would wait...

She clutched her arms across her chest and stood still, looking at the gates a few hundred yards away. Any moment, any moment, Uncle's Richard's carriage might appear. It must appear. She could not bear it if it did not.

*　*　*

When the carriage turned through the gates of Pembroke's estate, Drew sat up straight, lifting off his hat so he could lean his head against the window and see ahead.

Good God. A lone woman stood by the side of the drive a few yards away, far out from the house. He pulled the window strap, to pull the glass down. As it fell the scent of damp grass swept into the carriage, it must have rained. Throwing his hat aside he leaned out to look.

Mary.

Her hand lifted.

He ducked back in and knocked on the carriage roof.

"What is it?" Wiltshire asked.

A lopsided smile tugged his lips as the carriage slowed, love swelling inside Drew's chest. "Your niece, daft girl. Heaven knows what she is doing right out here?"

Love; a painful but beautiful ache running through his blood, Drew, turned and sprung the door latch as the carriage drew to a halt.

He leapt out, his fingers gripping the handle, then ran the few paces to meet Mary as she ran at him.

He caught her up off her feet and hugged her hard. Her arms wrapped around his neck and she kissed him.

He could grow to like these homecomings too much. The feeling was addictive.

When he set her down, she pulled away. Tears made her eyes appear like glass, and her palms pressed to his unshaven jaw.

"I smell like a sewer and look like a vagrant, I know, but I did not want to waste time I could spend getting back to you in tidying myself up." His voice rasped with emotion, hoarse.

"I cannot believe you are here. I feared they would not let you

411

go."

"They would not have done, I'm sure, had not your uncle become involved. I am in debt to him. But Mary, it is good to see you." *I feared never seeing you again.* He hugged her once more, his fingers laying over her soft hair.

"I thought I'd lost you." she whispered against his soiled neckcloth.

"Not this time, and not ever now." The emotion swelling in his chest again he set her away, looking at her. "And what on earth are you doing this far from the house?"

"I walked out to wait for you, in the hope you'd come. I wanted to greet you alone, not with everyone watching."

"Which means they are all wondering where you are, and becoming frantic. Come." As he turned he tucked Mary protectively beneath his arm. "I cannot say I look forward to meeting any of them in this state. Do you suppose we can avoid it?"

"We could have them take the carriage to the stables and go in through the servants' hall." She smiled up at him, her pale eyes glinting with happiness.

"Then that is what we'll do."

"Uncle Richard," she said in greeting as they reached the carriage. Drew knocked down the step and handed her up, shouting up to the box for the driver to take them directly to the stables, and not as far as the house.

"Mary." Richard smiled.

Mary hugged her uncle. "Thank you."

"You are more than welcome."

Drew took a seat opposite them thinking Mary would sit beside Richard, but she did not, she turned and sat next to him.

"I have asked the driver to run us into the stables, Mary is going to take me in through the servants' hall so I can clean up."

"As you wish." Richard smiled at Drew. "But you will be expected to attend dinner, you cannot hide forever, but until then I will have them send up hot water for you to bathe." He looked at Mary, and raised one eyebrow. "To your room?"

She nodded, blushing.

As the carriage turned into the stable yard Drew saw a row of footmen lined up before the house. They had seen the carriage coming but unless they ran across the drive they could not reach it.

"Quick," Mary laughed as the carriage drew to a halt and grooms began surrounding it. Drew sprung the door, and leapt out, then knocked down the step for her and took her hand.

She glanced back at her uncle smiling, and Drew looked at him smiling too. "Thank you."

"Come." Mary tugged on his hand. "This way."

Drew heard Richard laugh as Mary pulled him away.

She led him along a stone flagged hallway, lined by servants, who stiffened and bowed in a stream of movement which followed them.

Mary spoke acknowledging a few of them, but not stopping.

Then when, what Drew presumed to be the housekeeper, appeared from a room to see what the commotion was, Mary said. "Please send some tea and cakes up to my room. Thank you."

They ran up the narrow servants' staircase, no longer holding hands, as Mary lifted the hem of her dress, and when they reached her room, Mary laughed, drawing laughter from Drew's throat too.

Chapter 40

Mary was sitting on the bed, her knees bent up and clasped by her arms, her stocking feet balancing on the very edge of the mattress, toes peeping from beneath the hem of her dress.

"You look charming, my love…" Andrew's head rested against the rim of the tub and he grinned and winked at her. "You are a sight for sore eyes. Why do you not come and get in with me?" He deployed his roguish half smile.

"And be even later for dinner and have my entire family know why I am late. Thank you, I shall resist."

He gave her a devil-may-care grin. "We could abscond."

"You have just won their favour; do not antagonise them again"

He sat up, then stood, the water streaming down his bare body… "So I am sentenced to their company."

"You are." She smiled, knowing his nakedness was another ploy to win her over. Her eyes followed his movement, her heart longing to give in.

"If you like what you see, sweetheart, we can dally here."

"Or…" She uncurled her legs and slid from the bed, smiling at him as she reached for the towel. "You could stop procrastinating and get dressed. Then we can go down to dinner." She threw the towel at him.

He caught it laughing, but then threw it back onto the bed,

and moved quickly grabbing her arm and her nape and pulling her mouth to his.

She indulged for a moment, but then pushed him away. "Andrew. Now I am soaked,"

"You're changing anyway," he said on a low seductive whisper.

A brief light knock hit the door leading from her sitting room. "My Lady, are you ready to dress?"

"And now she will think we have done what you intended…" Her damp dress clung to her breasts and her thighs.

Andrew laughed.

"Wait there Betsy! I will come out to you!" Mary tossed an annoyed look at him, though internally she was not annoyed at all. She was full of joy as she saw his eyes dance with humour.

"Just remember, Andrew Framlington, I am on to you now. No shocking my family to set up smokescreens, no hiding behind games and deviltry. I want them to know you."

He grinned wickedly

* * *

The fine ivory muslin of her dress slid against the skin of her thighs as Mary walked down the stairs beside Andrew.

"You look gorgeous, by the way." Andrew whispered through the edge of his lips, his eyes on the footmen in the hall below. His breath caressed her bare shoulder. Her dress had very short sleeves, a low bodice and back. His fingers caressed her waist, as the single strand of pearls about her neck caressed her skin.

When they had left her room he'd offered his arm, and said, "You may take me to my sentence."

"It is not a sentence," she'd chided, resting her satin gloved hand on his arm, over his black evening coat. "Please do not upset them."

"I will behave, Mary, I promise, no nonsense."

But even though he had promised, her heart beat in a firm pace, a little afraid of what was to come.

"How many are here?"

The hum of conversation rose from the rooms below.

"All my uncles and aunts and their families, and my older cousins with their husbands. The younger children are in the nursery, but the older children will be dining with us. The boys are back from college."

"So we are speaking of hordes then, and your father?"

"Of course."

Andrew stopped and took a breath.

Mary looked up at him from a step below, her hand gripping his evening coat. "Andrew?"

He took another breath, and then with a non-roguish smile he gripped her hand and pressed it against his chest. "You asked for my honesty, for me to show you how I feel. This is how I feel right now." His heart rate pulsed swiftly beneath her hand.

She smiled reassurance. "If you are nice to them, they shall be nice to you…"

"And your father?"

"Only wishes to know you make me happy, and care for me."

He let her hand go, sighing, his expression changing. "I would prefer to speak with your father before we go into the drawing room. If I wait in the library would you fetch him?"

"Why?"

His curved finger brushed her cheek. "Because I need to put things straight, sweetheart."

* * *

Drew waited alone in Pembroke's opulent library for ten excruciating minutes. His hands were actually shaking. He gripped them behind his back. He had never been strong on admitting his faults. Admitting faults, gave others a point to attack.

He stared up at a portrait of Pembroke's duchess, her hair was half up and half down, and her shoulder turned to the room,

showing the side of her that did not bear the look of a duchess
– just a woman.

The door handle turned. Drew's heart pounded.

Damn.

"Mary said you wish to speak with me in private, Framlington?"
Marlow did not look pleased about it. "You do realize you are
keeping us all away from the dinner table."

Drew sucked in a deep breath. Humble pie had a bitter taste.
"Lord Marlow, I wish to ask you for Mary's hand in marriage."

The man looked at him askance. "It is a little late, don't you
think."

Drew sighed. "Yes, Sir, I know, but I did not ask, and now I
wish to rectify the matter."

Marlow's arms folded over his chest. "What folly, what game,
is this, Framlington?"

"No folly, no game, sir. I love your daughter. I have done so
from the commencement of my courtship. I know my only means
comes from Mary, but I shall look after her, love her and cherish
her. You should know it. I understand why you do not approve
of me, but I will make her happy."

"You did not do so in London, you made my daughter miserable." Marlow's dark gaze bored into Drew, cold and assessing.

Drew swallowed back his pride. "I felt humiliated before her,
by my family. I did not think she would want a man like me—"

"But she does, it would seem."

"Yes, sir, Mary does, and I thank God for it…"

"You ought to trouble yourself less over your birth, Framlington.
I do not judge you by it, and nor will anyone else here. We judge
by actions. Actions speak far louder than words. Your actions
towards your sister speak of what is underneath your anger…"

Marlow turned away and walked to where a tray of decanters
stood on Pembroke's desk.

"Sir?"

Marlow turned back, a glass in his hand. "Would you like a

drink?"

Drew needed to keep his head clear to survive this evening. "No, thank you."

"You have not treated my daughter well to date. But Mary has told me you've sworn to hold your temper and not segregate yourself with antagonistic outbursts. This conversation implies you mean what you've said."

"You must understand my family's circumstances—"

"I know it. Mary has told me everything."

Drew fell silent. Unsure what to say.

Marlow, drank the brandy and set the glass down. Then walked forward. "The slate is wiped clean. I will judge you on today and tomorrow and onwards."

Drew swallowed as Marlow approached. No one had ever spoken to him like this. Given him a chance to merely be who he was.

Marlow gripped Drew's shoulder. "You have my consent. Or rather you have my endorsement."

Drew's heart thumped harder, as Marlow's hand fell. Then he held it out.

Drew shook it.

"Do not let me down, son."

Son? Emotion tangled up in Drew's chest, an odd pain – longing. He shook his head. "Lord Marlow—"

"Edward, at least, or father if you wish, as you have none of your own. Now may we eat? I am hungry."

"Thank you," Drew said as Marlow turned away.

Lord Marlow looked back, smiling slightly. "You are welcome. Now do you see how things could have been, if you had done them right."

Drew took a breath, uncertainty and shock rattling inside him. He was on unsteady ground. "I am sorry I did not."

Marlow's smile twisted, wryly. "Well, Mary has forgiven you. So I shall forgive you. I am man enough for that. But remember it is on a provision, no more foolishness."

Lord in heaven. A tight pain gripped in Drew's chest. This is what he had longed for, to be a part of a family like hers, only he had never thought it would come like this, he had thought he needed to keep Mary to himself and make his own family.

Marlow walked ahead of him as they left the room.

Mary stood in the hall outside.

She crossed the distance to his side, only glancing at her father and clasped Drew's arm above the elbow, with both hands. He remembered her doing the same when they'd run away, as he'd driven the curricle.

The pain in his chest was cupid's arrow. It flew through his heart.

Mary talked to her father, taking the attention from Drew.

Bless her. She understood his confusion, *she always understood*.

But he still had her whole family to face...

Mary's grip slid from Andrew's arm to his hand as he held back, letting her father enter the drawing room first.

Andrew was nervous and tense, but she knew her father had given him his blessing, he had told her he would, and he had walked out from the library smiling.

The conversation in the drawing room fell silent.

Oh she wished she had thought to come in here and tell them all not to make a fuss. They began applauding.

Andrew tensed even more, when the applause ceased and her uncles approached. "I admire your courage, Framlington."

She let go of his arm as his hand was shaken. But she stayed close, knowing he needed her – he was so confident on the exterior and so unsure at the heart

"I am proud to know you."

"Well done, Framlington."

Andrew accepted their comments with nods and dismissive gestures, as he was told not to bother with titles and pomp.

His hand searched for hers.

She took it, and he gripped hers hard, as her uncles moved away and then her cousins came close. To have their say.

She remembered the feel of his heartbeat as they had stood on the stairs. The grip of his hand and the hesitancy in his responses said he was bewildered by this.

Her brother Robbie came forward, holding out his hand, with the eagerness of an adolescent. "Lord Framlington, I am pleased to meet you. I should imagine life was pretty grim in a prison cell?"

"Robbie…" Mary chided.

"It was extremely miserable, it is not a place I would like to be again."

"My brother, Harry, and I, are infamous at college. Everyone wishes to know us because our sister ran away with a scoundrel."

"Robbie!"

"The lad is not offending me, Mary…" Andrew's fingers squeezed hers. "I am glad to have brought you notoriety. Where is your brother?"

"With the children." Robbie laughed, glancing at Mary. "He was in trouble at college for a prank so Papa would not let him come down."

Mary rolled her eyes. "Typical Harry."

Andrew's fingers squeezed hers. "Where is Caro?"

"Over there. You may quiz Andrew later, Robbie."

Robbie grinned. "I will speak with you later, Lord Framlington."

Andrew's smile looked uncomfortable and a little forced. "Thank you."

Robbie turned to Mary and smiled. "Congratulations, Mary."

"Thank you, Robbie." She kissed his cheek.

But then she turned away. "Come on, I'll take you over to Caroline."

As they crossed the room her aunts and cousins continually stopped them and greeted Andrew.

Andrew's jaw stiffened as they were stopped for the tenth time. It was becoming too much.

Caroline was sitting in the farthest corner, with Mary's mother, quiet and doing her utmost to be lost among the crowd, although everyone had tried to include her, she did not wish to be included.

Caroline looked up as they neared. She had only come down to see Andrew.

Neither of them were comfortable here.

When he reached Caroline, Andrew let go of Mary, sank down onto his haunches, and gripped Caroline's hands. "How are you, Caro?"

She leant forward and hugged him, and Mary heard her whispering to his ear, but not what she said.

Mary had always been close to Robbie, there was only eighteen months between them, but the closeness between Andrew and Caroline ran deeper. It was born of mutual suffering.

Tears streamed from Caroline's eyes as Drew whispered back to her.

Something touched Mary's arm. She glanced back. Her father held out his handkerchief.

She took it. Then tapped Andrew's shoulder. He looked up. Mary offered the handkerchief to Caroline.

"Thank you." Caroline smiled, glancing at Mary's father for only an instant.

"All will be well, now," Andrew said, his hand patting Caroline's arm.

Then he stood and looked at her father. "I thought you were hungry, are we not going to eat?"

Her father laughed then turned away lifting a hand to signal to John. Within moments the gong rang to call them through to dine.

Andrew threw an apologetic smile at Mary, then lifted his arm for Caroline to take.

Mary's father offered his to Mary, and when Andrew walked on ahead, he said quietly, "I like him, now, I think. But he is still on trial."

"He thinks this his sentence," she whispered.

"I can see it is difficult for them both, but they will become used to it, to us. We will give them time to adjust. Had he been honest in the beginning I would have supported him then and we need never have come to this."

"You would have accepted his suit?"

"I would have listened if he'd said he loved you. I would then have watched and given him a chance to prove himself. He did not give me that chance and when he walked away with that cheque less than an hour after you were wed, a cocky grin on his face – I have never wished to kill a man more. I shall never approve of that. But now I understand his motives, I am giving him the chance I would have given him before."

"Thank you, Papa. He will not let you down. I know he won't." Mary lifted to her toes and kissed her father's cheek then turned to take her seat.

One of Mary's cousin's husband's sat on Mary's left, as her father walked further along to join her mother, who Robbie had led in.

The whole table broke into raucous conversation and laughter, as they dined, and discussions passed across the table, in a variety of volumes, while Andrew and his sister spoke exclusively to each other in low tones. Mary talked with her cousins, and Robbie who sat across the table.

Chapter 41

When Kate rose to lead the women from the room, Caroline turned to Andrew. "I shall retire."

"Then I will come with you and walk you to your room." He gave Mary an apologetic smile as he turned to walk Caroline from the room. "I will meet you in the drawing room."

Mary nodded.

When Andrew came down, her cousin Margaret was playing the pianoforte and singing as the men drifted back into the drawing room in groups.

Mary gripped his hand, seeking to protect him, and drew him away from conversations.

She would guess none of them knew he was uncomfortable, but she could see it in his stiffness.

"Let us dance!" Mary's cousin Eleanor called, clapping her hands to silence the room. Immediately the men began shifting chairs aside to make space.

"I am only participating if we are dancing waltzes!" Her father shouted at Eleanor.

"And he will then only dance with Mama... Will you dance with me?" Mary whispered to Andrew.

He smiled. "If you wish me to."

He'd promised her tolerance, and he'd tolerated her family thus far. She'd sit it out if she must. But she did wish to dance, and she wished to dance with him, not with anyone else. They had never danced a waltz.

His smile twisted and he leaned to her ear. "You want to very much, don't you? I'm sorry if I seem reluctant, it is just all evening I have felt your family watching. I do not like to be the entertainment."

"Then look at me, and do not think of them."

Margaret began a slow waltz, there were too many couples in the room for them to dance boldly. Andrew's hand slipped to Mary's back and urged her into movement.

Her knees weak she stumbled through the first steps as her stomach turned somersaults, dancing its own waltz.

"Happy?" he asked, as he spun her over exuberantly.

"Now you are here. *Only* when you are here."

He smiled. "I'm glad me making a fool of myself has some worth."

"It has significant worth. You have even charmed Mama and Papa."

His smile pulled sideways, then he leaned a little to her ear. "Your father called me son."

"Then he approves of you."

"He approves if I am good for you. I am being good."

"You were always good for me, even when you were very bad."

"So I have permission to be bad then?"

"As if you have ever awaited permission."

His breath brushed her neck and his lips touched her ear, and then she was pressed flush against him, her thighs moving against his, as her breasts crushed against his chest.

She would have backed away and told him off, but every couple in the room danced close.

It was entrancing.

When the music ceased and they stopped, the onyx pupils at the heart of his eyes were wide and deep.

She knew what he was thinking.

Margaret began another tune. Hunger and longing shone in his eyes as they began to move again, and his fingers slipped a little into the neck of her gown at her back. Then his head bent and his teeth nipped her neck.

She nearly fell, but he held her, a note of humour in his throat.

"You are being wicked."

"I am wicked, Mary. Please do not wish me dull." He missed a step, gripping her lower back, as she tripped. "Look how you have me muddled."

He did it again, and made her laugh out loud. It was what he had intended.

But as she nearly fell and Andrew captured her, she bumped into her father's arm.

"Sorry, Papa. Andrew is making mistakes to make me laugh."

Her father lifted an eyebrow, smiling and spinning her mother out of the way.

"Don't irritate him needlessly," Mary whispered.

"It was humour or ravishment, I will ravish you before them if you wish… Which would you rather have?"

"Ravishment," she answered, laughing. She did not wish him dull.

"Naughty girl; that would have me tossed out." He leant to her ear. "Have you told your parents about the child? Your father said nothing to me."

Mary leaned back and met his gaze. "No."

"Your uncle knows. I told him in town. So we had best tell your parents before they hear it from him."

The music trailed to a close.

Gripping her hand, Andrew pulled her the few steps to where her father and mother stood. "Sir?"

Her father turned. "Edward, as I you told, son, at least that."

"Edward, then, sir, we would like a word if we may?"

"What is it?" Mary's mother clutched Andrew's arm and drew

him aside as another tune began.

"My Lady, I—"

"It is Ellen, Andrew, until you feel able to think of me as a mother. Now speak."

Andrew took a breath. "Mary is with child, she has just let me know she has not told you and I thought you would wish to know." His fingers threaded in between Mary's clinging.

For a moment they were silent, and Mary bit her lip, but then her father reached to shake Andrew's hand, moisture glinting in his eyes, and Mary's mother grasped her into a hug openly sobbing. "Oh, I am happy for you, I have been so worried…"

"I hope this is a good thing. You are pleased, Drew?"

"Sir, I mean," Andrew sighed, "Edward, yes, I am pleased." He glanced at Mary as her mother let her go. "More than pleased, and John, Pembroke, is selling me a property adjoining his. We will live near here so Mary will have her brother close—"

"You are inferring I would not trust you…" Mary's father interjected.

"No, I mean, yes, Edward. I just wish to set your mind at rest."

"It will be at rest if you keep making her laugh and smile. And I know about the property, John might be my stepson but he does talk to me." Mary's father laughed and slapped Andrew's shoulder.

Andrew looked awkward. But her father turned to the room then lifted a hand.

"A moment! Let us have your attention! My son-in-law has some news!"

Margaret stopped playing and couples swung to a halt.

Andrew fingers closed more firmly about Mary's, and she looked up and saw him swallow, as though his throat was dry. Then he took a breath. "Mary is with child."

Handshaking and kissing followed with numerous good wishes, and then Margaret's husband shouted. "I wish for more waltzes, but someone else shall have to play; I wish to dance with my wife!"

The room broke into laughter, then Eleanor swapped places

426

with Margaret, and then they were all dancing again, although Eleanor ignored the size of the room and the number of couples and played a rousing, raucous tune, which had them all bumping into each other and laughing.

But after three dances Andrew whispered to Mary's ear. "I have had my fill of playing happy families, Mary, darling, do you mind if I go outside for a smoke?"

"I do not mind, but I shall come with you."

He smiled, tugging her hand, and pulling her towards the open French door.

The night was tepid but not cold, and bright, a full moon hung in the sky throwing silver light across the grounds.

"I am sure you should not be out here with me when I'm smoking, your father would not like it." He took a thin cigar from his pocket.

"And I'm sure I do not care what he thinks." She turned and walked backwards across the terrace.

He followed.

"The night is lovely, the stars are really bright."

"You are the brightest."

She leaned back against the balustrade. "Idle flattery will earn you nothing."

"So you said when I sent you that damn poetry." He struck the match on the stone, then lifted the flame to the cigar's tip, illuminating his face.

He had a rugged masculine beauty.

He shook the flame out and tossed the match away. Then he looked at her. "Brooke put so much effort into those words. They were mostly his. If you would ever like prose tell me and I'll call on Peter. I have asked him to be godfather by the way. I hope you do not mind."

He rested his buttocks on the balustrade, one hand on the stone, the other, holding his cigar.

"I don't mind." With him etched in moonlight this felt a little like a fairytale, only she'd not fallen for the prince but the villain. Except that the villain had been masquerading – just misunderstood and unloved; a little like beauty and the beast.

She touched his cheek with her fingertips, turning to face him. "Perhaps if it is a girl, *she* will like prose."

Andrew smiled. His free hand lifted to capture hers and draw it down, and then the grip pulled her closer as he opened his legs so that she could step between.

Her fingers touched his midriff beneath his evening coat pressing against his waistcoat.

"Are you surviving?"

"Your family?" A low deep sound slipped from his throat. "Yes, they are just a little overpowering when one is not used to them, sweetheart. But I shall cope. I generally do. I could not write sweet nothings, but when I sat down and rewrote what they'd scribbled half drunk, it flowed from me. I can even surprise myself sometimes."

She frowned at him. "You wrote? I thought they wrote the letters."

"The last paragraph of the second letter was my own poor attempt, and those thereafter," He gave her a self-deprecating smile.

"You are mine. You are, you know, mine"

His lips twitched, a smile hovering but not forming, "As much as you are mine, you always have been from the beginning." He sucked on his cigar and blew the smoke out upwards, away from her.

Mary's heart thumped hard against her ribs. "You and I are meant to be one, hand and glove, half and whole. Put us together, darling, make us one, a single being. I want you... Were they your words?"

He frowned, "That you are quoting back to me? Yes, probably, I do not remember them in that much detail. I just know I sat down that morning and they came spilling out of me. I did not want to lose you."

She'd read those words again and again in the last few days, even though she'd believed they were not his, she had hung on to the sentiment within them. But they were his... "I want you. I cannot say I love you, not yet. I do not even know what on earth love is, but I do know that I cannot sleep for thinking of you, or dreaming of you. I think of you and I lose my breath, I see you and my heart begins to pound, I hear you and my spirit wants to sing. I am yours, Mary. Be mine. I cannot simply walk away. I will not.

"Think of the possibilities. If this was love? If this is our only chance at finding each other? If we are meant to be? Would you throw that away? Throw me away?"

He smiled his roguish grin and shook his head. "You memorised it. No wonder you were so hurt when you found out it was not written by me."

"The other nonsense was not. I did not memorise that, but those words... They were yours?"

He sucked on his cigar again, eyeing her with amusement.

"Andrew, it was only those words which made me believe in you and want to see you again. Not your friends' words."

Tears misting her gaze, her arms slipped about him, and clung. "I am very glad I did not throw you away, we are meant to be aren't we..."

His fingers gripped her nape as her cheek pressed against his shoulder. "I think so yes, and I wanted it to be just like this."

"Like this?" She straightened looking at him as he drew on his cigar. "I am sure you did not imagine us here, with my family a few feet away."

"No." He laughed. "I did not imagine them. But you loving me as I loved you. That is what I longed for."

She kissed his jaw and then the corner of his lips. "That you have always had."

He broke their embrace, turned and extinguished his cigar then threw it out into the darkness. "Come on, let's be naughty. I don't want to go back in there really."

"Be naughty?"

"Abscond. I have a better idea than more waltzes."

"Andrew?" she glanced back at the open French doors, the music played on.

"Come on, be a rebel with me. They know you're safe."

She looked at him. Her loyalty belonged to him first, and she did not want to bridle her wild, restless stallion tonight when he'd only just earned his freedom again.

He must have seen the decision in her eyes as he grinned. "Come on."

Mary caught up her dress and followed as he tugged her towards the steps, and ran down them on to the lawn, then he began racing down the slope.

"Where are we going?"

"To the lake!"

He pulled her on as she lifted her beautiful dress above her knees so she could run with him, the long grass swiping at her lower legs, the scent of clover flooding the night air.

She was breathless and breathing hard when they reached the water.

It was absolutely still, reflecting back the dark night sky with its pinpricks of light and full moon.

Andrew pulled her on about the lake, until they were out of sight of the house.

"Here." He stopped, and began slipping off his evening coat as he breathed heavily too.

"What are you doing?"

"We are going for a swim, sweetheart."

"Andrew, I am in an evening gown."

"Did I say we were swimming in our clothes? Undress."

"What if someone comes?"

"They will hear us and leave us in privacy. We'll make lots of noise so they do."

"They will think…"

"That we are enjoying ourselves." He dropped his evening

coat onto the grass. "I promised your Papa I would keep you laughing…"

"Andrew—"

"Mary, we are married, no one will judge. Do not deny me…" His fingers worked the knot of his cravat loose. "If you say no, you will always wish you had said, yes. You like being naughty you just lack courage…" His cravat slid from around his neck.

"Here let me undo your dress for you." She turned her back.

His fingers brushed against her skin.

But then his hands hesitated.

"You are not wearing stays, or a chemise."

Her head tipped back against his shoulder, as his hands slipped about her, beneath the satin, to cup her breasts and his lips brushed against her neck. "I love you, but I wish you'd told me earlier you'd not worn underwear. I would not have bothered dancing"

Mary laughed. The nights she had met him in the dark, hiding from her family, crept through her soul. He had touched her like this then, and it had been dangerous and desperate. Now the danger felt like home… A place she wished to be. "I only did not because the fabric is so fine, underwear spoils the silhouette of the dress."

His fingers slid away. "Then, this has just become my favourite dress." He released the last of the buttons and helped her step out of it.

The night air caressed her skin, cool but not cold.

He folded her dress carefully and laid it on his coat. Then while she stripped off her long gloves, stockings and shoes, he stripped off his shirt; watching her hungrily, in silence, his eyes travelling over her body as she shivered.

"You do not even realise how beautiful you are, even now, do you?" He threw his shirt onto the ground and kicked off his shoes. "I love your skin, it's flawless." He took off his stockings, then slipped the buttons of his flap free. "Head to toe, perfect."

Her body shone luminous in the silver moonlight, except for the cleft of dark hair between her thighs.

He'd thought she would have tried to cover her body, but she did not. She merely let him look as he finished stripping.

"I cannot swim,"

He smiled. "I'll hold you." Urgency thumped in every vein as he moved towards her.

"My hair," she whispered, her fingers lifting to the ornate decoration, which twinkled with sparkling pearls, like those about her neck.

"Come here. I shall take out the pins, and you can plait it."

When she turned her back to him, her bottom brushed his hip. Desire pulsed in his blood. But he ignored the urge to lay her down and began plucking pins from her hair.

Her body shivered a little as he worked. He was shivery with need too.

He placed a cupped hand full of pearl-headed pins into a pocket of his coat.

"Will they be safe here?"

"We shall not swim very far out, and I am sure none of the servants will come down here at night."

She had undone her necklace. She slipped it off and passed it to him.

Once he'd taken it, her fingers began weaving her long dark hair into a braid.

He slipped the necklace into his other pocket.

"Are you ready?" He said when he stood, holding out a hand to her.

"Yes." He pulled her close and kissed her. His other hand gripping the back of her head.

Then he let her go. I shall dive in, and then when you jump I shall catch you.

Andrew slipped like an arrow into the water, fracturing the shining jet as he entered. A dozen ripples stirred, trembling across the surface as he disappeared beneath it.

He reappeared a few yards from the bank, shaking the water from his hair. A devil-may-care grin on his lips.

"Jump in!" He beckoned. "Be brave, darling, I'll catch you and I'll hold you up."

The dark water shimmered around him, painted with silver lights.

She had never swum, her brothers had, with her father, but she had never...

"Come on!"

If she was to trust him now, then she should trust him in everything.

She leapt into the water. It consumed her in a cold grip, and her legs became tangled among the weeds. She took a breath, but her mouth flooded with water.

Her arms flailed, her heart pounding.

Then a solid band caught below her breasts, pulling her up.

She coughed, choking, her arms swiping out.

"Relax, I have you."

She tipped her head back onto his shoulder, breathing hard and then coughing as she sucked in the cool night air. Her fingers shook as she gripped his arm, which braced her middle. She could feel his legs kicking at the water beneath her.

"Don't let me go," her fingernails clawed into his skin.

"I would not would I, Mary, darling. I do not want to lose you. Let's swim out a little bit shall we. Lift your legs, just let them trail, I will swim for both of us."

With that she felt his body brushing beneath hers, his chest against her back as his legs moved under hers.

"Let your body float, Mary, and trust me." She lay her head back against his shoulder and let her body rise. The water lapped and played with her breasts, caressing her skin as he swam backwards, further out into the lake.

Her grip on his arm eased, but then it began to slip away. She grasped it.

"I won't let you go, I'll hold your arms, stretch them out and let your body lay on top of the water. Relax, let every muscle slacken, as if you are falling asleep on a bed of water."

Mary looked up at the stars, and felt her body rise as his hold slipped to her arms. His fingers gripping her skin. Her feet bobbed up on the water, and her stomach touched the surface too. The lap of the water was a gentle caress.

"There, stay just so, I am going to let you go, you'll not sink if you stay relaxed. I shall be here, just behind you."

Her heart thumped, but she could feel him close, as the water stirred when he kicked it, and moved it with his arms.

She floated, alone on the dark lake, watching the stars above. For a moment it was wonderful, but then her feet began to sink, and she forgot how to be weightless and turned to grab his arm.

He was right behind her…

She laughed.

"Put your arms about my neck and I will swim."

Kicking her legs clumsily in the water, she set her arms about his shoulders loosely. To ride on his back.

"Ready."

"Yes." He began to swim, his legs and arms moving like a frog. They cut through the water, easily. His body sleek and strong beneath her.

The moonlight played with the ripples they created.

The park seemed even more beautiful in the darkness. Like a secret place. She let her body float, flowing through the water.

He turned suddenly, spinning in her arms, so he faced her, and his body floated up under hers so his chest pressed to hers, and his legs moved beneath hers to keep them afloat.

"This or waltzing?" One palm lay on her naked back while the other swept through the water.

"This. You." She felt like a Goddess of the night.

"Do you want to try and swim?"

434

"No,"

"Wrong answer, Mary, darling. Of course you do, you are just afraid. I will hold your hands, put your legs out straight and kick them."

She did as he bid her, while he eased her grip from his shoulders and swum back, an arms-length away, holding her hands.

"Just kick your feet."

She did and they splashed on the surface.

"Keep them beneath the surface, it will propel you better."

She did so, feeling her body cut through the water, forcing him to swim backwards, his legs kicking out froglike beneath the surface.

"I am going to let go of your hands, slide them forward and then push the water back with your palms."

Panic caught in her throat as he let her go, but she did as he said, and her body moved without sinking, she kept kicking and moving her arms as he swam before her, slowly, speaking words of encouragement.

"You said you could not swim, but you can, Mary."

"Like you can make my family love you."

He shook his head, smiling. We will swim in the river when we have our own property. "Come." He slipped back beneath her, facing her, and she clung about his neck.

"Happy?"

She kept kicking her legs. "More than happy. I love you." This was the life she had dreamed of with him.

"And I love you. Are you ready to get out?"

Her gaze ran along the shore. "How will we get out?" There were no shallow places.

"The boating jetty." His body floated beneath hers, brushing chest to chest, hip to hip and thigh to thigh.

"The boating jetty? Did you plan this?"

He smiled, his roguish, rakehell smile. "I'll admit to having noted the places where the lake cannot be seen from the front of the house after Pembroke said he'd watched us when we sat

435

down here. Then while you spent afternoons resting and I walked about the park I noticed the best places to get in and out. But the opportunity to indulge never came… until now.

"You are wicked."

"And you love me for it."

"Yes, I do." She pressed a kiss on his cheek.

"Come on, let's get out." The strength of his kicks increased.

The jetty stretched out into the water. Reaching from the shore.

"You climb out first, press your palms down on the wood and I will push you up."

While he gripped the jetty with one hand his other pushed her bottom as she lifted herself up. She tumbled on to the jetty laughing.

His palms pressed down on the wood, the muscles in his arms bunching, as he rose from the water. It streamed across his skin, moonlight highlighting the ridges and hollows.

She was a lucky woman to have a man like this.

When he was on the jetty, he stood and held his hand out to help her up. Mary took it. He pulled her to standing, then they walked back along the jetty, her hand in his and her breathing rapid, but not from the exertion… She knew what would come now, and she ached for it to happen.

When they reached the trees, behind which, their clothes were hidden, he gripped her nape and brought her lips to his. The pressure was strong and warm. Then his tongue slipped between her lips and danced with hers as his erection pressed against her stomach.

His hands slid down to her buttocks, and hers ran over his damp skin.

"I wanted to be patient, to be slow, Mary, but I cannot. I love you too much." His grip lifted her and she wrapped her thighs about his hips.

"I would take you against the tree but the bark would be abrasive on your skin, so we must use the grass as a bed."

436

He dropped to his knees. With her still clasped about his waist, and then he leant her back and lay her down carefully.

The grass was cool, and the sweet scent of clover rose in the air.

"Let us find heaven together."

He slid into her, pressing deep inside her soul as well as her body.

"I love you." He withdrew and pushed back in, the rhythm slow and firm. His lips pressed kisses across her face, on her cheek, her eyelids.

Enchanting.

Her fingernails clawed into his back. "Andrew."

His movements became swifter, and harsher.

Pain and pleasure flooded her body.

His movement changed to a little pulse.

Then his hands gripped her thighs and pulled them wider apart, and his strokes became ruthless and desperate with hunger.

"Mary," he growled her name, over her lips. "I love you. Cry out for me. I want you undone – unravelled! Have no restraint..."

"I love you too." She said into his mouth, as the tide of desire rose, brimming at the top, lapping at her senses.

The soles of her bare feet gripped at his thighs, as her fingertips clung to his shoulders.

Her passion ran over, slipping across the edge, and washing away her grip on sanity.

His pelvis struck hers with a force that rocked through her body and stirred her breasts, firing sparks of ecstasy into her nerves. He took control of her body – all that she was, his weight pressing down onto her repeatedly, as her bottom bounced on the crushed grass.

"You are everything I have ever wanted..."

Her thighs trembled as she sought to grip his hips, but he moved too fast.

A delicious whorl danced a waltz through her senses as sighs and cries of pleasure filled the air around them.

She fell again and he withdrew fully, then plummeted into her, breathing hard as his climax came too.

Wet heat soaked about him, seeping into his soul. He held still, letting the feelings ripple through his veins. He had thought himself a dead man only hours ago, now he had gone to heaven, but he was still alive.

When they ebbed away he met her gaze.

She smiled.

It touched his heart.

He felt like a conquering king.

He smiled too, withdrawing from her and rolling to his back. "Beautiful woman."

She rolled against his side. One arm and leg slipping across his body as her palm settled on his chest.

He did not move for a while, listening to the music from the house.

They could sleep here, but he supposed that was a bad idea. They would be far more likely to be found at dawn. When the grooms rose.

His hand ran over her damp hair. "We must dress and go back."

"But I am still wet, the water will ruin my dress."

"Then wear my shirt. We can go in via the servants' hall. Come along. Let me get you to the warm comfortable bed you deserve."

She rolled away as he rose. He held out his hand to her.

"The servants' hall will be full at this hour. They will be tidying up after dinner and preparing for the morning. I am not going through there half naked."

"Then go in through the front door and hope no one is in the hall. The choice is yours, sweetheart."

She sighed as he picked up his trousers and slipped them back on.

"Mary those are your choices, walk through the servants' hall and do not give a damn what they think, walk through the front hall, and hope no one is there, or get your pretty dress wet and ruin it... and as I now love that dress I would discourage that choice." He gave her a wry smile, as her lips pouted.

"You did not plan this very well." She huffed and then bent and grabbed up his shirt.

He laughed. "Yes well, you ought to know. I am no good at thinking beyond a certain point, Mary."

She slipped his shirt over her head. "You mean like stealing me and not thinking about how you shall fit within the family you had made an enemy of."

He laughed again. "Yes, that is a good example." He gathered up the rest of their clothes careful not to let her hair pins or her necklace slip from the pockets of his coat. Then with their clothes tucked under one arm, his free hand gripped Mary's.

"Come. I suppose, in future, I ought to include you in my planning, and then you may point out the elements that I may forget."

She laughed. "That is a good idea."

His shirt fell to her mid-thigh, covering very little, and the white cotton caught the moonlight, making them standout as they walked up the slope, towards the house.

Drew hoped no one looked out from the windows.

When they reached the gravel drive, she stepped tentatively onto it, then squealed as it cut into her bare feet.

"Wait." Drew slipped on his shoes, "Here take these." He passed her the pile of clothes, then swung her up into his arms.

She squealed again. "If you are trying not to be seen, making all this noise is not the way to go about it, Mary, darling."

When they reached the smooth stone steps of the portico he let her feet fall and held her while she got her balance. Then he took their clothes back from her, gripped her hand and led her up the steps.

He turned the door handle and the door gave inwards.

Luckily there were no footmen in the hall. They would be in the drawing room ready to answer any of Pembroke's or his guests' needs. Voices and music still echoed about the house.

Drew smiled at Mary, wondering if her family would really be scandalised or whether they would simply laugh.

They hurried upstairs, her bare feet silent on the treads, and encountered no one.

When they reached her rooms, inside and out of sight of anyone in the house, he pressed her back against the door and kissed her hard, their clothes slipping to the floor.

Then he carried her to the bed.

An hour later and Mary slept deeply beside him, tangled up in the sheets and tucked beneath his arm, a precious savoured thing.

But sleep would not come to him. He no longer felt like the wolf having stolen a lamb, he felt like a lion with his lioness and he could not cease thinking of the infant nurtured in her womb.

Once he'd asked her if she thought she'd stepped from her heaven into his hell, now it was the other way about, he'd walked from darkness into her light. She was his beacon, she would love and care for their child and she would be the heart of their loyal and loving family. Just as he had hoped and longed for, and not known how to achieve.

In future he would include her in his planning.

Chapter 42

"A carriage is approaching, Your Grace."

"How far away?"

The family were breaking their fast. Drew glanced up at the clock, his heart thumping. Eleven.

Would Kilbride be fool enough to come here? Drew stood.

Pembroke glanced at him.

Caro had not come down, she'd chosen to eat in her rooms. At least if it was Kilbride she would be nowhere near, and she would not have to endure any verbal abuse.

His heart thumping Drew walked from the room. Mary's chair scraped the floor as she rose.

Others were rising too.

He walked out towards the drive.

A footman held the door.

Pembroke caught Drew up as he reached the steps and Mary's hand slipped into Drew's.

He clung to her, as Marlow and the other men also arrived to watch the progression of the carriage.

Drew saw the shield emblazoned on the side. "Brooke!"

He let go of Mary's hand and jogged down the steps smiling as the carriage pulled onto the drive before the house, the gravel crunching beneath its wheels as several grooms ran forward to take the horses heads.

The door opened and a footman raced to set down the step when Peter appeared, smiling. "Good-day, my friend. I told you I would see you here."

A smile rose up from within Drew, the sort of smile he had never known until he'd met Mary.

As Peter descended, Drew saw Harry and Mark behind him.

His heart thumping hard, he walked forward to embrace his friends, realising that he had always known love. He loved them.

Harry and then Mark gripped his shoulders, making humorous comments about his situation, among the Pembrokes, in his ear.

Drew laughed.

He saw through their tactics, they'd arrived on mass to make it harder for Pembroke to turn them away.

But when he looked back at Pembroke, the man merely smiled and nodded at Peter, then the others, "You are welcome here, as friends of Drew."

Looking at each other, the pride of lions turned away. But Mary hovered.

"Would you mind if I walk through the Park with them, sweetheart."

She shook her head, then turned to follow her family.

He was a fool, to have so maligned and fought her family. They'd never been against him, just for Mary. They'd always been on the same side really. He'd been wondering all through breakfast, when no one had said a word about last night, if it was normal for couples to disappear in this house. Certainly all the men were deeply attached to their wives, he had seen constant looks and gestures passing between couples, silent conversations like he and Mary had.

Brooke gripped his shoulder turning him and laughing. "Oh ye of little faith, did I not say all would be well."

"The rest of the world shuns you and your wife's family take you in. I shall attempt that ploy and do something utterly scandalous when I pick out my future wife." Harry grinned.

"You may pick her out, but she may not take you, you would be lucky to have anyone take you," Mark jested.

"Mary, took Drew," Harry bit back, my reputation is nowhere near as bad as his.

"Drew has a charm that you do not," Mark responded.

"And my prose," Peter inserted.

"Ah, about your prose…" Drew felt a smug smile pull up his lips. "It had nothing to do with it."

"It did? You said she was charmed by that letter," Peter protested, smiling.

"That letter, yes, but it was not your prose, it was a paragraph I had written at the end. Mary, quoted it to me last night, every word. I'm sorry old friend, she could not recall your prose." Drew slapped Peter's back and laughed, as they walked on down the slope.

"Damn, that is my chances lost. You shall have to write my love letters then, when I need them."

"I think Mary would be better at it, you may ask her." Drew looked at Mark and Harry. "Has Peter told you, Mary is expecting."

"No I saved that thunder for the proud papa."

Mark and Harry looked their shock.

"My God."

"Good grief, I am to be an uncle."

Yes, they all were, they were his family. His surrogate brothers. He wished them in his child's life.

After an hour of walking and talking, Drew saw Mary striding out towards them from the direction of the house.

She held her youngest sister's hand in hers, and the child looked up at Mary with adoration in her eyes.

It touched his heart to think of their children thus.

Drew smiled at the child who he remembered playing with her doll that afternoon in town. "Do you wish to come into the house to take tea?" Mary asked Peter, Mark and Harry.

All of them declined. They were not a home and hearth bunch

by nature. They would rather be back in London at Jackson's, pounding each other with their fists.

Drew looked through a window into his old life.

He preferred his new one.

He could live this life, and be proud of what he had.

Mary stayed with him as he said farewell, and they all kissed her cheek as she begged them to visit again, making sure they knew they would be welcome, for his sake. Drew gripped her waist as she held her sister's hand, while they waved goodbye.

This was his future, he had a place – a home. Someone who loved him. Someone to love.

Epilogue

Leaning back against the broad trunk of an oak, Drew cradled little George in his arms, crooning to the child. He'd taken his son from the nursery while Mary slept. George was already two months old, and summer was setting in again, springs bright light and blossom turning to green leaves to shade them from the more golden sunshine which would nourish and then dry out the crops.

The child's fingers opened and then grasped his thumb.

He adored his son but he'd hated naming him Framlington. Yet it was the name he had and thus it was his son's.

But a name was not the thing that made a man. His son had strength of will and purpose, presented in the grip on Drew's thumb. His son would grow up well, and be nothing like the others who bore the Framlington name, because his blood was half Marlow and part Pembroke.

A name was just a name.

Drew looked into his son's dark grey eyes.

Mary had gone into labour three weeks before the child was due, her stomach ripe and round.

They'd been walking through the gardens with Peter, who'd been staying with them, and she had complained of a little back ache through the day, but nothing else. She'd been laughing and then suddenly she had doubled over in pain clutching her stomach as her waters vented in a flood.

Drew had sent Brooke hurtling off to fetch the doctor and a midwife and to call at Pembroke's; while Drew had carried her upstairs.

She'd been told the first labour was always slow and there was no need for panic and yet the pain had seemed severe from the outset.

She had clung to his hand and not let him leave her, as her maid had sent for linens and hot water.

He had seen her contractions clutch at her stomach, even through her gown, clamping like a buckling belt.

The terrified maid had urged him to help her undress Mary, while every few moments her stomach would grip solid again and she'd grip his arm and not let him move.

The child had arrived barely half an hour later slipping from her body in a slimy bundle just as the sounds of the doctor's arrival echoed through the house.

Mary's maid had picked the child up, while Mary gripped at Drew's hand and they both stared half in shock as the woman slapped the baby's bottom hard.

Then George had opened his lungs and wailed.

Mary had let go of Drew and reached for the baby and Drew's heart had dissolved.

He'd thought he'd learned the full extent of love. He had not. Not until the moment he'd met his son. A life he and Mary had created – through love.

The doctor had burst into the room, and ordered Drew out then mustered all the women into action with a bewildering efficiency.

Drew could still not quite believe he'd done the unthinkable and seen his child born, this little tiny human-being coming into the world, a piece of him and a piece of Mary put together in life.

He doted on the child; while Mary walked about with a half-smile all the time, a look of love and affection that was as much for him as it was for their son.

The hardship was to leave George alone in his cradle. How had he ever feared that he could not love his child?

George gurgled, kicking a single leg free of his loose blanket; a strong firm healthy leg.

Drew had embarrassed himself and shed a tear before Peter, when George had been born. Peter had merely poured a brandy from Drew's decanters and given it to Drew.

But Peter was enchanted too, and now considering finding a wife for himself.

Drew kissed his child's soft cheek, and absorbed the infant's sweet baby smell. But the boy was getting fractious, hungry for a feed, the one thing his son could not get from his father. But everything else, *everything else*, he could.

Drew cautiously rose, then walked across the front lawn to the house. Caro was sitting outside on a bench, her face turned to the sun. She doted on his son too, but every time she looked at the baby he could also see her remembering the children she'd carried who'd never been born.

He touched her shoulder. "Do you wish to hold George for a moment? He's due a feed and getting fractious but it will do him no harm to wait a moment, before I take him back to Mary?"

"No. He wants his mother and his milk." She smiled, but it did not touch her eyes.

She was sad, her life virtually empty. She had told him she felt like a failure because she had not been able to succeed in a marriage as he had done. He'd told her it was Kilbride's fault, not hers. She did not believe it, though. She considered herself worthless and unworthy and he knew how that felt. It had become something more for her, though. A monster that seemed to roar at her. She suffered with some nervous disorder. Yet she refused to speak to the doctor.

He wished he could change things for her, he had tried, but she'd expressed no interest in any social engagements. She'd cut herself off from the world, she would not go beyond his gates and when Mary's family visited she retreated to her rooms. She said she could not breathe among people.

But when it was just he and Mary here, she would read and sew, and she liked to work in the garden cutting flowers and gathering seeds, and occasionally she would dine with them.

She would be free of Kilbride soon at least. He was divorcing her. It was progressing through the courts.

He sighed, not really knowing what to do or say.

"Go on, go," she urged as the child made sucking sounds and rooted, wriggling and burrowing against his chest.

He smiled. "Will you eat with us tonight? John and Kate are coming."

She shook her head.

His fingers pressed her shoulder again before he turned away.

She may be physically free of Kilbride, but she had not escaped his wounds. She was still imprisoned by him.

When he entered the cool large hall, Mary stood with her hand on the newel post of the dark oak staircase, her eyes looking glassy from sleep.

She looked beautiful, womanly, with her breasts swollen with milk.

She smiled holding out her arms for George.

As Mary undid her bodice, Drew sat in an armchair beside the bed.

Mary leaned against the pillows on the bed and held her nipple to George's mouth.

Andrew's eyes glowed warm, as he watched.

She could not have imagined this in her wildest dreams, a happiness which was so bone deep.

George latched on to her nipple and sucked hard; the tug a wonderful sensation which pulled at her soul.

She looked up at Andrew. "Where were you?"

"Sitting out beneath the plane tree, enjoying the day, he likes the leaves swaying above his head."

"Happy?" she asked him.

"Happy?" He laughed. "My goodness, what a meagre word. I am ecstatic with joy, and peace, and contentment, I cannot even begin to describe in words the well of bliss I feel each moment. If it were not for Caro's sadness I would be enthusing over it constantly. But that does not seem fair to her."

She glanced down at George, whose eyes were shut while he sucked and his little hand rested on her breast.

She looked back up at Andrew. "My father has a theory that you are more devoted to me than most men would have been because you know that what we have is special. He thinks it makes life more difficult for Caro, because she sees what she has never had."

"Your father thinks me devoted? Damn, he has seen past my camouflage."

"What camouflage? He does not think it, he knows it. Every look you give me, or now give George says it. You cannot hide it."

"And that is because I adore you both."

"Papa, admitted to me when they came to see, George, that you are the best thing that could have happened to me"

That did make him laugh. "I seem to recall some rather vicious denouncements that I was the worst thing and no better than a viper, a year ago."

"But that was before he knew you, and you know both Mama and Papa love you now."

His eyes held hers dancing with amusement, devil-may-care thoughts shining in them. Fatherhood and marriage had not made him any less of a rogue. But his hard shell had shattered and his soft centre was now fully visible. What was left was a man with endearing fun loving qualities, the first to set her family laughing, the last to settle to a quiet night and the one to propose the most boisterous activities.

When the family met at John's, he was always whipping the boys up into a riot, establishing boisterous games in the woods, or the lake, and he had even had the girls playing cricket on the

449

last occasion in a team against the boys. The girls had won with Andrew helping them bat.

For a man who had shied away from her family, he was now a pivotal part.

Mary only wished that Caro could find happiness too.

"What is it?" Andrew must have seen her sadness.

"I was thinking of Caro."

"We will keep supporting her, she is at least content here, and hopefully with time, she will be happy too."

"Yes."

"But do not let it spoil your happiness, Mary."

"I shall not."

A smile twisted, his lips "I think, the next time I see Edward I shall call him father, and see how he reacts."

"You will rock him completely off balance…" She laughed.

"He did propose it once, but I doubt it was done seriously."

"Papa would never jest about that. He would love it if you did. John is not his son, but he has always called him papa. He thinks of you as his son, I know he does, more so because of your own family's disregard. He told me he has stared your father down a dozen times in town."

"Except the Marquis is not my father."

She shook her head. "No, but my father would be if you let him."

"He is," Andrew answered his smile turning tender, "to all intents and purposes, as your brother is now mine. It is John and Edward after all who have set me up here and shown me how to manage this estate. Have my family even contacted us since we announced George's birth? No. It hardly needs saying who is my family – you are, and yours."

"See you cannot hide how you feel."

Little George slipped from her breast gurgling, as milk spilled from the corner of his mouth. Andrew stood and leant forward, to take him from her, then raised George to his shoulder.

While she secured her bodice, Andrew rubbed the child's back, and sat down again.

Mary rose and moved to rest a hand on Andrew's shoulder, then she leant and pressed a kiss on his temple.

"You are my family, you and George."

His light brown glowing eyes turned to her; amber and honey. "And you and George are everything to me."

"You have been everything to me since that night in the darkness."

He smiled. "Since we swam in the lake."

"No, since the night in town, when I met you outside at Uncle Richard's. Do you remember?"

He smiled. "Yes, I remember. You were the sweetest thing. I'd stood out there watching you among your family, waiting to see if you'd take the bait. I was wooing you physically then as I recall, until you said no to me in that glasshouse, and then I had to think again and woo your heart and mind instead."

"You owned my heart, long before that, Andrew."

"I wish I'd known it, and then I would not have hurt you so much."

Her fingers cupped his shaven cheek. "It does not matter, I think those first weeks have only made us stronger now."

She pressed a kiss on his lips.